THE BOOK OF STANLEY

THE BOOK OF

TODD

STANLEY

BABIAK

McCLELLAND & STEWART

Library and Archives Canada Cataloguing in Publication

Babiak, Todd, 1972-
    The book of Stanley / Todd Babiak.

ISBN 978-0-7710-0989-1

    I. Title.

PS8553.A242B66 2007   C813'.54   C2007-903761-5

We acknowledge the financial support of the Government of Canada through the Book Publishing Industry Development Program and that of the Government of Ontario through the Ontario Media Development Corporation's Ontario Book Initiative. We further acknowledge the support of the Canada Council for the Arts and the Ontario Arts Council for our publishing program.

Typeset in Sabon by M&S, Toronto
Printed and bound in Canada

This book is printed on acid-free paper that is 100% recycled, ancient-forest friendly (100% post-consumer recycled).

McClelland & Stewart Ltd.
75 Sherbourne Street
Toronto, Ontario
M5A 2P9
www.mcclelland.com

I 2 3 4 5   II IO 09 08 07

For my late father, Allen Roy Phillip Babiak

THE BOOK OF STANLEY

ONE

Stanley Moss silenced the Cuban music and glanced at his watch. Frieda looked up at him and sighed. Apart from her sigh, the only sounds in the house on 77th Avenue were the turning pages of her novel and the random plunks and creaks of furnace and settling softwood. Outside, the neighbour's modified Honda Civic accelerated from its parking spot and whined down the avenue.

"Why does he do that?"

"I don't know, Stanley."

"Why would someone pay extra for a noisy muffler? The word itself: *muffler*."

Frieda didn't respond. The novel she was reading for her book club, as far as Stanley understood, concerned life in India. It seemed every novel she read was about life in India, with poetic descriptions of vegetation. In the silence, as the minute hand slid forward again, Stanley considered pursuing this with Frieda: the political and social foundations of her obsession with India.

The spring sun was about to set, sending an orange light into a corner of the house. It illuminated the dust, revealed the window streaks, and illustrated the particularities of his wife's beauty: small green eyes, long fingers, a larger than average nose.

Five past seven – the hour had now officially passed. Stanley shrugged. "That's our boy."

"Why are you surprised?"

"Because in the e-mail he promised to call."

"He promised, he promised."

Their son, Charles, lived in New York City. Charles was an investment banker with one of the most prestigious firms in America. When they visited, once every two years at Christmastime, Charles attempted to be a good host. But he rarely had a free moment between seven in the morning and ten at night, even on Christmas Day. Stanley and Frieda rode around the park in a carriage pulled by steaming white horses, while the big bells rang. They went to museums and restaurants and delis recommended by guidebooks, and partook of Broadway shows that met Frieda's standards for musical theatre. Stanley and Frieda accepted that being a proper host demanded skills that Charles had never acquired; it had to be good enough that they were in their son's city, spending his money. At times, however, times like these, Stanley attempted to be angry with Charles instead of hurt. But Stanley understood he was the architect of his son's flaws.

"So what should I do?"

"E-mail him again."

"How do I go about phrasing it?"

Frieda closed her novel about life and vegetation in India and slid a finger across her bottom lip. "Dear Charles. Hello, how is your money doing? Good? Good. So, remember that shortness of breath I mentioned? Turns out I have advanced cancer. I wanted to tell you over the phone but you're too busy to call us back." Frieda took a deep breath and looked up at the white stucco ceiling. Stanley followed her gaze to a cobweb above the framed map of Clayoquot Sound. Finally, she finished. "I'm dying. Love, Dad."

Instead of arguing with Frieda about Charles and his maddening insensitivity, Stanley lifted the remote control and turned the Cuban music back on. "Which song were we at?"

Frieda dabbed at her eyes with the pink handkerchief she kept handy and shook her head. It didn't matter. Neither of them spoke Spanish, so the lyrics would not become repetitive. "Put it on shuffle."

"I don't like shuffle. It ruins the artistic progression." Stanley did not wait for Frieda to respond. He started with song number one.

The oncologist and his family doctor had agreed that radiation and chemotherapy could prolong his life but would make Stanley miserable with nausea. Instead, they prescribed some drugs to dull the pain in his chest and aid his breathing. There was planning to do. The doctors figured Stanley and Frieda had a few months before things turned ghastly. Why not take a nice trip somewhere?

Frieda was furious at the medical establishment for not catching this sooner, at Stanley for smoking until 1991, at the oil and gas industry and the Alberta government for environmental pollutants that might have sparked the illness, and, most profoundly, at Charles for being Charles. "We should have given him up for adoption. Or fed him to jackals at birth."

"Frieda."

"He defines selfishness."

"He doesn't know."

"And at this rate he never will." Frieda stood up from the chesterfield and dropped her book on the coffee table. "Let's order Korean and drink champagne until we pass out."

"That's the spirit."

It took some time for Stanley to get out of his leather club chair. The tumours in his lungs had spread, and his body's hopeless reaction to them left little strength for standing from a sitting position. Once he was up, he pulled his wife in for a hug. Stanley waited until he had enough breath, and then said, "Let's go to the computer this instant and book a holiday."

"No."

"To Havana or Delhi or wherever you want."

Frieda shook her head. "You'll get diarrhea on the first day and die. Gosh, that would be wild fun for both of us."

The song, a slow blend of acoustic guitars, hand drums, and horns, was a sultry provocation. Stanley forced Frieda into a dance. "We can lie about on a beach somewhere and read. The ocean air will open my lungs. I'll be cured by cheap papaya."

"Stop talking."

For the rest of that song and half of the next one, Stanley and Frieda danced between the umbrella plant and the dining-room table.

Frieda held his hand, which had gone cool and moist. "What time is your appointment tomorrow?"

"Two."

She asked something else about the nature of palliative care but Stanley was not listening. There was a Korean restaurant in town and he wanted Frieda to phone it, but the name had fled from his memory. A result of the tumours that now lived in his brain, or possibly a side effect of the drugs. Something. It started with a *B*. Bap?

"Is it designed to prolong your life?" she said. "Or do they just make death a more pleasant experience?"

Bim. Bul?

Frieda left the room and returned with a bottle. In the moment it took for her to strip the foil and wire away and ease the plastic cork out of their thirteen-dollar champagne, Stanley felt a buzz of anticipation. It reminded him vaguely of that instant before a teenage kiss or the first time he held his son. The cork popped, bounced off the ceiling, and rested in front of the stereo. Champagne gushed and fell on the hardwood floor with a slap.

"Our final champagne." Stanley smiled.

In the silence between songs, the fizzing alcohol lay between them like a dog's accident. Frieda shook her head and pointed the bottle at her husband. "Don't say that again."

"I love you."

"Don't."

TWO

The house on 77th Avenue was in a post-war subdivision three blocks from an industrial park. The park, a collection of manufacturing depots and warehouses, was bordered by car dealerships, gas stations, fast food outlets, a strip bar, and the most depressing Sheraton hotel in western Canada. From the subdivision – a collection of bungalows and semi-bungalows covered in stucco and vinyl siding – the industrial park was a constant, rumbling reminder of the blue-collar commerce that defined the city. On the uncommonly warm morning of Stanley's visit to the palliative care specialist, Frieda was breaking the dirt in their backyard vegetable garden and cajoling him to sit on the patio and read newspaper articles aloud. One of his wife's few superstitions: vigorous vocal exercise might just frighten cancer from the lungs.

Stanley wore his grey suit. There were others, but since he had lost weight Stanley felt insignificant and ghostly in them. It was an old suit, stitched and tailored more than two decades ago. On special days, Stanley wore it with a vest. He liked the idea of the woefully unfashionable three-piece suit, and saw it as a gentle act of rebellion in a world that no longer valued rituals and manners. Once rituals and manners were gone, at a vague date and time he associated with his own death, only blue-collar commerce and its accoutrements – snowmobiles, unnecessarily large trucks, ripped blue jeans, automatic weapons – would remain.

The story he read aloud was about Afghanistan. As he said words like *Kandahar* and *Taliban*, Stanley could not summon their meaning. It wasn't just the names of Korean restaurants that he could not recall.

In recent weeks, whole chunks of Stanley's memory had disappeared like dreams in the morning. One afternoon, he'd been looking at a black-and-white photograph of a man and a woman sitting on the shore of a lake in the Shuswaps; until Frieda commented on his parents' youth, Stanley had assumed these were two strangers. Dead celebrities.

Since then, many of the most important events in his life had faded into shadow. The smell of barbecued meat, a show tune, a striped tie in his closet, or the bent spine of a book would inspire the fragment of a memory he knew was significant, even essential, but more and more often he couldn't grab the whole of it.

And Frieda was beginning to suspect. She tried to trap him. At the end of the article about Afghanistan, she stood up from the hard soil, removed her gloves, and scratched at her grey-blond hair. "Remember that baseball game?" The morning of Stanley's trip to the palliative care specialist, Frieda wore a turtleneck sweater, a jean jacket, a straw hat, and sweatpants with stripes on the side. She waved her gloves. "The night that boy from Lacombe went crazy and hit Charles on the head with the bat?"

On the patio, the newspaper rustling, Stanley remembered the summertime breeze in the Avonmore schoolyard, a warm breeze that slid in over the Rockies from the distant coast or farther, from the mysterious place where wind begins. It smelled of lilac and freshly cut grass, May trees, and leather. He remembered dogs barking in cheap apartment court-yards. Someone's alcoholic husband playing country music out his window and yelling, "Shattap!" The chant of lawn mowers on 77th Avenue and the mosquitoes that always descended upon the diamond to collect the blood of parents. A symphony of crickets. Wheat trains piloted by lonesome and sleepy men, their horns wailing as they passed through Edmonton to cause traffic jams every hour. And *crack* – a hit, a single, *clap, clap, clap*. Was this what Frieda wanted to know? Did she want to know if he remembered parents smoking and taking nips from Pilsner cans in the late 1970s, only pretending to watch the game? Other parents, the parents who suffered their sons' potential failures and successes before they fell asleep at night, screaming at their children, the umpire, and their saviour? The yellow and blue of the blanket Frieda wrapped around her shoulders when the sun threatened to dip beyond the houses on 81st Street?

"I remember."

By the look of pinched disappointment on her face, Stanley knew that no one had hit Charles over the head with a bat. If Frieda asked what he had done in his flower shop for thirty-five years, what would he say?

Stanley glanced up at the sky, which was in the midst of transformation. Dark clouds eased in to colonize the light ones, and swirled gently. There was a crackling sound above them, distant thunder. In 1987, the great tornado had passed through the city just to the east of their house, and Stanley remained haunted by the monstrous deep green of the wind that had mopped the earth and killed twenty-seven people. Just beyond those clouds, as they'd torn up the land with the sound of a crashing jet, white-and-blue sky of the greeting-card variety. As he looked up, Stanley was reminded of that day in 1987. The dark clouds did not appear or sound ominous at first, only odd. He thought to call out to Frieda, "Look up!" But before he had a chance, the clouds swirled and a jolt went through Stanley. There was within him a pressure so great he thought his heart had stopped – or exploded. Now he desperately wanted to summon his wife, but as the desire reached his lips it became impossible.

The sound in the sky, conversing with the soil and clay of their backyard, progressed from a crackle to a rumble to a roar. It was the roar of the natural world, finally swallowing the city and its dull commerce. But it was also a voice. One voice magnified a thousand times. It did not seem to Stanley that he was *hearing* the voice, exactly. There was only pain, discomfort, the urge to communicate with his wife – all of it overwhelmed by an awful feeling of his own singularity. His fears and regrets and humiliations folded at once into a flash of abandonment. Everything he had learned about death was wrong. It was not easeful or romantic. There was no release in this, no connection or understanding. This thing, whatever it was, wanted to tear him apart. A pulse of blue light filled the yard and the land underneath the back deck quivered.

He gripped the arms of his chair and searched through the light and the sound for Frieda. But she was not with him, and neither was the deck or the chair or the garden or the house on 77th Avenue. It was over.

Then it *was* over. The blue light and the sound and the pressure and pain went as suddenly as they had come. His backyard three blocks from an industrial park returned to him. Stanley shivered with heat and lost control of his bowels. He looked down at the newspaper, which had remained on his lap, and felt a flock of geese flying overhead. Now, finally, his body obeyed him and he called out to his wife. Before she walked over to put her arm around him and ask if he was all right, Stanley knew she would put her arm around him and ask if he was all right. He knew the precise tone of her voice, the anxiety in it that she did not want him to hear. He heard bulbs and bugs quivering under the soil.

"Something just happened." He looked around. "My heart. Or I might be going crazy."

"Let me help you."

"You'll have to check me in somewhere soon. I don't want you changing my diapers."

"Let's just see what the specialist has to say." Frieda tried to guide him out of the chair and toward the door.

"What can he say?"

Just then, the intercom at the Ford dealership beeped its introduction. "Garry, line one. Garry, line one."

"This is what we worked so hard for." Frieda pointed toward the Ford dealership with one hand, and their small backyard with the other. "Retirement. *This.*"

Stanley was not yet in the mood to go inside. He dismissed the state of his underpants and regarded the majesty of their backyard in May. The budding branches of a sick fruit tree – what fruit? – leaning toward them like a beggar. The chain-link fence on one side of the lawn and the tall cedar hedge on the other. Peeling white paint on the 1951 stucco of their slumping garage. White and brown siding on their small semi-bungalow, crying out for a spring pressure-wash. All to the tune of their neighbour's schnauzer, Ray Ray, barking at nothing, and a Harley-Davidson rumbling across the alley. "*This,*" he said, and wished Ray Ray would shut up for a minute. He wished the man across the alley would shut off his Harley-Davidson.

Ray Ray stopped barking. The motorcycle went quiet. Stanley heard the man across the alley slap the bike and cuss. He cussed again. A coincidence, Stanley thought, and then, for an instant, he thought otherwise.

"The fuck's going on here?" said the man across the alley. "How does this thing work?"

THREE

The red Oldsmobile shook, stuttered, and finally stalled at a set of lights in front of Ed's Pawnshop on 97th Street. As Frieda turned the key to restart the car, Stanley beheld a middle-aged man in a thin leather jacket in front of the pawnshop, presumably Ed. With one hand, Ed held a can of pop to his lips. With the other, he adjusted his crotch.

With a lengthy stutter, the car came back to life. Frieda frowned at the steering wheel. "This isn't good."

Stanley wondered what circumstances had led Ed to be Ed. For that matter, what had led Stanley to be Stanley, on his way to meet with a death consultant in the northernmost major city in the continent? An airplane passed overhead, destined for the municipal airport, its echoing yawn a harbinger of nothing, really. Trips not taken. Increased emissions. The slow halt of innovation. Retreat.

"Stan."

"Yes?"

"We're going to end up stranded. What should I do?"

"There's cheap parking in Chinatown. Take the next right and we'll park and hop a bus to the hospital."

Stanley was so aware, so newly aware of his surroundings, he wanted to put his hands over his ears and shut his eyes. The signal light was a jackhammer, the sunshine a dagger. He throbbed all over, yet, oddly, he felt healthier than he had in weeks. Months. Years. Stanley released his right ear and gripped the armrest on the passenger-side door. First he squeezed it and then, with a quick jolt, he ripped it off. Bits of plastic and fluff covered the sleeve of his grey suit.

"Jesus!" Frieda pulled into a parking lot behind a Vietnamese restaurant and XXX shop. "What happened?"

"It must have been loose."

"Loose?" Frieda stopped the Oldsmobile.

The inside of the door was filled with a synthetic mush. "This pink stuff must be for noise."

Frieda furrowed her brows and sniffed. "I'm confused."

So was Stanley, but the balance of their marriage forbade him from admitting it. When Charles was born, Frieda was anxious so he was calm. Whenever sickness or financial crisis arrived, they switched roles; Stanley stared at the ceiling all night while Frieda snored in peace.

"It's a cheap car."

"Since when is $25,000 cheap?"

"Let's just park. I'll call the dealership when we get home."

It was mid-afternoon, a school day, so Stanley had not expected to see children. Six large teenage boys and a thin girl, with professional sports logos stamped on their puffy jackets, sat against the rotten parking lot fence smoking cigarettes and passing a Big Gulp container back and forth. Stanley pulled out his wallet to find some loonies for the ticket machine. Before the kids stood up in unison and began walking toward them, Stanley knew they would come. The two tallest boys swaggered in front.

"*Come on*, you guys," said the girl, hesitating by the fence. "We already got enough."

Frieda pulled Stanley away from the ticket machine. Through her teeth, she said, "Let's go."

There was a practised hardness to the one Stanley picked out as the leader, enhanced by the yellowing remains of a

black eye. He had brown hair with canary highlights. With
the others behind him, the boy stopped and took a long sip
of his undoubtedly spiked Big Gulp.

"How can we help yez today?"

Frieda pulled at Stanley again, as he plunked in a coin
and ripped a ticket from the old machine. "Leave us alone,"
she said.

"We plan to, Grandma," said the boy with the black eye.
"We're the security guards. You pay us, not the machine."

A couple of the other boys laughed nervously and shuffled
their feet. Stanley cleared his throat. "That's all I had."

"Three bucks? Bullshit. I bet you got a hundred-dollar bill
in there. Just the wallet and you can go. The car stays safe."

Stanley loathed their pimply faces, their voices, their puffy
jackets. He loathed their stupidity and their parents who
facilitated it.

The leader's younger and slightly smaller friends, twitching
and biting at the pieces of dead skin on their lips, scratching
at the backs of their heads where the dandruff was hearty,
were just afraid. They wanted this to be over. They wanted to
be at home, playing video games, or even at school.

Without a word or gesture of warning, Stanley dropped his
ticket into the mud, stepped in, and grabbed the leader's
jacket below his throat. Stanley thrust his right hand
forward, so the boy swallowed and screamed at once. The
boy struggled, and with his left hand Stanley grasped a
handful of his sweatpants above the crotch. He picked the boy
up. In one motion, Stanley spun around and tossed the boy in
a high arc so he landed with a plop in front of a distant SUV.
Frieda screamed, and screamed once more. The boy had dog-
paddled through the air but he had not released his Big Gulp
until he landed. The cup lay dolefully under a K-Car.

The boy honked and gasped, winded. Stanley took another step into the crowd of children and said, "Isn't this a school day?"

They backed away.

Stanley walked calmly to the car, placed his muddy ticket on the dash, and led his trembling wife to the bus stop. The girl and one of the boys followed them. The girl said, "Can we come with you?"

"Go to school."

"Now?"

"Now."

The girl and boy turned and ran south, without looking back. A bus rumbled toward Stanley and Frieda. Frieda pulled at the lapel of his grey suit. "Stan. What happened back there?"

"I'm not sure."

"You hurt that boy."

"Not badly."

The bus stopped in a puddle. A day earlier, Stanley would have asked the driver to lower the hydraulic door. Today he helped Frieda over the puddle and jumped over it himself, without a running start.

"Whoa," said the driver. "Nimble."

Stanley dropped four dollars into the slot.

"Moving like that, I don't think you deserve the seniors' rate." The driver, a squinting woman in her forties, held eye contact with Stanley before looking up into the rear-view mirror. "All right, move back. Move. Back. If you don't move back, people, I don't drive."

The riders didn't move. Squeezed in now among fellow old men in outdated suits, students reading Jane Austen and *Introductory Thermodynamics*, and recent Latin American and African immigrants with plastic shopping bags, Stanley kissed his wife. "Don't worry."

"If you want to sit, sir, ma'am, just tell someone to get up." The driver reached back for Stanley and twirled her long fingers. Lovingly, Stanley thought. "They're supposed to. But if you're too bashful or whatever, let me know. I'll raise hell."

"I'm fine, thank you."

The bus started away and stopped at a red light. Again, the driver looked into the rear-view mirror. "Do we know each other? There's something super-familiar about you. Something . . . I don't know what."

Stanley smiled and shrugged. He felt Frieda staring at him like a flashlight in a dark room. Frieda held on to the support bar and stared at him the way she might stare at a dead body.

"It's hot in here, and smelly," he said, just to say something.

"Stan, yesterday you couldn't lift a pot of minestrone off the stove. How is it you can throw a teenager fifteen feet in the air?"

"I'll ask the palliative care specialist. Maybe it's a dying thing, a final burst of strength. Like those women who lift cars to save their babies."

"That's a myth."

"Sometimes, myths are true."

"No, they aren't, actually." Frieda reached up and touched the wrinkles around Stanley's eyes. She ran her fingers down his cheeks to the deep grooves around his smile, his jawline. "You look different."

"I'm not different."

"Is your right arm aching? Or your left arm? Do you smell burned toast?"

"I'm not having a heart attack, and I'm not epileptic."

Frieda whispered into his neck. "When you went in your pants this morning, was there anything funny in there?"

"I don't know, Frieda. I just scraped and flushed."

"That's how you tell if newborns are sick, remember, by their BMs?"

"For God's sake don't say BM."

Someone behind them sneezed. Years ago, when someone sneezed on a bus or even in the flower store, Stanley would hold his breath for a few seconds until the germs dispersed. He would breathe in through his nose for a time, so his nose hairs might filter the pathogens. Now, on the bus, he cavalierly sucked it all in. *Do your worst – viruses, bacteria, beer breath.*

"Earlier today, when you said you might be going crazy, what did you mean?"

"I felt odd."

"What sort of odd?"

"Just odd, Frieda. I don't know."

"What happened back there, it's not right. Not only for a cancer patient, but for anyone. It was . . ."

"Shh. Let's just see what the doctor says about it."

"The doctor won't believe you. I saw it and I don't believe it. That was *not right*, Stan. Are you listening to me?"

The driver glanced at Stanley through the mirror again as she accelerated left through a yellow light. "You didn't work at a TV station, did you? Weatherman or something? You're not that guy, are you? Did you used to be fat? Sorta jolly?"

Frieda whispered a laugh.

"I owned and operated a flower shop."

"Where?"

"Calgary Trail south of Whyte."

"Oh, south side. I'm never on the south side. Seen you somewhere else I guess."

"It's a small city."

The driver sipped coffee from a giant Tim Hortons mug. Stanley could smell it was light roast, with heavy milk, sweetened with aspartame. Church coffee. "A million people now. You call that small?"

Stanley wanted to end the conversation. Something was happening behind him, in the hot chaos of the bus, and he wanted to listen. They passed a 7-11 and Stanley pretended to be interested in some feature of the convenience store so the driver might look at the road instead of the rear-view mirror.

"Well, I call that a pretty darn big city," said the driver. "Just look at the way traffic's changed the last few years, all these people movin' in. Pretty darn big, my friend. I know: do you write for the newspaper maybe, in the garden section or whatever?"

Behind Stanley, the noise in the bus began to swell. Passengers had begun to talk out loud. Not in a conversational style but rambling, chanting, even singing. Without turning around, Stanley received it as a warbling concerto. A cacophony. One woman sang "We're in the Money," her voice deep and grand.

"Hey, it's your favourite."

Frieda shrugged. "Favourite what?"

It cheered Stanley that an entire busload would simultaneously break one of the most important rules of contemporary society. Why shouldn't they feel free to talk and sing to themselves at once, packed in among fifty strangers? Frieda, for all her ease and confidence, always fell silent in buses and elevators. How had this happened? Had it started with one or two schizophrenics and moved through the bus like a yawn?

A giant fog was easing into the city from the west. Could mean rain. Could mean anything, really: death for Stanley or the end of the world. "The song from *Gold Diggers*, the dance number. And all this talking."

"All what talking?" Frieda, who faced the rear of the bus, shook her head.

Stanley turned to behold the babbling riders. It was clear by their eyes and their expressions, all the apologies and hopes and hymns and ordinary wonderings, that these people were speaking. "If she doesn't, fine, I don't either," said a man in an Oilers cap, as he tapped his index finger on the window. "*Necessito ir a la izquierda*," said a girl with bad skin. The singer was a large woman with a stretched plastic Safeway bag full of mittens. Her voice rose but her lips did not move.

No one's lips moved, yet no one on the bus was silent.

We're in the money, the skies are sunny,
Old man Depression, you are through,
*   you done us wrong.*

FOUR

In the rotunda of the Royal Alexandra Hospital, a pianist played a Chopin nocturne. The man wore a black suit with a white shirt opened at the neck, and closed his eyes in mock-ecstasy when he stroked the high keys. On the mezzanine, several patients sat or stood and listened. The very young and very old, thin and stricken, sat quietly and reverently in wheelchairs, their wrists attached to saline bags. One woman in a red spring dress and black cardigan stared at the pianist through thick glasses. An elderly gentleman, her father, shivered in a wheelchair. She held his hand as she watched. With her other hand, the woman pushed her glasses into place. She wondered whether the pianist's choice of music was appropriate in the daytime. This was the sort of music the woman in the red spring dress wanted the pianist to play at night, in her apartment, as she sipped wine and schemed to unbutton his crisp white shirt.

As he continued past the woman and toward the elevator, Stanley endeavoured to shut off his ability to listen. He heard everyone in sight, the patients and doctors and nurses and janitors, all but Frieda. The empty elevator, finally, was silent.

"Are you nervous?" Frieda rubbed the back of his neck as the car rose to the sixth floor. "You look it."

"Something like nervous, yes."

Like all doctors' offices, Dr. Lam's was deliberately unimpressive, with fading paint on the walls and thin vinyl chairs in the waiting room. An infant sat near the coffee table with a communal Fozzie Bear, sucked by thousands of toothless mouths, pulling the bear's arm and screaming intermittently. The baby's mother sat talking on a cellphone, something about picking up a box of frozen dry ribs on the way home. Four others read *People* magazines from the previous century and various sections of the day's newspaper, and Stanley heard them aloud.

"Are you sure?"

Stanley moved his arms around. "No."

"How do you feel?" Frieda squinted. "Right now. I mean, do you feel nauseous or weak or forgetful?"

"Forgetful isn't a feeling."

"What's your mother's name?"

"Frieda . . ."

"Ten seconds. Your mother's name." She looked at her watch and began counting down, silently.

Stanley pretended to be insulted by the simple question. Even though he had just looked it up a week ago, just written it in his notebook so he would not forget, Stanley had forgotten his mother's name. He wanted to guess Alice but it didn't seem to match the quivering image of her. One good memory: a hayride at Lake Wabamun, his mother and father sharing a thermos full of hot chocolate and whisky. His youngest sister, whose name he also could not recall, had already died of polio. It was just Stanley, his other sister, Kitty, and their parents. How old was he? Seven or eight. "Alice."

"Alice?"

"Yes. My mother's name was Alice."

"Your mother's name was Rosa."

"Damn."

"I'm coming into the room with you."

Stanley wanted to be alone with the doctor. His new sense of strength frightened and puzzled him, yet he also felt so strong, so vigorous, that he could walk through a wall. In case this was a sign of something horrible, in case his three or four months were about to be downgraded to a week, Stanley wanted to protect his wife. In old novels, sufferers of consumption became increasingly hopeful and optimistic as they coughed up more and more blood, singing happy tunes unto the end.

The nurse walked into the waiting area with a tan file.

Before she said his name aloud, Stanley told the nurse without speaking that he had to be alone for this interview.

"Stanley Moss."

Stanley and Frieda stood up.

"I'm sorry, Mrs. Moss," said the nurse. "You'll have to wait."

The woman showed him into the consultation room, empty save for a large desk and books about death lining the shelves, a few of them written by Dr. Lam. There were also two worn leather chairs. "How long will it be?" said Stanley.

"Dr. Lam will be here shortly."

Shortly. Shortly. To be certain all of this was not a mirage, a dream, a psychotic episode inspired by the pressure of expanding brain tumours, Stanley waited until the nurse closed the door and then jumped forward into a handstand. On his hands, he walked to the centre of the room and did twenty-six upside-down pushups. He laughed and drooled on himself. His suit jacket came down over his head, blinding him. Yet he did not feel blind. He could not remember his mother's name but he knew, intuitively, where he was in relation to all other objects in the small room. And, when he focused, in relation to the entire floor of the hospital.

The moment he heard soft footsteps in the hall, rubber soles on old ceramic tile, Stanley hopped from his hands to his feet. He adjusted his jacket, plopped into one of the leather chairs, and exhaled.

Dr. Lam opened the door and Stanley stood to greet him. The doctor was younger than Stanley had expected. Thin, handsome, of Asian extraction. He wore casual trousers and a bland blue sweater, with an open white lab coat. Was this middle-class facade part of every public health system?

"Doctor."

"Mr. Moss. How are you?"

"It's hard to say, really. I have no precedent."

For a long time, Dr. Lam nodded. He tilted his head slightly, and spoke with soft concern. "In our society, we are not trained for what you're going through, Mr. Moss. We don't talk about it and we certainly don't understand it, even though the basis of our spiritual and even artistic culture rests on our relationship with death. Did you not come with your wife?"

"She's in the waiting room."

"Wouldn't you like her to be with you today?"

"Frankly, no. Or not yet."

"How is she coping with your illness?"

"The same way she copes with everything. With patience, intelligence, compassion, sarcasm."

"Do you and your wife have faith?"

"In what?"

"Are you believers?"

"No."

Dr. Lam smiled artificially and looked down. He took a pen out of his coat pocket. "All right. What I'd like to do with you now is talk about what we call a death plan. I know it might sound a bit macabre, and some of my colleagues have developed gentler phrases to describe it, but I don't see why we shouldn't be honest about what's happening to you. What will happen to me, to all of us. You see?"

"I see."

"Now. You have children?"

"Dr. Lam, I can't think of anything I'd rather do than make a death plan, but something odd happened to me this morning and I'd like to bounce it off you."

"Certainly." Dr. Lam lowered his pen. "Certainly."

"There was a flash, a voice. A rumble." Stanley swallowed and smiled. "Now I seem to have special strength and, every now and then, the ability to read, well, minds."

Dr. Lam squinted. It was a long and ponderous squint, accompanied by a silence that unnerved Stanley.

"Is it common," Stanley said, "this delusion?"

With a gentle clearing of his throat, the doctor picked up the phone and informed his secretary that the Moss session would run late.

FIVE

Stanley lay awake that night with his eyes closed until Frieda fell asleep. Then he waited another half-hour, for her Somnol pill to take effect.

It was wearisome to stare at the ceiling, so Stanley turned to Frieda and willed her to be happy. She continued to frown, faintly, in her sleep. Next to the bed was a framed photograph of adolescent Charles and their black Labrador retriever, Dennis, on the beach at Skeleton Lake. He tried to move the photograph with his mind; he tried to make chunks of white paint fall from the stippled ceiling into his hand. But it seemed his powers of persuasion did not extend to inanimate objects – yet.

When Frieda's breathing patterns shifted, Stanley sneaked out of bed and found his swimming trunks. He put on his grey suit and hat, and slipped the trunks and a towel into a white plastic Planet Organic bag. Thieves and marauders never seemed to visit their neighbourhood, so Stanley did not lock the door as he left. It was a Friday evening, not yet eleven. He stood in the cool air for some time before sprinting north through his neighbourhood of identical and nearly identical bungalows and semi-bungalows, across Whyte Avenue, and past a few grimy pubs and retirement complexes. It took him no more than a couple of minutes to run several blocks, and he was feeling so untroubled he did not care who saw him.

Dr. Lam, as it turned out, was a curious gentleman. He had asked Stanley to tell his story, very slowly, into a tape recorder. Stanley skipped over certain matters, like soiling himself.

"The voice you heard. Was it in English?" the doctor asked.

"I don't think so."

"Expand on that."

"On what?"

"On *not thinking so*."

"Well . . ."

"You heard the voice but you didn't hear the voice. Is that what you mean?"

"There was so much pressure in my head I couldn't really hear it. Even though I was hearing it. Whatever the voice said, it was slow. Maybe it was a female voice. Like three or four high notes on the biggest organ in the world. But it wasn't an organ, either."

"Can you reproduce the sound for me?"

"No."

"Can you try?"

Stanley cleared his throat, attempted to find the voice.

Once, when Charles was doing his master's degree in Palo Alto, they'd gone to a karaoke bar. Charles had convinced Stanley, after several drinks, to sing "I Only Have Eyes For You." But once he was in front of the people and the music started up, the "I am an old fool" element overpowered him and he couldn't sing. The crowd booed him. This was how he felt now, as though Dr. Lam, despite his curiosity, would boo him.

"No. It's a thing that shouldn't be attempted."

Dr. Lam lowered the recorder. While staring intently at Stanley, he picked up his pen and twirled it on the back of his thumb.

"Have you seen anything like this before, in a dying patient?"

"No. No I haven't, Mr. Moss."

"You don't believe me?"

"I believe you feel something has happened to you, and to the extent that it is a positive change it can only be –"

"I can show you."

"Show me what?"

Stanley remained seated for a minute. He knew he could do the handstand pushups, but this called for something new. A scene from *Singin' in the Rain* popped to mind. He stood up and prepared to explain himself to Dr. Lam, but decided it would be best un-introduced. Then he sprinted to the nearest wall, ran a couple of steps up it, and executed a back-flip. He landed hard, with his legs straight, took a couple of bracing steps forward, and turned to face Dr. Lam.

Dr. Lam had stopped twirling his pen. "Can you . . ."

"Do that again?"

"Yes."

Stanley did it again, and this time he landed it solidly.

"Cirque du Soleil!" said Dr. Lam, applauding. "Bravo. Now, what am I thinking?"

Stanley listened. Dr. Lam was definitely thinking of fly-fishing, in the mountains. "Fly-fishing."

"Bravo!" Dr. Lam stood up and clapped some more. He smiled and said, into his tape recorder, "Patient just read my mind. Just read my . . . *effing* mind."

"So?"

"So," said Dr. Lam, as he pulled out his handkerchief to wipe the sweat off his forehead.

"So what do I do? What does this mean?"

"I am going to study you, how about that? And I am going to write a paper about this, and we are going to be famous. More than famous, Mr. Moss. I don't think there is any sort of model for what we're dealing with here, not with peer review, anyway. Can I call you Stanley? Stan, even? Cognac?"

Earlier that day, before he heard the voice in the backyard, Stanley had read in the newspaper that city pools were open until midnight as part of an initiative to combat childhood obesity and youth crime. The change room bustled with youngsters, their slick torsos and metallic voices, pushing each other and cackling about girls. They were boys, not men, the chubby boys of the new millennium, video-game champions, all of them too young to enjoy the nightclubs of Old Strathcona on a Friday night. Some took their post-swim showers, carefree with expletives, while Stanley took his pre-swim shower. They bumped him and did not apologize.

Stanley walked into the echoing hall of water and found the two lanes designated for laps. The giant clock hung directly across from him, its red second hand moving through another minute, and another. When the second hand reached twelve, he dove.

Despite his awkwardness on ice skates and in football cleats, Stanley had a sort of grace underwater. Though he had not been in a pool since the 1970s, he remained an elegant swimmer. Now, Stanley was also a powerful one. At the end of one hundred metres he stopped and turned to the clock. Forty-three seconds had passed.

"What the ass?" A young man in a red shirt, the lifeguard, stood over Stanley. He had crumpled a white hat in his hand. "What the *sweet mother ass* was that, man?"

Stanley sniffed, pretended to be out of breath. "Water's fast tonight."

"The world record for one hundred metres is just under forty-eight seconds. Some Nordic guy. You just slayed that." The lifeguard glanced at the giant clock, accusingly. "Dude, you were under forty."

"No, I wasn't."

"You so were. I watched the whole thing." The young man lowered himself to the slick deck as though he had become faint, and put his head in his hands. His hat fell into the water. "This is so messed up."

"It must have been a minute."

"Shut up. Let me process this. I feel sick sorta. How *old* are you? I mean, who are you?"

Stanley understood, as the young man rocked back and forth like a madrasa student, that it would be prudent to be more careful in the future. Several thoughts came to him. He might continue lying to the young man. He could pretend to be a great swimmer, visiting from California. Or he could kill the lifeguard, destroy the living memory. "I'm nobody."

"Dude, you are *not* nobody. I train sixteen hours a week and I can't even approach that pace. And you're like, fifty. I don't understand."

"Actually, I'm sixty-two."

"Can you do it again? I want to grab some other guys. No one'll believe me."

"I'm pooped."

"You aren't pooped. Don't pretend to be pooped!"

Stanley lifted himself out of the water and helped the life-guard, a tall and fit young man of seventeen or eighteen, to his feet. "I'm sorry."

"Who are you?"

On his way back to the change room, Stanley realized that others in the pool were watching. The splashes and screams and echoes of screams had quieted, due to the life-guard's loud incredulity and, perhaps, other more peculiar reasons. As Stanley took his shower, the lifeguard stood next to him.

"Who are you?" the lifeguard said again. Tears had formed in his eyes. "Please."

SIX

Dear Allah –

In my dreams you are white. How can that be? You look like that man in Pretty Woman, *only older. This is not what I have learned. You know what I have learned and IF IT IS WRONG AND YOU KNOW IT, and if you are*

*real, and if you know All Things, why have you
deceived us for so long? Why have you chosen me to be
doubtful? Why now? You know what we believe. If we
are wrong and you know we are wrong, and surely
someone is wrong (I believe the Christians are wrong),
why do you not stop us and correct us in a civilized
manner? We would only be angry and ashamed for a
short time and then I am certain we would be pleased.*

Thank you sincerely. Allahu Akbar.

*Maha Rasad
Montreal, Quebec*

Ms. Charlebois was so pregnant she could not reach
down for a piece of chalk that had fallen to the floor. Yet
there she was, in front of Maha Rasad and the rest of her
class, discussing Kirchhoff's Second Law. It seemed to Maha
that Ms. Charlebois should be at home, doing whatever it is
women do right before they give birth. Sterilize bottles?
Sweep the stairs?

Tomorrow, Maha would begin writing her final series of
high school examinations. But she could not concentrate on
physical laws of electricity. Maha checked over her fifteenth
letter to God, for spelling errors and grammatical peculiari-
ties. Very quietly, she read it aloud to herself. This was what
she had learned in both English and French composition tuto-
rials: we do not discover our mistakes until we hear them.

Just as she was about to slip her fifteenth letter to God into
a pocket at the back of her physics binder, Ms. Charlebois
appeared before her. "Maha."

"Yes?" She covered the letter with her elbows.

"May I see that?"

"No."

"You weren't paying attention."

"Yes, I was."

Ms. Charlebois sighed and leaned back, crossed her arms over the giant belly. "Tell me what I was saying."

"You were discussing Kirchhoff's Laws, which concern energy. The conservation of energy and the conservation of charge. There are two laws."

The teacher sniffed, clearly disappointed. "Why are you writing letters in my class?"

"I'm sorry, Ms. Charlebois."

Maha knew the material and knew she would get between 90 and 100 percent on her exams, but she also knew Ms. Charlebois would demand the letter. This was not because of any rule or regulation. No, Ms. Charlebois was curious. And Maha was a special case, a student with a *history*. At Wagar High School, the jewel of Côte St.-Luc, a suburban city in the western quadrant of the island of Montreal, a teacher was entitled to see private letters composed by Maha Rasad.

"Hand it over."

After a short pause, the extent of Maha's rebellion, she took her elbows off the letter and gave it to Ms. Charlebois, lifting it so the woman would not have to bend over. Silence filled the class as Ms. Charlebois read the letter. When she was finished, she looked down at Maha.

"What's it say?" Jonathan Talbot, whose voice was like a knife on sheet metal, wore a T-shirt that advertised for a motorcycle company. Ms. Charlebois ignored him.

"We'll deal with this later?"

Maha nodded.

Now her classmates stared and talked among themselves. In the five or seven seconds it took for Ms. Charlebois to resume her position at the front of the class, Maha heard several theories. Most of them, of course, concerned sex. Maha imagined the particular act that had rendered Ms. Charlebois pregnant. Unlike many other teachers at Wagar, she was a beautiful woman. Thin, clear-skinned, with a deft hand in eye makeup and excellent taste in scarves. Yet it was difficult to picture Ms. Charlebois without clothes, without the giant belly, writhing and calling out as they do in the movies. Repeating "yes" or "*oui*," addressing God, tearing into or slapping the man's flesh. Was it in the dark, the instant of Ms. Charlebois's impregnation, or on some bright Saturday morning in a township farmer's field?

Electricity. The conservation of electricity. Jonathan Talbot was staring across the aisle at Maha's breasts, her hair. She imagined his sour breath, streaked with hot dogs and Coca-Cola. His erection.

He leaned toward her and whispered, "What'd it say?"

"Nothing."

"Was it a *make me real* letter?"

Maha did not answer, or turn to him. She stared straight ahead.

"A fuckin' *make me real* letter?"

Somehow, even though Jonathan Talbot had whispered, Ms. Charlebois heard him. The heightened senses of a pregnant woman. "Jon. Out!"

"What?"

"Out!"

"I didn't say anything."

"Right. Out."

"This is prosecution."

"The word is *persecution*, Jon. Either way, get out. You're done here."

Jonathan turned to Maha, opened his mouth, and moved his tongue around in a crude manner. "Fine."

He stood, and Ms. Charlebois paged the office to prepare the administrators for Jonathan Talbot's arrival. Kirchhoff's Laws were illuminated for another seven minutes until the buzzer sounded. Maha's classmates filed out while she sat in the acid of her shame. *Make me real.* Ms. Charlebois eased into the ergonomically correct chair at her desk, exhaled mightily, and smiled.

"Come closer, Maha."

She did, with her gaze fixed firmly on the blackboard behind the teacher.

"How are you?"

"Fine."

"Things are all right?" The teacher reached down and cradled her belly. "Really all right?"

"If there's something you want to say, just say it."

Ms. Charlebois frowned thoughtfully. "You're writing letters to – how do you say it? Allah? – in physics class. Now, you aren't like other students. I can't warn you that you're about to fail and ruin your prospects for university. You could ace the finals in your sleep."

"Yes."

"But given what happened in January. Given your file. I just want to . . . make certain your health is sound. Are the other students still bugging you? Jonathan. Is he?"

"He's insignificant."

"Should I call your parents, I wonder?" The teacher lifted the letter to God and used it as a fan. "Should I be concerned

about this? You're not getting *extreme*, are you? Because we
have strict guidelines around these things now, with the fire-
bombings and shootings here in Montreal and all the strife
in the Gaza Strip . . ."

"I'm not an extremist."

"They taught us about warning signs at the convention."
Ms. Charlebois leaned forward on her desk. "You don't hate
Jews or anything, do you?"

Maha Rasad swiped the letter from Ms. Charlebois,
gathered the supplies from her desk, and marched out of
the physics lab.

"There's a hotline!"

In the hallway, Maha walked upright, proudly, just as
her mother had taught her, until she turned the corner.
Then she backed into a set of lockers with a hollow clang
and lowered herself slowly to the floor. French class was
underway but she lacked the strength, energy, or resigna-
tion to go. There were two posters on the wall across from
her, one with a photo of a black female sprinter grunting
over the finish line and the other featuring a smiling male
student in a wheelchair, surrounded by supportive peers. In
large white letters the posters announced "DEDICATION"
and "UNDERSTANDING," respectively. Underneath, poems
of the greeting-card variety.

Just as she had done with the other fourteen letters to God,
Maha ripped this letter into tiny pieces and began to swallow
them, one by one.

SEVEN

Maha and her one true friend, Ardeen, sat on the upper floor of the Faubourg Sainte-Catherine, eating bagels and clementines as afternoon passed into evening. It was not a particularly warm day, but Ardeen wore a short black skirt. Every minute or so, she reached up to touch the new silver ring in her eyebrow. Under their table sat several bags from BCBG.

"What do you mean you don't like shopping any more?" Ardeen popped an orange wedge into her mouth.

"It used to make me feel good. Now it doesn't."

"That's crazy."

"I know."

Ardeen ran her tongue over her teeth. "It's just a terrible phase. Don't think about it too much."

"Ardeen, don't be mad. But I think I'm leaving."

"Leaving what?"

"Montreal."

"Why? When?"

Maha shrugged. "I don't know. Sometime after exams are finished."

"I thought we were going to Cegep together." Ardeen kicked one of the bags under the table. "What the hell's going on here? Did you apply to U of T without telling me?"

"No."

"This is about what happened, isn't it?"

Maha took a small bite of bagel and shrugged her shoulders. The bagel was at least a day old, though the bag claimed it was made that morning.

"It was so long ago." Ardeen waved another piece of clementine in the air. "No one even *remembers* it any more."

This was false. Maha knew, from several sources, that Ardeen had told and retold the story of that night in January several times. The quiet, studious, by some accounts snobby Maha Rasad screaming out "Make me real!" while lying naked on the parquet in front of an open door in a grubby east end townhouse.

Maha preferred not to think of the public aspects of the *make me real* business, and wanted at times to scrub her own skin off to cleanse herself of those three words. But she didn't remember calling out. All she remembered was the face of the Lord, the voice of the Lord, the Lord choosing her.

The others saw the grunting blond man on top of her. Maha saw Him.

"Everyone remembers."

Ardeen finished chewing and adjusted her scarf. "I don't want to say this, Maha, but I guess I have to? You have to get over yourself. You're seventeen. We're writing our final exams this week. No one really cares which loser Nordique you had sex with."

"Then why can't they . . . why can't *you* shut up about it?"

"Me?" Ardeen opened her mouth wide, as though she had just been accused of stabbing a kitten. "Girl, I am worried about you. It's a sign of mental illness, you know, to think your friends would betray you. I got your *back*."

Maha smiled.

"Who *found you* in the first place, last year, all meek and lonesome and, like, wearing Village des Valeurs and those gay shoes? Little miss play the piano and pray with your flippin' mom?"

"God called me."

Ardeen stopped unpeeling her second clementine. "God called you."

"Yes."

"What, on the phone?"

"The night of the party. He came to me that night."

"You were wasted."

"While that guy was on top of me, during . . . *it*."

"That wasn't God, Maha. That was vodka and green apple syrup, remember? Maybe it was the big O."

"I heard Him. He spoke to me. He wants me to come to Him, so I'm going."

"Don't tell me you're committing suicide. What a cliché."

"No. I'm going to find Him in person."

"God. In person."

"Yes, Ardeen."

"All right. So where does God live?"

"I don't know that yet."

"But you're saying he's a man. But he's also God?"

"Yes."

"You're walking on the path to Jesus here, if you ask me. If I started talking like that, my parents would send me to camp. *Serious* camp. I can't even guess what Zaki and Sara Rasad would do." Around them, the seats on the upper floor of the Faubourg filled with single downtowners who ate Subway and takeout Thai green curry for dinner. The men among them stared, especially after Ardeen got up to sit on Maha's lap and began stroking her hair. "You're just confused, baby. It was traumatizing for you. Your mom, the school. That dude you're supposed to marry."

"If you don't believe me, fine. But don't talk to me like I'm your . . ." Maha looked around, to make sure no one was listening. She prepared to say a word she did not use habitually. ". . . bitch. Just leave me alone."

"Maha. Socially speaking, you don't exist without me. I heard Jonathan Talbot was gross to you in class today. I heard about that, and you know what I did? I asked Dylan to kick his ass, make him think about his actions. I did that for no reward, no glory. I did it quiet, sneaky, like a doer of good things in the background of the world, you know? And how am I repaid for getting Jonathan's ass kicked? I'm insulted, like some cat that pissed on the couch."

There was an opportunity here for Maha to apologize, to thank Ardeen for being a superb mentor and protector. But as Ardeen waited for the apology and expression of profound gratitude, Maha could not find the words. Or the will. "Go."

Ardeen jumped to her feet and slammed her half-peeled clementine on the table. "I hope you *do* commit suicide." And then she fetched her bags, turned, and walked away, her black high-heeled sandals clacking.

A bagel remained on the table, and three clementines. It was still bright outside, the late-day sunlight crashing through the giant windows. Maha continued peeling Ardeen's clementine and stared at the orange perfection that was revealed. *This* was the domain of the Lord. She would not allow herself to feel guilty for what she had just done. If Ardeen did not understand, Ardeen was not a true mentor and protector.

Above her, a grunt of introduction. Maha looked up to see a man in a tight black T-shirt, nodding. "Mind if I join you?"

"Yes."

The man smiled with half his mouth and sat down anyway. His cologne inspired an instant headache. "So, what's your name?"

Maha began to gather the bagel and clementines and drop them into a plastic bag. It was best, she had learned, to ignore people like this.

"*Tu parles français? Ça tombe bien.*"

"Please just stop talking. To me and to everyone. Really."

With her bag of food, Maha ran to the top of the stairs. Two steps down, the man called her a lesbian.

EIGHT

Maha crept into the yard behind their house on the West Island so the Lord might notice her. It had been stifling inside, glutinous with the smell of boiled chickpeas, one of Maha's least favourite foods. She had worried, in her bedroom, that ceilings and the fog of cooked vegetables might hamper the Lord's perceptive powers. Not that it was any clearer or fresher outside. It had rained and the city reeked of dog droppings.

From the yard, her mother's round face was visible in the

kitchen window. The fruit trees were beginning to bud and the early flowers were up. Only one small spot of filthy snow remained, between the garden shed and the old brown fence. She waited in the wet yard for some time, listening to the random calls and cries of neighbourhood children, the muffled ring of the family telephone, the hum of the expressway.

The Lord, it seemed, was not looking for her. So Maha kicked at the lump of snow and went back inside. The smell of boiled chickpeas hovered in her bedroom as she sat before a blank sheet of paper, preparing to write and devour her sixteenth note. Until recently, she had addressed the Lord as Allah out of respect for her family and community, but ever since the January night he came to her on the parquet floor of that apartment near Metro Fabre, Maha suspected the Lord was not exactly Allah. When she swallowed the letters, as an offering to He who knew her blood and bones intimately, Maha closed her eyes and imagined this new Lord. He did not look like Allah or dress like him or sound like him. The Lord's voice was that of a man who has smoked too many cigarettes, the host of a jazz music show on public radio.

"Maha?" Her mother knocked on the door. Her mother's knock, always the same. Three quick taps, followed by entry. Only Maha had taken to locking the door. She heard her mother's sigh through the hollow wood.

"Just a sec."

Maha opened the door and her mother entered. Sara Rasad, in her red sweater set and apron, peeked subtly around her daughter toward the desk. Their relationship, like everything else, had been transformed since that night in January. Whenever they shared a room, *shame* hunkered in the corner, panting and salivating.

"Dinner is almost ready."

"I'll be right there." Maha didn't make eye contact with her mother, hoping she would go away.

Sara Rasad didn't go away. She crept closer to the desk wiping her hands unnecessarily with a dishtowel. "Are you studying, then?"

"Yes."

Several walls separated them from the family room and the television, where Maha's father and younger brother Arun had stationed themselves. Maha wanted her mother to rouse them for dinner. Speeches had become common in the past six months, and Maha wasn't sure she could bear another.

"Do you need any help?"

It was obvious that her mother was not there about dinner or homework. "No. Thank you."

Sara Rasad swung the dishtowel about. "We're very proud of you, you know. For your schoolwork."

"Thanks. I'll come for dinner right away, Mom."

"But . . ."

Maha straightened her posture, prepared herself. Someone at the Islamic Centre weekend potluck had perhaps offered some new guidance to ward off harlotry. What wisdom? What opportunity for ablution?

Sara Rasad spoke quietly. "While you were outside, your physics teacher telephoned."

Through the walls, Maha could hear the deep bass of her father's snores. Arun's somewhat less than enthusiastic "Ha," accompanying a laugh track.

"What did she say?"

Sara Rasad, who grew up in a suburb of London, England, reverted to her childhood accent in stressful situations. "She's worried about you, as am I. In January, you –"

"Please, Mom."

"Don't you *please* me, Maha. I've done my very best to understand what you're going through. First you get drunk and –"

"Stop."

"– and copulate. In public, no less. Now you're writing letters to God and giving them to your teacher." Sara Rasad managed a tortured smile and placed a hand on her daughter's shoulder. Again, she lowered her voice. "I thought we had made a set of rules. I thought we would communicate more effectively when you felt troubled. This is what families do. Silence and scheming will only lead to . . . further humiliation."

"Yours or mine?"

Sara Rasad dug her fingernails into the wool of Maha's sweater. She breathed, forcefully, through her nose. "Why can't you understand the consequences of your actions?"

"Why can't you leave me alone?"

"We love you. We want you to live honourably, with dignity, according to –"

"Mom, I've said sorry, hundreds of times. I don't drink any more. I don't stay out late. What else can I do?"

Sara Rasad looked away from her daughter for a moment, at the geometric design of the bedspread, and left the room. Maha did not turn back to her sixteenth note to God or follow her mother to dinner, because she knew Sara Rasad would return. With a newspaper article about post-traumatic stress syndrome, maybe, or words of good judgment from the imam. A quotation she had transcribed from a viewing of the *Dr. Phil* show.

While she waited, Maha fingered a stack of graduation flyers and pamphlets. An advertisement for summer jobs in

Banff fluttered to the ground. She picked it up and learned that she could be a chambermaid at the Banff Springs Hotel. Maha also learned that the hot springs on the eastern slope of the Rocky Mountains had been discovered by accident in 1883 by railway construction workers. According to aboriginal legend, the springs had magical healing powers.

Sara Rasad knocked three times on the door jamb and re-entered Maha's room holding the black cordless telephone. She covered the receiver with her hand. "Gamal is on the telephone."

"I don't want to talk to Gamal."

"You must."

"Did you call him?"

Sara Rasad closed her eyes for a moment. "Please. This one thing, for me."

"He can't help and I don't need help. Please leave me alone, so I can study."

The patience and compassion left Sara Rasad's voice as she held the phone in front of her daughter. "Do as I say."

Maha didn't know Gamal, not really. They had met once, during a formal meeting at his parents' house in Mississauga. It was an emergency measure, one month after she'd had sex with the boy on the parquet floor, a happenstance that was meant to remain a secret from Gamal and his family. The only sounds she heard in Gamal's house, as they sat on the couch together with a tray of sweets and strong tea before them, were from his stomach and the tick of the gigantic Iranian clock. When Maha broke the silence to ask about the extravagant clock, Gamal told her the ancient Persians had crafted it. Maha said she didn't know the ancient Persians had clocks. Gamal grunted and scratched at his nascent beard.

It was clear Sara Rasad was not going to leave the room until Maha took the phone, so she took the phone. "Hello?"

"Hey."

"How's it going?" Maha waved her mother away.

"Dinner," said Sara Rasad, as she departed.

Gamal snorted. "Your mom says you're having a crisis."

"She reads too many sentimental novels."

"Huh," said Gamal. A few conversations ago, Gamal had confessed that he thought novels had a detrimental effect on society. So, in ensuing conversations, Maha brought them up as often as possible.

She stared at the ad for Banff as the stillness on the line became uncomfortable. *Magical healing properties.*

"Your mom asked me to come visit this weekend, to cheer you up."

"Come here?"

"Yeah. Do you want me to come?"

Maha watched her father stumble down the hallway, newly awakened from his sleep, like Frankenstein's monster. "No."

"Well, then I probably should. We should sort out how you're feeling." Gamal cleared his throat. He was seven years older than Maha, and sometimes he talked as though he had acquired a lifetime of knowledge and insight in those seven years. "Sometimes it can feel overwhelming and frightening, the uncertainty of the future."

The digital alarm clock said it was 7:19, Eastern Time. Maha was certain her future was in Mountain Standard.

NINE

During the second intermission of a Saskatoon Soldiers game, Kal McIntyre learned to appreciate poetry. The Soldiers were in Kelowna and losing by three goals, which was their custom. Kal was on the toilet at the time, drinking from a Gatorade bottle filled with the cheapest rye whisky he could find, which was his custom. The bathroom door was open so Kal could hear Dale Loont, the coach, berating his teammates for lackadaisical forechecking and general sloppiness of character.

"Is there fire in you?" he said.

A few of the players, young guys, answered variously: Yeah. Oh yeah. Hell yeah.

"Come on, that ain't even kindlin'. I said, is there *fire* in you?"

More joined. "Yeah!"

"Are we a bunch of hick pussies like they say?"

"No!"

"Are we Soldiers?"

"Yeah!"

"Are we gonna do some killin' out there?"

"Yeah!"

"I'm talking about intestines on the ice! Pumpin' hearts!"

"Yeah!"

Dale Loont started quietly and worked louder with each syllable unto the final word. "Now, my boys, my men, are we gonna shed some Kelowna blood out there in the third motherhumping period?"

In his twenty years of hockey, the rhetorical questions posed by overweight coaches in sweat-drenched locker rooms had constructed a cumulative feeling of nausea and dread in Kal. He leaned back on the cold porcelain of the white tank and read the messages etched into the grey paint on the bathroom door.

"Suck it!" commanded one, next to a crude drawing of the male sex organ. "Only homos play hockey," noted another.

If Kal was going to shed some motherhumping blood out there – Dale Loont was born again and therefore unable to say *fuck* – a short nap was in order. Not that bloodshed would serve any purpose. There were only three games left before playoffs, and the Soldiers, a farm team for the Carolina Hurricanes, were eleven points out of contention.

As he closed his eyes, Kal noticed a third message, near the bottom of the bathroom door. It was different from the others. It had been written with a black Sharpie, by a careful hand.

> . . . *for here there is no place*
> *that does not see you. You must change your life.*

> – *Rilke*

On the toilet, Kal read these two lines again and again, and wondered when he had last looked at some poetry. High school, but even then. Had he looked? Had he allowed the words to do this – whatever *this* was – to him? Moments of great insight happened on the ice from time to time, but they were so automatic and over so quickly there was no time to chew on them and wonder why they had come. This was different. It was curiously physical. Here in the locker room, in Kelowna, there was *no place* that did not see him. Over and over, he repeated the lines out loud. When he was ten and twelve, in the arenas of Thunder Bay, Kal had been the best young player anyone had ever seen. The more he'd played, the more powerful he'd felt. No, maybe not powerful. Something. Hot oatmeal and lightning, thrashing in his gut. And now, in the locker room, on the toilet, Kal reclaimed that feeling.

Kal did not believe in conversion experiences. Yet it seemed to him he was in the midst of one, hot and cold at the same time, happy and sad, hopeful and fearful. All that made him Kal – the past and present and the doleful future he could not deny – existed at once and rattled inside him. All of this was more exquisite and commanding than anything rye and yellow Gatorade could provide.

"Who you talking to?" It was Gordon Yang, the backup goalie and probably his last friend on the team.

Kal did not answer. He could not.

"Are you pissed?" Gordon Yang rapped on the cubicle door. "Wake up."

No, they were not friends. Kal had no friends left, and it was his own fault. He continued to read the words, whispered them.

"Kal!"

He stopped reading. "Coming, sorry. Got a touch of the green apple quickstep."

"Bullshit." Gordon Yang punched the door. "Just get your ass out here. I'm sick of making excuses for you."

Alone in the bathroom again, Kal looked down at his bottle of Gatorade. It seemed old and insincere all of a sudden, like a bottle of politics. He stood up, lifted the toilet seat, and poured the rye inside.

At the sink, Kal stared at himself in the broken mirror. Since the day he'd turned twenty, Kal had considered himself middle-aged. Four years later, there were wrinkles near his eyes and around his mouth when he smiled. He drank too much rye whisky and entertained dark and vengeful thoughts as he fell asleep at night. Yet in the afterglow of the words he had read on the back of the cubicle door, Kal rediscovered a sort of purity. He could only conclude that the third period of this game in Kelowna would be special, a new beginning. Kal – *that* Kal – had arrived.

On his first shift, he made a decent play in his own end, stealing the puck from a Kelowna forward and sending it up the ice onto some new kid's stick in front of the red line. The new centre didn't know what to do with the puck when he got it, of course, and in most circumstances that would have been frustrating for Kal. But not tonight. He understood the kid's frustration afterward, sitting on the bench in a fume. Instead of ignoring the kid, Kal crashed his glove down on the boy's shoulder pad and said, "Next time."

The kid looked up and said, "Real sweet pass."

Kal's ex-wife Candace and their daughter Layla were in the stands, just above an advertisement on the boards for Home Depot. He waved but they weren't looking. Suddenly, a memory of the night of Layla's birth hit him. February 4, 2001. They were living in an apartment in Windsor when Candace's labour pains kicked in. According to the book they had purchased about pregnancies, walking helped ease the baby down into the birth canal and often took the mother's mind off the contractions. Between three and four in the morning, with a vicious wind howling off the Detroit River, they had shuffled up and down their dark block. Kal had been freezing but Candace couldn't get cool enough. She had made him promise, between contractions, with her teeth clenched, that he would never leave her.

On Kal's next shift he glanced up at Candace and Layla after shooting the puck past the Kelowna blue line. At that moment, someone plowed into him and he went down. Ordinarily, Kal would stand up, throw off his gloves, and see what might happen. Instead, he took his position on the Kelowna side of the blue line while the man who hit him, a notorious meathead named Luciak, called him a pussy. Some men in the stands, sporting goatees and baseball caps, booed.

You must change your life.

When the puck was on the opposite boards, Kal took his eyes off it just long enough to glance up at Candace and Layla again. This time they were looking. Layla waved and a shiver of love and pride zipped up his spine. Instead of waving at his daughter, Kal nodded and turned his attention to the game just in time to see the puck slide past. A Kelowna forward was already three strides ahead of him, on a break-away. He chased the forward, watched him score, and skated back to the bench in silence.

"That was real pretty, Mack." Dale Loont walked over and bent down, spoke quietly into the top of Kal's helmet. "If you don't want to play, walk. Just walk away."

TEN

After the game, Kal was forced to wait until his teammates had left Prospera Place for the hotel bar. Dale Loont wanted to have a frank discussion about his performance on this road swing, but Kal was not interested in rebuttals. As Dale Loont spoke, Kal sat in his jeans and T-shirt, repeating the lines of Rilke to himself.

"Do we understand each other?" said Dale Loont, at the end of their frank discussion.

"Absolutely," said Kal.

Candace and Layla waited in the lobby of Prospera Place, near the bulletin board. When she spotted Kal, Layla ran to him. His daughter's hair, as he hugged and kissed her, smelled of orange peel. She wore a black skirt and pink tights with black boots and an authentic-looking white fur jacket.

A rich girl.

"I'm sorry you didn't win, Daddy."

"We didn't deserve to win."

"You know I figure skate now?"

Kal took Layla's hand and they walked to the bulletin board where Candace stood, with that knowing look about her. In their last seven or eight phone conversations, Layla had mentioned the figure skating thing. "I *didn't* know that. I think it's plain terrific and I'm real proud."

Since Candace and Layla had moved away, Kal had come to understand that he was slowly becoming another one of his daughter's relatives, another old man to charm. For now he was Daddy, but he knew that Layla referred to Elias Shymanski the same way. In time, Kal would only lose more and more of his daughter, particle by particle, until they became shy and strange around each other. Like all spurned fathers, he occasionally considered sneaking into Layla's bedroom one night and spiriting her away to Guatemala City. But this was selfish thinking. Kal had nothing and, therefore, nothing to share. He wished, briefly, that he could drop to his knees and tell Layla about the lines of Rilke, and that she would understand and sympathize.

It hurt Kal to see that Candace was obviously happy, more comfortable, and more hopeful without him. It hurt to remind himself that she was a noble beauty. Her fur jacket was most definitely authentic, as were the designer jeans and high-heeled boots.

"Good game."

"Oh, it was not."

"Don't mess with Kelowna."

Kal shook his head. "Never again."

Together they walked out of the arena and into the parking lot. It was a warm late-spring evening, with the scent of lilac in the breeze. Music played from one of only four trucks that remained on the lot, a pickup with a few men gathered around the open tailgate.

"Can Daddy come over?"

"I already told you, Layla. No."

Kal smiled. Elias Shymanski, the Ford-Mercury dealer who had stolen Candace from him two years previous, was under the impression that Kal was an explosively violent and vindictive man, keen to shiv him with an edged weapon. This was not so distant from the truth. A cordial dinner at a newish hotel restaurant was not in their future. "I'd behave myself."

Candace turned to Kal and faked a cough. A warning. If he said anything further, she would restrict phone calls and visits to punish him.

The truck with the open tailgate was seven parking spots from Candace's Expedition. There was a red cooler on the tailgate, and an aggressive hybrid of rock and rap music thumped and sawed from the cab. The young men spotted Kal's hoodie, with the Saskatoon Soldiers logo on it, commented loudly, cackled, and walked over with their beers in hand.

This was rare. Not that grown men would openly harass each other, but that he was alone. Players were encouraged to enter and leave arenas en masse, to prevent broken noses and bad publicity. In high school, or even a day ago, Kal would not have allowed the drunk men to approach unchallenged. It was always best to pummel the leader quickly and savagely to frighten the others. But the way Kal saw it, he had to change, and here was an opportunity.

"The pride of Saskatchewan," said the smallest of the three men, who had large ears and a tiny face that made Kal think of a gerbil. The gerbil in a jean jacket stopped several feet in front of Kal. "What're you lookin' at? You got a problem?" He tossed his full can of beer away and it landed on the pavement with a thud.

Candace hurried to open the back door of the Expedition and lift Layla inside. It only took a minute to buckle her into the booster seat. "No," said Kal, "stay. I want to talk to you."

"I don't want Layla to see this."

"There'll be nothing to see." Kal turned to the men. "Thanks for your interest, fellas, but no, actually, I don't have a problem. As for what I was looking at, I was just admiring the pickup truck and the heavy metal hip-hop thing you got going there. What's the name of the band?"

The men, who appeared to be about Kal's age, turned to one another. All three had goatees.

"And I want to thank you so much for coming out, for supporting minor league pro hockey. I know I'll be going back to Saskatoon with my tail between my legs. Between my legs, fellas."

The gerbil bent down to tie his shoe. Then, in a flash, he stood up and tossed a handful of dirt and tiny pebbles in Kal's face.

Kal heard Candace say, behind him, "Oh, for Christ's sake."

The dust got in his eyes and the men were on him. Kal got low and grabbed a couple of legs, flipped one of the men on his back. But the other two continued to kick and punch, landing blows about Kal's upper back, shoulders, arms, and ears. It ended when Candace stepped forward and bear-sprayed the attackers. They held their eyes and stomped and cussed so loudly that Kal was sure Layla would hear them through the doors of the SUV.

"Fuck, I'm dying. I'm dying," said the gerbil.

"Call an ambulance!" said another.

While Kal wiped himself off and allowed his ex-wife, her breath smelling of coffee and cinnamon, to examine cuts on his forehead and in his mouth, the drunks writhed on the pavement and wailed about blindness and retribution.

"Goddamn you." Candace smirked with affection and nostalgia and, Kal figured, a vast sense of relief that they were no longer married.

Kal opened the back door of the Expedition to discover his daughter crying. Through her sobs, she asked why the men had attacked him. Since there wasn't a satisfying answer to that question, Kal unhooked Layla from the seat, lifted her out, rocked her in his arms, and told her how big she was getting. Twice he had to spit the blood out of his mouth with as much daintiness as he could muster.

"They hurt you!"

"No, Layla. Daddy isn't hurt. Those men couldn't hurt Daddy."

Candace opened the driver's-side door and tossed the bear spray inside. "That isn't happening again."

"I know, sweetheart. That dirty shoe-tying trick."

"Not your sweetheart any more, Kal."

He whispered into his daughter's ear. "Just let Dad get a few things in order, change his life, and then he'll come get you and Mom and we'll all live somewhere nice and pretty together. With palm trees, probably. Right?"

"Yeah," Layla said, into his blood-splattered hoodie.

"Time to go," said Candace.

"Not without Daddy!"

"You got playschool tomorrow. You need a bath."

"No!"

Candace yanked Kal away from the vehicle, buckled Layla in, and closed the door. The child screamed again.

Candace sighed. "Thank you. Really. For a swell evening."

"Something happened to me tonight. I see things differently. And I want you and Layla to be a part of it."

"You just got in a fistfight, Kal."

"I'm changing my life."

"To what? You don't know how to do anything else."

"It doesn't matter what I do, really, it's how. Anyway, it's a feeling more than a plan."

"I don't get it."

"Candace, I need you to help me change. And I can help you. We don't want Layla growing up spoiled and fancy."

"You saying I'm doing a bad job?"

"I'm saying we could be happy together, and Layla could be happy with us. I feel a big transformation coming on. See, there was this poem, this call to me."

"A poem. You, and a poem."

"I'm a new man."

"From the handbook of ex-husband clichés."

"No. Really."

"Kal, I think you should change. It'd be good for you. But you know it has nothing to do with me any more and very little to do with Layla, right?"

Candace hugged him quickly, turned away, and stepped up into the driver's seat, slamming the door with a *thwock*. Kal waved as she roared away, but the rear windows were too tinted to see if Layla waved back.

The men were quieter now, in the nighttime parking lot. A part of Kal wanted to lay the boots, but another, more powerful part of him simply pitied the men before him, on their hands and knees, spitting and moaning. Kal bent over the gerbil.

"That was real sick, what you did to me there. In front of my daughter."

"Blow me."

"What sort of men are you? You're way too old for this sort of behaviour. Maybe you even have kids of your own."

Kal ambled down the sidewalk toward his hotel. The gerbil cussed again and called out, "Sorry, man."

ELEVEN

The following night, in Saskatoon, Kal wondered about Hell. He was back in his apartment on Tenth Street at Dufferin, playing Halo 2, destroying the Covenant one by one in order to save mankind. Gordon Yang was over, and they were drinking beer and eating Old Dutch salt-and-vinegar.

"There's no Hell," said Gordon, as he wasted a small pack of aliens near what appeared to be a pile of burning tires. "It was invented to stop people from being bad."

Kal nodded, but he wasn't sure he agreed with Gordon. Usually, in these sorts of conversations, he would nod and hope it would be over soon so they could talk about hockey or maybe video games or women. Tonight he actually considered Hell, and decided he believed in it. Not the exotic one he'd learned about at Sacred Heart School, but a different sort of place, smelling of white toast and shoulder pads. Hell was playing hockey all your life, skating for seven years on the verge of the show, only to wake up one morning and realize you were slow, drunk, angry, and uneducated. To have a wife who divorced you because she thinks you have no future and a daughter who's forgetting you more and more every day.

"You barely touched your beer."

Not only was Kal suddenly bored with beer, he was bored with Halo 2. It was as though he had eaten a bad hot dog, only the rot was in his head instead of his stomach. In twenty years of video games, from the old Pong console hooked up to the black-and-white TV in his bedroom to the new Xbox, Kal had never been bored. Yet here he was, in his dark and smelly apartment off Broadway, stricken by the meaninglessness of what was possibly the greatest video game ever created.

Earlier that evening, before Gordon Yang showed up with the beer and potato chips, Kal had staved off panic by fetching the small canvas bag of pornography from his bedroom closet. Even his favourite flick, *Indiana Joan and the Black Hole of Mammoo*, couldn't cheer him up. It struck him, for the first time, that the girls of *Indiana Joan and the Black Hole of Mammoo* couldn't possibly be having any real fun. Kal removed the disk from his DVD player, tossed it into his canvas bag of pornography, and dropped it all into the garbage chute. After listening to an Otis Redding disc, an emergency tactic, he began to weep. Then he dialed Candace's number in Kelowna.

Elias Shymanski answered in that phony high-class voice of his, and Kal paused. "Hello?" the man said again, as though he were auditioning for the role of James Bond. Since Kal had not remembered to block his number before dialing, the Ford-Mercury dealer who was having sex with the love of his life already knew who was on the phone. There was no point trying to prank the man. There was no point asking for Candace, as she would not speak to him. It was past Layla's bedtime. "You must change your life," said Kal.

"What?" said Elias Shymanski, and Kal ended the call.

Gordon Yang sensed Kal's lack of interest in Halo 2 and dropped his controller on the chipped coffee table before them. "Let's go to Vangelis, shoot some pool."

"I don't want to."

"Let's smoke a bowl."

"I don't want to do that either, Gordon."

"What the fuck? So you got jumped in Kelowna, get over it."

"It's not them." Kal bit his top lip and turned his video game avatar in circles until the Covenant swarmed and destroyed him. "I've decided to change my life, that's all, and once you decide a thing like that you can't take it back. It's a venom."

Gordon Yang turned from the television. For a moment or two longer than usual, he stared at Kal. He chewed at his thumbnail quizzically. Then he winked. "Change your life tomorrow, man. Tonight, we get retarded."

With some rhetorical flourishes, Gordon convinced Kal that only a night at the strippers would cheer him up. So they phoned a taxi.

The driver, whose name was Abdelahi according to his tag, did not speak. He listened to soft drum music. Gordon made lewd invitations to groups of university girls out his open window. When the car arrived at Showgirls, Gordon paid the fare and slid out. As Kal followed him, Abdelahi turned and said, deeply and slowly, "Prepare yourself."

"What?"

Abdelahi seemed confused. In a different voice, an accented voice, he said, "I said nothing, sir."

"Prepare myself for what?"

After a pause, Abdelahi smiled. His teeth were wonderfully white. "I do not understand, sir. Enjoy!"

For an hour, Kal and Gordon sat at a table drinking very expensive Coke. Stringent liquor-control laws meant Showgirls could serve beer only in the adjacent bar, so most of the men shuffled in and out of the strip club. Gordon gave a standing ovation to Lana the Bulgarian Bombshell, the most beautiful woman ever seen in Plovdiv. "I want to go home now," said Kal.

"Absolutely not. I heard the next chick's only got one leg."

"Gord, I can't. Something weird's happening to me and I can't concentrate properly on strippers."

"Okay, wait. I got just the thing to cheer you up." Gordon jogged over to the manager.

It was clear what was happening here. Five minutes later, Kal was alone in what appeared to be a former accountant's office. The fluorescent lights had been removed but there were two stand-up lamps, fitted with orange bulbs, one on either side of a red, faux-Persian rug. On the wall, framed photographs of nude and almost-nude women leaning art-fully over motorcycles and Trans-Ams. The room smelled of cigarettes and perfume and cleaning solution. The small sign on the wall instructed Kal, in both of Canada's official lan-guages, to sit and stay in the padded lounge chair. If he stood up at any time during the performance, he would be forcibly removed and fined. Kal sat, inspected his fingernails and the cigarette burns in the chair arm, and wished, briefly, that he would fall asleep and not wake up for several years.

With a quick knock, a tall Indian-seeming woman entered. Kal recognized her earlier, from the Kama Sutra and 1001 Arabian Nights performances.

"Kal, I presume?" she said.

"Yep. Hey, nice job earlier."

The woman wore tight black yoga sweatpants and a thin satin shirt. "Should we get started? Clock's ticking."

"We might as well."

The woman unbuttoned her shirt. "You're a professional hockey player?"

"I am."

"The NHL?"

"The AHL."

"You like it?"

Kal answered the way he always answered. "It's what I wanted ever since I was a kid."

"That's terrific." The woman dropped her shirt on the Persian rug – her stage. "This was my childhood dream too, to dance naked in front of slouching strangers."

"We're damn lucky people."

"God should strike us down for our happiness." The woman pulled her sweatpants down. Underneath, she wore a pair of pink thong panties. "You want me to take these off now or slowly, as part of the show?"

"Slowly."

"Good choice. High heels on or off?"

"Definitely off."

"Another good choice, and a rare one." The woman pressed play on a small CD player that was also an alarm clock, and began to sway. It was contemporary R&B: a bass line, a drum machine, and a woman singing about someone's baby. As the music was not very loud, Kal could hear the dancer breathing. Her exhalations were slightly raspy, due to an apparent cold or lung disorder. Kal could also hear the cartilage in her knees as she placed her hands on the arms of his chair and bent low. Her hair was so black in the dim light that it shone blue.

"You believe in God?" he said.

The woman stood up and slipped her thumbs under the waist string of her thong as she moved her hips. "What do you mean?"

"It isn't a trick question."

"I guess I do."

"What do you think of him?"

The woman turned around, so her bare behind faced Kal. She bent over and looked up at him between her legs. "I think he feels sorry for us. He can see we're suffering."

"Us?"

"You and me, everyone. Us. We're pathetic, don't you think?" The woman stood up and gestured with her arms as part of her dance, indicating *here and now.* "Exhibit A."

"Right."

The woman lowered herself backwards, limbo-like, until her palms hit the rug. Then she extended her pelvis upward. A yoga move, Kal figured. The woman's hair brushed the floor. "For an extra fifty I'll let you touch me."

"I know."

"Do you want to?"

"You betcha, especially right now. But . . ."

"But what, hockey boy?"

"I'm trying to change my life here. Paying to touch strippers doesn't fit into my new plan."

The woman shifted so she was on her hands and knees, a classic. Even in the dim light Kal noticed her shaving rash. Her rash and her scratchy voice, her cavalier use of the phrase *strike us down,* it was all endearing. She moved with the song for a while, which had given way to a "guest performance" by a rapper. The dancer went flat on her front and shifted, with a small grunt, to her back. She opened her legs, signalling that the performance was nearly over. "So what are you doing at Showgirls?"

"My friend Gordon figured it would cheer me up."

"Gordon Yang?"

"Yeah."

"He's a sweet guy. He understands tuition costs these days. Gordon always pays the fifty bucks."

"I'm sorry."

The woman closed her legs and the song ended. It was silent in the room but for the distant thump of the sound system and the poppy consonants of the DJ. Kal stood up and extended a hand to help her up, and she took it. "You aren't supposed to stand."

"Again, sorry. I don't know what I'm doing."

"Who does?" The woman coughed and extended her hands toward the ceiling for a moment, turned her head from side to side. More yoga.

They were only a few feet apart now. Kal had spent fifty dollars on dumber things. There was a sheen on the woman's stomach, from oil, perhaps, or sweat. Or moisturizer – this was Saskatchewan, after all. She smiled and nodded, and turned to collect her clothes.

To Kal's disappointment, she did not take her time getting dressed. She pulled on her yoga pants and her shirt, and dished him a queenly wave.

Kal sighed. "I want to thank you for everything you did for me here."

The entertainer cleared the phlegm from her throat. "Say hi to God for me, when you find him."

TWELVE

"Prepare yourself," as uttered by Abdelahi the cab driver, gurgled and echoed in the bedroom as Kal tried to sleep. Since his return from Kelowna, he had been waiting for an agent of change to appear. It would be a woman, he thought. One of those new tough-lady NHL scouts in a grey skirt and blazer, chewing gum and making fierce eye contact. Or someone from the broadcasting industry looking for an honest and handsome, but not fancy, colour man. But the agent had not come.

Now Kal suspected she would never come, that he had prepared himself defectively for the coming change in his life. The bedroom window was open and the night was cool. Kal was too lazy, or stunned by anxiety, to get up and close it. As dawn broke, Kal reflected on Abdelahi's words and realized there was a fair chance he was going crazy. One of his teammate's older brothers, a completely normal young man apart from a compulsion to masturbate in public, had apparently turned into a schizophrenic overnight. Now he was on drugs, a drooler, living in some halfway house in New Brunswick.

Or, *or*, maybe Kal had a brain tumour. Maybe he was turning homosexual. That certainly would have explained his new and shocking lack of interest in pornography and video games.

Kal did not wait for his alarm to sound. Shortly after six he showered and *prepared himself*: he filled a large backpack with clothing and zipped up his jacket. It was cold and bright outside, a typical spring morning in the prairies. The city felt as though it had hardened overnight. A sort of shellac had been brushed over the stout buildings and thirsty old trees. Dogs barked. An airplane ascended for the trip west to Alberta. Kal walked toward the river, past the playground and park benches to Gabriel Dumont Park with its fake Métis village. Long before Kal had arrived in Saskatoon, this had been the site of a dump. Now it was a collection of short trees and shrubs along the twinkling South Saskatchewan, with a canoe launch and play village. Once, before Kal had met Candace, he'd pretended to be Métis in order to impress and have sex with a Blackfoot girl he'd met at a hockey camp in Lethbridge. Unfortunately, his ruse failed. The Blackfoot girl had been saving herself for men of greater means and potential.

Birds were out in great numbers. Kal was one of the few people on the paths that morning. He passed a homeless man and a couple of veiny joggers and ventured over the shrubbery to the muddy bank of the river. Standing by the gurgling water, he closed his eyes, shut out all his thoughts, and listened. Sparrows. Water. Wind in tall grass. The distant freeway.

Kal walked back to Broadway, found a cab, and rode to Credit Union Centre with the back windows open. He had hoped Abdelahi might still be working, so together they could explore the true meaning of "Prepare yourself." But this morning, the cab driver was an obese white fellow who smelled of feta cheese that had been left on the counter too long.

At the vibrating bus parked in front of the arena, coach Dale Loont stood with his arms crossed. "Where you been?"

"I took a walk along the river."

"You took a walk along the river."

"I took a walk along the river."

Dale Loont looked up at the blue blue sky. There were plenty of strong chins out there but Dale Loont had a weak one, which had always disturbed Kal in a way he knew was unfair. It was a miserable instinct, to dislike a man according to the strength of his chin. Now he saw the sorrow and wretchedness at the core of Dale Loont.

"You're hungover I expect?"

"No, actually."

"You're supposed to be a model for these kids, Mack."

Kal was twenty-four, which made him only five or six years older than the average player. How much wisdom was expected of him, really? "Sorry, Dale."

"What are you sorry for, exactly? For being a slob and a boozer? For throwing away your talent? For being a goddamn *zombie* out there when I need you on fire?"

Around the lips of Dale Loont, the remnants of toothpaste. Kal looked away. "That's exactly what I'm sorry for, Dale. All of that."

"Good. Now, what are you gonna do about it?"

Kal knew what Dale Loont wanted to hear. Bons mots about passion, sacrifice, one hundred and ten percent. Instead, he gripped Dale Loont's fleshy arm and pulled him away from the rattling bus. The weak chin was getting to him. Kal was careful not to raise his voice or squint as he spoke. "You don't have to tell me what's not important, Dale, because I'm an expert in that field. So let's just get on the bus and avoid each other for the next, I don't know," Kal looked down at his watch, "three hours. Okay?"

On the bus, Kal sat next to Gordon Yang. "Where'd you go last night?" said Gordon, whose eyes were dark and puffy. "I waited for you at Showgirls and then I waited for you next door. For a while I was hoping you scored with Rupi."

"Who's Rupi?"

"The Arabian Nights? The fucking lap dance I spent twenty bucks on, thanks for saying thanks?"

"Sorry, Gord, thanks."

"But then I saw her later, in the bar, and you know what she said?"

"What?"

"That you're clinically depressed."

The driver plopped into his bouncy seat. "Winnipeg or bust."

As the Yellowhead flattened into the sunny east, Gordon Yang fell asleep. It felt wrong to Kal, this direction. A few kilometres out of Saskatoon, he shook Gordon.

"What? What? Please, Kal, I am so, so tired."

"Remember your uncle, who owns that place in Banff?"

"I remember my uncle, Kal. What do you want?"

"You think he'd give me a job?"

"You got a job." Gordon sighed and sat up. "You wanna be a dishwasher now or something?"

"Yes. I want to be a dishwasher."

"Piss off."

"Gord." Kal shook his friend's head, and then manoeuvred his face so they looked into each other's eyes. "When we stop for gas in Viscount, I'm getting off this bus."

"What if we stop in Yorkton? We sometimes stop in Yorkton."

"Forget Yorkton. Just promise me something. When you get to Winnipeg, I want you to call your uncle and tell him I'm coming. Tell him I'm a good worker."

"All you've ever done is play hockey."

"Tell him I'm a *very* good worker."

"This is stupid."

"Phone your uncle."

Gordon closed his eyes. "Fine. I'll phone my uncle and say the finest dishwasher in Saskatchewan is on his way west."

"Good. Thank you."

"Idiot."

Gordon drifted back to sleep and a familiar quiet settled over the bus, broken only by Dale Loont's cellphone conversation with his wife. Kal wondered why Rupi the stripper had diagnosed him with clinical depression. Was it the atmosphere of failure in Showgirls seeping into him? The question of God? Kal couldn't recall why he had asked a stripper about God or what he had expected to learn from her. A number of people would have been better suited to exploring the notion with him. Priests, for instance.

Before his father died of Non-Hodgkin's Lymphoma, when he was in grade three at St. Thomas Aquinas in Thunder Bay and his family was most like a family, Kal attended Sunday school. He had one outfit: a pair of black pants, a beige dress shirt, and a black vest. Each week Kal would wear one of his dad's clip-on ties and stand before the sliding glass mirrors in his parents' bedroom, amidst the musty sleeping smells of his mother and father, and he would be *so handsome*. Every Sunday, so handsome. His father would declare, from time to time, that Kal would grow up to be a lady-killer.

At Kal's father's funeral, the preacher declared that God had taken him. Sunday school was all about the majesty of God and Jesus, who seemed to be the same thing, yet when God and Jesus *took* someone – his father, for instance – it was terrible news. When Kal's mother wasn't around, his father had called the preacher a Big Gay and mocked the Sunday school teacher, Mrs. Reyes, for her backfat. None of it made sense then, and almost twenty years later, on an eastbound bus, it still didn't make sense.

In Yorkton, Dale Loont and some of the players went inside to use the toilet and buy coffee. Kal took his backpack and left Gordon sleeping. The bus driver, Stu, stood at the pump. "I hate Yorkton," he said. "You have to stand here and hold the nozzle. It doesn't have that thing on it."

"Stu, where's the bus station?"

"Downtown on First Avenue. Why?"

"I'm changing my life, Stu."

The bus driver looked up. "There were a couple times I figured on changing my life but I never did 'er."

"I lost the magic."

"You think so?"

Kal nodded.

"You're finished? Really?"

"Really."

Stu reached up and placed his non-pumping left hand on Kal's shoulder. "That's a damn good thing to learn now, before you get old and mean. What should I tell Loont?"

"Tell him I went off to find my fortune."

"Is that what you're doing?"

"I don't know. First, I'm gonna be a dishwasher."

Stu stopped pumping and offered his old, lumpy hand for a shake. Kal took it. "Kid, good luck. I hope you find that fortune."

"I probably won't."

"No one ever does." Stu shook his head. "Except sons of bitches. And, unfortunately, you ain't one of those."

THIRTEEN

When Tanya Gervais researched and bought the urban assault vehicle, she knew it wouldn't be popular with all of her friends and acquaintances. But Tanya also knew the most unique and maligned automobile on the road today had a lot in common with the woman who sat behind the wheel. Durable and a bit intimidating on the outside, refined and complex inside, and utterly dominant in its sphere.

The Hummer H2 was still relatively new, with less than a thousand kilometres on the odometer. The cabin was still shiny with the unmistakable fragrance of leather and freshly moulded plastic. Ownership had a retroactive effect. She now could not imagine herself driving anything but a bright-yellow Hummer. When Tanya put it in gear, the sound of her black coat squeaking against the leather seat verged on erotic.

At dinner parties, after a few glasses of wine, when the West Coast crunchies felt empowered to blame her consumer preferences for the war in Iraq, farmed salmon, Hollywood movies adapted from comic books, climate change, deforestation and desertification in Africa, that funny taste in the tap water, religious fundamentalism, and Vancouver house prices, she answered the way her Hummer might answer, if only it had the capacity to speak.

You don't like it, move to Cuba.

A lot had changed recently. Though it had taken almost twenty years in the business, the most miserable of them in dread Toronto, Tanya was finally being recognized for her talent, experience, vision, and commitment. A month after her thirty-eighth birthday, she had become vice-president, marketing and development, for Canada's newest and hottest entertainment and lifestyle brand, Leap.

Leap Television, Leap Satellite, Leap Mobile, Leap Fashion, Leaptv.com. There were even plans for a youth-oriented discount airline if one of the current players in the North American market showed signs of an impending bankruptcy. Her cellphone – a Leap product – linked to a new-generation intercom on the Hummer's dash. The ring was her current theme song, "The Woman In Me" by Shania Twain. Tanya was not a fan of her music, or that of any other country-crossover artist, but Shania Twain had fashioned herself into an international brand, with extensions into a number of cultural sub-industries. "The Woman In Me," every time Tanya heard it, was a reminder that limitations were for the feeble. Crunchies who disparaged Tanya's Hummer were also inclined to dismiss Shania Twain and her *chanteuse doppelgänger* in Las Vegas, Céline Dion. But the crunchies, drunk on inferior wine, were jealous and pathetic. Were *they* beautiful Canadian multimillionaires living in warm climates? Were any of *them* on the *Forbes* list of Top 20 Richest Female Entertainers?

"The Woman In Me" began to play, and Tanya whispered an affirmation to herself as she pressed talk on her cellphone. She was stopped at a set of lights in the transition zone from East to West Hastings Street downtown, a buffer between one of the richest and one of the poorest neighbourhoods in the country. Rain joined the strong wind that jolted the Hummer. On the sidewalks, the hipsters and the homeless, the sane and the prophetic, battled their umbrellas.

"Gervais."

"Tanya, my sweet."

It was her boss, the thirty-six-year-old genius Darryl Lantz. The man who'd shown her it was folly to pretend she didn't find inspiration in Shania Twain and luxury SUVs inspired by military transports.

"Darryl, my liege."

"I'm in the Vancouver office here with a couple of the lawyers. Where are you?"

"East Hastings, in the rain."

"The welfare cheques came out today. I hope you brought nunchucks."

"Hi, lawyers," Tanya said.

They greeted her, through the intercom, formally. It was her thing, to disarm men in expensive suits with a tone of easy confidence. She allowed phrases like "Hi, lawyers" to carry certain messages, like poison on the tips of arrows. *Yes, I am a woman. Yes, I dye my hair blond. Yes, I've had a teensy bit of pre-emptive work done on the eyes and around the mouth. But if you toy with me I will devote all of my vigour to your undoing.*

"Tanya, we're working on the British co-pro and we're stuck on a couple of the details here. You have a minute?"

She had to drop off a package of raw digital video footage several blocks away, at the Pacific National Exhibition, and traffic was tight. Her lane was clogged with a garbage truck and a bus turning left, so she flipped on the signal light and began creeping into the right lane. The car behind her, a little Jetta, did not approve. *Haink*, the Jetta said. So Tanya flattened her hand on the Hummer horn, a real horn. A *go fuck yourself* horn. "Always for you, Darryl." The rain came down even harder, in waves, so Tanya adjusted the wipers as she half listened to Darryl Lantz and prepared for the light

to change. Her plan was to accelerate through the intersection, return to the left lane for the open road, and come
back into the right lane in time to miss the pothole repair
crew up ahead. The air smelled like tar, one of Tanya's least
favourite smells.

The light turned green and the pickup truck in front of
her paused momentarily. Again, Tanya honked. She despised
slothful, inattentive drivers. Finally, the pickup accelerated
and Tanya deked left to get around it. The road opened up.
All she had to do was get past the pickup truck and move
into the right lane without clipping the smelly pothole crew.
Darryl Lantz talked on. But the pickup didn't slow down.
The truck kept pace with her so she had to cut back in
behind it. She cussed quietly, and the Jetta driver *hainked* at
her again.

Tanya waited to accelerate, just long enough to flip the
Jetta driver the bird. She flipped it, hoping the driver could
see through the wet windows, and slammed on the brakes as
a rectangular slab of concrete, half the size of the Hummer,
smashed into the pavement ten feet in front of her. Tanya
screeched to a stop not two inches from the slab, which had
burrowed into the pavement like the unexploded bombs of
Second World War movies. Above the Hummer, the claws
of a crane swaying back and forth like the pendulum of a
grandfather clock, next to a burgeoning condominium.

"Tanya? Are you there? What was that?"

It had been so loud and so unexpected and so massive and
so heavy that Tanya forgot she was on the phone with Darryl
Lantz and the lawyers. "Nothing," she said. "Nothing." She
said this by reflex because *nothing* was supposed to bother
the vice-president, marketing and development, of the hottest
new entertainment and lifestyle brand in Canada. A crowd of

curious pedestrians gathered in the rain to stare at the slab of concrete. It was aged and uneven, veined with rebar.

"Good."

Darryl Lantz continued, but Tanya had lost the ability to process what he was saying about the British reality television concept they were trying to import. She could hear him over the increasing buzz around the slab but the words were not properly linked. Already, she could hear sirens. "There's a concern here, Tanya, that tempting husbands to cheat on their wives with former girlfriends will create some rather complex legal challenges. There's a sinister quality to this concept and I love it, love it unreservedly. But Canadians are becoming more litigious, as you know, inspired by their American cousins. We're wondering how your contacts in London got around this."

There was an answer to this question, of course. Somewhere. The grey of concrete slab that would have killed her if she had not paused to make an obscene gesture at the driver of a Jetta met the grey of the sky and the grey of the Hummer's interior. Was that how death worked? One instant, everything, and the next, nothing? Maybe it was an outlook formed by a career in the entertainment business, but Tanya had always envisioned her life as an epic. The churchy lower-middle-class upbringing, the idiosyncratic education, the ugly relationships, the rise to power. Once she reached a plateau of sorts at Leap, she would adopt a child and hire a nanny from the developing world to care for it. By forty-five, she would take over from Darryl Lantz, or head up a similar company, her own company. In New York. The first magazine profiles and unauthorized biographies would appear as she eased into her fifties.

The randomness and chaos of the world had always seemed a colourful backdrop for the meticulous strategizing of Tanya's adult life. Real estate prices confirmed that the appearance of randomness and chaos were desirable. Tanya wanted to spend her middle years in New York, the capital of randomness and chaos, because her success, the elegance of her success, would look and feel most artful there. But how many concrete slabs were out in the world, in New York and London and Paris, ready to fall on her Hummer?

"Tanya?"

"Yes."

"Did you hear me?"

Did she hear him?

Darryl Lantz chuckled, but it was clear he didn't find anything funny. "I'll repeat."

Even though the climate-control mechanism contended it was twenty-two degrees Celsius in the H2, Tanya was freezing. There was a jaggedness, a moist blackness about her. She attempted to connect the feeling to others in her past – influenza? food poisoning? bladder infection? – but all she discovered was a series of nightmares from her childhood. The earth, or a facsimile, covered in ash and dark angles, Tanya standing utterly alone and abandoned in a clearing. When she tries to reach some of this world, to touch or even understand it, the edges stretch out to infinity.

In sessions with her therapist, years ago, she recalled this recurring nightmare. The therapist, Dr. Huston, said it was one of the most common dreams among career-minded people living in the west end of Vancouver and, indeed, in all major cities in the developed world. Tanya had rejected her evolutionary and social impulses to find a mate at a young age, reproduce, and purchase a minivan. Dr. Huston leaned forward over the linked fingers on his lap. He said something that ended with "the realization that we are alone."

But Tanya never felt alone. Not *alone* alone, in the way Ebenezer Scrooge was alone. Tanya was unencumbered, free, available, prepared for anything. Anything except the concrete slab that crushes fabulously successful people in the middle of a rainy afternoon on East Hastings Street. Now she repeated his diagnosis aloud, into the receiver of her cellphone. "The realization that we are alone."

"Tanya?"

"Yes?"

Darryl Lantz did not chuckle. "Tanya, can you hear me? We can hear you. I'm in the office with a couple of the lawyers."

Workers from the condo development were on the street now, in their hard hats, screaming at one another. Several men and women under open umbrellas spoke into cellphones. More sirens, getting closer. Tanya turned off the phone.

It wasn't aloneness she feared but the instantaneous unravelling of her dreams and desires, her idea of herself, her plans. The unwriting of those magazine profiles and unauthorized biographies. For all the tepid religion in her formative years, she believed only in Tanya Gervais. But when a concrete slab can fall from the sky and crush you in an instant, in a *thonk* of crushed yellow metal and a malfunctioning alarm – *whoop whoop* – why believe in Tanya Gervais? Of all that is available to the believer today, the buffet of men and women and icons, past and present, why her? What did Tanya Gervais mean, anyway? Where was she going? What was she doing?

Tanya tried to do that thing she did on the day her parents kicked her out of the house for smoking marijuana: push it aside, file it away, use it as fuel. But she couldn't put the Hummer in park, let alone open the window for the bearded man in a hard hat and blue overalls, screaming in the rain. "Are you okay?" said the man in the hard hat. "Miss? Missus?"

FOURTEEN

Two years ago, in her previous position, Tanya Gervais was production manager on a documentary shoot about the health care system in Costa Rica. On a break one day, bored with the heat in downtown San José, she went for a hike in the hills behind her hotel and saw the most beautiful thing in the world: a blue morpho butterfly. The colour of its wings reached through her chest cavity and fluttered there. And for the first time in her adult life, Tanya was moved to tears.

Luckily, there was no one around.

No words in her vocabulary – lustrous, translucent, iridescent – came close to describing that blue. She continued along on her hike, obsessed with discovering why such a colour should exist. What evolutionary advantage? On the airplane back to Vancouver, she wondered how a woman might make money off the blue morpho. Was there a market in the U.S. for such a thing? No matter how hard she tried, Tanya could not find a way to reduce the butterfly to a commodity, to sell her experience on the well-worn trail behind the hotel in San José.

Now, Tanya attempted to package her near-death experience on East Hastings. Perhaps it was the sort of thing others might relate to, if she were able to reproduce the slab and its psychological value. Its purity. The new quality of her aloneness that the slab illuminated. When the police and fire trucks arrived, the large and gentle men helped her shut off the Hummer, gave her a cup of substandard coffee, put a blanket over her shoulders, and asked her a number of questions about the slab. Tanya could hardly remember what she said, though she did take a photograph of the slab with her phone. The slab had not crushed her, but it had crushed something. A presence had become an absence.

An hour or so later, she delivered the package to the PNE without informing the client that she had come, thereby negating the value of making the trip herself instead of calling a courier. After several failed attempts to speak with her on the cellphone, Darryl Lantz finally advised her, in a stern voice-mail message, to go home, get her shit together, and contact him about the British import in the morning.

Tanya parked the Hummer in the garage under her west-end condominium. She marvelled at the separation between the chemical smell of her garage and the peachy freshness of her building's elevator. Normally Tanya worried that a crack addict would break into the garage and vandalize the Hummer, but today she found herself wondering about the infomercial industry. Maybe she could write a slim volume, produce a set of six compact discs, and sell them on late-night television.

In her 1,400-square-foot condominium, she sat on the couch and watched night fall over the mists of English Bay. Tanya checked her messages. Three from Brian. Brian, the chief financial officer of Leap and her current boyfriend. Brian had heard, from Darryl Lantz, that she had been acting strangely.

Tanya took a bath with a notepad, in case any ideas about packaging and branding the slab came to her. To her displeasure, she cried in the bathtub and accomplished nothing. Instead of Shania or Céline or any of her other mentors, Tanya listened to a satellite radio special on Mahler. Though he had been dead since 1911, Gustav Mahler seemed to understand, with absolute precision, the way she felt in the echo of the slab. She put on a black dress and sat at her dining-room table, staring at the notepad. Blue of the blue morpho. Slab of the slab. No ideas came to her, yet the slab did not allow her to concentrate on the British co-production about cheating spouses, or Brian, or anything else related to Canada's newest and hottest entertainment and lifestyle brand.

When Brian knocked, he was twenty minutes late. The flowers, pale-pink peonies and some baby's breath, looked and smelled fresh enough. Brian, a tall man with a deep voice who wore a lot of aftershave from Paris, kissed her on the lips with his eyes closed.

"You look stunning."

"I know."

"What happened today?"

"Nothing major."

In his car, a Lexus, Brian described his day. He so often felt like the only one in the company who truly understood the relationship between revenues, expenditures, and profits. In the restaurant, Wild Rice on Pender, not far from the strip of East Hastings where the concrete slab had nearly killed her, Brian whispered that maybe, just maybe, Leap would not survive three years without a takeover by a larger media player. Usually, Brian and Tanya exchanged stories and opinions like fencing opponents, each waiting for a millisecond of silence to strike. Both wanted to be in the position of Darryl Lantz one day, visionary and captain of the digital revolution, and in conversation together they often competed for the right of succession. But tonight, Tanya had nothing to counter Brian's contention that Leap was doomed. She cared neither for the future of Leap nor for the bearing of her own career in the entertainment and lifestyle media.

The restaurant was designed, like so many in the city, in the spirit of Asian minimalism – the cherrywood and stainless-steel accents of western opulence. All around them, fellow Vancouverites whispered and laughed inoffensively. After two glasses of wine, and an uninterrupted monologue concerning his majesty, Brian leaned forward and placed his hand on hers. Did the appetizers not agree with her stomach?

Their seats for the touring National Ballet production of *Swan Lake* were in the third row, centre right. Tanya had difficulty paying attention until the corps de ballet. The sight of all those beauties in white tutus, their youth and their innocence, their perfection, their immortality in the context of falling slabs of concrete, brought Tanya to tears again. She tried to fight it by biting the insides of her cheeks and performing Kegel exercises. Tanya closed her eyes, to wipe them without ruining her makeup, and pictured herself in Banff. She was leaving in less than twenty-four hours for the television festival. There, she would have meetings with desperate fools she had known far, far too long. Perhaps the fatigue and frustration, in concert with the high-threadcount sheets on her hotel bed, would cure her.

At the intermission, her eyes a mess of black mud, Tanya rushed to the ladies' room. In front of the mirror, surrounded by rich women and their talk of everything that did not matter, Tanya felt nauseous. So nauseous she threw up in the sink. The women gasped, one screamed, and they all backed away. When Tanya stood upright from the regurgitated grilled rare ahi tuna and kabocha and butternut squash pot-stickers, she looked at her reflection and did not recognize the vice-president, marketing and development, of Canada's newest and hottest entertainment and lifestyle brand.

For the first time in many years, Tanya wanted her mom. But her mom, unlike the ghost of Gustav Mahler on the radio, would not recognize or appreciate her.

Without fixing her eyes or even wiping her face, Tanya walked on to Hamilton Street without her coat. She hailed a cab and, in the back seat, prepared herself for the implications of unemployment. Drugs, institutions, dry hair, chanting, incontinence.

Instead of sleeping that night, Tanya searched the Internet for a possible treatment. But she did not find it. The next morning, she packed her bag for Banff and arrived at the office before 7:00. She stared at the eighty-three new e-mails in bold on her computer screen. Outside, near the floatplane terminals, workers smashed giant support beams into the beach for something about the Winter Olympics. Carol, the executive assistant to Darryl Lantz, phoned at 8:30 to request a 9:00 in his office. Her employees arrived, the shiny young women of marketing and development, with their bleached teeth and black pinstriped suits from Winners. Winners.

They chattered in their usual manner, joined their team-mates in the oval of cubicles, and fell eerily silent. Tanya's phone call with Darryl Lantz and the lawyers had already become office mythology. *The realization that we are alone.* Her senior manager passed the office and peeked in as though Tanya were a zoo animal masturbating.

"How *are* you?"

"Fuck off."

Her senior manager, who knew she would soon be the next vice-president, marketing and development, tilted her head in mock sympathy. "Lovely. Let me know if I can help with anything?"

At 8:55, Tanya stood up from her desk. She passed Carol and the office of Darryl Lantz and hit the call button for the elevator.

FIFTEEN

Stanley Moss sat in the open lounge of the Edmonton International Airport, looking down at a cup of Tim Hortons coffee. He had asked for black but the teenage girl at the counter had poured some sort of mock-dairy product into it, giving his coffee the consistency of spoiled butter. A discarded newspaper next to him featured a columnist analyzing the Progressive Conservative Party of Alberta: too progressive or too conservative? The ruined coffee and the

trite column conspired against his good mood. He looked up
from the paper to see Alok Chandra standing in front of him
in an orange patterned muumuu and white turban, arms
outstretched. "Brother-in-law."

Released from his embrace, Stanley walked around Alok,
looking for his bags. Alok had grown tremendously fat and
smelled of sandalwood. The last time Stanley had seen him,
in 1989, he'd worn business suits with ironed handkerchiefs
and the occasional flower in his lapel. "Luggage?"

Alok winked and tapped the shoulder strap of his backpack. "This is it. I learned in my treks through rural Asia
never to bring anything more than a small bag."

"This isn't rural Asia."

Alok started toward the revolving doors. "We hear in
Toronto that everyone's rich and arrogant here now. Is that
true? I definitely feel an energy I don't recognize."

"In the airport?" Even though Stanley could suddenly lift
heavy things, toss teenagers, break swimming records, and
occasionally read minds, he remained skeptical about Alok's
ability to *feel an energy*. Twenty-two years ago, Alok had still
been married to Stanley's sister Kitty. Alok had been a prac-
tising psychiatrist then. One afternoon, he'd suffered a hernia
in a bowling alley and, upon recovery, in the afterglow of
painkillers, received an epiphany. Alok decided he had been
called to quit his practice and move to Toronto, where he was
obliged to open a New Age bookstore and Reiki centre. He
was also obliged to engage in ritual group sex, thereby
ending his official status as Stanley's brother-in-law.

In the Oldsmobile, on the stretch of Queen Elizabeth II
Highway that linked Edmonton with its airport, Alok opened
his window. "Smells the same."

"Like what?"

"Grass maybe? Dust? The Platonic form of dryness?"
Alok reached over and squeezed Stanley's shoulder. "When
the phone rang and I saw your name and number on the call
display I thought, 'Here we go, Stanley Moss is calling to
bring me home.'"

"Wow."

Alok nodded. "I've become quite good at predicting the
future." Though he was in his late sixties and obese, there
remained a youthfulness about him. He applauded, hollered
"Canola!" into the wind, and closed the window. "I love
you, Stan. Always have."

"That's nice of you to say."

"Well, I'm really thrilled to be here. I don't know why I'm
here, because you're the mysterious gentleman you always
were. On the airplane I had a dream that you were going to
present me with proof that I'd committed a murder. I'm sure
my dream interpretation book would have a lot to say about
that, but I didn't pack it. I pack light. When's the last time
we actually spoke? Kitty's funeral? Oh look! A tractor!"

Sure enough, a tractor moved down a field to the west of
the highway, in silhouette. The long, orange dusk of summer
in the prairies had begun.

"I love tractors."

"Is the store going to be all right while you're gone?"

"The store runs itself. To be honest, Stan, I only go in
when I'm lonely. My staff does everything. Everything. That's
why I've been able to take those trips. You know what I saw
in Nepal?"

Stanley attempted to see what Alok saw in Nepal. A train.
Odd vegetation. The sun and the brim of a hat. A skinny boy
with his eyes closed. "Nope."

"Buddha. The new Buddha. There's this kid who doesn't eat and doesn't sleep. He just meditates and receives wisdom from the impersonal godhead."

"Did you talk to him?"

"Oh no. Absolutely not. He was meditating really hard, you know, and his handlers kept onlookers at a distance. It wouldn't have been proper to yell something out."

"How do you know it wasn't a hoax?"

"I knew. I just knew, Stan. This is my life's work, right, to be plugged into these sorts of things?"

Stanley smiled.

"You look different. Vibrant. Sneaky." They passed a series of overpasses and freeway junctions, big box stores, and strip malls wrapped around giant parking lots. "The city, I see, now looks like every other city in North America. By which I mean to say doomed."

Even though Stanley was the sort of man who complained about oil refineries, strip coal mining, urban sprawl, and the unrestricted growth of the province, he felt a little bit proud of the small giant the city had become. "If this highway corridor were a country, it would be the second-richest in the world, after Luxembourg."

"I think you should keep that sort of trivia to yourself, Stan. Really. It's nothing to brag about." He stayed quiet until Stanley entered Old Strathcona and stopped, randomly, at a café named for New York bagels. Alok got out of the Oldsmobile and walked to the edge of the gravel parking lot, which was tucked between a jazz club, an old mill, a theatre shaped like a wheat silo, and a number of condominium towers. He crossed his arms and looked out over the river valley.

It was simple to read Alok's thoughts of reflection and nostalgia, of this neighbourhood and winter and the smells particular to cities of the plains. Stan wondered if it would be best to leave his old friend for twenty minutes.

"Are you hungry, Alok? If not, I could come back."

"Always hungry. Always."

"I think I should probably tell you why I flew you out here."

"To get a load of my turban, perhaps?"

"I *was* going to ask you about that."

Alok reached up and massaged his turban. "Picked it up in Nepal."

"You don't say."

In front of the café, just as they were about to enter, Alok hugged Stanley again. Mid-hug, he kissed Stanley and picked him up. In the air, Stanley glanced to his left and saw several patrons of the café, frozen in mid-chew, as they watched a large, elderly Indo-Canadian in an orange muumuu lifting and kissing a gentleman in a grey three-piece suit purchased in 1987.

SIXTEEN

The owner of the New York Bagel Café turned on the hanging lights as the sun eased behind the houses and hills to the west. Alok Chandra removed his turban, a one-piece, and shook his head. "Why didn't you call me, or send an e-mail, when you found out?"

"Alok, we haven't spoken in years."

"I know hundreds of holistic practitioners who might have cured you. This whole 'medical management' approach to cancer is a sham. What you have to do is convince the cancer cells to back off. Make them trust you. It's like taming a dragon."

"Dragons." After a sigh, and a sip of his wine, Stanley continued. "Anyway, it's in remission now, or something. My symptoms have disappeared."

"Hallelujah. What treatments did they use?"

"None."

"You're self-medicating. Good. Good."

A woman wearing large spectacles put a plate of organic beef goulash in front of Stanley and a spinach pie in front of Alok.

"This looks delicious," Alok said. Then he took the woman by the hand. "Might you also bring us another half-litre of wine?"

The woman nodded and took her hand from Alok. She stared at Stanley, stuck her tongue into her cheek, almost said something, and walked to the bar.

"God bless this *food*," Alok said. "You know?"

Stanley nodded. "I just feel better. A lot better. Too much better."

"I don't understand."

"This is it, Alok. I don't either. That's why I asked you to come."

"There's no such thing as a free trip to Alberta. Is that what you're telling me?"

"Yes."

Alok took his first bite of spinach pie, and pointed at the pie with his fork, as though the pie had figured him out.

"When I began to notice these changes, I looked on the Internet to see if maybe it was a common thing. But it isn't."

"Maybe you tamed the dragon without even knowing it. Do you have any crystals at home, lying around in the eastern and northern extremities? Do you chant, as a rule?"

"Alok, shut up for a minute."

"Certainly." Alok gulped the final bit of his wine just as the woman with large spectacles set down their second half-litre. "Thank you, my love."

Stanley pushed his plate and glass away. "I have powers."

"Am I allowed to ask questions?"

"Yes. Sorry for telling you to shut up."

"It was very rude. Very *Alberta* of you."

"Shut up."

"What sorts of powers, Stanley?"

He was embarrassed, all of a sudden. All this fuss. "It's probably nothing."

"Come on."

"I seem to have acquired a touch of superhuman strength."

"Keep talking."

"And I can hear thoughts."

"Really?"

"Really."

"All right." Alok closed his eyes and placed his index fingers on his temples. "What am I thinking right now?"

Stanley saw what Alok was thinking in a series of flashes: sex with Frieda, as she was in the 1980s. Poofy hair, tight jeans. "You prick."

"Sweet Susan. You got that?"

"I did."

"Wow. Wow. How do you do it?"

"No trick. I just hear and see, if I want to hear and see."

"Why? How?"

Stanley shrugged.

"Hence the plane ticket. I'll consider this very seriously, Stan, using each area of my expertise. How is Frieda, by the way?"

"Twenty years older than your fantasy."

"Do you think she's still mad? At Kitty's funeral she wouldn't even look at me."

"She'll be all right."

"What does she think of your mind reading?"

"She doesn't know about it. I mean, *I* don't even know about it. Is this something that happens to cancer patients, by chance, just before they die?"

Alok took another bite of spinach pie while he considered Stanley's question. The server with the large spectacles was staring at Stanley from behind the counter, as she had been throughout their meal. Finally, she walked over, pulled up a chair, and sat down. "May I?"

"If you could give us another moment," said Stanley.

"I was wondering," said the woman. She smiled, shook her head as though embarrassed, and removed her glasses. "I was wondering if I could see you sometime."

"Oh. I'm married."

"Not that way. Necessarily. I just feel I'd like to talk to you. These things have happened in my life. It's like this mould has grown over everything. In a couple months I'll be forty-nine, and what have I accomplished so far?"

"Well," said Stanley.

Alok pulled out his wallet and stood up. He dropped sixty dollars on the table and beckoned Stanley out the door with a head tilt. "So sorry," he said to the server. "Mr. Moss is very tired. Perhaps we'll return and you can talk then."

"But . . ."

"Good night."

Outside, in the warm night air, Alok rubbed his hands together. He led Stanley around to the rear of the New York Bagel Café.

"Alok, did you eat enough? We left a lot of wine on the table. I could have spoken to that woman afterward."

"Forget her. Let's see something."

"Like what?"

"Something. Whatever you can show me. Your super-human strength."

During the Fringe Theatre Festival, Old Strathcona was the most densely populated piece of land in Canada, but it was currently deserted. Stanley looked around.

Alok did a 360. "I don't see anyone."

Stanley took a short and focused breath, jumped ten feet into the air, and thrust himself into a backflip. In the midst of it, with sky and gravel, tree and distant condominium whooshing past, it occurred to Stanley that he should prac-tise backflips before performing them. He knew, instinctively, when to stop spinning and straighten out. But as he prepared to land, Stanley leaned too far forward. His feet hit the gravel and he stumbled forward into Alok. "That wasn't very grace-ful. Sorry."

For the next thirty seconds, Alok said nothing. The city hummed. Then Alok said, "Frick," followed it up with a "Fuck," reached back for something to sit on, and fell into a chain-link fence near some unused railroad tracks. "Moses. You are Moses."

"Shh. Don't talk like that. I'm not Moses."

"Whatever you say. Whatever you say." Alok pushed himself off the fence and approached Stanley. Though Stanley felt uncomfortable, even frightened, he didn't back away. He allowed Alok to lay his hands upon him – on his chest and shoulders, in a frantic and searching manner. Alok closed his eyes, and in one motion he dropped to his knees and took Stanley's right hand and pressed it against his cheek. "Master."

"Stop it. I want you to tell me what this means."

Alok adjusted his knees on the gravel, said "Ouch," and looked up at Stanley again. "Master."

SEVENTEEN

Frieda was not fond of Alok Chandra. Taking him home for cocktails or coffee was not an option. So after Alok had sat for half an hour on the railroad tracks, mocking the phony Buddha in Nepal and marvelling that God had chosen his new messenger here in Canada's fifth-largest city, Stanley coaxed him back into the Oldsmobile.

"Maybe that's it, Stan. It's an unlikely place and you're an unlikely person. An old florist, sick with cancer. I mean, how dull can you get?"

"Thanks."

"Say, can we stop at a liquor store? I could really use some Grand Marnier."

"Is it necessary?"

"This is a spiritual phenomenon on a global scale, Stan. I mean, I'm sitting next to the most important man in the world. That is, if you're still a man. Do you feel like a man?"

"As much as I ever did, I suppose."

Stanley parked in front of a liquor store near Alok's hotel. While his old friend waddled inside, Stanley watched a black-haired couple in ponchos spray-painting wooden panels on the sidewalk. A crowd stood before them, sucking up the aerosol fumes. The artists had some finished pieces around them, wet-looking fantasy scenes like three-breasted women on horseback, looking sufficiently thoughtful by the light of a bleeding moon.

The idea that he was God's new messenger was comical, and he already regretted flying Alok Chandra out. It would have been just as easy to walk into a holistic health centre and bookstore or the Russian Tea House during palm-reading hours if he had been looking for that sort of insight. And Stanley did not appreciate the "prairie rube" insinuation in Alok's surprise.

A homeless-looking man, dressed in soiled jeans, knocked on the Oldsmobile window. Stanley opened it. The man did not speak. Instead, he shuffled warily from foot to foot with his hand out. Normally, Stanley did not give money to beggars. He worried that sustaining their way of life with financial contributions could harm their chances for renewal. But tonight he felt different. He took out a change purse and dropped almost four dollars into the man's cupped hand.

The man stuffed the money in his pocket and looked at Stanley. Really looked. Stanley felt compelled to reach out and touch his arm. "You should really stop this. It's not doing you any good. You can."

"I can."

"You can."

By now, Alok had appeared. "My destitute, angelic brother," he said, and put his arm around the homeless-looking man. He pointed at Stanley. "This, right here, is your salvation. Your greatest hope. Come with us."

"No," said Stanley. "I gave him some money."

"Get in the back seat."

Stanley did not want the man in the back seat. His jeans were really very dirty. "No. Don't."

Alok sighed. "Did you give him some wisdom? A nugget?"

"Yes."

Alok turned to the homeless-looking man. "Did he give you a nugget?"

The man nodded.

"What was the nature of this nugget?"

"Uh . . . I forget now. Something nice."

"Something nice." Alok shook his head and turned to Stanley. While he did, the homeless-looking man peeked inside the liquor bag. "Stan! This has to be your bread and butter."

"What has to be?" Stanley knew the homeless-looking man wanted to leave. "Let him go, Alok."

"Are you sure you can't perform some sort of miracle? Make him look, smell, and think better?"

The homeless-looking man was becoming impatient and a little insulted. "Excuse me, guys. I got an appointment over there."

Alok shook his head in profound disappointment and released the man. A few paces away, the man pulled a pile of money out of his pocket and proceeded toward the liquor store. "Damn it, Stanley. See what you did?"

"Get in the car."

There were several hotels in Old Strathcona but Stanley had decided on the Varscona for Alok. It was conveniently located near cafés, restaurants, liquor stores, and left-wingy retail outlets that sold recycled toilet paper and books about crushing *the man*. This way, Alok wouldn't be too needy. While Stanley checked him in, Alok inspected books on the decorative shelf. The clerk offered an upgrade to a suite for an extra fifteen dollars a night, but since Stanley was already keen to send Alok back to Toronto he quietly rejected the offer. Stanley handed the key card to Alok and they hugged again in front of the fireplace.

"Breakfast tomorrow?"

"Sure."

"Will Frieda come?"

"Maybe. But you can't tell her I brought you here. She doesn't know about this and, well, you know how she feels about you."

"All that was so long ago."

"Yet so vivid, if you allow yourself a second to think about it."

"Right. Right." Alok chewed on his thumb. "Anyway, tonight I'm going to consult a few bookstores, the mighty Internet, and my own internal databanks through meditation and Grand Marnier. Bringing me here, it was destiny. It *is* destiny, Master."

The automatic wooden doors opened for Stanley. "If you call me Master one more time, or Holy Teacher or Almighty or anything else of that nature, I'll use the muumuu to hang you from the nearest lamppost. Yes?"

Alok clasped his hands together. "He is beautiful in his wrath."

EIGHTEEN

At home later that evening, Stanley and Frieda listened to John Coltrane and played a couple of rounds of Boggle.

"What's he doing here?"

Stanley had prepared for this query. "There's some sort of spiritualists' convention. They use Ouija boards, conduct séances, read tea leaves, that sort of thing. It's in a different city every year."

"Where's he staying?"

"The Varscona."

Frieda looked up from her list of words. "There aren't any convention halls in Old Strathcona. Shouldn't he be staying downtown?"

"I'm not a convention planner, sweetheart."

Since the day Stanley threw the kid across the Chinatown parking lot, Frieda's eyebrows had been permanently raised. The only mind he wanted to read was hers, but Stanley had no access. For a full five seconds, even as she sipped her tea, Frieda stared at her husband. "How are you feeling today?"

"*Comme çi, comme ça.*"

"I noticed you snuck out of bed again last night. I woke just after one in the morning and you were gone."

"Yeah, sorry, I've been restless. I watched TV downstairs and fell asleep in front of some movie."

"That's odd, because I went downstairs. You weren't there."

Stanley had not prepared for this. "That's right. I went for a stroll."

"A stroll." Frieda smiled through the chanty bit of *A Love Supreme*. "In our neighbourhood, a stroll."

"Yep."

She looked down at her watch. "Are you up for another stroll tonight? If so, how about I join you?"

Stanley traded his slippers for shoes, and they stepped out into the heavy and moist night air. There was no wind. Fumes from oil refineries east of the city tasted like a rancid biscuit. He had to work hard, reaching and grabbing and gently wheedling with his pinky finger, but eventually he convinced Frieda to take his hand. They walked without speaking for several blocks, televisions flashing in every window, until they reached the Mill Creek Ravine. Instead of asking his wife's permission, Stanley led her down into the trails along the creek. Here the air was cooler and cleaner.

They passed a young man and a woman in matching flannel, walking two black Labrador retrievers in the moonlight. They smiled at one another, said hello. Once they had passed, Frieda said, "Usually, when I see couples like that, I think about your illness. I wonder how many walks we have left."

Stanley nodded.

"Now I'm almost nostalgic for that feeling of hopeless certainty. There was my husband, dying. It was . . . clear. I know it's grotesque but there it is."

"What are you saying?"

"Stan, I'm saying I want you to be honest with me. You don't cough any more. You threw a boy fifteen feet in the air."

"It wasn't fifteen feet."

"You haven't returned any of Dr. Lam's phone calls, and you've been secretive."

"When I get news, I give it."

"Bullshit." Frieda stopped walking and yanked at Stanley's hand so he would stop as well. They were on a cedar bridge, the creek tinkling underneath them. "I picked up the extension when the oncologist called. I know what he told you about the latest results."

"That something is wrong with them."

"What's wrong with them is they show you're *healthy* again. Now, that seems like something you should have shared with me. I'm going to ask you some questions, all right? And I want you to answer honestly. Can you do that?"

This was not how he had planned his confession. They were supposed to be in Frieda's favourite restaurant. The sushi was supposed to be on its way. Warm sake. There were supposed to be tiny rocks about, and slivers of burning incense.

"When's the last time you slept?"

"A week or so ago."

"Are you short of breath any more?"

"No."

"Headaches?"

"No."

"Why don't you remember anything?"

"I can't answer that one."

Tears welled up in Frieda's eyes. "What's happening to you?"

Stanley embraced his wife. "I really don't know. To be honest, that's why Alok is here. I asked him to help me figure this out."

"Alok couldn't figure out junior high math." Frieda wiped her eyes and nose on Stanley's sweater. "What else is going on?"

Stanley took a step off the trail and into the bush. Clouds moved off the moon again and the ravine glowed. Wildflowers were alert in the dew. As Stanley looked around for something, he could hear the crackling maturation of leaves and the flutter of bats. "I can sometimes hear thoughts. But never yours."

"Whose?"

"Whomsoever's."

Stanley eased through the bush. It reminded him of years ago, hunting for lost golf balls in the aspen parkland. In between a diseased pine tree and a birch, not far from the pillars of the cedar walking bridge, he found a boulder. The boulder was lodged deep in the creek bank, and fallen trees lay on top of it. Frieda had followed Stanley's progress, but she stayed on the trail. He called out to her. "Is anyone around?"

"The couple and the dogs are way ahead. Around here now, no. Only loonies are out in the ravine this late. What exactly are you doing in there?"

It was not difficult to slide the boulder up on to the soft, mossy ground. The trees crashed into the creek. Stanley lifted the boulder over his head and the dirt and wood chips, buried twenty or fifty or one hundred years ago, fell into his thin grey hair. He carried it out of the woods and on to the path.

Frieda saw him and took a couple of steps back. "No."

"I can do this."

"Is it real?"

Stanley braced himself and allowed the boulder to balance in his right hand – it had the weight of a softball –

before he tossed it straight up, way up. The boulder crested, spun lazily, and landed with a powerful thud in a clearing next to the trail. The ground shook so hard that cars in front of the $700,000 houses looking out on to the ravine began to beep and honk and howl. Frieda had watched the progress of the boulder but now she turned to address Stanley. She lifted the index finger of her right hand to make a point, and her legs went wobbly. She stumbled, her eyelids fluttered. Stanley moved as fast as he could to catch his wife before she fell into the creek.

For a few minutes, he tried to rouse her with words and kisses. Had Stanley ever held Frieda like this? In the honeymoon, threshold-of-the-hotel-room position? She was breathing, so Stanley was not concerned.

Out of the ravine and in the neighbourhood again, Stanley passed a gentleman smoking on his front porch. "Hey!" the gentleman said. "Is she alive, or . . . ?"

"Yes."

The man took a drag of his cigarette and walked out on to the sidewalk. He wore a beige fleece jacket. "What did you do to her?"

"Nothing. She's my wife."

"Did you hit her?"

"No. She was frightened and she fainted."

"Does she do that a lot? My brother-in-law is a doctor, so . . ."

Stanley walked quickly to discourage the man from following. "Yes. She has a condition."

"What condition?"

"Leave me alone."

"Maybe I should call the cops. What's your name?"

"Stanley Moss."

"Stanley Moss, eh? How do I know you're not lying?"

"Take the wallet out of my pocket."

The man looked down at Stanley's pocket while they walked, but didn't reach for it. Instead, he sucked from his cigarette. "You didn't hit her?"

"No."

"You must be strong, carrying her like that. She ain't skinny."

Stanley continued along.

"There's something weird about you. Where you from?"

"Please, leave us alone."

"Maybe I should and maybe I shouldn't. Maybe a good citizen should follow you, see where you live, call in the heat."

Stanley stopped again. "I know things about you, Mr. Davis. I know you were in Whistler last winter. After some drinks with your friend Jason from Richmond I know you walked past a sporting goods store and tried the door, just for kicks. The door was open, wasn't it, Mr. Davis? Did you enjoy your new skis and boots and jackets? Mittens?"

"Are you a security guard?" Mr. Davis dropped his cigarette.

"Pick that up."

Mr. Davis picked up his cigarette. "How did you know that?"

"It's an indictable offence, Mr. Davis."

The gentleman turned and started back to his house along the ravine.

"And stop snorting cocaine or you'll go bankrupt and die before you meet your grandchildren."

Mr. Davis began to run.

A few doors from home, Frieda opened her eyes. She put her arms around Stanley's neck. "My head hurts."

"I'm sorry, darling."

"Did you throw a big rock in the air?"

"I did."

She lay back in his arms. "I thought I was waking out of a bad dream. I'm waking into one."

"Shh."

"What are we going to do, Stanley?"

That night, while Frieda rolled and coughed and sighed in their bed, he flipped through the Old Testament. Some of it, the war bits and bad temper, was just as he remembered. Other sections didn't make any sense at all, with the same God wrestling the Hebrews *and* speaking from the clouds. When it grew frustrating, he crept downstairs and watched reruns of *The Simpsons*.

NINETEEN

The rhythm of their marriage: if one cried, the other could not. If one laughed excessively at a cinematic comedy or the misfortune of a televangelist, the other could not. Together, they composed a single creature easily embarrassed by its own emotions. When Stanley grew sick and despondent, Frieda became a cautious optimist with bouts of sarcasm. When Frieda was frightened or annoyed or frustrated, Stanley tried to be droll and light of spirit. Even though years of experience had taught him that he was grotesque when he tried to be droll and light of spirit, like a clown eating raw poultry, Stanley did it anyway.

While they waited at Tasty Tom's for Alok to arrive, Stanley searched for ways to cheer his wife. That morning, after the boulder-tossing incident in the ravine, she'd woken up quiet and thoughtful. She'd spoken formally, without using contractions, as though she had been infected with a degree from Oxford.

"Now, think of this one." Stanley waited for Frieda to take a sip of her coffee and look up, slowly, from her menu. "Shrub. Now that is a bizarre word, when you focus in on it. Absurd, really. Shrub."

Frieda adjusted the collar of her shirt.

Stanley wanted her to be snappy Frieda, skeptical and sardonic Frieda. Since they had forgotten to take the newspaper to the restaurant, she couldn't even make merry about local, national, and world events. In Tasty Tom's, surrounded by Spanish guitar music and the smell of frying onion and egg, he understood her situation. Despite being the daughter of a Baptist preacher, Frieda was a confirmed atheist by her early teens. For a woman without any faith and belief muscles, recent changes in her husband would be, at the least, alarming.

"I'm sorry, sweetheart. I've been insensitive."

She folded the menu. "Can you fly?"

"No." Stanley laughed. "Of course not."

"Have you tried?"

"What are you going to have? Let me guess: some sort of omelette with spinach and cheese, tomato salsa on the side."

"Can you walk through walls? Do you have X-ray vision? Can you produce webs from your wrists or stretch your arm from one end of the room to the other?"

"Frieda."

"Stanley."

"We're not in a comic book. We're in a restaurant."

"I am having trouble understanding."

"So am I."

Alok appeared next to the table, his hands clasped together, wearing the orange muumuu and white runners again. Upon his head he displayed a thin layer of white hair instead of the turban. "Frieda Moss. The radiant, the intelligent, the sublime . . . stand up, my lovely, and give Alok a hug."

A long silence passed. Finally, Frieda extended her hand for a shake. "How are you, Alok?"

"Violently fat, as is evident." Alok sat down next to Frieda, put his arm around her briefly, removed his arm as though her shoulder were made of barbed wire, and clapped his hands. "Smells good in here. How's the coffee? Of course, I already had some down the avenue. I'm a bit shaky from it, actually. But a little more couldn't hurt. And isn't that sun glorious? Warm and *sharp*. Why did I ever leave this place?"

"Because there were more kooks in Toronto."

Stanley reached across the table and took Frieda's hands.

"I am sorry, Alok." She looked up at the ceiling fan. "That was rude."

"No, I'm sorry. I wronged Kitty and I wronged you. But I'm better now. I'm enlightened. My friends, I have become a vessel of goodness."

Frieda smiled at *vessel of goodness*. "Stanley told me you were here for a convention." She turned to Stanley. "I assume that was a fib, Mr. Fantastic?"

"You're stretchy?" said Alok.

"No. I am not stretchy."

"Maybe I could be The Thing." Alok squeezed his bottom lip, a gesture of mock-thoughtfulness. "I'm certainly huge enough, and orange. Of course, I'm very weak, physically. But maybe –"

"Please stop it, both of you." Stanley was about to deliver an improvised lecture about not being a superhero, about not being anything special at all, really, when the waitress, chewing a wad of cinnamon gum, arrived to take their order. Coffees, omelettes, whole wheat toast.

When she left, Alok pulled a small notepad out of the canvas purse he carried over his shoulder. "I've consulted various sources, about what's happened to you. And I think I have the answer."

This was how Stanley had felt during the tests that led to his cancer diagnosis. He had been ready to fall on his knees before the specialists, even though some of his friends were doctors and he knew them to be deeply fallible. *Save me, save me.*

"The good news is, Stan, you're not going crazy. The bad news is, I don't think you're a superhero."

"Obviously not."

"I think you're God."

Stanley and Frieda, rarely aligned, raised their eyebrows at Alok and uttered versions of "Ha!"

"Wasn't finished."

"I hope not."

"Or, or," he said, "some sort of *messenger*. A messenger from God. A prophet. What aspects of your former life have passed away?"

Stanley leaned over the table and spoke quietly. "Certain memories. Though I remember you quite clearly, for some reason."

"What else?"

"I suppose I'm not as modest. I find myself more willing to, I don't know, express myself."

"Good, good. Right. Any specific things bothering you? About humanity, say?"

Stanley thought about it for a moment. Global warming, terrorism, the United States of America, super-viruses, noxious chemicals in household products. "The usual, I guess."

"Splendid, here's the thing. In history, when folks get powers like these, the ability to perform miracles –"

"I don't know if we can call them miracles, Alok."

Frieda opened her eyes widely. "What are they, then?"

"When people acquire the ability to perform miracles, certain feats are expected of them. You, Stanley Moss, have been called. You have a duty. And I am here to help you discover it."

Stanley briefly entertained the notion that he had been called. Yet in the time it took to pull a napkin out of the dispenser and wipe his mouth unnecessarily, he decided Alok was wrong. Agnostics are not called. The weak of heart are not called. Florists are not called. "It's the cancer, I think. The cancer has pressed some sort of button in my brain, next to the memory mound."

Frieda and Alok looked at one another, briefly, and turned their attention back to Stanley. He looked away from them, at the whole of the small restaurant, open to all the thoughts and concerns of the patrons and staff at once. The smell of bacon and coffee and burned toast mingled with thoughts and feelings of hunger, lust, boredom, and financial crisis. A thin woman near the door, reading the paper, was so hungry she could hardly concentrate on the words. A young man in a group of five could not focus on the conversation around him, which concerned former American vice-president Al Gore, because he was so completely desirous of the thin woman near the door. The teenage daughter did not want to be out for breakfast with her parents, and wished for it to be over soon so she could meet her friends at the skateboard park. The young husband tried to smile as his wife said admiring things about the brie and fruit in her omelette, but he could not forget that they were dipping into their line of credit every month, that a restaurant breakfast was irresponsible. It was just brie and egg and blueberries with coffee. They could make all this at home for a quarter of the price.

His powers were dizzying but Stanley could hold them together, even direct and compartmentalize them now. On the bus and in the hospital, on the day of the blue tornado, he had been frightened. Now, as he attempted to reconnect with that fear, he could not find it.

"I don't want this," Stanley said, though he didn't believe his own words.

TWENTY

They sat at a small table in a University of Alberta library, looking through religious texts. Frieda closed a scholarly interpretation of Zoroastrianism and chuckled. "You'd better learn how to write poetry, if you want to be a prophet."

Stanley looked up from the book he was skimming, a short history of Florence during the reign of Savonarola. "I'm sorry, Stan." Frieda exhaled shakily. "I can't seem to understand why this is happening."

Stanley smiled fondly.

"It feels like we should call the police, or the prime minister. Someone who can protect us."

"Did you find anything in there?"

"There is one God. He asks from us that we think good thoughts, say good words, practise good deeds. Quite decent, actually. You?"

He whispered, as several students had glared at Frieda for speaking at full volume. "Faith can be a dangerous thing."

"Stop the presses."

Alok waved as he returned from the room full of computers. He held a piece of paper high in the air and said, even louder than Frieda, "I've got it!"

A chorus of "Shh," rose up from the library floor.

"Do you know anything about the old Grail myths?"

Stanley and Frieda shook their heads in unison.

"They're about finding some magical *thing* that will save the land, and the people, from dying. That's what humans have always had in common, a fear that the world around them is fragile and may not sustain them. You should see, or rather smell, Toronto on a hot day in late July. Have you talked to a scientist lately? There are environmental manifestations but it's *social*, too. We're in exile from our own values."

"What values?" said Frieda.

"Human civilization as we know it began crumbling and liquefying years ago. This explains the success of my store, of the whole New Age movement. We're an intuitive species.

There's a worldwide, barely conscious desire to *do something.*
Only we're doing all the wrong things. Can't you feel it?"

"It isn't the land or our values, Alok." Frieda leaned over
the table, so he would listen. "We feel fragile because we're
senior citizens."

Alok touched his temples, undeterred. "As a people, we
need that magical thing, that atmosphere of sacredness, that
one answer. This hunger explains all the giant churches, with
the waterslides and rock music for Jesus, and martyrdom
operations. We're desperate, as a people. Even if we don't
know it, we *know* we're doomed."

"So?" said Frieda.

"So we have to go to Banff."

"The whole species or just the three of us?"

"Why Banff?" Stanley reached for Alok's sheet of paper.

"It's nothing but an outdoor mall now," said Frieda. "I
prefer Jasper. Actually, I prefer Cuba. Can *we* go there while
you go to Banff?"

Alok held the paper away from Stanley and cleared his
throat, prepared to deliver a lecture. Then he looked around
and paused. "Let's go outside. It's warm out there and I hate
whispering."

They gathered their notes and started out of the library,
and a table full of young people dressed in faux-cowboy
outfits quietly cheered.

"You little miserables," said Alok. "Have fun paying for
my retirement and health care."

In front of the Arts building, they found a spot of warm
grass. Several magpies hopped near a bluff, waiting for
dropped food. Alok lay on his side. "Will I sound sufficiently
authoritative like this, or should I stand and deliver? Stan,
how's my voice? Weak and strained?"

"You're fine, Alok. Whatever's comfortable."

A bank of dark clouds had eased in from the north and west. The hem of the storm was uneven, drooping with moisture. It would miss the valley, but a mini-rainbow had formed below and behind it. Alok pointed. "Proof God exists," he said.

Frieda sighed. "It's proof that moisture refracts light, actually. I know these are bewildering times, Alok, but can we please try to keep the moronic comments to a minimum?"

"Over 98 percent of the world believes in a sort of God. Are you saying all those billions of people are morons?"

Alok pulled a few blades of grass and tossed them into the air, apparently to judge the speed and direction of the wind. "In 1889, an American woman called Mary Schäffer arrived in the Rockies. I've read that she and her then husband were naturalists and do-gooders, interested in photography and writing – the late-Victorian upper-middle-class stuff. I've read that she was just an adventurous sort of girl. But I've also read that she was *called* to Banff on that first trip, and that claim is backed up by her own writings."

A bright yellow warbler settled on the branch of a birch tree, above Alok. He nodded at the bird knowingly, as though it too had been called.

"Her dreams, in Philadelphia, were suddenly disturbed. During her childhood and early adulthood, she was a devout Christian. By the time she arrived in Banff, it's clear that Mary was looking for something else. Proof of something. And, by all accounts, she found it."

Stanley and Frieda waited. Alok merely smiled and took a deep breath in through his nose.

"Two sisters from Hydesville, New York, developed a way to talk to the dead in 1848. They were basically the first spiritualists. The movement spread quickly, and Philadelphia is not far from Hydesville. Anyway, by the time Mary Schäffer arrived in Banff, she was dabbling in spiritualism. This is my theory, and it's a good one. She settled in the Rockies, some time later, as the secret leader of a growing movement of spiritualism, and a devotee of the natural world."

"I, for one, would like to see the source material for this theory," said Frieda.

With great effort, Alok rolled on to his stomach and pushed himself up to his knees. "Frieda, please. I know our past is lousy with . . . complications. But I want to help Stanley, and you, understand this. I'm sorry about the way I acted in the 1980s. But really, my friends, I was younger then and stupider and afraid to die, I must say. I thought that by sleeping with several women, and even a few men, I might –"

Frieda put her hands up. "Okay. Thank you. You're forgiven, as long as you never say anything like that again."

"Agreed."

Stanley was pleased. It was an odd truce, but a truce nonetheless. "Mary Schäffer."

"This is my theory: botany was a cover. Mary was called to Banff or, specifically, Lake Minnewanka near Banff. She pulled together a group of native elders, spiritualists, and disaffected religious strivers, and they discovered something." A group of students passed, and Alok waited until they were gone before he continued. "In the language of the Stoney Indians, Minnewanka means 'water of the spirits.' It was haunted, you see. By 'fish people.' Do you follow?"

"Nope," said Frieda.

"Minnewanka was settled in paleolithic times. People

lived there when Agassiz, the inland sea, was still draining into the Hudson Bay. Of almost anywhere in North America, it's the oldest in terms of settlement and legend. Ask any Stoney today. But why? Why there? The climate is severe and you can't grow anything. Why would nine thousand years' worth of First Nations people, and then Mary Schäffer and her band of spiritualists, be drawn to Banff?"

Frieda shrugged. "Real estate has always been real estate. It's pretty there."

"I have a hypothesis, and it concerns Stanley." Alok seemed to savour the silence, and their anticipation, for a moment. "It's said Mary Schäffer and the other spiritualists believed native legends about something *extraordinary* happening in Minnewanka. In Banff."

"Oh, all this makes terrific sense. You want Stanley to go to Banff because some loons in the nineteenth century liked the place."

Alok lifted his finger again. "We North Americans are atheists, tolerant agnostics, and blind zealots. The moderates among us are drunk with our own selfishness. We're the walking dead! I can smell it, and so can those magpies. The magpies are waiting for us, and the continent, to die. And you, you, Stanley Moss, have been called to remedy the problem. In Banff."

"What problem?"

"*The* problem."

"I'm really not convinced that Banff is the key to *the* problem." Frieda sniffed. "Why not . . . Washington? Ottawa?"

Stanley took a deep breath and lay back on the grass, looked up at the blue of the sky. If he was supposed to do something extraordinary, shouldn't he know why the sky was blue?

"It's not just spiritual, either." Alok's voice had risen. "Banff is a vortex of meaning, social and political."

Frieda leaned over and repeated, flatly, to her husband, "Vortex of meaning."

"When the railwaymen discovered the hot springs, they wanted to own it." With some grunting and a whispered cuss word, Alok stood up. He appealed to the bough of a large cedar and, presumably, the heavens. "So did others. *Individuals*, you see. The matter went to the courts. In another country, the United States for example, the most powerful individual would have won the right to, in effect, own Banff. But this is Canada. The federal government stepped in to resolve the dispute and made it into a national park. *Made it public.* You see? Like it or not, this act helped create the *Canadian spirit* more than anything else in the nineteenth century. Banff is Canada, and Canada is dying. If Canada dies, the whole world dies."

Stanley watched the university students, summer session kids, throwing Frisbees and reading in the sun. Usually sitting out in the heat made him perspire, especially in the lower back, buttocks, and forehead. Today, he was dry. Wholly comfortable. He was nearly overwhelmed by a desire to tell Frieda and Alok that he could beat world records in competitive swimming.

His wife coughed, and coughed again. Stanley reached over and tapped her on the back, though he knew from experience that it accomplished nothing.

Despite receiving a number of self-help books as birthday gifts from people who figured he was too uptight, Stanley was not the sort of person who could stop sweating the small stuff. Worry and fear and beauty and civility lived in the cracks between the small stuff, and this was everything to Stanley. He was a florist.

The scent of French fries dipped in both vinegar and ketchup filled the air. A skateboarder rumbled on the sidewalk, listening to music on headphones. The magpies yelped. In the distant campus bar, a punk band rehearsed for a concert. A hot-air balloon floated overhead, advertising for a realtor.

By this time tomorrow, Stanley knew, they would be in the Rocky Mountains.

TWENTY-ONE

Maha Rasad tiptoed out of the change room and peeked from behind a sprawling potted palm tree to see that the hot tub remained empty. She hurried across the cold floor and stepped into the water.

The hot tub in the Chalet Du Bois was really a warm tub. And the water smelled faintly of her father's undershirts. She discovered a button near the palm tree that might heat and agitate the water, and reached out of the tub to push it. Maha was half out of the water when a large man in a grey sweatsuit walked into the room. There was an ape on the front of his shirt, dressed in fatigues and aiming a hockey stick as though it were a gun: "Saskatoon Soldiers." She returned to her seat in the tub.

"What's up?"

Maha said nothing.

"You work here?"

She shook her head, no.

"Oh, good. I sneaked in the back. This is my third time and no one's caught me yet." The man knocked on the imitation cedar wall and placed a backpack on the floor. Instead of going into the men's change room, he simply pulled off his sneakers and socks and sweatshirt. Maha turned her back and the man laughed. "My trunks are already on. When a guy sneaks into hot tubs, he's gotta be agile, ready to roll."

The man pressed the button next to the palm tree and the room rumbled. Maha moved toward a jet so she might obscure the white bikini she had bought at the snowboarding shop. It was the least revealing bathing suit she could find in Banff but it remained far too revealing. The most profound shame was in cartoon letters on her behind: "DAMN."

"I hope it's warm in there. My upper back's on fire." He stepped into the water and looked down at his chest, covered in uneven patches of dark brown hair. "Right up until I was twenty-two I was completely bald, chest-wise. Then this stuff whupped in and turned me into Chuck Norris. You ever see *Return of the Dragon*, the Bruce Lee film?"

Maha looked out the steamed window, at the shadows of cars and trucks and pedestrians on Banff Avenue. She thought briefly of the figure in her bank account, and of delivering those job application forms she had collected. In Montreal, her path had seemed so clear. Coming to Banff was not inspired by desperation or whimsy but divine obligation. Now that she was here, enduring a chest hair confession, Maha speculated about the Lord's sense of humour.

"I was married then. Maybe my follicles figured, well, he doesn't have to attract any more ladies. Then, all of a sudden, *divorce*."

If she'd been wearing a one-piece bathing suit, Maha might have taken this opportunity to escape. But she worried the man might see "DAMN" on her behind and make unfair assumptions. No, Maha would wait him out, like a French citadel surrounded by drunk Italian soldiers.

"Guess what I ate for breakfast this morning."

Maha closed her eyes and wished herself into the hotel room, in front of a home decorating show that involved confident homosexuals from the United Kingdom. When she opened her eyes, the man in the hot tub was smiling. He was missing a couple of teeth, and a tattoo on his arm proclaimed his love for someone named Layla.

"All right, I'll go ahead and tell you. Chicken soup from a pouch with wieners chopped in. It was wicked. My mom used to make me that. With wieners! Really took me back."

In Montreal the rule on the metro, in the mall, down Crescent Street when the Bostonians were visiting in the summer, was to pretend you were a ghost. Eventually, they would turn their gaze elsewhere.

"Where you from?"

Maha said nothing.

"You know English?" The man tilted his head appraisingly. "No, no, no. Let me guess – Pakistan. Afghanistan? Iran. Sri Lanka. Egypt. Kuwait. The Congo. What else is over there? Iraq! Iraq? No. Syria. Wrong direction? India."

"Canada," Maha said, finally. She had a strong urge to pull a few branches off the palm tree and whip him. "Montreal, actually."

"Oooh. Your English is excellent."

"English is my first language."

The man crossed his arms. "Isn't that terrific. You learn something new every day. So. You here with your family?"

Maha recognized it was time to be silent again.

"You want a peanut butter cup? They had this two-for-one deal at a gas station on the way here, so I got six cups. You in?"

"No. Thank you."

He pulled himself up onto the edge of the hot tub, so only his legs dangled in the water. First he poked at his small beer belly and then he sighed and slouched. "That pretty much decides it. I'm shaving my chest. Chuck Norris did it, eventually, to succeed in Hollywood. Everyone still respects him."

What to do? Maha wanted to tell this man, who was actually in rather fine shape, and not significantly hairy compared to her father and uncles and cousins, that he should stop talking and fidgeting. Maha wanted to slip into the detergent-smelling sheets of her king-sized bed and nap. Maha was here to meet *the man who is a god*, not to spend time in a lukewarm, smelly pool of water with a redneck. Perhaps all this was a bad dream. Perhaps she was sick. She had definitely missed the deadline to apply for a decent space in Cegep.

"How about this." The man straightened his posture. "How about you and me go out for burgers tonight."

"No."

"You don't eat burgers?"

Maha furrowed her brow.

"You know why I came here, to Banff?"

Again, Maha furrowed. She also looked at her fingernails.

"Let me back up a little. You familiar with a guy called Rainier Maria Rilke? I know he has Maria in his name but he's a dude. You know him?"

"No."

"He writes kickass poems and, I think, letters to people. Anyway, check this out: '*ornamental clouds compose an evening love song.*' I memorized it, from a book in the library. '*You must change your life.*' You know?"

The water was not warm enough. A chill had eased its way into Maha.

"I read that on the door of a shitter and decided, all right, I get it. So I stopped drinking rye, for starters, and quit the team. Here I am, if you can believe it. Just today I realized the lines are from a poem about a *statue.*"

Maha understood she would have to get out of the water and hide in the women's change room.

"I like your bathing suit, by the way. The name's Kal. I'm from Thunder Bay, originally. I used to play pro hockey but now I wash dishes at Far East Square."

Maha took a deep breath and stepped up out of the hot tub. She tiptoed through the cool air toward the change room, waiting for it.

"Damn!" said Kal.

TWENTY-TWO

A gentleman in his fifties, with acne scars and a $1,600 black suit, stood up from the conference table at the Banff Springs Hotel and rubbed his hands together. In the silence before he spoke, Tanya Gervais wondered where the gentleman had found the money for his Armani suit. She knew it was Armani because Brian had two of them, and because this gentleman had flashed the label inside his jacket. But Brian was a chief financial officer, not a Canadian independent television producer.

"All right, close your eyes," said the producer, whose name was Seth. One of Seth's two partners, a tiny woman Tanya recognized from a similar meeting in 2003, motioned at her from the other side of the table: *Really, close your eyes. Please.*

Tanya closed her eyes.

For the next few minutes, Seth described a forest of cedar and Douglas fir, raindrops on leaves, wild ferns and lichen. Skunk cabbage. Totem poles everywhere. All to locate a dramatic series set in the eighteenth century, just as James Cook and other white sailors began arriving on Vancouver Island. It would be a comedy, about the wacky travails of aboriginal peoples.

"You know," said Seth, "the hunting, the gathering, the totem pole building, the eating of dogs. Can you see the humour in this? Not that we'll shy away from tough, edgy issues like incest. But most importantly, it's about joy. Laughter, Tanya. Mother Earth, etcetera. What I want to get across to you is these people are *real storytellers*, and what we don't do enough of, as producers, is tell their stories. We'll focus on a young girl, a Pocahontas type. She'll have an interior monologue and address the camera from time to time, you know, in that exasperated tone of a teenage girl. She can speak with an accent, or not, depending. All the usual pressures of being a teenage girl, plus being aboriginal, plus all these white guys all over the place? The grants'll write themselves."

It seemed to Tanya that Canadian film and television had already done a more than ample job exploring incest. And why Pocahontas? In some ways it was the ultimate male fantasy, to arrive among the natives and pluck a sexy teenager out of the group for sex and "education," but in another more important way it made her want to throw up.

Tanya opened her eyes. "Sorry. I have to pass."

The three producers, Seth and his partners, shared a quick glance. In less than five seconds, Seth was leaning forward and rubbing his hands together again, ready for pitch number two. "Close your eyes," he said. "This one is gonna *kill you.*"

"I'll listen to one more, if it's quick, but I'm not closing my eyes again."

"Yeah, but –"

"Sorry. Clock is ticking. The eyes stay open."

Seth looked wounded, but he recovered quickly.

"There's a young lawyer, a defence attorney. She's cute, not beautiful. Birdy, sorta. Nervous about things, but in a quasi-sexy way. Asian, we're thinking. The series is set in Calgary."

Tanya stood up. "Thank you."

"Winnipeg? Halifax? It doesn't matter where we set it."

"I have another appointment in a few minutes, unfortunately, and –"

"Toronto! It's set in Toronto!"

Tanya shook hands with Seth's fellow producers. Instead of admitting defeat, Seth, steward of the country's national self-image, placed his hands together in prayer and blocked the door.

"We both know how the game's played, Tanya. You have to spend money and we need to develop something. *Anything.* It's a match made in heaven."

"No, it isn't."

"What don't you like about the ideas?"

Tanya had been doing this too long, in their position and hers, to respond to his question with any degree of candour. This was her seventh such meeting in two days, and each one of the pitches she had heard was appallingly derivative and sad and, well, Canadian. A loser sandwich covered in loser gravy garnished with fried loser, all in the context of multiculturalism.

"Let me out."

"Not until you answer the question." Seth reached up and dabbed his forehead with the sleeve of his jacket. "This is our livelihood."

"Get out of my way or I'll kick your nuts."

"Please," said the tiny woman, in a voice so desperate and tired Tanya wanted to turn around and crush every bone in her body with a hug. "Please."

"Try the CBC."

Seth moved away from the door as though he had been pelted with machine-gun fire. He whispered, as Tanya started out, "We're *human beings*, you know."

In the lobby again, surrounded by other men and women with binders and lanyards, Tanya felt a panic attack coming on. She looked down at her schedule of interviews – five more and then a dinner with the Canada Council – and walked out of the Banff Springs Hotel. Instead of hailing a cab, she took the stairs down to the Bow River and stood among the fragrant pine trees and tourists snapping photographs of the falls. She breathed.

It was a warm day, with just enough cloud in the sky. She removed her jacket and walked north and west along the rolling white river, from the Banff Springs Hotel toward town. The path wasn't ideal for high-heeled footwear but, to her surprise, Tanya wasn't annoyed by its imperfections. Not far from the bridge that arced over the Bow River, near an exposed boulder in the cold water and a sign advising against swimming, Tanya decided that her career in television was officially over. So was her relationship with Brian. She couldn't imagine herself in the yellow Hummer any more. In sum, this constituted a grave psychological crisis. But it didn't feel like a crisis. Knowing that the slab hovered above her, ready to fall again, mysteriously freed Tanya from the need to call her analyst and get better.

Tanya climbed up to the road again and stepped on to the bridge. A Japanese man asked her to take a picture of him with his family, the town and Cascade Mountain behind them. Holding the camera and looking through the digital viewfinder at the love and authenticity of the small Japanese family – their utter lack of interest in licensing or development money – calmed her.

"Beautiful," she said, after she had taken the picture. "You're beautiful."

In her hotel room at the Chalet Du Bois, Tanya lay on her bed and turned on the television. She flipped through the seventy-one channels and found precisely nothing she wanted to watch. Tanya had devoted her entire career to precisely nothing.

She turned off the television and sat in the silence of her hotel room, until the ambient noise rose up around her. The air conditioner, the traffic on Banff Avenue, the voices of other guests through the ceiling and walls, random clicks. The particular beige of the beige curtains, a colour that someone, somewhere *actually planned*. Dust on the side table, in the grooves of her reading lamp. Lint on her black pants. The rogue pubic hair an inch below her belly button.

Tanya got up off the bed, sat at the computer desk, and turned on her laptop. It powered up and a schedule of events appeared before her, prepared by the secretary in Vancouver. She closed that window, opened her e-mail program, and began writing to Darryl Lantz.

Dear Darryl,
I resign. Please do not send a psychiatrist. This is an act
of acute sanity.
Love,
Tanya

TWENTY-THREE

Until Kal slept with the wrong Soldiers fan and gave Candace that nasty bout of syphilis, their only regular disagreements had been over dirty dishes. It was one of the significant shocks of married life at eighteen, all that time he had to spend at the sink. If Kal made dinner, it seemed reasonable that Candace wash up afterward. Unfortunately, she never saw it that way. Candace preferred to be improvisational about dirty dishes, which usually meant that she played with Layla while Kal did the work. He would wash the dishes and clean the small kitchen in Windsor and then, moments later, it would be a mess again. The smell of a wet rag after a week's employment, a stainless-steel pot caked with oatmeal, cheese microwaved to the side of a plastic bowl, lettuce and spinach drowned in oil and vinegar: for Kal, it was a question of human rights.

Yet here he was, in the back of an Asian fusion restaurant in Banff, the door open to the pale-yellow dusk, deeply enjoying his job. The spray nozzle, which he used to rinse the plates and wine glasses before stacking them into the tray, was not only stretchy. It was also mighty.

Every few minutes, one of the servers would stack a pile of food-encrusted plates and lipstick-stained glasses to his left. Piece by piece he would go through them, first scraping the plates into the garbage and then spraying them clean. Then Kal would artfully separate them on a grey pallet and send them on a conveyor belt through a stainless-steel washing machine. The plates emerged on the other side of the machine, hot and nearly dry. Once or twice, when no one was looking, Kal pressed a hot plate to his cheek.

The owners of Far East Square, Chip and Wendy Yang, thought music in the kitchen was vulgar. So Kal listened to the radio on a nine-dollar Walkman. Since the Calgary radio waves bounced off the mountains before they could reach Banff, all he could pick up was the local CBC, in French.

Tonight's program featured a special on European music before the Second World War. The songs were sad and romantic, and provided a sense of dreamy grandeur while Kal scraped clean a platter of Singapore beef jerky and spinach risotto, decorated by two balled-up napkins, an opened sugar packet, an empty lip gloss container, and a chewed piece of gum. What stood out, for Kal, was the accordion in the French songs. It was a sullen and mysterious sound, sexy too, and unembarrassed by its earnestness. The explanation of a thing that can't be explained. He was moved to tears by the instrument, by his memory of the woman in the hot tub, and how it all related to the poem.

There was a tap on his shoulder. Kal wiped his eyes and turned to see Wendy Yang frowning behind him. He turned off the radio and removed his gloves.

"You want dinner?"

Wendy grumbled as she took over at the dishwashing station. Kal hurried to the small staff table, where Chip was already eating. There was a plate of tofu and mixed vegetables, curried fish Singapore style, and three crab cakes. A large, steaming bowl of coconut rice sat between them.

"I met the most beautiful woman yesterday, Chip."

Chip's mouth was full of curried fish Singapore style. He just nodded.

Kal scooped a little bit from each bowl onto his plate. "I never thought I could ever feel like this, after Candace broke my heart so hard. I figured my heart'd be a dead thing forever."

"Feel what?" said Chip, once he had finished chewing.

Since his dad's death, Kal had known that a reserve of energy and hope and goodness and joy was stored in some inaccessible corner of him. In his teen years and beyond, the rye had kept it buried under layers and layers of gloom. The Rilke poem had cracked him open, like an axe, and now all this stuff kept spilling out. Kal had trouble in moments like these, harnessing the bounty. There was no way to explain how he felt when he saw the beautiful woman in the hot tub, or the great grandeur of the accordion, so Kal smashed a wine glass on the floor. "You know what I'm saying?"

The kitchen went silent for a long while, until Chip stood up. "That was stupid. Get the broom."

Kal fetched the broom and started sweeping. "I met her in a hot tub across the street. In the Chalet Du Bois."

"Did you knock boots?"

"*Gosh*, Chip. I just met her, and she isn't that kind of girl, I don't think. To be honest, I've had plenty enough of those kinds of girls in the last few years, on account of my broken heart. I never thought of it this way before – I never thought of it at all – but it leaves a guy feeling even emptier, you know what I mean?"

"I have been married for thirty-seven years." Chip leaned forward over his bowl and looked toward the dishwashing station, to make sure Wendy wasn't listening. "Sometimes I want to feel empty. And I mean *empty*."

Kal didn't want to imagine Chip Yang engaging in sexual intercourse, so he looked down at his broom and the broken glass on the floor and thought about the accordion. It all made perfect sense, why he had been drawn here to change his life. Kal was meant to hear the accordion music on Radio-Canada and become a musician. He was destined to meet the woman in the hot tub, whose ass said "DAMN." Now that the tiny iceberg of frozen rye whisky in his heart had been axed, Kal was doubly inspired. He would write accordion songs about Layla, her cuteness and superior intelligence and tiny shoes and talent for gymnastics, and the woman in the hot tub.

Chip finished eating abruptly and pushed himself away from the table. With his hands on his soft belly, he said, "Sometimes I want to go into a nightclub and say to a tall woman from Germany, 'Hey, girlfriend, do you want to try something that was once illegal in this country?' But you know I'm old now, and fleshy. Look: my teeth went yellow from cigarettes and tea."

"Listen, Chip. I did that a couple of times when I was married, and you know what? Now my wife and daughter live with a Ukrainian car salesman in Kelowna. You don't want that, do you?"

"No."

"Well then."

Kal sat down to finish his meal while Chip rose and put his black Nehru jacket back on. Before he departed, Chip burped and washed his hands. The Yangs' cat, Philip, appeared in the doorway. Though he had been working at Far East Square for only a couple of weeks, Kal understood the patterns of the restaurant. One of them involved Philip showing up around nine o'clock. The cat walked into the kitchen from the alley, thereby breaking health code regulations. Eventually, Chip spotted Philip, picked him up, screamed at him in Cantonese, smacked him in the head, and tossed him outside. Each time he witnessed the punishment of Philip Yang, another small piece of Kal McIntyre died.

"Get," Kal said, to Philip. "Go away."

It was time to get back to the dishwashing station. Kal took his plate and Chip's plate and tried to shoo Philip away with a fake kick. But this was ineffective. Philip – a thin, Creamsicle-coloured cat – sneaked under the giant steel island where Wendy and the other cook, Yip Suen, usually prepared salads.

At the dishwashing station, Kal strapped on his radio again. "Philip is here."

Wendy shook her head. "Did Chip see him?"

"Not yet."

"Where did Philip go?"

"Under the island, I think."

Wendy took off the yellow gloves. "Don't worry about Philip, you know. I think this is a game he plays. If he did not want Chip to hit him and throw him and scream at him, he would stay outside."

"You mean it?"

"I have given this plenty of thought. And it is a secret that Philip comes in the kitchen. If an inspector arrives, we have to throw him out. You cannot tell anyone. If you do, I will fire you and then I will hunt you down. It is not worth it for you to open your mouth about Philip."

"Wendy?"

"Yes?"

"Something wonderful is going to happen to me here."

"Does this have to do with Philip?"

"I don't think so. It has something to do with the beauty of the accordion."

Wendy raised her eyebrows.

Kal noted, in Wendy's simple eyebrow lift, a note of apprehension. This job, he saw, would soon be finished. He vowed not to break any more glasses or tell fellows about the beauty of the accordion, especially if the fellows happened to be his employers.

TWENTY-FOUR

Stanley turned off the highway, and the view astonished Alok and Frieda into a rare silence. On Banff Avenue, crowds of shoppers in sunglasses hurried up and down the sidewalk as though carrying a La Senza bag was a job and they were all late for their next appointments. For Stanley, who had not been there in many years, the stores and restaurants – the artificial heart of a national park – made the treeless peaks of the Rockies seem like another commodity, a mirage, a joke.

Alok sat up and placed his index fingers on his temples. "We must resuscitate the soul of the western world here in Banff, among all these field stations of the global corporate agenda. From here, the soul will spread and save us all. I'm confident of that."

Frieda giggled as Stanley pulled in behind the last hotel on Banff Avenue before the Bow River. The Chalet Du Bois was essentially a commercial motel with a newish log cabin facade, but it was economical. There was an empty parking spot next to a giant luxury bus. Alok asked to get out in case the space between the car and bus was too small for him.

As Stanley parked, Alok stood in the middle of the lot, his arms out, sniffing it all in. Through the windows of the Oldsmobile, Stanley and Frieda heard Alok hollering to himself and, potentially, others.

Frieda took Stanley's hands. "Turn the car back on, please, and let's go home." She spoke slowly, pronouncing each syllable. "I have a terrible feeling."

"Let's just –"

"Oh, let's not." Frieda lifted Stanley's hands to her mouth. "We can go to Lake Louise and the icefields. The icefields are shrinking and we ought to see them one last time. In case all this is . . . you know. We can stay in Jasper tonight, at the Lodge. Go for a hike tomorrow. Sit in some hot springs."

On the other side of a fence, a child sat on the hood of a Volkswagen. The child wore a thick black sweatshirt and stared at Stanley as though, somehow, he were expected. It was not clear, from this distance, if the child was a boy or a girl. Or, perhaps, a dwarf. Stanley could not read the child's thoughts but felt genuinely nervous, so nervous he stopped listening to Frieda's quavering voice. He went cold and then hot again. For a moment, he was sure the illness had returned all at once. His heart beat so quickly it seemed to vibrate.

"Stan."

He turned to his wife for an instant, and when he looked back at the child, the child was gone. "Did you see that kid on the Volkswagen?"

Frieda released Stanley's hands. "You remember when Charles was called into the gifted program in junior high school and you thought it would turn him into a pompous ass? And I decided it would just stimulate him?"

"He did become a pompous ass."

"You registered your objection but he went into the program anyway, didn't he? And in the end it turned out you were right. Yes?"

"I think Charles was destined to be a pompous ass independent of us."

"The point here is I am strongly registering my objection."

Again, Stanley looked toward the Volkswagen. He shivered.

"And I'm going to make you eat shit for the rest of your life if this little adventure turns out to be ridiculous and embarrassing." Frieda opened her door and stepped out. Stanley looked to the Volkswagen one last time and followed his wife.

Alok stood at the back entrance to the hotel, waving his arms like a giant summer snow angel. He activated the automatic doors. "Let's go, lovebirds. The land is dying here!"

"Lovebirds," said Stanley, as he put his arm around Frieda and pulled her close.

"Don't."

"Maybe there's a Jacuzzi in our room. We can have one together."

"I'll have a Jacuzzi by myself, while you and Alok save the land. Then, when you're finished with this twaddle, we can go home and sit in the garden like proper old people."

They entered the Chalet Du Bois arm in arm, three abreast. It reminded Stanley, for just a moment, of *The Wizard of Oz*. Instead of a buoyant song, they had a soundtrack of sighing beverage coolers and snack dispensers in the foyer, and a man arguing on his cellphone in German. Frieda was unhappy, Alok was ecstatic, Stanley was . . . he couldn't say, exactly.

In the lobby, a pretty young woman spoke with the clerk at the desk. It appeared they were negotiating the price of a longer-term stay. Stanley recognized the young woman, who had brown skin, shiny black hair, and big brown eyes, but he did not remember her name or how he knew her. That Greek restaurant at home?

The young woman abruptly stopped speaking, moved her hair away from her eyes, and turned to Stanley, Frieda, and

Alok. "Oh," she said, and walked to Stanley. She hugged him and her voice broke.

It wasn't memory, exactly, but he knew this girl. Despite his wife's unhappiness, Stanley smiled with the comfortable recognition that he was in exactly the right place at exactly the right time. The anxieties that hung from his thoughts at all times, like heavy ornaments, had dropped away. It was so full, this feeling. He had to stop himself from laughing out loud.

"I'm Maha," the young woman said, into his chest. "But you know that. I was worried you weren't coming."

Alok clapped his hands.

Frieda turned away. "I'll get the luggage."

TWENTY-FIVE

In the liquor store on Bear Street, Tanya Gervais reached inside the wet paper bag that was her heart and discovered a love forlorn. It was the love she'd once held for France: French cheese, French bread, *la langue* itself, and, most poignantly, the wine.

Australian wine had conquered her with its marketing prowess. As much as she appreciated their techniques, Tanya reviled the consequences. Like some yob addicted to season nine of *Survivor*, here she was, a sophisticated woman, standing before the spiritual emptiness of Wolf Blass Yellow Label.

Did she actually enjoy Wolf Blass Cabernet Sauvignon? Or had the product seduced her with its ubiquity? The stately air of its raptor mascot?

"What's your best-selling wine?" she said, aloud, without looking away from the bottles.

"Wolf Blass, by a mile," said the thin man behind the counter.

"Why?"

The thin man scratched his arm. "Everyone buys it 'cause . . . everyone buys it."

"That's *right*." Tanya had not noticed that the clerk sported a rather full and regal grey moustache. "It isn't wine quality or even the quality of the marketing campaign. It's about mass delusion."

"You're one of those TV people, aren't you?"

"I was." Tanya turned away from Australia and returned to the France of her youth. Yes: *Appellation Hermitage Controlée*. She carried a bottle to the counter and pulled out her American Express corporate card. "I figure they owe me this, at least. As consolation for destroying my life."

The slim man grasped a corner of his regal grey moustache. He didn't seem capable of processing her remarks. "You gotta do whatcha . . ." he trailed off.

Tanya signed her name to the sales slip. "We're all going to die, you know. You, me, Wolf Blass – if that's someone's real name. And at the moment of our death, we're going to look back on these consumer choices we made. Aren't we?"

The thin man opened his mouth just slightly, a long bubble of saliva connecting his dry lips.

"Will we die proud of all the television we watched? All the Australian wine we bought? Or are we –?"

"I'm sorry, lady. I don't want to be rude, but can you go away now?"

Tanya collected her wine and exited the store. Outside, the mountain wind continued its struggle with the heat of the sun. Couples and families from around the world filled the street, awed by their journeys in and out of sporting goods stores rather than up and down mountains. She had hoped that quitting her job would make her cheerful and optimistic. But just a few hours later, at the corner of Bear and Caribou, Tanya was lost.

A man in a toque and a "SAVE ANWAR" T-shirt strode past her. Tanya stopped him. "Do you see me?"

"Huh?"

"Am I here? Do you see me?"

The man glanced about suspiciously. "Yes?"

"All right, how about this." Tanya tilted her head and nodded. "Do I *mean* anything?"

It appeared the man was going to answer her question. Then, with a determined pivot, he said, "I fix mountain bikes, lady," and hurried down Bear Street.

The lobby of the Chalet Du Bois was connected to a Tony Roma's. Tanya entered the lobby and her first, destructive thought was thus: *I am going to eat a large plate of ribs tonight, and sleep with the pimply waiter.*

An Indian gentleman wearing the largest Rush concert T-shirt in the history of progressive rock blocked the stairway.

"Excuse me," she said.

"Of course. But. Have you been crying?"

Tanya wasn't aware of crying. She looked down and hid her eyes, in case the makeup had smeared her into an Uncle Fester lookalike, and tried to muscle past the gentleman.

Instead of standing aside, he put his hand out for her to shake. "My name is Alok Chandra. We're here to help."

The Chalet Du Bois was a three-storey hotel with a small and ridiculously slow elevator, but Tanya would take it. She walked past a beautiful young woman and a quasi-elderly man with vivid blue eyes. He opened them widely to her, and smiled. Tanya couldn't help but conclude, in that first instant, that the quasi-elderly man would have outstanding screen presence.

Tanya stopped. "Are you a delegate?"

"No," he said.

"How do I know you?"

The beautiful young woman reached over and rubbed his arm. "This is the Lord."

The Lord shook his head. "You have to stop saying that, Maha."

An older woman, standing on the other side of not-the-Lord, braced herself against the fake log wall. She looked as though she might faint. Alok Chandra put his arm around Tanya. The big man smelled of the chips one spreads along the bottom of a hamster cage. "You were destined to find us here, in the lobby of this hotel."

"This is my hotel. I stay here."

"Just as we do," said Alok Chandra. "Just as we do."

The faint woman brought her hands to her face. Tanya was bewildered, and still feeling lost, so she stepped out of the man's embrace and pressed the call button. "Pleasant to meet you all. Mr. Chandra. Not-the-Lord."

"Wait," said Alok Chandra. "Who are you?"

She did not pull a business card from her jacket pocket. "Tanya."

"All right, Tanya, what I'm asking is: *who are you and what are you doing here?*"

She had trained herself to answer questions quickly and definitively. A reputation for dithering or excessive thoughtfulness was detrimental to the career of a marketing and development executive. Now that she was no longer in the television business, she paused. She waited patiently and passively for the answer to arrive, and it did not arrive. The response was stalled, like the elevator.

Not-the-Lord looked down at his watch. "We just got here. We're going upstairs with our luggage and then we're going out for dinner. Would you like to join us?"

Usually, during her yearly visit to Banff, Tanya dreaded dinner invitations. The artificial friendships, the small talk about government funding and political threats. The flirting, wine, and inevitably bad hotel-room sex followed by guilt and lies and headaches the following day.

"No, thank you." Tanya gave up on the elevator and walked determinedly back through the crowd and up the first set of stairs. With each step she felt less whole.

In her room, Tanya opened the bottle of wine and filled her glass. Without sniffing the cork or oxygenating the Hermitage, she swallowed it back. Her breath, in and out of her nose, was noisy. The dry air. The dry wine. The moisture evaporating from her body ounce by ounce, leaving only crooked ditches and dead pores.

She poured a second glass, with the heat of the first wiping away the cardboard wall that separated her from tears. So *that* was where her body stored moisture. Tanya turned on the television, watched the first five minutes of *Wife Swap*, went into the bathroom, and locked the door. Then, without splashing any water on her face or even wiping the mascara from the hollows of her eyes, Tanya ran out of the hotel room, down the hall, and into the empty lobby.

"Where did they go?" she said, to the clerk.

"Um," said the clerk.

"They were putting their bags in their rooms and going out to eat. Where did they go?"

"Um."

Tanya considered pulling a decorative antler off the wall and punishing the clerk for his obviously chronic methamphetamine use. Instead, she took a small dining magazine from the information rack and ran out onto the street.

TWENTY-SIX

A hockey team can be hot for a month, only to fall into the most inept and awkward spell. The simplest things, like passes into the neutral zone, become impossible. The mysteries behind these inconsistencies applied, Kal learned, in the restaurant business as well.

Sometimes, for an hour or more, the dishes arrived at a perfect pace. Kal would wash constantly, without any pauses long enough to inspire boredom, listening to a lengthy violin sonata or something gay by Gershwin. Then, even though everything about the diners remained the same, a great idleness would arrive, with no dishes, followed by a momentous pile for which there was no room on the stacker. And Kal would panic. Forks would emerge from the washing machine with cheese baked on their tongs. Cups with rings of hot chocolate inside.

During one of the lulls, Kal walked into the dining room to draw a ginger ale. And there she was: the woman in the hot tub. Only now she wore a sleeveless black turtleneck sweater and sat next to an obese man in a Rush T-shirt. Across from her, an elderly couple.

Kal waved at Chip, on the other side of the bar. "You have to do me a favour, buddy."

Chip did not seem to appreciate Kal calling him "buddy." The proprietor of Far East Square backed away and snorted. Behind the sounds of conversation, laughter, and cutlery on plates were trickles from the wall fountains.

"I need to buy a drink for that girl." Kal pointed. "Whatever she's drinking. Chip, my man, that's the girl I was telling you about. Check out that posture."

"No."

"Please, Chip."

"Maybe you should call me Mr. Yang from now on."

"Mr. Yang, this is very important."

"Not to me. You know, Mrs. Yang thinks you're crazy. You're on her shit list."

"I'm not crazy. I'm smitten. They're two different things."

"Go back to work."

"Only if you find out what she wants to drink, and give her one on the house."

"On the house?"

"The house is me."

"The house is *me*."

"Right, Mr. Yang. Say the drink is from a secret admirer. No, no. From me."

"Does she know your name?"

"Kal from the hot tub, say. Say that. No, say it's from Kal – the *awesome* guy from the hot tub."

Chip filled a glass with mineral water. "I don't know if I can say that. Now, get back into the kitchen. Your apron is filthy."

Kal formed his hand into a mock six-shooter, emptied the cartridge into Chip, and returned to a new stack of plates and cutlery in front of the dishwasher. The song on his earphones was about being caught in the rain. Kal danced while he washed.

"You better not break anything else," said Wendy, loud enough for Kal to hear over the lyrics. Wendy had never been friendly with Kal, but in the last few nights she had turned hostile. Some people, Kal knew, lacked the proper chemical connection to be teammates. You could force it, but the team never felt right. With time, annoyance turned to distrust and eventually hatred. In his hockey career, it had taken Kal a few seasons to understand this. He'd fought with teammates, even sabotaged their play, because he'd failed to recognize the biological facts. Human life was finite. A guy was better off surrounding himself with sweet chemical connections. "One more glass and you're fired."

With Wendy, it went beyond chemicals and beyond the usual pattern of annoyance, distrust, and hate. Kal recognized in Wendy Yang a profound sadness, the sadness he himself had felt since he'd left high school to become a full-time hockey player. It was everywhere in the kitchen of Far

East Square. The stacked plastic white lard bins were sad. The blank walls and fluorescent lights were sad, doubly sad as it all reflected off the stainless steel of the cooking station. And it was more than sadness he saw in Wendy. It was fear. As a hockey player, Kal had worked to strip the fear from his decision-making processes. If a guy was too thoughtful on the ice, he wouldn't take risks. Yet Kal knew that a wall of fear stood between him and greatness. No matter how much rye and Gatorade he drank, Kal could not strip the fear from his play.

He removed the earphones and leaned on the shiny counter where Wendy assembled the dishes. "You're thinking too much, Wendy. It's making you anxious and shaky. Look at your shaky hand!"

"Get back to your station."

"Do you want to be a mediocre chef, or a great one?"

Wendy looked up at Kal and frowned. "Leave me alone. Stop talking and get to work."

"Put that cilantro down, Wendy, and focus. *See* the meal. The perfect meal. You want the people out there to have a special experience, don't you? Not just a sorta-good experience?"

"Get to work, Kal, or go home and never come back."

"You're scared, Wendy. You're scared of greatness. I used to be scared of greatness, but I'm not any more."

Wendy stood up from the plates and stared straight ahead, at two bowls of soup on the warming tray. Her rosy cheeks had turned fully red, and her head quivered along with her hands.

Chip walked through the door and placed another tub of dishes on the stacker. "She won't accept your drink."

"Make Kal work or fire him."

"Wendy." Kal walked around the stainless-steel island and put his hands on Wendy's arms. They were tiny and tense. Every muscle was active. "You must change your life."

Before the fork made contact with the skin of his cheek, Kal spotted it out of the corner of his eye and wondered whose mouth had wrapped around it. He had time to hope the fork had been inside the woman from the hot tub's mouth. The pain was more explosive than, say, a cross-check in the mouth, because he hadn't partaken of rye whisky.

Wendy released the fork and it remained in Kal's cheek. Kal backed into the stove and stopped when he felt its heat. If Wendy had not been scared before, she was now. She screamed and pointed at Kal's face. Then she ran around the island and stood with Chip at the dishwashing station. Kal pulled the fork out of his cheek and held it out. There didn't seem to be any blood on it. Chip drew a butter knife from the dish tub and brandished it before Kal's fork like a sword.

Years of hockey had built a web of nuance around Kal's reaction to pain. It hurt quite a lot to be stabbed by a fork, and it hurt even more to pull it out. But every smart player knows that if you react too quickly, if you surrender to rage and revenge, you will only end up in the penalty box and hurt your team. So Kal placed the fork in the sink and cupped a hand under his right cheek, where the blood was now dripping. "I was just trying to help, Wendy."

He passed the other chef, Yip Suen, and stood over the deep sink in the corner near the door. First Kal washed his hands and then he began splashing cold water on his cheek. Yip Suen stood next to him with a clean white handtowel, and once he was satisfied the wound was relatively free of black bean sauce, Kal held the towel to his throbbing face. "Yip Suen, thank you."

"No, thank you," said Yip Suen. "I will pluck the fear out of my cooking, and become a master."

"That's terrific."

Kal fashioned a large bandage from another clean towel and taped it to his face. The cat, Philip, was walking through the kitchen unharassed now. Wendy was already back at work, her chest heaving with sobs. So was Yip Suen, with a new air of delight about her. This truly pleased Kal, despite his light-headedness and the certainty that he would need a tetanus shot. Chip had already written up a crude liability agreement, releasing Wendy from any wrongdoing.

Chip presented the handwritten sheet to Kal. "If you do not sign, and if you try to bring action, I will tell the truth. You sexually assaulted my wife!"

"No, he did not," said Yip Suen. "Don't sign it, Kal."

Kal dished Yip Suen a high-five and walked out of the kitchen into the dining room. At the table of the woman from the hot tub, he smiled and cleared his throat.

TWENTY-SEVEN

The Lord would not allow Maha to call him the Lord, so she called him Stanley. It was such an old-fashioned name, a salesman's name. In her heart, the Lord would remain the Lord, even if on her lips he was Stanley.

In Montreal, she had walked past places like Far East Square hundreds of times. The wall fountains and tiny chairs, the simple marriage of dark wood and glass. But she had never eaten in a place like this. Her parents thought restaurants were too expensive, and she only went to food courts and cheap cafés with Ardeen.

Maha was about to ask the Lord how he came to be the Lord when the hot tub man, who had already tried to buy her a cocktail, arrived at the table with a square of cotton taped to his right cheek. It was soaked through with blood. He cleared his throat.

"My name is Kal McIntyre." He stared at Maha, so she looked down at her plate. She didn't want to be embarrassed by this mentally handicapped man in front of the Lord and his wife. The appetizers had just arrived – deep-fried prawns in the form of lollipops, with a ginger sauce for dipping. Maha focused on the dollop of ginger sauce, the non-colour of a vinyl-sided condominium.

Alok Chandra engaged him. "What happened to your face?"

"Wendy Yang stabbed me with a fork, but that's not important."

"Right you are, my son." Alok gestured at the table. "We're here to find what *is* important."

Their server, an excited Asian man, ran out of the kitchen. He was waving his arms about, smiling at the diners and laughing. "It's a wild night, folks, no tax. No tax on your meals." Yet when he reached Kal, his whispered threat was loud enough for Maha to hear. "If you do not leave right now, I will make sure you die."

Perhaps the server did not understand whispering, for it was clear that everyone at their table and the table behind Kal had heard the server. The Lord reached up and took the server's hand. "He's going to join us for dinner."

The server struggled with this news. But he was also at the mercy of the Lord, whose touch had calmed him. The server no longer smiled or laughed nervously or grimaced.

"Do you understand?" said the Lord.

"I understand."

"And of course, you didn't mean what you just said to Kal."

"No." The server turned to Kal. "I did not mean what I said. I will not poison your food or hire someone to shoot you."

Kal rubbed the server's back. "Great news, Mr. Yang. I'll sleep better tonight, knowing that."

Once Mr. Yang was gone, Kal sat next to Maha. The back of her neck tingled. She did not turn and look directly at him, but she could feel him there, his breath and his beating heart.

Frieda and the Lord introduced themselves to Kal and he shook their hands. "I just have to tell you, Mr. Moss, that was something else. The way you calmed Chip down like that. I was just about ready to take a fork in the other cheek. Are you some sort of hypnotist?"

"No."

Alok reached across Maha's plate and squeezed Kal's hand.

Then Kal turned to Maha. His eyes on her like a heat lamp. "And you are?" he said, as though they had never met.

"Maha Rasad."

"Now that is one hell of a pretty name. I am delighted to make your acquaintance, Miss Maha."

Around the table, everyone started eating the deep-fried shrimp again. Maha sneaked glances at the Lord, who kept looking up and staring at something or someone across the room. A couple of times, Maha turned around quickly to see what it was. But there were only paintings on the wall back there, and the window to the street.

Frieda asked Kal what had brought him to Banff and he told his story. A story Maha had already heard in the hot tub. This delighted Alok, who informed Kal that he had been called here, like everyone else. "Young man, you *have* changed your life. In twenty years you will look back on this night with a sense of divine wonder."

"Divine wonder," said Kal. "I could sure use a wedge of that."

When they had arrived at the restaurant, the only available table was for six. Maha would have preferred a gathering of two – her and the Lord. She was lamenting the number of filled seats when the woman from the hotel lobby appeared, huffing, at their table. "Is it too late to join you?"

All right, this is enough, Maha wanted to say, but Alok welcomed Tanya Gervais warmly. Kal stood up and called her "ma'am."

The waiter brought cutlery and wine glasses for Kal and Tanya, and a sort of calm descended on the table. The music, slow dance beats behind a whale song, was gallingly perfect.

TWENTY-EIGHT

Maha asked Stanley a series of questions he could not answer: Why did you create human beings this way, with their taste for war and consumerism and beheading? Why do you allow class to exist, and poverty, and poisoned water sources? What happens, exactly, when we die? Do you know the devil? Are we alone in the universe? The Holocaust, for one: what were you thinking? Earthquakes, drinking and driving, volcanoes, nuclear weapons, pornography, cancer?

All of Stanley's answers frustrated Alok. Especially this one: "I don't think much of anything happens when we die, save decomposition."

At this, Alok laughed, bellowed, "He doesn't mean that!" and pulled Stanley to the bar.

Someone had spilled sake and Stanley smelled it and saw it. But he didn't warn Alok, who placed his bare arm in the puddle. Alok wiped his arm with the Rush shirt and prepared to engage in a lecture.

"I know what you're going to say," said Stanley.

"Well, then?"

"Do you want me to lie to them?"

"Stan. How do you think you got here? Why do you think they're here? This has all been preordained."

"By whom, Alok?"

As he considered this, Alok put his arm in the spilled sake on the bar again. "Pissing hell."

"I'm not an actor. I can't pretend. That girl thinks I'm some sort of god."

"Not some sort of god."

"All right, God."

"So?"

"So she's deluded."

"How did Maha recognize you in the hotel lobby? Please, Mr. Rational Explanations, enlighten me."

"That is curious, but it doesn't mean I'm –"

"Please tell me what it means, Stan." Alok finished wiping his arm again, and glanced back at the table. Maha was now questioning Frieda. Tanya, the television executive, looked as though she had been slapped a number of times. The young man with the bandage on his face stared longingly at Maha. "You have to admit there is more than coincidence to this. Somehow, for some *reason*, you have been plucked from the herd to accomplish certain goals. Spiritual goals, Stan, for a spiritually bankrupt time. I can't tell you what to say to those people, but I hope you think before you speak. Decomposition? Where's the hope in that?"

"I think a world without the rewards of Heaven would be much improved. Like a world without video games and machine guns."

"Well, keep that opinion under wraps for a while, what say? Until we figure this thing out."

"This thing." Stanley looked toward the windows at the entrance of Far East Square, and the busy sidewalk beyond them. "Maybe Frieda's right. I could do these people much more harm than good."

"Snap out of it, Stan. You're it. You're him."

"I don't know what I'm doing."

"All the great prophets made it up as they went along."

The child from the Volkswagen appeared at the door. Stanley could see, now, that it was a girl. She wore the same black hooded sweatshirt, and watched Stanley with crossed arms. "Excuse me," said Stanley, and he hurried across the polished floor toward the exit.

As he passed the table, Frieda called out.

Stanley opened the door and the child ran off. It was a warm night and the streets were full of boisterous tourists moving from restaurants to bars. Stanley pursued the girl, but not so quickly as to frighten her. The girl ran backwards, facing Stanley with a smile. Yet, somehow, she weaved expertly through the crowd.

Not once did he take his eyes off her. But in front of the chocolatier, she vanished. Stanley stood in front of the shop and looked around. Gone.

Since he was there anyway, he stepped into the shop and purchased a dark bear claw for Frieda. He bought one for himself, too, and back on the street he tried to eat it. Bear claws were his favourite, but he could not summon an appetite for chocolate. Instead of hurrying back to Far East Square, Stanley leaned against a brick wall in front of a café.

Stanley watched the people pass and listened to them. Their hopes for the evening, their enthusiasms. Their children and the amount of credit remaining on their VISA cards. What would God, if there were such a thing, make of tourism? What was Stanley supposed to *do*, really do, now that he was here? What was expected of him? Even as his memory of the strange little girl faded, Stanley was afraid. He looked down at the sidewalk and wished, briefly, that he were dying after all.

Back in Far East Square, the members of his dining party welcomed him back. No one asked where he had gone. The

THE BOOK OF STANLEY

television producer, Tanya Gervais, announced that her
lawyer friend in Calgary would certainly help Kal negotiate
compensation for his injury that evening. "We can't be too
Canadian about this sort of thing. We have to go for the
carotid artery."

No one, not even Kal, responded.

So she continued. "How much is your rent?"

"Including utilities, $850. But I don't want to inconven-
ience anyone, and I think they're probably nice people, deep
down. Besides, I had way worse, back when I was playing
hockey. My teeth are all messed up." Kal opened his mouth,
to show everyone. Some of the deep-fried prawn batter was
visible in there.

Frieda was watching Stanley. "Not hungry?" she said.

"No. But I got you a treat for later."

"That's nice of you."

He turned to face the others. They stared at him again,
expecting something. Something wise. "Please," he said, with
a sweeping gesture. "This food isn't going to eat itself."

Maha cleared her throat. "Stanley. One quick question.
Are the Sunnis right, or the Shiites? The Wahhabis are way
off, I feel that. I'm not sure about Ismailis. But my personal
feeling, and tell me if I am wrong, please, is that the Sufis are
the soul of Islam."

"I don't know anything about that."

"Yes, you do. You must. You *are* Islam."

Alok nodded. "That is a superb question, Maha, about
where Stanley fits among the ancient religions. But I don't
think it's relevant any more, really. Stanley is here to clear
the board and create an altogether new game. Something
fairer, cleaner, more reasonable, more peaceful, closer to our
hearts and our minds."

"You guys are making up a religion?" said Kal.

Maha shook her head. "No. It's already –"

"Yes." Alok slammed his chopsticks on the table. "That is exactly what we're doing. Stan can perform miracles, wonderful miracles. I'm sure most of you feel, in some secret corner of your heart, that we're all in big trouble – humanity-wise. Well, Stan's here to basically save the land from dying. Right, Stan?"

Stanley decided to present Frieda with her gift of chocolate now. He passed the bear claw under the table into her lap and she sat motionless, stunned. It was clear she did not want to be in Far East Square, with Alok and these strangers, talking about her husband as though he had become . . . Allah? She looked down at her lap. "That's why you hurried out, to get bear claws?"

"Yes."

"Really?"

Stanley was incapable. "No."

TWENTY-NINE

In her hotel room that evening, after dinner, Maha searched the Koran for references to Stanley or a man like Stanley. There was, as she expected, nothing. So she watched television until it bored her, and then lay in bed. When she could not sleep, Maha drew a bath and lowered herself into it.

The Lord did not operate according to human reason. Yet he was married to Frieda, a quiet woman with sad eyes and a lovely black pendant on her silver chain. It was all so normal, boring even. *Banal.* There was a musty smell around them, like an old car that has been sitting too long in the sun.

It was her holy duty to bear witness to the unity of God and Mohammed – peace and blessings be upon Him – as His messenger. Unless the Lord was an angel, or a prophet. A new Mohammed, with an Oldsmobile.

Maha turned on the hot water, as her bath had gone cool. Soon, she would be out of money. The hotel cost $91 per night, plus taxes. She had already spent the bulk of what she had saved working for three years at Torino on Décarie Boulevard. Now, in the bathtub, a part of Maha wished she had stayed home. Perhaps, in time, the Lord would have made the trip to Montreal.

Maha wanted to phone her mother. But she knew how it would go if she heard the voice of Sara Rasad. They would argue, and apologize, and cry. Surely, the imam had been consulted, not to mention every man and woman Sara Rasad knew in Montreal and London and Beirut. Woe to the mother of the lost daughter! Guilt would gush through the fibre optic cables and Maha's bones would vibrate with it, like a plucked bass string, for hours. They would have her coordinates, finally, and her father would arrive the following morning – sleepy and annoyed. He would pretend not to have noticed the Rocky Mountains on the shuttle bus ride from Calgary to Banff. When pressed, he would shrug and say they were not nearly as beautiful as the mountains of Lebanon. Zaki Rasad would pay Maha's bill at the hotel and, shortly afterward, feign a heart-related illness. They would eat at McDonald's and they would take the next shuttle bus to the airport.

She imagined herself, with fragrant steam rising out of the bath, as a plant with rotting roots. A strong wind could blow her away, and when she fell to the ground, in some distant land, Maha would not have the energy to get up. The television commercials about mood-enhancing pharmaceuticals echoed in the silence of her room, amid the deep rumble of the climate-control mechanisms and the dripping water.

Even though he seemed not to believe in an afterlife, seemed not to know why he had created the earth and its murderers, the Lord was supreme. He had to be. The Lord suffered from a strain of amnesia, that was all. The body he inhabited was aged and sick, burdened by marriage and all the ordinary responsibilities and ornaments of a white, middle-class Canadian senior citizen. It would arrive, the rapture, and the Lord would loose himself from these chains.

A knock. Another knock. "Maha?"

She stepped out of the water and wrapped the white terry towel hotel robe around herself. "Just a moment."

There was a peephole in her hotel door. Tanya Gervais stood on the other side, with a notebook in her hand. "Can I come in?"

Maha opened the door. Of all the people she had met today, Tanya was most like her friends in Montreal. She dressed like a *Montréalaise* and spoke just a bit louder than everyone else. There was a frantic air to her, and hints of a fake British accent, and it made Maha feel tired and suspicious. "Is everything okay?"

"Fine, fine." Tanya sat on the edge of the bed.

Maha waited for a moment, for Tanya to explain herself. But the explanation was not forthcoming. Maha stood and Tanya sat. Outside, on Banff Avenue, a bus passed.

"I can't sleep."

"We have that in common," said Maha.

"What do you think of him? Of Stan? Do you buy this? I don't want to bore you with details of my personal history, but I'm at a very vulnerable point in my life right now. I had what they call a near-death experience in Vancouver last week. This slab. I got here for the festival and all I saw was meaningless, meaningless, meaningless. And then . . . tonight."

"I think he's –"

"I go back and forth. Maybe it's a scam. I'm single and I've been careful, Maha. The real estate market's been very good to me. But maybe, just maybe, this is genuine. Maybe that's why I came to Banff."

"In Montreal, my parents –"

"What makes it seem authentic is his reticence, don't you think? It's like he doesn't trust what Alok says he is."

"Well, in Islam –"

"If the guy was cocky, if he was going on about making the blind see and that crap, I'd probably run screaming. But he's so sincere. It's like he's frightened, isn't it? He's like a baby who wakes up one morning able to walk and talk. There's something really special about him, isn't there? I'm not just crazy, am I?"

"No. But the angel Gabriel –"

"Let's just see, right? Alok says the guy can perform miracles. I say we challenge him tomorrow morning. We want to see a miracle. Is it too much to ask? I don't need anything huge. God damn it, I'm fragile. Really, really fragile. If I were home right now, I'd be all over my therapist. All *over* him. I got this great guy, on Pender. He just lets me talk, mostly. Anyway, all I mean to say is I'm ready. I'm ready for whatever Stan is about. Aren't you?"

"Yes."

Tanya started to the door. "Thanks so much for the talk, Maha. Really, it means a lot. Tomorrow morning? Breakfast? Miracle?"

THIRTY

In Tony Roma's, where the breakfast buffet smelled overwhelmingly like a breakfast buffet, Tanya Gervais rested her head on her arms. She had stayed up all night, drawing up plans. All good religions, like all good entertainment products, created and fulfilled mass desires. What the people wanted were granite countertops in their kitchens.

So what would a religion of granite countertops look like? It would not be demanding. With work and family life and the rigours of a nightly television schedule, the people did not have time to attend church or some facsimile regularly. That said, real estate remained the number-one long-term investment an individual, or organization, could make. So the religion would need a holy place – preferably with shopping and daycare. Thoughtful interior design. Good lighting. Giant-screen televisions and – why not? – a wine bar. Followers could visit whenever they had time, pray, watch a hockey game, and pick up an organic cotton T-shirt.

A religion also needed a good story. If Stanley were the real thing, he would need something heroic in his past. On the Internet, Tanya had discovered a career-by-career list of the most and least respected professions. Politicians and journalists were near the bottom. Teachers were near the top, along with firefighters. Florists, unfortunately, were not represented.

Then again, Christians had the Jesus fish. Maybe there was something she could do with a flower. Stanley Moss: the florist of men. No, the florist of people. No. The florist of humans. Watering, weeding, fertilizing, protecting from frosts. In Tony Roma's she gazed at her notes, and her flower sketches, and the fatigue was like a bomb waiting to go off behind her left eye.

"More coffee?"

The young waiter had a goggles tan. He carried a carafe and blinked in slow motion. The name tag on his chest said "ANTON." Tanya nodded, "Please." As the thin young man in the white shirt poured, Tanya asked if he was a Christian.

Anton stepped back from the booth. "Are you giving out pamphlets or something? There's no soliciting in the restaurant."

"Just asking, Anton, that's all."

"Can I get you anything else? Another soy milk?"

Tanya declined and considered the exchange, made another note. For Anton to become a believer, they would need to shatter his expectations. And it couldn't be something commonplace or easy, because Anton and his peers had grown up in the digital era; he would have been a toddler when *Jurassic Park* came out. It wouldn't be easy, but the risk was worth taking. The overhead, for a nascent religion, was so low. The product was abstract. Shipping costs were nil.

Her booth was nearest the lobby so she would see Stanley and the others. The first was Kal, who waved and hopped up the stairs into the restaurant when he saw her. "I called your lawyer this morning. He's awesome."

Tanya nodded. She didn't want to look away from the lobby for long, and worried suddenly that Stanley and his wife had slipped out of the hotel while she was staring at the table or questioning Anton.

"He called the insurance company already."

"Do you know if Stanley was ever a firefighter or a teacher?"

"I just met him last night."

Soon, Kal gave up on socializing and went to the buffet. When Stanley did appear in the lobby, a few minutes later, Kal was drenching his eggs and potatoes with ketchup and talking about the magnificence of the accordion. "I must have heard accordions before, right? But they weren't speaking to me like they do now. The accordion is the secret language of the human heart, don't you figure?"

Tanya ran toward the lobby and slammed into Anton. He dropped his carafe and briefly watched the coffee leak into the carpet. "Oh sweet," he said, "sweet cherry fucken pie."

Stanley's white hair was wet, parted on the side, and he wore a distinctly unfashionable blue suit – to match the grey suit he had worn the previous evening. His tie was thin and old, all wrong, and the knot was too tight. This was Tanya's special gift: instead of seeing this as flawed, she saw it as beautiful. Believers looking for someone uncorrupted, in these cynical times, were growing tired of vain and vigorously coiffed men, riding to their mega-churches in limousines and helicopters.

"I have an idea," she said.

Stanley smiled. "Good morning."

"Yes, sorry, hello. Did you sleep well?"

"I don't sleep."

"Of course not. You're . . . what are you again?"

"I don't know, to be honest."

"We'll work on that. Your brand."

"My brand?"

"I'll need to see a miracle, Stan, and *tout de suite*. If we have something here, we have to get out ahead of it. Web presence, media coverage, press kits, viral marketing. Round two: products."

"Frieda and I were talking this morning. I'm not sure if this is something I can do, Tanya. Alok's enthusiasm is Alok's enthusiasm. To be honest, I don't see how we can create a religion here when I don't believe in God. Never have."

"Every problem is an opportunity, Stan. Let's take that, your doubt, and run with it."

"Run where?"

"The people can relate to doubt. I bet, in our hearts, we're all a bit doubtful. All but the loons. If there is something *inside* that doubt, something resonant, we can package and distribute it."

"Why would we do that?"

To make money. To become famous. To spin it off into books and films, get on *Oprah*. Was he really so naive? "To help people, of course. To, uh, save the land."

The elevator door opened and Frieda stepped out, with a walking stick. She wore a sun hat and smiled neutrally. "Hi, Tanya. Ready, Stan?"

"Where are you going?"

"On a little hike."

Tanya lied. "I love hikes."

Stanley and Frieda had no choice. They invited her along.

THIRTY-ONE

Walking up Tunnel Mountain with Maha, it occurred to Kal that he didn't know what a miracle was, really. The first thought that came to mind was of an extremely tall black man performing a slam dunk, as one of the all-sports channels called its nightly highlight reel "The Miracle Plays." Catholic school had provided him with a few biblical examples: walking on water, making water into wine, bringing a dead man back to life, surviving a crucifixion. But these miracles didn't seem to fit the time, the place, or the weather, and Stanley wasn't much of a sports figure. When Kal was small, his mom had once taken him to the Thunder Bay Community Auditorium to see a man called "Raveen, the Impossiblist." Raveen was supposed to be a miracle-worker. He was supposed to cure Kal's mom of her smoking habit and give her a new lease on life. There was a spinning disco ball, and manufactured fog, and loud music. Raveen seemed determined, if nothing else. The miracle lasted three days.

There were plenty of pitiable things in the world that a proper miracle-worker could fix. Starving babies in Africa and Ukrainian car dealers who waltz right up and steal a man's wife from him, to name but two. Kal didn't share these thoughts with Maha, who walked up the mountain with Raveen-like determination.

They passed clumps of fir trees and wildflowers, and the air smelled faintly of smoke. Kal wanted to comment on

the trees and flowers, or on the distant forest fires of northern British Columbia, or the accordion, but he was mindful
of appearing frivolous before this serious girl.

Stanley and Frieda walked in front, and Kal noticed that
Maha wanted to keep her distance. When Frieda stopped to
inspect a flower or point out a bird, Maha stopped too, and
turned to gaze upon the town. Alok and Tanya were below
them on the trail.

They were halfway up the little mountain overlooking
Banff before Kal thought of something to say. It concerned
him that he was almost out of breath, as he hadn't done a lick
of exercise since stepping off the team bus in Saskatchewan.
"Do you know what an impossiblist is?"

"No." Maha didn't slow down or stop.

"Tanya was saying Stanley's going to perform a miracle,
so I figured –"

"A magician?"

"What?"

Now Maha did stop. "An impossiblist. It sounds like a
fancy name for a magician."

"I guess so, yeah."

"What about it?"

Kal wished he hadn't worked so hard. Silence was much
more relaxing. Maha had her big brown eyes fixed on him,
and swiped her hair to reveal the full shine of her forehead
in the haze. "I was just thinking that maybe that's what
Stanley is."

"He isn't." Maha started walking again.

It pleased Kal that she wasn't staring at him in that accus-
ing manner any more. His lower back had broken out in an
instant sweat, before that stare. She was a powerful girl, inside
and out. "Okay."

"You're Christian, right? What if I said Jesus was a magician?"

Kal had to give her that. It didn't seem right at all. But he did have questions about Jesus, now that Maha had brought him up. "Why did he spend all that miracle-working power on turning water into wine, anyway, when he might have – I don't know – got rid of deserts? So babies wouldn't starve in Africa, for instance. The miracles of Jesus, when you sit right back and think about them, are pretty damn selfish. If you were his friend or in his town or whatever, it was a pretty sweet deal. If you lived in a different desert, though: look out, Charlie."

"Look out, Charlie," said Maha, as though hearing it had disappointed her.

The only sounds on the path up Tunnel Mountain were their footsteps on the small pebbles and the odd breeze moving through the boughs and branches. Now and then, a couple passed, going down, and said "Hello," with their various accents: Japanese, German, French. Up ahead, Stanley and Frieda stopped. They appeared to be arguing, very quietly. Maha stopped, and turned, and together they looked at the town some more. Alok was way down, bent over.

"This is so weird," said Kal.

Maha didn't concur.

"Do you sometimes step out of yourself and see yourself doing something weird and think, 'I can't believe I am where I am.'? I did that a lot, playing hockey. I'd be on the blue line and the puck'd be in our end, in Syracuse or Rochester, and I'd think: *I am playing hockey in Syracuse.* Or Rochester or whatever. I'm definitely having one of those moments right now, up here on this mountain with you."

It appeared Maha wasn't listening. She took a deep breath and blew it out.

"Maybe later on we could head down to the hot tub again."

"I don't think so, Kal."

"You got a boyfriend back home, don't you?"

"Not exactly."

"Someone you like? Or love?"

"I have a fiancé in Toronto."

It was like someone had sneaked out from behind a juniper bush and kicked Kal in the face. He half expected his nose to start bleeding. Stanley and Frieda continued along and so did Kal and Maha, up the switchback. Kal had a great idea for a miracle, if Stanley was fixing to dole them out and the babies of Africa were already taken care of. He could go ahead and give Maha's fiancé a nice bit of rectal cancer. Then, a bouquet of shame bloomed in Kal and his stomach ached fiercely.

"Well, congratulations to you. I bet he's real handsome and rich and smart. Lucky guy. Your family likes him, probably. That's good. Why rock the boat, right?" They walked past a thorny bush and Kal grabbed a handful of it. "Great news."

THIRTY-TWO

At the summit of Tunnel Mountain, everyone but Alok looked out over the deep valley and commented on the view.

On the slope of the mountain not far from his wife and new friends – were they friends? – three mule deer stood together in sweet silence. Stanley watched them for several minutes, their smooth and careful movements. It was easy to see why deer inspired longing in humans, for a purity lost to avarice. Knowing what he knew, or half knew, since the powers had come to him, Stanley saw this longing as yet another expression of weakness. All that was pure was contained in the vain hope for purity.

All morning, Stanley had been wondering if it was ethically sound to deprive the world of special powers, if one had acquired them. Sometime in the late 1970s, he supposed, Stanley had stopped believing in good and evil. It wasn't easy to catch up. Where should special powers be directed? What *was* good?

Like the hunt for purity, goodness was a mirage. So far, the special powers had moved Stanley to empathy and pity, to a fuller understanding of weakness, but not much else. Every time Maha called him "Lord," he flinched. He continued to distrust the conceits of religion, of a comprehensive historical and spiritual world-view. At the same time, he didn't feel capable of driving home with Frieda later that afternoon.

Alok lay on some moss, breathing heavily and moaning about the ugliness of morning hikes. His skin, in the flat light of an overcast day, had a somewhat green quality about it.

"Never again before breakfast," said Alok. "Never again!"

Two women with a distinctly European mien about them took pictures of the deer and started back down the mountain. Stanley helped Alok to his feet. "I think Frieda has some water."

"I don't need water. I need to be in town, with eggs, bacon, potatoes, coffee, and a small glass of Grand Marnier, and you know it."

Stanley led Alok to the far end of the summit, where the others looked down at the Bow River half a kilometre below. Kal was telling them about a plaque he had read; it turned out there was no tunnel through Tunnel Mountain.

"Someone wanted to build a tunnel, or something, but everybody else figured it was a bonehead idea."

The wind came up out of the valley in cool gusts and whipped their hair about. Frieda looked away from the valley and into Stanley's eyes. Since arriving in Banff she had been uncharacteristically quiet and docile. Her manner now was inscrutable, but Stanley knew what Frieda wanted. She wanted, even more than before, to walk down this mountain immediately, load the Oldsmobile with their luggage, and drive home, preferably by way of the Columbia glacier.

The light, even with the cloud cover, was bright up on the mountain. Frieda squinted and the beautiful lines above her cheekbones, lines she had inherited from her mother and her mother's mother, were long and deep. It occurred to him that the relevant fact of being God in a godless universe, thanks to a chemical reaction in his backyard, was simply this: Frieda would die and he would live.

"Well," he said.

Frieda hugged herself. It was not a warm day and she wore only a zip-up sweater over her blouse. Alok spoke into the wind now, about the majesty of the view. The sacredness of this place, the good omen of deer, the significance of mountains in nascent religions. "Someday," Alok said, "the people will look at Tunnel Mountain and they will see much

more than a mountain named after a stupid idea. The plaques
will say, 'Hark!'"

Alok continued but Stanley stopped paying attention at
"Hark!" He took a few steps back from the ledge and Frieda
followed. "What do you think they want from you?" she
said, just loud enough to be heard over the wind.

"They want answers."

"Do you have answers, Stanley?"

"Not yet."

Frieda sighed. In these last days, she had become a world-
class sigher. Not long ago, she had concentrated all of her
powers on making sure her husband got through each day
with a morsel of hope. She had been an unpaid nurse, psy-
chologist, and cheerleader. Now she merely followed him,
and sighed. Frieda did not even argue any more. Of all the
answers Stanley hoped to receive – from where? on high? –
he awaited a strategy for Frieda with the most impatience.

"I love you."

"I love you too, Stan." She stepped in close, took his hands.
"Let's get out of here."

Another gust came out of the valley, this one so strong
that Frieda stumbled. She let go of Stanley's hands and
looked up, perhaps for rain. Stanley wanted to tell her what
he was about to do, but he didn't know how. "Don't worry,"
he said.

"How can I not worry?" Frieda spoke without looking at
him, and laughed. "You and I, that's what we do. We worry."

"We can stop now."

"Stan, there's more reason than ever to worry. Unless, of
course, you're keeping something from me."

Stanley took his wife's hands and kissed her. He took three
steps toward the edge of the mountain. And he jumped.

THIRTY-THREE

For a moment, the Lord could fly. Trivial things blew away and belief clung to her insides like melted iron. This, *this* was what Maha had been waiting for. This was why she had been born, why they were here, to bask in his greatness. To serve the one God. To transcend themselves through him.

Nothing she had learned in school was important, no piece of history or chemistry. Books were insignificant – dust-collectors! The clothes upon her, symbols of vanity. Her family consisted of three talking mannequins. She reached out and grasped a handful of Kal's shirt at the chest. He flexed his pectoral muscles.

In the next moment, the Lord could not fly. The Lord fell into the valley stomach first, his hands and feet swimming along. He did not cry out. As he plunged to the dense forest of pine and fir trees far below, the Lord tilted forward. He crashed into the canopy headfirst, with a ferocious cracking of branches audible even in the strong wind, and then the Lord disappeared from view.

His wife fell to her knees on the summit of Tunnel Mountain and cried in whispers.

No one said a word. They waited a moment. Maha had not heard the thud of his body crashing into the tan riverbank. She backed away from the ledge.

"Jesus H. Christ." Tanya turned to Alok and slapped his mighty breasts with the back of her hand. "You said he had

powers and I actually believed you. I actually *believed you.*"
She addressed the others. "Do you understand the trouble
we're in here?"

Alok filled his cheeks with air and blew. Kal continued to
look down.

Maha put her hand on Frieda's shoulder, waited for her
own sadness and disappointment to come. But they were not
there. Even though the Lord had just plummeted to his
death, Maha felt no sense of loss. "Don't worry," she said,
to Frieda. Maha hugged the Lord's wife around the shoulders. "He's okay."

Then she addressed the others. "Don't worry. The Lord is
not dead."

"Are you fucking blind?" said Tanya. She motioned
toward the Bow Valley with her thumb. "Hello!"

Frieda pulled at some weeds as she sobbed, her hands
shaking. She seemed not to have heard Maha. Frieda seemed
to be in another place, mentally. Maha kneeled beside Frieda
and prepared to explain things to her.

"Let her grieve." Alok pulled Maha away.

"But she doesn't need to grieve. He's not dead."

Tanya looked at her cellphone. "I bet the Mounties are
pretty bored around here. They'll investigate us. No one'll
believe he jumped. We're screwed, blued, and tattooed."

"Kal. Will you listen to me?" said Maha.

"You bet."

Maha looked over the cliff with him. "You see, he's
testing us. Our faith."

"Of course." Alok joined them, and clapped his hands.
He closed his eyes and shook his head. "I'm a fool. That's
why he dragged us up here. It's like Abraham and Isaac."

"Ishmael," said Maha.

Tanya stuffed the phone into her purse and jogged toward the path. "On second thought, I won't call from my own phone. Let's go, you guys. We have to get our stories straight."

Maha helped Frieda up, and Kal and Alok followed. As they reached Tanya and the path, Frieda pulled herself away from Maha and walked determinedly into a bluff of shrubbery and spruce.

"Let her go," said Alok. "She knows the way down."

"Frieda's a problem." Tanya gestured toward the shrubbery. "She could tell the cops just about anything."

The Lord would not appreciate Tanya's doubt. Maha wondered what would have happened if Abraham, peace be upon him, had not followed the Lord's directions. What if Abraham, peace be upon him, had stayed in camp, protecting his beloved son from the eye of Allah? What if his faith had been weak, as Tanya's faith was weak? Allah surely would have destroyed the prophet and his son, and Abraham, peace be upon him, would not have led his tribes out of darkness.

"Maybe we should pray," said Maha.

Tanya did not slow her pace. "All right, he was a crazy person. Everyone agree? Good. If they press us on it, we can say he led us up a mountain to show us a miracle. That isn't a lie. We'll look naive, maybe a little stupid. But it's better than a holding cell. Even cops understand simple human curiosity, right? Alok, you shared some history with him. It was cordial?"

"I wish I had an accordion right about now," said Kal.

It was much faster going down Tunnel Mountain than up. Maha wore sandals and the leather straps rubbed at the backs of her heels. But she would endure the pain without complaint. There were much greater things to consider. The Lord, she imagined, watched them somehow. Not from the riverbank but from nowhere and everywhere at once. His human form was only a shell, a vessel. This was the flaw in Maha's narrow imagination: she used the model of western reason to comprehend the incomprehensible. She wanted to look through the Koran again, for hints of the Lord's return and all that he expected of her.

Kal touched Maha's arm and smiled at her. "I know why he chose you, Maha."

"Can we walk slower?" said Alok.

They neared the bottom of the mountain and Maha recalled the visit, to her mosque in Montreal, by an imam from London, England. She'd still been a child then. The angry imam had recited various prophecies about the last day, and claimed they were coming true on what was then the verge of the millennium. These stories had terrified Maha, for she'd feared she was one of the unrighteous. Her thoughts were not pure. She had seen pictures of men and women fornicating on the Internet. She had sneaked chocolate bars at school during the fast of Ramadan. Desperately, desperately, she had wanted her parents to be rich so they might buy her a horse.

In the presence of the British imam she had felt irredeemably far from God. On the way home, in the blue minivan, Maha had wanted her mother to say he was a silly man, a medieval lunatic from a depressing suburb. But her mother had said nothing about the imam, even when they'd stopped for ice cream at Dairy Queen. The imam's words and his beard and his long fingers, the peculiar, well-travelled accent to his Arabic, kept her up that night and for many nights thereafter. Maha realized, in view of the Tunnel

Mountain parking lot and two shirtless men with goatees drinking beer from cans, that this was the first time she'd felt entirely free of the imam's prophecies.

THIRTY-FOUR

During his fall, Stanley experienced a few regrets. Number one was the way he had handled things with Frieda. He really should have told her he planned to fly off the back of the mountain. Number two was going public before a couple of practice sessions.

Stanley passed through a hot and mysteriously fragrant pocket of air. In the newspaper, or perhaps in a book, Stanley had read that when people jump off buildings they die of fear before they land. He questioned the science of this. How could scientists know such things, unless they had hooked monitors to a volunteer?

Stanley was falling faster than he imagined possible, and he was not afraid. He experienced a more potent, ecstatic, and comprehensive version of empathy – not only for Frieda and his new friends but for Asian restaurateurs and nasty teenagers and his son in New York City. He thought, for the first time, that he understood Charles.

From a distance, the boughs of Douglas fir and lodgepole pine trees appeared soft. Downy. Up close, however, they were anything but. Stanley slammed into them and it sounded, and felt, like he was being ripped to pieces. He clenched his fists, closed his eyes, and concentrated.

And that was the secret: intense concentration. Stanley could not worry about Frieda or fragrances, and he could not concern himself with the science of fear. His body went hot. He slowed and landed softly on the spongy ground, simply by willing himself to do so.

It was shadowed here, much cooler, a refuge for mosquitoes and twinkling spider webs. There were deep cuts on his face and hands, and he was something like sore, but otherwise Stanley felt well.

His blue suit, which no longer made him feel insignificant and ghostly, was covered in ashy soil and pine needles. Nearby children playing among the hoodoos and in the cold Bow River screamed with joy. Birds sang. Stanley lay on the ground for some time, his soreness easing, completely bewildered. All of this must – must – mean something. In earlier, less-skeptical times, it would have felt more natural to consider oneself a prophet or even a god.

Instead of standing and hiking up to the road immediately, Stanley took the opportunity to practise his newfound skill. The sensation originated in the back of his skull and radiated down from there. His heels ached and rose before his chest hopped up off the ground. It was difficult to control his body as he levitated into the branches. He attempted to remain horizontal but tilted back, upside down.

Stanley practised floating under the boughs of the spruce trees, easing into a somersault and opening his arms in a Superman imitation. He tucked and spun, slowly, and laughed the way he had laughed the first time he'd snorkelled in the Caribbean. Then he remembered where he was. Stanley remembered how he had come to be here, in this mossy fort of northernness. Frieda's concern hit him like a baseball, splintered his concentration. He dropped, awkwardly, on his neck and shoulders. A fall that would have killed him a month ago.

He ran up the bank, swerving around trees and shrubbery. The sun came out from behind a cloud and lit up the mountainside. Stanley scoured the forest for his wife, first the path and then non-traditional routes created by wildlife. He found Frieda easing over a slab of white rock, holding on to a juniper branch for balance. There were tears on her face and the characteristic pink had drained from her cheeks. She saw Stanley and, after a moment of gaping at him, she snorted, sarcastically. "Of course," she said, and let go of the branch.

She began to slide down the rock and Stanley caught her. They stood on the root of a pine tree. Frieda buried her face in his suit collar and clung to him. "You son of a bitch."

Stanley ran his fingers through her grey and blond hair, untangling the bits at the end. "I'm sorry."

"If you knew you could suddenly break the moon in two, or kill the President of the United States, would you do it?"

"No."

"You jumped off a mountain."

"I should have warned you."

Frieda placed her hands over her eyes and held them in place for several minutes. A raven landed on a branch nearby and cawed. The sun came out from behind a cloud. Stanley wanted to say something to comfort his wife but all of his instincts ran contrary to her wishes. She took a deep breath and dropped her hands from her eyes.

"There must be a reason for this, and I intend to find it," he said. "I can do some good here."

"You *can* do some good. Sign the RRSPs over to the Cancer Foundation. Volunteer at the Food Bank, or construct some affordable housing. Read to poor kids at the library. Trade the Oldsmobile for a Smart Car."

Stanley lifted his hands. "Half an hour ago I had deep lacerations on my hands and face. They're gone."

"I don't want to hear that." Her voice broke and she attempted to walk away. But off the root, the rockface was too steep. Stanley caught Frieda's arm before she fell, and she fought to get away from him. Once she gave up, he picked her up and carried her to the path. They passed a group of Japanese tourists who whispered to one another.

Near the parking lot, her breathing returned to normal. He lowered his wife to her feet and she fixed her clothing. Her hands were criss-crossed with scratches from the juniper bush, and she blew on them. She straightened his tie and wiped debris from his collar.

"Tuck in your shirt," she said.

"What if these people were called here, to me?"

"I think you know my feelings, Stan."

"You think we ought to jump in the car and drive home, without saying goodbye."

She nodded, and started walking down the path again. At the Old Banff Cemetery they looked over the bear-proof fence at the blanched tombstones.

"Isn't religion supposed to be about losing the ego? Shouldn't it be about *giving up your worldly power*, in order to think harder? Comprehend the incomprehensible?"

"So I should go home and meditate? Waste this?"

Frieda shrugged. "This frightens me. It doesn't frighten you?"

"No. That isn't the right word."

"You aren't the same person you were a week ago."

"I'm not. It's true."

"Maybe it's immature or selfish or unadventurous of me, but I don't want a husband who jumps off mountains." Frieda pushed herself off the fence and rubbed another errant pine needle from Stanley's jacket. She started back down the street to the Chalet Du Bois and, to his amazement, he did not know whether to follow.

THIRTY-FIVE

The day had taken on a curious aspect for Kal. First, an old man had jumped off the side of a mountain. Now, Tanya was talking to the police from a pay phone in Cascade Plaza – with her voice disguised to sound like a hillbilly's.

"We were hikin' up that there mountain you got in town there, yep," she said. "No, sir, we don't know him for nothin', constable. He was a white-haired fella in a very dated suit. Wool or somethin'. I remember sayin' to my husband, Roy, I says, 'Isn't that peculiar, a man in an old suit goin' for a hike?' And the next thing you know, the fella went and *jumped*."

To impress Maha, Kal whipped up his most disapproving glare.

"No, there was no one with him nohow. He was all alone, constable, and talkin' crazy. Like some sorta crazy person.

No sir, no, I won't be providin' my family name, sir. This
here's an anonymous tip."

Tanya hung up the phone without saying goodbye. She
looked up and pointed at what looked to be a light with a
black shade.

"We're being surveilled!" She sprinted toward the door.
"Let's beat it out of here."

Alok chuckled. "I don't run."

"Come on, you retards." Tanya covered her head with
her hands like a captured serial killer and bolted.

Maha and Alok walked at a leisurely pace. So did Kal,
behind Maha, so he could stare at her legs in the athletic
short-shorts she had worn for the hike. Alok seemed to think
Stan was dead and not-dead at the same time, and he questioned Maha about how she could be so certain he was alive.

"Is it a hunch?"

"No, not a hunch. More than a hunch. I'm certain."

"But it's not like you're receiving messages, is it? He
hasn't sent me anything, unless I'm not tuned to the right
frequencies."

Kal didn't know what to add, or what questions to ask.
He just wanted to be sure that his relationship with Maha
outlasted Stanley's funeral. With the money coming in from
his settlement with Far East Square, he could learn how to
play the accordion. He longed to describe the mountains
surrounding him, the pretty and spooky aspects of the mountains, in song. He longed to hear and understand musical
notes the way he saw colours and smelled smells. It would
make him a full man, worthy of love.

Far ahead on the Banff Avenue sidewalk, Tanya wove
through the pedestrians. "She's going to end up feeling really
stupid," said Maha.

"So stupid," said Kal.

The weather was hot and dry now, the sky an unblemished blue. As much as Kal was worried about Stanley and everything, he was keen to change the tone of the conversation. "One thing I was wondering about is swimming. Does anyone want to go?"

"I think we should wait to hear from the Lord," said Maha.

"Maybe after we hear about him or whatever?"

Alok suggested they stop for Grand Marniers, so he could learn more about the spotlessness of Maha's faith. Maha wanted to get back to the hotel. So they compromised in front of an ice cream store. While Maha and Alok talked about Stanley, Kal bought three ice creams. When they arrived at the Chalet Du Bois, Tanya sat in the lobby on a bench made of logs. Her arms were crossed. "Where have you been?" she said, through her teeth.

Kal took a demonstrative lick of his ice cream cone, which had pecans in it.

"Has Stan been through here?" said Alok. "Have you checked with the front desk?"

"Get up to my room, all of you, now."

Kal turned to Maha, because Tanya made him tired. Maha shivered as she stared into the darkness of Tony Roma's. "Oh no," Maha said, "no, no, no," and rushed to the elevator. She pressed the call button several times and kicked the door.

A man in his late twenties or early thirties, with a healthy growth of stubble on his face, emerged from the restaurant and walked past Kal and Alok. He approached Maha and spoke urgently to her. "Your parents are ill with worry."

"How did you find me?" Maha pressed the elevator button again.

"There was a pamphlet in your bedroom. I phoned the hotels. It was simple."

"Leave me alone."

"Who are these people? What are you doing here with them?" The man gestured toward Kal and Alok, briefly. He said something to Maha in a language Kal did not understand, and grasped her arm.

"Hey, fella." Kal stepped in close to the man and breathed into his face. "You're gonna take your hand off her, I think."

Maha led the man through the lobby, to a chesterfield underneath a majestic portrait of elk. They spoke too quietly to hear.

"Who the hell's he?" said Tanya.

Kal shrugged. He didn't want to talk about it.

"Boyfriend," said Alok.

"Oh, she's way too pretty for him. It won't last. An imbalance like that'll destroy a relationship."

Maha led the man, who was actually a bit too handsome for Kal's taste, back to them. "This is Gamal."

Kal shut off momentarily, like a generator on its last dribble of gasoline. He flickered, slumped, and cronked slowly back into operation. By the time Kal was ready to process what this meant and challenge Gamal to a bench-pressing competition, the stranger had already introduced himself to the others. Now, he held his hand out for Kal to take. He said his name a couple of times. *Gamal. Gamal.* It sounded like a cuss word, the way he pronounced the final *l*. And yes, his advantages were clear: he had infuriatingly clear and brown skin, and an expensive-looking wristwatch.

"Kal," said Kal. Gamal's grip was soft. The drowning husk of pre-poetry Kal, swirling around in his stomach acid, flailed to the surface and nearly called out, "You wanna fuckin' go, pussy?"

Gamal put his arm around Maha and she shook it off. "Maha tells me you've been good friends here. Thanks for looking out for her. She's very young and, as you can tell, an inexperienced traveller."

"Shut up," said Kal. Then he said, "Sorry."

Silence crackled through the lobby of the Chalet Du Bois. The elevator door opened. "I'll help you pack," Gamal said.

Alok laughed. "She isn't leaving."

"Absolutely not," Maha said.

Gamal took Maha's hand and led her into the elevator. Kal feared saying goodbye to her, or offering a note of warm regard, because he was certain his voice would come out as a squeak.

THIRTY-SIX

"I love her."

"You can't love her, Kal." Sitting on the king-sized bed in her suite, Tanya switched from one news channel to another, looking for news of a dead elderly man in the Bow Valley. She stopped at Leap. "You guys just met. She's hot and emotionally unstable, so of course you'd like to *make* love to her."

Kal covered his ears. "Don't say that."

"Look, she's obviously promised herself to this Gamal character. It's a cultural thing. These people come to Canada and marry within their group because they think we're inferior."

"I am inferior." Kal growled up some phlegm and, to Tanya's great dismay, swallowed it. "Did you get a load of his watch?"

Tanya looked over at the young man leaning against the headboard of her bed. He wore a tight blue dryweave shirt that highlighted his pectoral muscles. There was a firefighter aspect to him that would appeal to certain women. But he slouched and he was losing his hair. There was a pimple between his nose and his lip that needed attending to. How could Kal not know that snorting up phlegm drew the sexual energy out of a room faster than a tube of Preparation H?

Not that she wouldn't sleep with him, under the right conditions. "You want a glass of red wine, Kal?"

"No, thank you."

The phone rang. Tanya turned down the television and answered.

A deep and smoky voice said, "You might want to come see me."

"Is this Alok?"

There was a pause. Then he said, "Who the hell else would it be?"

"I don't know your phone voice." Tanya hung up. "Let's go down. King Kong has something to show us."

They took the stairs. Kal slowed as they passed Maha's room. He put his ear to the door and frowned.

"What?" said Tanya.

"I don't hear nothing."

"Anything."

"What?"

"Nothing." Tanya continued to the next room and knocked. "Maybe they went out."

"Maybe they're *sleeping*."

Alok opened the door and stepped back with a bow and a flourish. "Presenting, the next great international prophet and man-god, Stanley Moss."

He sat in a chair by the window, next to a small, round table. Frieda stood across from him, her arms crossed. It took some time for Tanya to adjust. First, she suspected that she was being conned. These people were actors, in stage one of converting her to their cultish religion and taking her money. It was ingenious.

Too ingenious, actually. Kal appeared ready to faint or throw up, and the look on Frieda's face — a mixture of fear and impatience and resentment – could not have been manufactured. "What are you . . . how?"

Alok distributed champagne glasses and opened the mini-bar bottle with a mini pop. "I want you all to appreciate this moment for what it truly means. We're witnessing the beginning of the new spiritual age. And we've been chosen to be part of it. Please, before you drink, consider that." He filled the flutes with champagne and lifted his.

"This is impossible," said Tanya.

"Here's to the great, great glory of the impossible."

As much as she wanted to exercise proper manners, Tanya finished her champagne in a gulp. She looked down at her feet, to stop herself from crying or shrieking in delight or horror. "Did the trees break your fall?"

"I suppose, but not enough to save me. I slowed myself down."

"In the air you slowed yourself down?" said Kal.

Alok clapped. "Just think, people. When is the last time something like this happened? The beginning of Islam? Christianity? Think of the parts the early disciples played in these religions. We have a profound responsibility, here, to protect this man. This more-than-a-man."

"It seems I can float, when I put my mind to it."

"He can *float*." Alok opened the mini-bar again and pulled out bottles of red and white wine. "Show them, Stan. Flaunt the laws of gravity again, you wonderful humming-bird of a man."

Frieda stood up and kissed Stanley. "I'm going to bed early tonight, sweetheart." Without saying good night to anyone else, she walked out of the room.

"Stan," said Tanya, unable to keep her voice and hands from shaking, "can you show us?"

"I don't know." He sighed. "This is fairly new to me, and I want to be sure we aren't making too much of it. Let's not entirely discount a scientific explanation."

Stanley walked over and lay on the bed. He closed his eyes and his feet shot up in the air, as though sucked from the ceiling. Then the rest of him, chest first, levitated. Stanley allowed his hands and arms to hang below, and then brought them up above him. He seemed to be conducting himself, like a symphony.

"I've been working on this," he said, his voice perfectly, ludicrously calm. "On staying horizontal. My body naturally wants to go up feet first for some reason."

Kal fell and no one caught him. He smacked into the mahogany chest of drawers, then careened forward onto the bed and bounced onto the floor with a loud thump. Alok reached down and tried to turn Kal over, grunting as he exerted himself. Eventually Alok gave up and sat on the bed with his head between his knees.

Tanya couldn't hold herself back any longer. She started to cry. Not at the spectacle but at the palpable glow around Stanley. There was such quiet goodness about him, and sincerity, and humility, and grace. Historically, these were not qualities Tanya admired. She had mistaken them for powerlessness. She had mistaken so much that was venerable for powerlessness. Tanya had remained hungry even when she was full. She had been a giant, devouring mouth.

Stanley lowered himself back onto the bed. "I'm getting better at landing," he said, and went over to check on Kal. Kal's eyes fluttered open and, with an expression of bewilderment, he struggled to his feet. He hugged Stanley and kissed him on the neck. Tanya convulsed with sobs.

"I didn't believe," she said, wiping the tears away quickly. "I'm sorry."

Kal clasped his hands. "You *are* the Lord."

"If we're going to do this, you'll have to think of some other name for me." Stanley walked to the window in the room and looked out. "That just doesn't seem right."

"God," said Kal.

"Director," said Tanya.

"The Stan," said Alok.

THIRTY-SEVEN

The lounge in the basement of the Chalet Du Bois was full of television executives, so Alok led the engineers of The Stan across a busy street to the Rose & Crown. Even in the two-storey pub, there was a thirty-minute wait for a table. A Celtic band presided over the raucous dance floor and teenage men clomped around like zombies drunk on brain, leering and shouting at mountain women in Lycra shirts – shirts that allowed no mystery about the size and shape of the nipple. Stanley waited in the lineup, witnessing this romantic carnage.

"We should continue along. There must be somewhere less sad than this."

Alok shook his head. "No, no, we've been led here. Remember, Stan, free will isn't possible in a deterministic universe. And you're the determiner."

"And I think this is the wrong place."

To Stanley's chagrin, Alok seemed to ignore this last bit. He had his giant arm around a young server in a black rugby shirt. She nodded at Stanley and said, "Whoa, really? Damn."

Five minutes later, they were sitting at the back of the Rose & Crown, near an underutilized piano. Kal asked what Alok had said to get them in so quickly.

"I told her Stan was Sir Anthony Hopkins."

While Tanya and Alok fell into a deep discussion of how they ought to proceed, organizationally, Stanley concerned himself with Frieda. He felt his transformation had not altered the Stanley Moss-ness of Stanley Moss. But if his wife did not recognize him as the man he had been, maybe there was something altogether more sinister at work here than he had previously thought. Maybe he had been inhabited. Possessed. Maybe none of this was happening at all.

"I can't stop thinking about Maha," said Kal.

Stanley smiled, grateful for a diversion. "Would you prefer to forget her?"

Kal bit his bottom lip as Tanya raised her voice at Alok and placed her hands on the wooden table. "Only the crazies buy religion, the real thing. But we want the crazies *and* the skeptics. Our market watches reality television, shops at Wal-Mart, eats fast food, drives minivans, plays video games, uploads videos to the Internet, dreams of plasma screens. We're attacking the great, numb bulge in the middle of America."

"I disagree completely." Alok reached for Stanley and pulled him close. The big man had not showered after his hike up Tunnel Mountain, and a ham-like scent attended him. "The Stan ought to address the essential meaninglessness of contemporary existence. Globalization, and modern religion, have made us into nothing more than clients."

The server arrived to take their drink orders, and stared at Stanley. "Can I get your autograph later?"

"I'm afraid my friend was dishonest with you. I'm not Sir Anthony Hopkins."

"Actually, he's better than some puffy actor," said Alok. "He's God."

"I'm not God, either."

"He can read your mind. Think of something."

The server frowned. "I don't get it."

Alok took her arm. "Picture your warmest memory."

It was easy. Stanley concentrated and saw the girl winning a bicycle race, hugging her parents, tears in her eyes. He described, in two sentences, her warmest memory.

"How did you do that?"

"Isn't he so much better than Sir Anthony Hopkins?" said Alok.

"That's freaky."

Alok whispered, "He floats, too. And he could pick up this piano, if he wanted."

"No, I couldn't."

The server stared at Stanley for some time, and then took their drink orders. Stanley saw that she was not curious. She did not sense *wonder* at their table. The woman was alarmed, even wounded. It was as if they had asked her to meet them in back for a round of blow jobs – the sort of thing that no doubt happened to people in her position on a regular basis. Orders taken, the woman did not linger.

"Did you learn anything from that exchange?" Stanley said.

Neither Alok nor Tanya answered. Kal raised his hand. "She was spooked."

Stanley had never excelled in the gardening and floral business, as others around him had, because he always ordered what he thought people *should* have, like native plants and perennials that didn't need much tending. Of course, what his customers wanted were exotics and the fad flowers they saw in glossy magazines. He wondered if there was a way to appeal to both types of customers, to sell native plants as though they were exotics.

"I think we have to take a couple of steps back here. The word *religion* could get us into trouble. In the gardening business –"

"We're not selling flowers here, Stan." Alok's face began to turn red with frustration. "We're not thinking micro. We're not over-thinking this, or making it into a dose of good medicine. What we're selling is a new world."

"But you said you're against selling stuff," said Kal.

Tanya slapped her forehead. "You can't sell a new world, you big fat jackass. You can only sell dreams and the signposts of dreams."

"Jackass? Jackass?"

"Kal, what are your dreams?" Tanya tilted her head, like a television interviewer.

The Celtic bandleader announced, in the next room, that they were going on a break. There was some applause and, then, near silence. Kal said, finally, "I want Maha. I want to play the accordion. I want my daughter. I want to change my life."

Stanley was pleased to see that neither Tanya nor Alok had an easy answer for this. The fulfillment of dreams, or even the promise of it, was more complex than they imagined. Even for someone they saw as simple. Kal excused himself and wandered over to the old piano. He opened the cover and slid his fingers along the keys. Instead of listening to Alok describe how deeply Tanya had wounded him by calling him a fat jackass, Stanley followed Kal to the piano and stood behind him.

"Play."

Kal slid his fingers along the keys. "If you can't play the accordion, you can't play the piano."

"Let's start with the piano and go from there."

"I can't."

Stanley focused on Kal's fingers. He concentrated on telling Kal he could play the piano. It wasn't a transfer, exactly, but to Stanley it was like filling a cup to the brim. When the cup was full, he placed his hand on Kal's shoulder. "Please, try."

The canned rock music coming out of the sound system was not nearly as loud as the band had been. Kal made sure no one was paying attention to him. He looked up at Stanley in a pleading manner, then shrugged and said, "What the hell." He straightened his back and lifted his fingers to the keyboard. Confused, he started to ask a question, directed not at Stanley but at himself. When Kal touched the keys, he started with a low note and followed with a high one. He continued along, in a slow rhythm.

Kal played the nocturne Stanley had heard in the rotunda of the Royal Alexandra Hospital. It rose slowly and gained prominence in the room. The song, its gentle power, hushed the drinkers. By the time Kal reached the flourish, four minutes into the song, someone had turned off the rock music. A small crowd had gathered around him. Alok and Tanya were not arguing any more. The "Nocturne in C Minor" ended quietly, as it had begun. Kal lifted his hands from the keys. He turned around, his breath quivering, his smile beatific, as the crowd broke into warm applause. Someone hooted. Someone else called out, "Attafuckinboy!"

The audience began to disperse. Kal grasped Stanley's hand. "I'll do anything. Whatever you want."

Stanley placed his index finger to his lips.

The server brought two glasses of wine, for Alok and Tanya, a beer for Kal, and a small bottle of fizzy water for Stanley. He wasn't sure he could drink it. In the last few days, his appetite – even for water – had diminished to just about nothing. Kal sat with his head in his hands.

"That was so beautiful," said the server. "Thank you."

Kal looked up and smiled at her. "You're welcome."

"Now *that* we can sell," said Tanya.

THIRTY-EIGHT

On his way out of the Rose & Crown, a number of the drunks thanked Kal for his piano playing. A woman his age, with glassy eyes and sticky-looking blond dreadlocks, grasped his hands and whispered, her face so close he could feel the heat and moisture of her vodka-cooler breath on his cheek, "I'm staying at Two Jack Lake, in a red tent. I got a bottle of white wine and a whole box of soda crackers. Meet me there in twenty minutes. That 'Rhapsody on a Theme of Paganini' was hot."

Tanya pulled him away from the woman and down the sidewalk. At this elevation, the warm air departed with the sunlight. Kal wished he had brought a jacket. Tanya shook her head and scrunched her eyebrows, as though she were in the middle of an argument. "This isn't a democratic religion, Kal," Tanya said suddenly. "All we need is a strong spiritual leader, with one or two trusted advisors and a heavy. You can be the heavy."

"I don't want to be the heavy."

She ignored him. "We'll book a venue at the Banff Centre, introduce Stanley to the media, write ourselves a gospel."

"Alok can be the heavy, how about. I mean, look at him."

"Stop it, Kal." At the intersection, they waited for the light to change. Tanya stuck her index finger into his ribs. "This thing's bigger than you and your petty desires. You're either with us or you're against us."

Coaches always found pleasure in being loud and miserable. They were most themselves when, like Tanya, they were on the verge of losing their voices. When someone in particular messed up, got a penalty at the worst possible time or didn't get back on defence, Kal always noticed a flash of joy in the eyes of his coaches before they turned monstrous and started cussing. If Tanya weren't a television executive, he figured she would make a perfect hockey coach.

Stanley and Alok walked ahead. They crossed the street and entered the Chalet Du Bois. Just as they did, Tanya pushed Kal up against a storefront. She spoke softly, and so close that he could feel her breath on his neck. "Listen to me. I need an ally here."

"Right."

"This isn't playtime. This is the real thing. Do you understand what I'm saying?"

Kal didn't have the faintest clue what Tanya was saying, and she was making him very nervous. "Yes."

"So if it comes down to it?"

He nodded.

"Are you still mooning about Maha? Come on, man. Focus."

Kal was focused, primarily, on the fact that he knew how to play the piano and, surely, the accordion. His instincts had been exactly right about music, about its ability to change him. Though he worried about losing Maha to her fiancé, the world seemed less chaotic now that

Kal could play the "Nocturne in C Minor." "I'm gonna do whatever's best for Stanley."

"Good." Tanya released him. "Good. My point is, sometimes a person doesn't know what's best for him. Sometimes he needs an advisor, and a heavy, to show him."

Also like coaches, Tanya lacked certain listening talents.

Upstairs, Kal passed Maha's room slowly. There were murmurings inside, and he wanted to stop and listen, but Tanya shoved him along. Alok met them at his door, where they had agreed to meet for a nightcap and brainstorming session.

Inside the room, Tanya hunted around. "Where's Stanley?"

"He's with Frieda."

Kal put his ear up to the wall, so he might hear Maha and Gamal.

"She's a problem, Alok. A big problem."

The big man opened the mini-bar, which at this point didn't offer much more than cans of pop and tiny bottles of hard liquor. "An unsolvable problem."

Tanya sat on one bed and Alok sat on the other. Kal pretended to be engaged in their conversation about possible names for the religion, but he remained open to sounds from the adjacent room.

"Mossery," said Alok.

"The Improvement," said Tanya. "No, too vague and brainy. Awesomism!"

"Church of the Last Chance."

"That sounds scary. I don't like it."

"Goodology?"

"I think that's taken. In university I dated a philosophy major." Tanya sipped from a tiny bottle of gin. "You don't like Awesomism?"

"It'll sound stupid when we're sober." Alok sloshed the Grand Marnier around in his glass.

"I'm not drunk."

"Of course not."

"Are you saying I'm a drunk?"

Kal gave up on listening through the wall. "I think The Stan is still the best."

It was noticeably quiet for a moment, as Tanya and Alok drank and thought. Both seemed ready to speak up when there was a slam in the hallway, and shouting. Maha said, "Go! Just go!"

In his haste, Kal forgot the hotel room door opened to the inside. He grasped the handle and slammed into the heavy door. It took a moment to compose himself and exit the room. Gamal and Maha stood together in the hallway like witnesses to a gas station explosion. There were tears in her eyes.

"Are you all right?" Kal said.

She nodded.

"You're pretty satisfied, I guess." Gamal's face was red. "Drafting her into your sex cult."

"It's *not* a sex cult, Gamal," said Maha.

"No one's having sex at all," Kal said, hopefully.

Alok and Tanya walked out into the hallway, their drinks in hand. "Everything all right, sweetie?" said Alok.

"There you go." Gamal looked as if he might spit on the floor. "*Sweetie.*"

Maha hurried inside her room and slammed the door, leaving the others to stand and marinate in discomfort. Kal couldn't hide his satisfaction at seeing them angry at one another. "We're gonna take real good care of Maha."

"Don't talk to me, meathead."

Maha came out of her room with Gamal's small black bag and shoes. Satisfaction turned to overwhelming joy. Kal wanted to sing but he remained calm. For some time, Gamal stared at Maha. Then he turned to the others, and his gaze lingered on Kal.

"There's all kinds of fish in the sea!" Kal said.

In hockey, you always know when a fight's coming. It commences with yapping and shoving, some stick work, and by the time the gloves hit the ice there's a feeling of inevitability about the whole thing. That's why Kal was so shocked when Gamal slapped Maha across the ear and said, "*Sharmouta.*"

Maha crumpled against the thin wall with both hands up, looking more in shock than in pain.

"It's on, fucko," Kal said, and took a swing at Gamal.

"No!" Maha said.

Gamal ducked the punch and backed away with a bounce. Kal stepped over the bag and shoes, and prepared to pound the smaller man.

No one in the AHL fought like Gamal. Before Kal had a chance to grab him, Gamal had punched him in the face several times, elbowed him about the cheek and neck, kicked him in the groin, and kneed his right eye in a jumping manoeuvre. All to a series of hisses and high-pitched whoops.

"Stop hurting him." Maha sobbed.

Kal knew he should retreat, but he hoped Gamal had only scored a few lucky blows. He was woozy and nauseous, but he didn't want Maha to think he was feeble. Again, Kal moved in to attack. He wasn't sure how it happened, but after receiving several more blows, he bear-hugged Gamal. Since his options were limited, he was reduced to biting

the man's shoulder. Gamal put his fingers in Kal's eyes.
"Let me go," said Gamal.

Kal had no choice. He did, and slowly lowered himself to
the floor. First, he sat down. Then, nearly overcome by
sleepiness, he lay on the rough carpet. Through his sore,
watery eyes he watched Gamal gather his things and walk
away without another word.

"I don't think I've ever seen anyone take a beating like
that," said Alok. "Even in the movies."

Maha crouched over Kal. "Are you okay?"

"It's mostly my pride."

"It's mostly your face," said Tanya.

Kal was on his feet no more than thirty seconds before he
excused himself to throw up in Maha's garbage can. Then,
with her, and the smell of her, in a state of something like
bliss, he began his second bloody journey to the Mineral
Springs Hospital.

THIRTY-NINE

The young doctor allowed Maha to sit in the examination
room while she stitched Kal's many wounds. His face had
already swollen to almost twice its natural size. The fork
stab had reopened and there were two cuts on his opposite
cheek, below his eye. His lips were puffy and cracked and
his cauterized nose was bulbous and purple. His shirt was

splattered with so much blood it looked as though he had eaten a live goat for dinner.

As she worked, the doctor refused to speak with Kal. Male hormones, she contended, were a scourge upon the planet. Proof that God was, at best, a buffoon. "You know how many faces I sew up every night?"

Maha did not want to encourage the doctor, who wore a ring in her left eyebrow.

"How many?" said Kal, the left side of his mouth frozen with anaesthetic.

The doctor ignored him. "Is he your boyfriend?"

"No."

Kal slouched.

"I told my fiancé I didn't see a future for us, and he mistreated me. Kal intervened."

"Oh, big hero."

Throughout the treatment, the doctor condemned the male of the species. As she did, Maha found herself thinking more fondly of Kal. There was a word that suited him, one she had never actually said aloud: *guileless*. The doctor was wrong about Kal, who seemed stripped of excessive self-regard and a capacity for cruelty. Not that Maha was in a mood to argue with the woman.

Maha led a newly stitched Kal out of the hospital. On the way back to the hotel, they kept to the dark and tranquil residential streets off Banff Avenue. The spruce trees in front of large homes and small, cedar hotels were decorated with pale-yellow Christmas lights. Locals in out-of-season ski jackets walked big dogs that hurried over to every stranger they saw, panting happily, wagging their tails.

Kal walked gingerly and breathed through his mouth. He

expanded on his new feelings for poetry and music, and his thoughts about mountains. "Their bigness points out your smallness, and keeps you honest," he said, his voice resembling a movie monster's after a couple of sleeping pills.

Was it Banff or was it the Lord? Maha couldn't say, but she agreed that her natural defences – the layers of protective falseness that made up what others saw as her personality – were on low. In Montreal, with friends and her parents, she had refused to discuss the night in January when she and Ardeen had acquired a bottle of vodka, Sprite, and green apple syrup. So when Kal asked her why she had been keen to leave home for Banff, she surprised herself by telling the truth. "At a party, I got drunk and had sex with a guy from Académie de Roberval while his friends watched."

Kal stopped. They were in front of a brick house with a white "Beware of Dog" sign attached to its low chain-link fence. "No, you didn't."

"I did." Maha examined the sign, which had yellowed and faded in the sun. She wondered if the dog were now dead, as there didn't seem to be much evidence of digging in the yard, and no stuffed animals or bones or ropes. She fought an urge to change the subject, toward the nature of dog ownership. "I yelled out 'Make me real' a bunch of times."

"Make me real?"

"And the Lord arrived. Stanley."

"You had sex with The Stan. That's . . . whoa."

Even in her jacket, Maha was chilly. So she began walking again. "I didn't have sex with the Lord. While the guy was on top of me, I *saw* the Lord but I didn't *see him*. I felt he was there, and knew exactly who he was."

"People found out?"

"An entire generation of teenagers on the island of Montreal found out, along with my teachers and eventually my mom and dad."

"Shit."

"They were horrified. Who wouldn't be, I guess. Things went badly with us and the next thing I knew, they were setting me up with Gamal."

"No wonder you left."

"But I wasn't just running away from something, coming here. I was running *to* something."

Maha and Kal arrived at the front doors of the Chalet Du Bois. It was late and she was tired. A hot bath was in order, along with some reading. But since he had taken a terrible beating for her, she felt obliged to invite Kal in for a hot chocolate. If he could drink through his messed-up mouth. Before she could offer, Kal extended his hand, awkwardly, for a shake. "It was real pleasant of you to come to the hospital with me."

"Of course."

"Where did Gamal learn to fight?"

"Thailand. I tried to warn you."

Kal continued to shake Maha's hand. His grip was too tight and his hand was moist. There was a lopsided aspect to his face, on account of the swelling, so she couldn't tell if he was making eye contact with her or looking at the Chalet Du Bois logo on the door. "Your hand is soft."

"Oh. Thanks." Maha gently pulled her hand back, and Kal released it. She looked down at her hand, to avoid his stare. "You're okay getting home?"

"For sure, yeah. I doubt there's any more Thai boxers about."

He didn't turn around, or even look away.

"Well," Maha said, buoyantly.

"Well. Yeah."

"Good night, Kal."

"Absolutely. Back at you."

Maha smiled one last time, opened the heavy door, and walked into the Chalet Du Bois. At the stairs, she glanced back and saw Kal through the frosted window, waving.

FORTY

Stanley and Frieda walked alongside the rushing and roiling Bow River, its power constant and – Stanley thought – random. It seemed he was now obliged to believe in a cosmic force that controlled and sustained rivers, mountains, snowmelt, clouds, and the human heart. This is what he kept secret from his new friends who called themselves his disciples: belief didn't lead to comfort. It only inspired more questions about the possibility of belief.

They passed a tour group from Italy. As they did, the round-faced woman leading the tour smiled and said hello. The Italians repeated it after her, like children trying a new word: "Hello!"

Each time Stanley attempted to hold his wife's hand she pulled it away. They had been speaking in bursts, unable to avoid arguments. It was simple, though out of love for one another they had attempted to make it complicated.

Frieda insisted they go home and Stanley insisted they stay.

"How could a god or prophet make them any happier?" Frieda pointed back at the Italians with her thumb.

Another question without an answer. "I'm not sure they're happy. Affluent, sure, but happy is something else."

Frieda placed her hands in the pocket of her thin, baby-blue windbreaker. "Happiness didn't exist before we could buy it."

A large hawk hovered over the river and the Italians, behind them, took photographs and called out.

"I disagree."

"Because you're a preacher now."

"I think the religious or spiritual aspect of humanity has been crushed by the desire to buy and sell, to acquire wealth and power. What I want to do, if I can do anything, is separate them."

Frieda shook her head. They were not far from the bridge that would lead them back to the hotel. Stanley was already due at the Banff Centre, to help prepare for his public debut as a man of miracles.

"When did religion, as we know it, begin?"

Stanley didn't know the answer to this question, so he guessed. "Old Testament time."

"All right. When did the market economy, as we know it, begin?"

He was trapped, as usual. "Old Testament time?"

"In Israel and India and China, it was a time of war and suffering *and* capitalism."

Stanley knew where Frieda was heading with this, so he pulled one of her hands out of her jacket and led her up the riverbank to the bridge deck. "I'm already late."

"That's all this is, you know that. It's a sell job." The

wind picked up as they crossed the Bow River Bridge, adorned with the heads of imagined aboriginals. "Religion and happiness are both products, like new cars."

At the Chalet Du Bois, Stanley opened the door for Frieda and they stood in the lobby together. He couldn't remember a more uncomfortable moment with his wife since their early dates. They stared at one another, and at the faux-rustic furniture. He was, at once, reluctant and enthusiastic about the afternoon's planned activity.

"This won't take long, darling. It's for lighting cues."

Frieda nodded, dispassionately.

"Hour or two at the most."

Another nod. "Whatever you feel you have to do."

Stanley wanted to shake this attitude out of her. There was, he was certain, absolutely nothing he could say to bring his wife to his way of thinking. The more he tried to discover a solution to this fundamental problem, the more he desired an escape from it.

Stanley was still thinking about Frieda twenty minutes later as he stood on the empty stage of the Eric Harvie Theatre, waiting for the lighting technician to finish his cues. Frieda's doubt was not regular doubt. Historically, it had more weight and nuance than his own, Roquefort to his cheddar, provoking innumerable crises of confidence. But the rental fees had been paid and Tanya was finished with the handbills and posters. He knew what had changed in him and his wife did not. Despite the abstract quality of his ultimate goal, for the first time in his life Stanley was thoroughly motivated. It didn't really matter, now, if he was ready. Readiness was a question for his audience.

In the aisle, Tanya yelled at the man in the booth as various colours and angles of lights flashed on Stanley's face.

"No," she said, with a stomp of her foot. "That's too much. Go soft, muted, subtle."

"I like the bright orange," said Alok. "It makes you look damn imperial, Stan."

Tanya growled.

There were more than nine hundred seats in the theatre, and all of them were empty. When the lights flashed on Stanley's face, he could not see out but he could certainly hear, and feel, Tanya and Alok, the absence of Frieda. That is, until the lights went down for ten seconds and Stanley spotted the pale girl from the Volkswagen and Far East Square. She sat next to an older woman in the back row.

He hopped off the stage and started up the aisle toward them.

"Get back up there," said Tanya. "We only have another fifteen minutes with the tech."

By the time Stanley reached Alok at the middle of the seating area, the child and woman were gone. "Did you see two people sitting back here?"

Alok shook his head. "Do you need a break, pal?"

"Bush league!" said Tanya.

The woman and child weren't in the lobby either, so Stanley rushed out of the theatre and down the sloping St. Julien Road until he reached Grizzly Street and the cemetery. He spotted them sitting on a bench, near some old grave-markers and a vase of dried-up flowers.

Worried the little girl might disappear again, Stanley approached without taking his eyes off her. There wasn't room to join them on the bench so he sat on the ground, at the edge of the path that ran before them. The woman wore a black dress and a gold-coloured cardigan. Her clothing didn't seem old-fashioned but her posture did, and so did the straw sun hat she wore over her light-brown hair. The woman avoided eye contact haughtily, as though Stanley had insulted her.

The girl spoke first. "Call me Darlene," she said. The girl, whose luminous skin was so beautiful it seemed to be made of tinted glass, was dressed the way children dressed when Stanley was young – like miniature adults. She wore a dress with a long coat that appeared to be cashmere.

"Pleased to meet you. I'm Stanley Moss."

"My name is Mary Schäffer," said the woman, who did not look at or even acknowledge the presence of the girl beside her. Stanley recalled the woman's name but couldn't remember why. She offered her hand, inside a tight black glove. "I am here to find out who you are."

"Stanley Moss. I'm from Edmonton."

"Are you a demon? Abbadon or Dagwanoenyent or Gaap?"

The girl laughed. She formed her right hand into a gun and pretended to shoot herself.

"I don't think I'm a demon."

"Well, demon or not, this is highly irregular. We have decided you must explain yourself immediately or risk expulsion."

"Expulsion from Banff?"

"Don't sass me. Don't you sass me."

The girl rolled her eyes.

"I speak for my entire community," said Mary Schäffer. "We've been watching you and we demand that you clarify your presence here."

Stanley smiled, as the girl seemed to indicate this was a joke. He looked around quickly for cameras. "You represent Banff, somehow. The town council?"

Mary Schäffer stood up off the bench, stepped around Stanley, and began walking down the worn path that zigzagged through the cemetery. Stanley got up to follow and then, with an elegant slide off the bench, so did Darlene. "I've been here in this capacity for almost seventy years but the community has been in place for much, much longer. Thousands of years."

"What community?"

"She's not a good listener," said Darlene.

"And you are the most potent irregularity we have come across." Mary Schäffer sniffed at some flowers in an old wooden barrel. "Now, who sent you?"

"I don't know."

"Are you here to rule us?"

"Rule who?"

Mary Schäffer sighed. "Do you have a list of demands? Have you come from Mictlan? Feng Du? Yomi? Rangi Tuarea?"

"I have no idea what you're talking about."

"You're hostile."

Stanley clapped his hands together. "I'm not hostile. I don't even know what I'm doing here. I was in Edmonton, dying, and this blue light and loud rumble came through me, from the sky, and . . ." It was clear Mary Schäffer was not listening. There were unripe berries on a small bush in the graveyard and she had busied herself in pulling them off and stuffing them in a breast pocket of her black dress. "Hello?" he said.

"Are you here to unseat me? To become mayor?"

"Mayor of Banff?"

"Fine, then. Perhaps I'll have you killed."

Stanley looked around. The child was now sitting up on a handsome plinth with its inscription worn off. He was having trouble understanding this conversation. "I haven't come here to take your job. And if you'll let me explain myself, I will. I have come here –"

"My patience has run out."

"Before you threaten me with further violence, can you tell me who you are? Maybe you can help me understand what's happened. I was on my deck one morning. I was quite shamed, actually."

"You take me for a fool, don't you?"

"No. No. Ms. Schäffer, is there someone else you're talking to? I really don't understand you at all."

Her front pocket was now full of berries. Stanley should have known the names of the bush, and the berries, but they were lost to him. This absence in his memory, and the frustration of speaking to this obviously crazy woman, was demoralizing. Mary Schäffer began walking away, and disappeared into a white spruce. Her child consort, Darlene, had not followed, but she was gone too.

Stanley sat on the bench in the Old Banff Cemetery and attempted, briefly, to figure out what had just happened. His black shoes were scuffed. A demon, surely, would have more impressive footwear.

FORTY-ONE

The television festival was over, but a number of Tanya's colleagues habitually stayed in Banff for an extra week. Officially, the development executives lingered to meet with industry professionals and spirited rookies in a less hectic atmosphere. Unofficially, it was an opportunity to drink excessively and commit a final round of adultery before flying back home to dirty diapers and unmowed lawns.

Tanya arrived at the Banff Springs Hotel wine bar on the evening before Stanley's coming-out party. The executives had shed their suits in favour of garden apparel – tan slacks and white shirts, spring dresses, unnecessary sunglasses. Eight men and six women sat at a couple of long tables pushed together, two bottles of Beaujolais and an Okanagan white before them.

It was the exquisite hour between day and night. The sun had just dipped below the peaks, so the valley was drowned in dreamy pink light. Judging by the gentle slurs in their voices as they welcomed her, Tanya's colleagues had retired to the bar before dinner. And then dinner had failed to happen.

The very important, very attractive people had already flown back to Los Angeles, leaving only Canadians and Australians and Brits – cynical protectors of their national identities. Tanya sat in a chair near the oak-framed window, under a chandelier. She recognized immediately the violent mixture of self-loathing and defensive pride that bubbled up

in Canadians, Australians, and Brits at the Banff World
Television Festival in the days after the Americans departed.
We'd never make that shit. Oh, to have an audience.
Of course, her colleagues had questions. There were
rumours that Tanya had resigned from Leap: who had head-
hunted her? A BBC producer named Johnson Quayle who
was blind in his left eye and, she had been disappointed to
learn on a drunken evening three years previous, function-
ally impotent, had heard she was moving to London to work
for MTV Europe.

Tanya answered the question by distributing the handbills she had so carefully designed, advertising the event as
"A Night of Mystery and Grand Amazement." She had also
brought five copies of The Testament, an eleven-page
booklet of The Stan's tenets and principles. It was a hasty
compromise, at this point, between her and Alok's interpretation of Stanley Moss and how best to attract six billion
people to him. "This is the future, my friends."

Johnson Quayle glanced at the handbill and led the questions. "A magician?"

"No." Tanya sighed. Why were people so damn literal?
Even smart people? "No, I'm talking miracle, here. This
man has genuine powers."

"Superpowers?"

She poured herself a glass of the Beaujolais, since none of
her former colleagues was sober or polite enough to do it
for her. "The word *miracle* has been hijacked by comic
books and glorified jugglers, hasn't it? I'm talking about
an old-time religious miracle that will initiate a new age
of spirituality."

"You're New Age now?" A woman from across the table,
heavily involved in the Toronto International Film Festival,

removed her sunglasses. Tanya could not think of her name. Her blond, curly hair seemed blonder and curlier than it had last year.

"This isn't a bunch of crystal-rubbing and drum-beating. It's authentic."

Johnson Quayle put his hand on Tanya's and squeezed. This news seemed to have aroused him. "A cult."

Tanya was glad she had come to the wine bar. It was an insight into the marketing and communications challenge that lay before her. Tomorrow night's event had come together so quickly that she wasn't quite prepared for its dangers. Tanya had to take control of the context straight away. Otherwise, her colleagues in the media – slaves to simple, mechanical thinking, she now understood – would have the power to interpret The Stan. Tanya decided not to finish her glass of Beaujolais. She would be up all night, preparing for tomorrow.

"It's not a cult. You have to forget everything you know and leave your skepticism in the lobby. You must be open to the transcendent, to the extraordinary."

After she delivered these lines, which sounded like lines even to her, the wine bar was silent except for Glenn Gould's *Goldberg Variations*, the soundtrack for every overpriced hotel wine bar in the world. Then, beginning with Johnson Quayle, her colleagues laughed.

For a moment, she missed the routine of her former life. Johnson Quayle had seen a dentist since the last time they'd met, and his teeth were remarkably straight and white. Despite his performance, or lack thereof, in days gone by, Tanya figured that if she had not decided to leave this world behind, she would be in the throes of a short-term affair with Johnson Quayle.

She felt sorry for the development executives of Canada, Australia, and the United Kingdom. They would never find what she had found, among the half-talents of their indigenous film and television industries. Soon, they would not look nearly so shiny in garden attire and unnecessary sunglasses. The tanning-bed tans and dental surgeries and eyelifts and bottles of wine would fail them, and the executives would be replaced by younger and perhaps even deader versions of themselves.

"Please come tomorrow night," she said. "It's an experience you'll never forget. In fact, if I were you, I'd order cameras and reporters to arrive here as soon as possible. If you don't get your own footage of this, you'll be paying for it."

Cynicism erupted like a puff of smoke from a tired volcano. Johnson Quayle couldn't quite convince himself that Tanya Gervais actually believed in something other than money and advancement. "What's this really about, cookie? You can tell us."

Tanya took one final sip of her wine, just to wet her lips and remember. "All I can tell you is I've seen something unusual and amazing here in Banff, and if you'll join us tomorrow night you'll see it too."

As she walked around the table and out of the little wine bar, Tanya knew she had hooked her colleagues. They would arrive as a group tomorrow night, tipsy, making sarcastic comments all the way up to the Banff Centre. But like everyone else in the theatre, they would secretly hope she was telling the truth.

FORTY-TWO

A giant bouquet sat in the corner of the green room, next to a five-page outline of the evening's activities and unsolicited "speaking points" from Tanya. Stanley could not name the flowers in the bouquet, so he attempted to classify them according to scent. The yellow ones were the sweetest, while the white flowers had a hint of spice to them. Five red flowers – he guessed roses – made him feel sad. Two or three of them, as far as he could tell, had no smell at all.

Stanley had forgotten the names of flowers but he had not forgotten this feeling. The empty ache in his chest, cold hands, fear of loneliness. Once, long ago, Stanley had entered into an affair with a customer. The woman was not discreet, and when Stanley realized it was a mistake and tried to end it she wrote a horrifyingly descriptive letter to Frieda. They separated for eight months, during which time Stanley felt *this*, and yearned for the only substance that erased it – equal parts blended Scotch and water.

The speaking points reminded Stanley of late-night television advertisements for self-actualization techniques. Instead of memorizing them, he stared at himself in the mirror and inspected his wrinkles. Muffled by the concrete walls, the symphonic music reminded him of the prelude to magic shows at the Calgary Stampede. He stared at the flowers and willed them to reveal themselves. When they refused, taunting him with their namelessness, he tossed them in the garbage. Then he regretted it and pulled them back out. The vase was broken so he propped the flowers, one by one, on the back of a chair against the wall. There was a knock on the door and Frieda entered the green room. "The theatre is full." She removed her jacket and hung it on the back of the door, revealing a pair of blue slacks and a white shirt. Stanley tried to commit this image of her to memory, as she leaned against the dressing-room table. Though he could not read his wife's thoughts, Stanley knew why she was here and how this would end.

Frieda examined the outline and speaking points, and shook her head. Her voice was fragile. "They want you to cure five or six cancers? Cause a mini-thunderstorm?"

"They provided suggestions."

"Have you tried creating a thunderstorm?"

Stanley wanted to say something cheery, even ironic, to bind them against Tanya and the rigidity of her marketing and communications plan. But he had already made his choice in this, and so had Frieda. It threatened to exhaust them, as husband and wife. All he could come up with was, "I don't think I can do it."

"I don't think I can do it either, Stanley."

He sat in a black leather chair in the corner of the room, and placed his fingertips on his temples. In the 1970s, Stanley had suffered from migraines, and this was the only remedy he knew. He wanted to direct their conversation away from what they had already discussed, endlessly, in their hotel room and on long, searching walks along the river. "I talked to some ghost-people, or something."

"Lovely." Frieda sat on the arm of the black chair and ran her fingernails lightly along Stanley's scalp, something he loved. "It can't be that easy, can it? Create a thunderstorm? It seems to me spiritual truth, if there is such a thing, takes time. Study. Even militancy. You can't just . . . I know *I* can't just . . ."

Stanley said what he had to say. "I need you."

"No, you don't. You did once and someday you might again. I hope you do, desperately."

"Frieda, don't do this."

She turned away from him.

"Frieda, please."

"I'm already packed. The car is full of gas."

"Wait one more day."

She smiled. "You don't want me to wait another day, or even another hour. If you're convinced this is what you want to do, I'll only be a nuisance to you."

"You'll never be a nuisance, Frieda. I –"

"I want my retired florist back."

"He was dying."

Her sob was almost imperceptible. "At least he was mine, and I knew him." She took her jacket off the hook and slipped into it. Then Stanley stood up and they kissed, awkwardly, and held one another. The sound of their clothes rustling together was uncommonly loud to him. With all his focus, Stanley tried to change her mind. Into his neck, she said, "When this disease leaves you, come back to me."

"Just tonight. Let me show you what I can do."

"I don't have to watch you do something special. I don't need to see anything to know something spectacular attends you. I've known that for forty years."

"The ghost-people today. They said I'm a demon."

"There are no demons, Stanley, or ghost-people, or gods. Men don't jump off the sides of mountains and survive. Cancer is incurable, and thunderstorms are caused by unstable air masses, not preachers in grey suits." Frieda rubbed the moisture from her eyes and buttoned her jacket. "I love you." Frieda walked out of the green room and closed the door very softly behind her.

FORTY-THREE

The Calgary lawyer had sent documents to the bank, and the bank had agreed to give Kal an advance on his coming settlement with the insurance company. The insurance company had been keen to dispense with the Far East Square matter quickly, and the lawyer had advised that a more lucrative settlement would take five years or longer.

Kal thought it would make him happy, but it confused him, if anything, to have more than a thousand dollars in his chequing account. He walked out of the bank and leaned against a tree in a mini-park surrounded by new construction, and stared at the small vinyl book where his new account balance had been typed by a computer. Mountain peaks were obscured by low afternoon cloud, and the air was still.

On his way to the Chalet Du Bois, to pick up Maha, Kal made two stops. At the Hudson's Bay Company, he bought a black Italian suit. The woman behind the counter clipped up his cuffs, in lieu of tailoring, so he could wear it that evening. The man at the flower shop was bored so he spent far too long arranging a bouquet for Kal that was "bound to make any woman fall at your feet in bliss."

He passed a mirror in the display window of a jewellery store and barely recognized himself. If not for the yellowing bruises on his face, Kal would have been an entirely respectable young man. He thanked Stanley aloud for his good fortune and a passing couple laughed at him.

Maha was not ready to go when he knocked at her door, so Kal leaned against the wood-grain wallpaper in the hotel hallway. A bit of his blood had stained the lightest corners of patterned carpet outside Maha's room. He could hear her hair dryer inside.

The flowers he held were wrapped in shiny brown paper. Kal picked at the tape and opened the top flap so he could admire and smell them. How had these flowers come to be here in this mountain town, where so few of them could grow? Why did flowers exist, and how had they come to represent love? Like architecture, locomotion, the postal system, and the design of the universe, the complexity and the business of flowers left him spellbound.

Maha opened the door. Kal tried to say good evening to Maha and close the unwieldy paper flap. Neither worked out. He knuckled the head off a gerbera daisy and said, "Piss," as it fell to the carpet not far from his bloodstain.

Maha picked up the stemless daisy. She wore a short white dress, somewhat nurse-like, with a belt around the waist. When she stood up again, with the daisy, she pulled the dress down. "Too racy, you think?"

Kal had a commanding desire to drop to his knees and kiss Maha's legs and pronounce her the prettiest girl in Banff. "Not at all," he said, and passed the now-closed bouquet to her.

"Please, come in."

Maha's perfume filled her suite. Inside, she peeled the paper away and gasped at the flowers. "Sorry about knocking that one's head off," Kal said. "And cussing. I'm working on it."

"You were a hockey player for a long time."

"'Piss' is a nice one, when you stack it up against the others."

Maha sniffed the flowers. "No one's ever bought me a bouquet."

"That seems wrong."

"What should I do with them?"

Kal went through the glasses in the room, but they were all too short. He poured out a small bottle of mini-bar white wine and filled it with water. Maha stuffed the flowers inside and arranged them.

Then, for a long time, they stood in a crackling silence. Kal felt a wave of gas coming on and fought hard to keep it bottled up. He failed, however, and coughed to mask the sound of its release.

"You have a cold?"

"No. I swallowed something wrong."

"You ate already?"

"No. It was gum."

"Why did you swallow your gum?"

Kal didn't like where this line of questioning was headed, so he picked up Maha's copy of The Testament. It was only eleven pages long because Tanya had argued that no one could read anything longer than eleven pages these days, ruined as humans were by visual media. When this thing caught on, they would hire a professional writer and expand – put in some pictures. The disciples had "worked together" on The Testament over the past couple of days, but none of Kal's suggestions had made it to the final draft. "I read this last night," he said.

"Me too."

"Don't you think they should have used words like 'thou' and 'thine' and whatnot to make it sound more Bible-y?"

"Absolutely not. That would have been a huge mistake."

"Yeah," said Kal. "A totally huge mistake."

It had been surprisingly easy to ask Maha out for a pre-show dinner. The beating by Gamal had conferred a sort of respectability upon him. When they were writing The Testament with the others, in Tanya's hotel room and at the Rose & Crown, Maha had been the least likely to ignore his suggestions. She had seemed genuinely impressed by his piano-playing.

So far, there was a cloak of innocence over their relationship. As a professional hockey player, he had learned a thing or two about the ladies. Whenever a woman had wanted to leave the nightclub, in Providence or Hamilton, and go have sex in the hotel room he always shared with Gordon Yang, Kal had known it. Maha wasn't dishing any of those signals, yet.

Over dinner at Magpie & Stump, Kal outlined his hockey career. As he told Maha about hockey, which was all he had really known since he was six years old, it began to sound to Kal as if he were talking about someone else. Some other Kal McIntyre from Thunder Bay, Ontario. Maha listened carefully and asked questions, especially about Layla.

"She was an amazing accident," said Kal.

"Do you get to see her much?"

"Almost never. She's hardly mine any more. Hopefully when she's a teenager and can make her own decisions, she'll want to see me. I figure I'll pay for her tuition, start a trust account with this insurance money. Don't know if I can afford living expenses, though. What if she wants

to go to school in Toronto or Vancouver or something?"
Maha smiled and they had another one of those silences.
They thought separate thoughts, obviously about each other,
and the mystery of Maha was so uncontaminated Kal wanted
to ask if she would like to buy a plot of land with him in
Saskatchewan and become soybean farmers.

They walked up Caribou Street and Kal purposely hit her
arm with his, to warm Maha up for some possible hand-
holding. She told him about growing up Muslim, which
sounded quite enthralling to Kal, much more exotic than
growing up Catholic.

"So did you ever know any *crazy* Muslims? With the
jihad and everything?"

By the look on Maha's face, Kal knew these were not
intelligent questions to ask. Hand-holding, suddenly,
seemed a remote possibility. They passed a large house with
an historical plaque in front. Kal wished they were walking
up Tunnel Mountain, so he too could jump off. "I'm sorry,"
he said.

Maha led them up a set of wooden stairs leading to the
Banff Centre. They passed a visual arts studio, where two
women in paint-splattered smocks smoked cigarettes on the
deck. Kal was too chastened to say anything else, even
about a subject as unrelated to suicide bombings as smocks.
Where did people buy smocks, anyway? Then, as they
approached the glass facade of the Eric Harvie Theatre, Kal
went over the stupid questions he had asked Maha and
decided they really weren't so bad. It wasn't easy to be a
Muslim, sure, but it wasn't easy to understand Muslims,
either. He wasn't in charge of putting things on the news.
As they entered the red lobby by separate doors, Kal chose
not to let defensiveness overtake him.

"Can I take your coat, mademoiselle?" he said.

Though it was obvious that Maha was still troubled by the jihad business, she granted him that pleasure and they walked among the audience, many of whom were dressed very casually, in fleece jackets and pants with many pockets. In his new suit, Kal was careful to say "Excuse me" and to thank the staff excessively.

Their seats for "A Night of Mystery and Grand Amazement" were in the back. Since Kal and Maha weren't involved in the production, their job was to watch and listen to the audience – take notes. They sat down and pulled out their dollar-store notepads. Fleece jackets and pants with many pockets, a sense of puzzlement, a variety of European and Asian languages, few children, more than half senior citizens. The music was at a decent volume and, to Kal, seemed mysterious and grandly amazing. While they waited for the curtain to rise on their religion, Kal sent silent messages to Maha.

I'm your man. I'm your guy. Not as stupid as I sometimes seem.

FORTY-FOUR

The curtain rose from the stage, and television cameras swivelled behind the last row of seats. A new fear gripped Maha. If Tanya was right about the media and the way these stories spread, her parents would see this.

Her parents and, more importantly, their community would regard Stanley as the embodiment of blasphemy. An abomination. Maha could have sex with a Québécois, in view of fifteen others. She could drop out of school or abandon her family without a word. These were shames from which the family could recover. But abusing the Prophet was something she could not do. The Prophet was the seal; no others were to come. If Gamal wanted to talk, he could make things very difficult for Maha's family in Montreal.

The previous night, perusing the Koran for possibly the last time, she realized there was no way to explain the Lord. The Lord seemed to remember nothing about his time in the desert with Mohammed, all those years ago. Maha herself had said the words, as a child: There is no god but Allah Almighty, Who is One (and only One) and there is no associate with Him; and I testify that Mohammed (peace and blessings of Allah be upon him) is His Messenger.

Maha pulled her sweater around her shoulders. Kal reached around to help her. "Are you cold?"

"Sort of."

"I could warm you." Kal put his arm around her, tentatively. "I'll never say anything else about jihad, I promise, and –"

"Stop, Kal, please."

"Right, great, super." He removed his arm, and fondled his notepad.

The lights in the theatre went off suddenly, and orchestral music began to play. It sounded like the final scene in an old action movie. Over the music, just faintly, Maha could hear the click of Tanya's shoes on the wooden stage. In the darkness, Maha had to fight off the images of her parents. She said, aloud, "I had not considered how dangerous this is."

"Why dangerous?"

A spotlight found Tanya, at the front of the stage, and the volume of the music decreased. She paused for a moment, and opened her arms to the audience. Tanya welcomed everyone and said, slyly, that if anyone had a heart condition, they should leave now. There was sporadic laughter, and someone asked to be given "a fricken break."

Tanya ignored them and launched into Kal's story, his journey from professional hockey player to concert-level pianist. Kal as the species in microcosm.

"I don't know about concert level," Kal whispered. "Do you think I'm concert level? I've never seen a proper piano concert. And *microcosm*. Can you –?"

"Shh."

While Kal was talking in her ear, Maha had missed some of what Tanya was saying.

". . . you read the news. It's no secret to many of you that the land is dying." Tanya wore a headset microphone, and she walked from one end of the stage to the other, arms in motion. She spoke slowly, enunciating every syllable, pausing for effect. For Maha, she was a spring, ready at each moment to unfurl violently and bounce around the room. Tanya crouched and said, quietly, as though the audience were a bosom friend, "Please, for the next hour or so, try to forget what you know. The land is dying. May I present its saviour."

Tanya bowed, and backed away, stage right, with a flourish.

No one came. A few people in the audience laughed.

"May I present Stanley Moss. Stanley Moss, everyone."

Again, nothing. A teenager near the front called out, "This is gay!" Tanya ran across the stage in her high-heeled shoes and disappeared.

"Uh-oh," said Kal.

Maha could not write fast enough. Sarcastic applause and smartass comments abounded. Someone booed. A few people stood up and gathered their belongings. One of the cameramen behind her began fumbling with his equipment and said, to one of his colleagues, "God damn it. I *hate* the Trans-Canada at night."

"Let's get drunk and stay," said his colleague.

"Could do, could do," said the cameraman.

Then new footsteps echoed through the auditorium and the audience went silent. The Lord walked out alone, in his grey suit, and lifted his hand. Maha wondered if others would *understand* him in the way she did, the special glow of his presence. But she need not have wondered. No one in the audience said a word, and the cameraman went back to work. There was nothing to write but "silence."

He did not adjust the microphone or speak, for the first while. The Lord inhaled and released a breath she could feel in the last row of seats. "I tossed my speaking notes in the garbage," he said. "I should say we worked hard on them. But I am here tonight with an invitation, not a lecture."

The Lord paused and said, "My name is Stanley Moss and I am an atheist. Was an atheist. Then, some time ago, on the morning of my first visit with a palliative care specialist, something happened to me."

Maha desperately wanted the Lord to surprise her, to say something about Allah or the Prophet. But he did not. Instead, he talked about his lifelong battle with doubt and the state of religion today, here and around the world.

He asked questions of the audience. "Are you happy? Do you know who you are? How many hours of television do you watch in a week? Please count. Do you feel good? Do you cough in the night? Are you lonely? Are you active citizens? What do you think I mean by 'citizen'? Does your water taste good? How much sleep do you get? Are you willing to sacrifice comforts for the broader good? Do you think religion is a positive force in society and politics? Do you talk to your god? To your children? Do you tell the truth?"

The spell in the crowd was broken. Audience members began to shift in their seats, to grumble. One woman called out, "What is this?"

Again the Lord lifted his hand, and again the crowd went silent. For some time, the Lord appeared either thoughtful or confused, as though he didn't know what to say, or do, next. It was terribly uncomfortable for Maha, who wanted the Lord to *be the Lord* for them the way he was for her. Almost half the audience was standing, and prepared to leave, when the Lord asked the technician to turn on the house lights. Maha wondered if he was going to ask who suffered from cancer or AIDS or other terrible diseases, to dole out some cures, but he did not. Instead, the Lord said, "Belief. Authentic, honest, frightening, horrible, and heartbreaking belief. This is what is missing from our lives." Then he pointed to a woman. This woman sat at the end of the first row, in a section designed for wheelchairs.

Alok brought the woman and her chair up onstage. The Lord waited for her to be next to him in front of the audience. She was elderly, with a visible tremble. The Lord asked her name and she said, in a quiet voice, "Anita D'Ambrosio."

"Are you a believer?"

"I'm a Catholic."

A few people laughed. The Lord looked up, briefly. "What does that honestly mean to you?"

She shrugged. "I'm a Catholic. You know what that means."

"Do you have any unrealized dreams in your life, Mrs. D'Ambrosio?"

The woman did not speak for some time. Then she smiled and said, with an embarrassed laugh, "To sing like Maria Callas."

This elicited some warm laughter in the audience. The Lord reached down and Anita D'Ambrosio took his hand. She stood up out of her wheelchair. They held eye contact and the Lord said something to her. Maha could not hear it, as he had not spoken into the microphone. Anita D'Ambrosio had the microphone.

"Are you sure?" she said, shakily, to the Lord. "Are you really sure?"

He nodded and released her hand, and she stood on her own, with a magnificent smile on her face. She prepared to address the audience and turned to the Lord again.

"I'm bashful."

It appeared, from Maha's seat, that the Lord and Anita D'Ambrosio communicated then, without speaking. She cleared her throat, curtsied to the crowd, adjusted her bulky floral dress, and began to sing.

She was a soprano. Maha knew the song from *Aida*, one of only two operas she had seen. Though she was in the back row, Maha could tell that Anita D'Ambrosio was not afraid. Her hand was pressed to her chest and her back was arched, her eyes were closed. "*O patria mia*," she sang, "*mai più ti rivedrò!*"

The aria reached an impossibly high section, and as Anita D'Ambrosio held the note, she rose gently off the stage. She did not stop singing. Soon, she was several feet in the air, and her voice – as improbable as the fact that she was floating – was full and fearsomely beautiful.

Maha fought an urge to close her eyes and simply listen. There were gasps and even a few screams in the audience. A man stood and pointed at Stanley and hollered furiously at him, but his voice was weak compared to Anita D'Ambrosio's. Fifteen or twenty people struggled out of their seats and rows, and ran out of the auditorium. As they did, Anita D'Ambrosio dropped the microphone onto the stage with a crash and sang without it, her arms outstretched. She held the note for an impossibly long time. The three women next to Maha were in tears, and so was Kal.

When Anita D'Ambrosio allowed the high note to fade, the song slowed and quieted, and she began easing back down to the stage.

The eight hundred people in the Eric Harvie Theatre stood up. A number of them rushed the stage. Nothing was audible but shouts. There was too much to write in a notepad, and Maha could not see around her any longer. She climbed onto her chair with Kal's help and watched Anita D'Ambrosio hug the Lord and kiss him and thank him just as a crowd of men and women arrived onstage.

"Who are you?" Anita D'Ambrosio said, near enough to the fallen microphone that she could be heard over the applause and howls of joy, of fright, of something like anger.

FORTY-FIVE

Media outlets in Europe, Asia, Australia, and South America called Tanya's cellphone, eager to speak with or about Stanley Moss. She had sent a press release to a friend in Vancouver who worked for a global public relations firm, and the results had been instantaneous. In the release, Tanya had referred to Stanley as "the prophet of the next great world religion."

Most reporters were skeptical of the images that had spread across the globe, over television and the Internet. Experts analyzed the footage, looking for digital debris, strings, harnesses, and lip-synching errors.

Though he had dismissed her advice completely and spoken off-message, Tanya respected what Stanley had done. She regretted the gap in her planning that had allowed Stanley to be mobbed onstage by religious nuts eager to touch him, and wished he had followed the script, if only loosely. But Tanya had to admit: the old woman was an inspired choice.

In her own television interviews, after the miracle, Anita D'Ambrosio was politely amazed by her performance in the auditorium. She was also clearly an old woman with a voice ruined by time and cigarettes, an unlikely soprano.

The Christian press wanted to know if Anita D'Ambrosio had been insulted by Stanley's subtle denunciation of her religion. Did she think this had anything to do with the end of the world? Was Stanley Moss the man of sin, the Antichrist, the harbinger of the great apostasy? Had Satan the seducer been loosed from his prison?

"I don't believe so," said Anita D'Ambrosio, back in her wheelchair. "He's actually a very nice man."

In Rome, the new pope dismissed the "Canadian miracle" as a bit of movie magic, yet another diversion from the truth. French media called Stanley a magician with philosophical and theological pretensions, and went through The Testament, point by point. Thierry Ardisson, host of *Tout le monde en parle*, phoned Tanya personally, asking her to bring Stanley Moss over the Atlantic immediately. Someone at CNN, in the middle of a thin biography, used the phrase "The Stan," from the press release. Soon, the other cable news channels in Canada and the U.S. were doing the same.

Since Tanya had the largest room in the Chalet Du Bois, the disciples gathered in her suite to watch the coverage on television and scan the newspapers. Stanley sat alone at the breakfast table near the window, staring outside. Next to Stanley, this cultural commodity she had stumbled onto, everything else Tanya had ever done seemed ridiculous to her. Leap was a sad little thing. Even her most extravagant dreams of a senior media job in New York, her own wildly successful company with a 10019 zip code, could not approach this. It was folly to believe one's own press releases, but The Stan was all about belief. Belief made her better. Tanya believed.

On the bed nearest Stanley, watching him, it occurred to her that a miracle-worker's offspring might turn out quite spectacularly.

"Maha," she said, "you look uncomfortable."

"I do?" Maha looked down at herself, perched on a

wooden chair in front of the television. "I don't feel uncomfortable."

"Hop up on the bed, sweetheart. You can watch from here." Tanya gave up her spot on the bed and sat next to Stanley. She rubbed his arm and spun her cellphone on the breakfast table. "Think you're ready to tackle some of these interviews?"

"Frieda warned me that all we're really doing here is selling something. That's exactly what I don't want."

Tanya smiled. "Don't think about it as something you're selling. Your job, if we can call it that, is to *communicate* a religion called The Stan. A religion without dogma, without guilt."

"Without rewards."

"Now, don't say that. We need rewards, or no one will join. We're not saying The Stan will make them rich, or make their hair grow back, but it will improve them."

Stanley looked out the window again. "Doesn't the idea of reward, of competing in the arena of rewards, just lead to abstractions and distortions and mental illness, in the end? Not to mention the justification of war and terror?"

"Whoa, whoa, whoa." Tanya lifted the cellphone off the table and slipped it into her pocket. "Let's you and I book some time for media coaching. This is a positive campaign."

CNN went to commercial, so Kal flipped through the channels until he found another newscast. The cellphone rang, now to the tune of "What's The Buzz?" from the *Jesus Christ Superstar* soundtrack, and Tanya answered it, "Gervais." Alok, who had been asleep on the second bed, opened his eyes.

It was the young BBC production assistant on the phone again, looking for directions from the airport. Tanya watched the television as she spoke. An Asian-Canadian psychiatrist and palliative care consultant appeared on the screen.

"Hey, I know him," said Stanley.

Dr. Lam claimed to have discovered The Stan and attributed his powers to an extremely rare genetic malfunction that he could trace back to the world's great prophets and spiritual leaders: Moses, Buddha, Jesus Christ, Julius Caesar, Mohammed, Bahá'u'lláh, the Dalai Lama.

"Oh yes," said Alok. "Yes and yes and once more, with whipped cream and a maraschino cherry on top, yes."

Stanley held his face in his hands.

The cellphone rang again. It was Fox News, looking for Dr. Lam's contact information. Then she talked to a reporter from *The Guardian*, in London. Was it true, the reporter wanted to know, that flights to Calgary and hotels in Banff were suddenly overbooked, heralding a worldwide pilgrimage to the home of, ahem, The Stan?

Before Tanya could respond, there was a knock at the door. Kal hopped up to open it. Tanya asked the reporter to hold the line as a man in a navy-blue business suit that was too big for him walked into the room.

"Kal, I said no media in the hotel room." Tanya waved the man away. "You have my number. Call it."

The man stared at Stanley for a moment, swallowed, and said, "I am sorry but I must ask that you leave the Chalet Du Bois immediately."

"Why?" Tanya flipped her phone closed, hanging up on *The Guardian*. "Who are you?"

"This room was booked, some time ago, by a tour group. We apologize for any inconvenience."

Tanya stood up. "Are you joking?"

"I'm afraid not, ma'am."

"You can't kick someone out for that reason. I have an arrangement with the front desk."

"I am the front desk, ma'am."

Stanley took a few steps forward and the clerk backed away. "Tell them the actual reason you're here."

"It's you. My manager, we, don't want to be involved in this thing."

Alok slid off the bed, bent down, and punched the air, like a winning pitcher at the end of the World Series. "Only two days old and we're already being persecuted. Pop the champagne, kids. We're in the bigs."

"Shut up, Alok." Tanya addressed the nervous man, who looked to be a virgin in his late thirties. He fidgeted with his watch. "Your manager made this decision?"

"Me and my manager."

Tanya threw her phone on the bed. "I want your manager's name. Now, you wimp."

The clerk was ready to cry, Tanya could see it. For a couple of years in the early 1990s, she'd watched boxing on television and had admired the way someone like Mike Tyson, at his prime, smelled blood and turned vicious.

"I . . . please, just . . ."

"Have you ever heard of the Charter of Rights and Freedoms? You're going down, *amigo*."

"Tanya," said Stanley. "Leave him alone. We'll find somewhere else to stay."

"No," she said. The clerk wouldn't make eye contact with her. He wore a wrinkled white shirt under his blue suit, and the top button was undone. There was a small gold cross on his necklace. "This is against the law. You can't evict us from your hotel because we aren't Christian."

"I'm Catholic," said Kal.

The clerk wouldn't look up. Tanya wondered, for an instant, if Stanley had frozen him or mashed his brain into bean dip.

"It's all right, son," said Stanley. "We understand why you're doing this. It's wrong, and you should reflect on that, but we understand."

"You have an hour." The clerk turned away from Tanya, opened the door in a rush, and left the room. His heavy footsteps, as he ran down the hallway, were audible.

Tanya shook her head, at Stanley and the rest of them. "What the fuck was that?"

"No room at the inn," said Alok. "Get it?"

"I don't *get it*. We can't allow a turnip of a man to thwart us. I had him."

"Ah, we haven't been thwarted," said Alok. "This just helps us, ultimately."

"All my clothes are hung up. My toiletry kit, neatly unpacked. The computer desk is actually comfortable, a rare thing, and –"

"Enough," said Stanley. "Where's the phone book?"

It did not take long to find new accommodations, despite the reports of pilgrims filling the airplanes and highways toward Banff. Stanley opened the local Yellow Pages and seemed to know exactly who to call – the owner of a bed and breakfast on Grizzly Street. He booked all three guest rooms.

"We might have to share a little bit," he said, after he hung up.

Kal put up his hand. "I, for one, would love to share. Can I join you guys?"

Instinctively, Tanya opposed this move. She had learned, in the television business, that displays of weakness always turned fatal, career-wise. But there was great potential in sharing. Close quarters, an intimate B & B, opportunities to sip a glass of eau-de-vie with Stanley Moss, in front of a crackling fire. Maybe there was even a bearskin rug. What would the son or daughter of a Moses, a Buddha, or a Bahá'u'lláh be like? Radiant, she figured, intelligent, famous, and hopelessly wealthy. And none of the sons and daughters of Moses, Buddha, and Bahá'u'lláh had a mother with twenty years of experience in marketing and development.

Tanya felt fertile enough, and Stanley appeared virile despite his calendar age. If a man could throw boulders, jump off cliffs, dole out piano skills, and make old ladies sing then surely he could impregnate a thirty-eight-year-old woman with hardly any cellulite. She went to pack.

FORTY-SIX

Four large men dressed in bland cowboy garb leaned against the travel-booking counter in the lobby of the Chalet Du Bois, pretending to look at brochures. Stanley and Alok, the first to finish packing, sat on a chesterfield made of stained birch, with wolf-print cushions.

"Have you sent flowers?" Alok said.

Stanley had shared his feelings of incompleteness without Frieda, not to elicit sympathy or possible strategies to bring her back, but just to say it out loud. As Alok offered other suggestions and bits of "wisdom of the thrice-divorced," Stanley watched the cowboys and listened to their thoughts. Each man had a natty beard and identical black workboots. They were connected in some way with the anxious and guilty clerk, and they were here to do something about Stanley and Alok. To take them somewhere. The cowboys were waiting for the right moment.

"My wife after Kitty, Gabriela, collected little dolls. It was creepy in her basement, where they all sat on shelves. Anyway, when she was pissed at me I always knew just what to do. Buy her a creepy doll. The secret was to know the dolls she already owned and the –"

Stanley placed his hand on Alok's arm and squeezed. "Don't fight back."

"What?"

"It's going to be all right."

"What's going to be all right?"

The clerk exchanged glances with the four cowboys and left the lobby through a door marked "Employees Only." A moment later, the cowboys were upon Stanley and Alok. Instead of tossing them through a wall, Stanley allowed himself to be led forcibly through the lobby and out the back door.

"If you scream, we'll kill you," said one of the cowboys, a man with giant front teeth and an overbite. "We have guns. Walk normal."

Alok reached out for Stanley. "What's happening?"

"Don't worry."

There was a young couple in the parking lot, lifting luggage from their trunk. The cowboy with the overbite nodded to the couple as they passed. Then he looked around, spat on the pavement, and continued hustling Alok and Stanley to a large, white, canopied truck with a double cab. The young couple disappeared inside the hotel.

One of the cowboys opened the tailgate and canopy, and two others tied Alok's and Stanley's arms behind their backs. Overbite stood guard, watching the parking lot. It was quick. The most anxious one blindfolded and gagged them. His hands trembled and he cleared his throat regularly. He and another man strained to lift and toss Alok into the back of the truck, but in the end they shoved him roughly inside. Stanley jumped in.

The truck rumbled and backed out of its parking spot. Alok lay on his stomach, and it was difficult for him to breathe. He grunted and rocked and whined. As soon as the truck sped up, Stanley pulled his hands out of the rope, removed his blindfold, and took the strip of cotton out of his mouth. "You're okay," he said, to Alok, and freed him.

Alok rolled onto his side, breathed normally again, and whispered, "Why are you letting them do this?"

"I'd like to understand who they are and what they're doing."

"What if they hurt us?"

"I won't let them."

Alok winked. "You can hear them up there?"

"I can."

Based on the vehicle's speed, Stanley guessed they were on the Trans-Canada Highway. Ten minutes later, the truck turned and slowed. Up front, the men argued about where to keep Stanley and Alok. One argued they ought to just kill the devils – tie them to a good pile of concrete and drop them in the middle of Two Jack Lake. Overbite countered that fighting evil acts with evil acts was the way of darkness. They would wait for instructions.

The truck sped up a hill, continued over a mile or so of gravel, and finally came to a stop. Doors slammed, and Stanley could hear the crunching of footsteps.

"What should I do, Stan?"

"Just stay quiet for the moment, and hide behind me if they have weapons."

"You won't let them hurt us, right?"

"Never. You're perfectly safe, I promise."

Alok smiled and rubbed Stanley's hair. There was a heavy *clonk* and the canopy door opened into the brightness. Stanley was briefly blinded. The nervous one opened the tailgate, grabbed Alok's arm, and pulled him out onto the ground. "Hey! They got loose!" The man kicked Alok in the chest and screamed for his mates.

Alok tried to roll away as the man kicked him again and again. He cried out, "Stan?"

Stanley jumped out of the van and grasped the man, whose thoughts were all hatred and fear, by the face. He shrieked and kicked Stanley in the leg. Still holding the man by the face, Stanley pivoted and whipped him into the side of the truck. There was a great, hollow crash. The man crumpled to the gravel and lay still.

Stanley bent down to look at Alok, whose eyes were half closed.

"I'm feeling damn poor, Stan." Alok's breaths were thin wheezes, and he held his chest.

Looking around, Stanley saw they were in an isolated

area south and east of Banff. He recognized the view of Rundle Mountain, capped with snow.

"You're going to be fine," said Stanley, though he didn't believe it. He quickly surveyed the property, a log house and garage.

"Hospital," said Alok.

The other three cowboys stormed out of the house, accompanied by a short, chubby woman. All three had guns. It was obvious she was in charge. In a high yet husky voice, the woman said, "Shoot him."

Stanley danced away from the bullets and rushed the men. Two of them dropped their guns and turned to run. The other, Overbite, shot Stanley just above the bicep of his left arm. It hurt, briefly, but did not immobilize him.

"I reject you," said Overbite, as Stanley took the gun from his hand and tossed it onto the gravel. "I reject you in the name of Jesus Christ."

"Do you have permission, to use his name?"

Overbite spat in Stanley's face. In a brief rage, Stanley slapped the man and he tumbled to the ground, semi-conscious. His compatriots, still running, rounded the log cabin and continued toward the base of the mountain behind. The stout woman remained, her chin raised.

"I have been waiting for you," she said. She carried no weapons, and was unconcerned with the health and welfare of her bodyguards. The woman had a faint moustache, and flecks of yellow in the whites of her eyes. She carried a satisfied look on her face, and a faint snarl. Her buttoned-up blouse matched the blue of the cowboys' shirts. "Your coming was foretold."

Stanley calmed himself, as he did not want to slap anyone else. "Foretold by whom? Who are you people?"

"It is enough that *we know you*, enemy. And we welcome you here, for the final battle. We are well prepared. We act according to the will of God the Redeemer and –"

"Shut up. Just shut up, you lunatic."

Stanley turned away from her to see to his friend. Alok continued to lie on the gravel, wheezing shallowly, his eyes closed. The sight of him nearly provoked Stanley to break the woman's neck.

As he helped Alok up and led him to the passenger door of the truck, Stanley read her thoughts. She was a vault of belief.

The keys were not in the truck, and Stanley could not will it to start. "Where are the keys?"

"I'm not going to help you, old serpent."

Stanley sighed and went to Overbite, who whimpered quietly. Blood dribbled from his nose. He rifled through the man's pockets and found the keys. Before he started it, Stanley yanked the limp cowboy from the side of the truck so he wouldn't run over his arm. A small cloud of dust rose up. The man was not dead, but several of his bones were broken.

The sun went behind a cloud, and the woman looked up, raised her arms, and began to pray. Stanley turned the vehicle around, knocking over a small wooden fence. He piloted the truck down the gravel road, through the hamlet of Harvie Heights, and onto the Trans-Canada Highway. A number of cars were stopped on the shoulder. Tourists photographed a herd of mountain goats.

"We aren't violent men," said Alok, without opening his eyes.

"I'm sorry I didn't do it sooner." Stanley reached over and touched Alok's forehead; it was cool and wet. "What hurts?"

"My chest, my shoulder, my arm." Alok could hardly get the words out. "Something bad is happening to me."

"You're just winded, that's all."

"I don't think so, Stan." Alok coughed, weakly. "There's doom in the air."

Stanley pulled into the parking lot of the Mineral Springs Hospital and hopped out. He flopped the big man over his right shoulder. Inside the doors of the emergency room, the first person who saw them – a woman with gauze wrapped around her head – dropped her can of Diet Coke. It plunked and leaked on the white floor.

There was an empty wheelchair near the door, so with his free arm Stanley lowered Alok into it. The nurse took one look at Alok and called a porter and an acute-care nurse.

"Don't leave me, Stan. I can't be alone. I need to know you're –"

"I won't leave you, my friend."

The admitting nurse held up her hand. "Are you immediate family?"

"No."

"Then I'm sorry, you'll have to wait."

The porter arrived, trailed by another man, and they wheeled Alok away.

"I need to be with him."

"You can't be with him, sir," she said.

"Yes, I can." Stanley focused on her mind.

For the first time, the nurse made eye contact with Stanley. "It's against hospital policy and it isn't safe."

Stanley willed her to allow him inside. The woman seemed to understand what he was up to.

"Listen, fella." The nurse took the little gold cross on her necklace and squeezed it, briefly. "I watch TV. I know who you are. But none of your black magic is gonna work on me."

"But –"

"We'll take good care of your friend. And if we can't do it, we'll rush him to the city."

The porter had taken Alok through swinging doors into what looked like a small operating theatre. Stanley called out after Alok, weakly, "You're going to be all right, pal."

The admitting nurse exhaled through her nose, grabbed her cross again, and walked backwards through the swinging doors.

FORTY-SEVEN

The bed and breakfast on Grizzly Street had been built in 1912 as a home for a Rocky Mountain explorer named Mary Schäffer. On the walls of the great room, built with shiny fir planks, Kal and Maha read about her exploits and admired the black-and-white photographs of the house in bygone eras.

Actually, only Maha read the stories and quotations. She wore a white T-shirt with a V neck, so Kal stared at the line of her collarbone.

"Oh, her first husband died," said Maha, "and she kept coming here from Philadelphia. To cure her heartbreak."

"Heartbreak," said Kal. Once again close enough to Maha

that he could smell her. She smelled of springtime, like a princess ought to, and an image of his own worthlessness flashed and faded. "Poor lady."

Tanya sat near the front window, on the telephone with a producer from *60 Minutes*. The producer wanted assurances that his reporter, Morley Safer, would have a lengthy, exclusive interview with Stanley Moss.

She hung up the phone, growled, and looked at her watch. "Where *are* they?"

"They'll be here," said Maha, without looking away from the interpretive display.

Stanley and Alok had not met the other three in the lobby of the Chalet Du Bois as planned, and Tanya was worried they had fled back to Edmonton. The lure of Frieda. "I swear to God I'll sue him from here to Stuttgart if he does this to me."

Kal didn't think Stanley and Alok were the types to leave without saying goodbye, but he didn't say as much. He wasn't keen on speaking with Tanya, who quivered with frustration. The owner of the bed and breakfast, a tall woman with bad posture who had asked that they call her Swooping Eagle, was eager to learn about Stanley. She set a tray of tea and biscuits on a table near the fireplace and turned on some music.

"So," said Swooping Eagle, "how was he chosen?"

"How was who chosen?" said Tanya.

"Why, Stanley Moss, of course."

Tanya looked up, and it seemed to Kal that she wanted some sort of help. So he said, "Lady explorer – neat."

"Yes," said Swooping Eagle. Then she turned back to Tanya. "I'm so curious about Mr. Moss. When will he join you?"

Tanya looked at her watch again. "It says on all your advertisements that your name is Janet. What's with Swooping Eagle?"

"That's my craft name. Does Mr. Moss have another name?"

"The Lord," said Maha. "But he doesn't like us calling him that. Religious language is polluted. We need to think up something better."

"Polluted, polluted. Yes." Swooping Eagle backed against the fireplace and mantel. "This is an obsession of mine, and other members of my coven. We meet for monthly salons, to discuss issues like this. How did language get to this state, do you think? What was the evolution of religious language?"

In case Swooping Eagle wanted him to answer this question, Kal pretended to lose a contact lens. He dropped to his knees and looked under an end table near the picture window. "Dang it!"

"Let's think about Europe, for a sec, as the root of our religious culture. You with me?"

Kal patted the floor as Maha said, "Coven?"

"So you've got the suppression of pagan religions and the rise of Roman Catholicism. This lasts for centuries and centuries, great darkness, all that. Then you get the Protestant Reformation and the confessional lunacy, the inquisitions. And, finally, Voltaire, the Enlightenment, and the French Revolution. Still with me?"

"Totally," said Kal, though in truth he had no idea what she was talking about. So far he had grasped "*blah blah* Roman Catholicism *blah blah blah*." But he was definitely eager to learn. "We're picking up what you're laying down, Ms. Eagle."

Tanya snorted and began to flip through a copy of *Sage Woman* magazine.

"God begins to depart from western Europe. I mean, as a social, political, and moral force. Yes? Then, after the Revolution, the Jacobins attack the Church. They suppress Catholicism and try to start *a new religion*."

"That's what we're doing," said Kal.

"Right. Well, they fashioned their pagan rebirth around the catastrophe of the Revolution. Where does this lead? Visions of triumph and binding spiritual ideals, talk of blood and race and aggressive human progress?"

"Well, um, there's the uhh . . ." said Kal.

"The Nazis," said Maha.

"Exactly." Swooping Eagle leaned over the back of the chesterfield, for emphasis. "And Communism. All the -isms, really. These were, essentially, religious movements. They followed all the same models, with rituals and holy places and godlike leaders. Even if they pretended to be finished with religion. Leading us where? Where?"

She looked at Kal, smiling, waiting for him to answer. "Here?"

"Yes! To the cult of the individual. Consumerism. Snuff films." She paused. "Do you think Stanley would agree with that analysis?"

No one answered. Kal shrugged and looked at the scones.

"I suppose it's best if I put my questions directly to him," said Swooping Eagle.

"It depends on the questions." Tanya inspected her fingernails. "We don't like to bother him with trivialities."

Swooping Eagle stared at Tanya for a few moments, turned to Kal, and said, "Please, help yourself to some scones and cookies. The tea is Earl Grey!"

"How kind of you," said Maha.

Swooping Eagle took a couple of steps back from the tray and hovered expectantly, until she had the room's full attention. The strange tension in the house, flickering among these three women, was like a bad smell. Kal wanted to stand in the backyard for a while, until it passed.

Then their hostess announced, with a smile, "I'm a witch." She said it the way some other people might say, "I like white wine."

Tanya barked out a laugh. "Meaning?"

"I mean I'm a witch. A Wiccan. A priestess of the sacred mysteries? I was initiated into the craft in 1994, atop Tunnel Mountain." She looked up in its direction, in case Kal, Maha, and Tanya were not aware of Tunnel Mountain. "What I find so fascinating about Mr. Moss is that he doesn't say any of the words, or dress in any ceremonial robes. How does he do what he does? This spiritual movement you're starting: what sort of rituals and initiations and celebrations are involved?"

Kal wished Alok were here. Alok would have known just what to say. A frightfully awkward minute passed. And another. Kal beat it toward the back door as Maha said, "We wrote a testament."

"A testament. How thrilling. Can I see it?"

Tanya sighed and pulled a copy of The Testament from her purse. "Knock yourself out, Swoopy." The owner took it from Tanya and spun it around in her hands. She opened it to the first page and sat on the couch across from the fireplace. At first, Kal, his hand hovering over the doorknob, was relieved. Then she began reading aloud, which only made things more fraught. Kal was torn. Was it polite to leave the room while The Testament was being read aloud? *"This is the book of a man called Stanley Moss, the atheist, who in the latter stages of his life became a Lord to us all."* Swooping Eagle looked up. "Classic." Tanya was furious. Maha didn't like Tanya. Every word between them seemed sarcastic, or filled with a double meaning Kal couldn't grasp. No one had touched the snacks. A woman named Swooping Eagle was reading a book out loud. Yes, Kal had to escape.

"Now, in the year when Stanley Moss was diagnosed with cancer of the lungs he prepared to descend into black black night, nothingness, and abandon his wife, Frieda, and son Charles, lately of New York City." Swooping Eagle looked around. "This is quite compelling," she said. "Can I continue?"

"Can I call you Janet?" said Tanya.

A large green van passed slowly on Grizzly Street, and Kal stood at the door in agony. He had ordered an accordion on his credit card, with rush delivery. But the truck continued along.

The B & B owner pushed her long, frizzy brown hair back behind her ears. *"Just as the frailty of Stanley Moss became apparent and his palliative care was to begin, in the lateness of his life, Stanley received a visitation. There was a thump, and great pressure, and the colour blue. A voice that shook the earth. This heralded the beginning of the* rebirth *of Stanley Moss.*

"The nausea did pass away, and the fear of death. Yet Stanley saw, in the phase of his rebirth, that we have nothing to fear in nothingness. There is great beauty, and honour, in receiving nothingness into our hearts. In receiving the black

black night and all its implications. The incomprehensibility of the universe and the rotting bones in the soil underneath us all.

"*That morning, as he travelled by motorized vehicle to see his doctor, Stanley was animated by his new strength. He was set upon by ruffians with poor hygiene, and he dispatched of them. On the bus, later, he did cement his connection to us all when he began to hear our inner thoughts.*"

Swooping Eagle closed the book and laid it on her knee. "He hears thoughts?"

"Usually," said Maha.

On Grizzly Street, the delivery truck beeped as it backed up. The driver looked at a sheet of paper, and then looked at the house. Kal seized his opportunity and ran out the door.

The accordion, a Roland FR-7 V, was in its gleaming box. He signed for it, denied a temptation to hug the driver, and stood with it proudly as the delivery truck started away. It was evening now, and the sun was easing below the mountains. Bees were about the flowers. There was a rumble down the street, of an approaching crowd. He guessed it was the multilingual tourists on Banff Avenue, in the midst of shopping and eating and drinking – being enthusiastically human.

It was so peaceful in the yard and such a relief to be out of the soup of discomfort that he decided to unpack the instrument on the lawn. Stanley's voice interrupted him just as he began to rip the tape.

FORTY-EIGHT

Tanya jumped out of her chair and hugged Stanley and kissed him on the mouth. "Where have you been?"

"The hospital."

"Will you do *60 Minutes*?"

Maha tossed her scone at Tanya's head. The oven-warm biscuit exploded in Tanya's ear with a puff of egg, flour, shortening, sugar, and water.

Tanya jumped. "Who did that?"

"Me."

Tanya made fists.

"Sorry." Maha got down on the floor to clean the mess.

"Why were you at the hospital?"

"I'm going to need more than a *sorry*, little miss. Do something, Stan!" Tanya picked the bits of scone from the inside of her ear and wiped the flour off her shoulder. As Maha crawled on the floor, she half expected Tanya to kick her.

"Alok had a heart attack this afternoon."

Kal stopped opening his accordion box and sat back on the wooden floor with a plop. Maha dropped her crumbs.

"We were waiting for the rest of you in the lobby of the Chalet Du Bois and several large cowboys attacked us."

Maha could not imagine this being possible. "How? How did they attack you?"

"They didn't seem too dangerous, and at the time I didn't want to hurt anyone. I was curious about their intentions.

I could have stopped them but I didn't, and look what's happened. It's my fault."

"Is he all right?" said Maha.

"Did you kick their effin asses?" said Kal.

"Does the name Morley Safer mean anything to you?" said Tanya.

Stanley removed his shoes, inspected the great room, and stopped at the information about the explorer, Mary Schäffer. "Huh," he said. Then he said, "Huh," again, and turned back to the group. "Luckily, there happened to be a heart specialist in from Edmonton following up on another patient. They've given him some clot-busting drugs."

"Can we go see him?" said Maha.

"Maybe tomorrow, based on how tonight goes."

The B & B owner stared at Stanley with a look that was somewhere in between a smile and a frown. He offered his hand. "You must be Janet."

She pulled Stanley in for a quick hug. "Call me Swooping Eagle."

"She's a witch." Kal addressed himself to the accordion box again.

"It's her craft name," said Tanya.

"Swooping Eagle, can I use the telephone?"

The Lord retired to one of the bedrooms, to phone Frieda. Maha collected the remainder of the scone and started into the kitchen. Even if Alok had not been in the hospital, the views from the kitchen window of the mountains in the summertime dusk would have been enough to make her weep. So no one would hear her, she ran cold water in the sink and splashed it on her face.

"All right," said Tanya, behind her. "Let's talk."

Maha stood up from the sink and dabbed her eyes with a tea towel.

Spotting the evidence of tears, Tanya took a half-step back in apparent horror. Then she ran toward Maha and held her. "I forgive you, Maha. I forgive you. I'm a good person and I forgive you."

Maha was keen to attempt one of the hip-tosses she had learned in elementary school judo. She was also keen to scream, and cry some more, to run into the great room, pull Kal's shirt up, and inspect his stomach muscles. She was keen to go to the hospital to see Alok for herself. She was keen to sit in a room, alone, with the Lord, and ask him what to do, think, and feel next.

Instead, Maha disentangled herself from Tanya and returned to the great room. She found Swooping Eagle and Kal around the coffee table. Swooping Eagle was describing the initiation rituals for her coven, including the casting of a circle. "A lot of what we do is ancient," she said. "Some of it we just borrowed from the Freemasons."

"Are they witches?" said Kal.

"Oh, no," said Swooping Eagle. "They're mostly old men with Buicks. One is mostly for men and the other is mostly for women. You can be a Wicca man but not a Freemason woman. Ours has more magic. And less billiards."

Tanya sat down on the couch behind them. "How did you get into it, Swoopy?"

"I was called," she said, turning to eye Tanya. "Before I joined my coven, I was in darkness."

Maha joined the men around the table. "I was called to the Lord. I mean, Stanley."

"Total darkness over here, too," said Kal. "*You must change your life.* So I did."

"Splendid, Kal. Just splendid." Swooping Eagle gathered the tea and scones, which had gone untouched but for the one Maha tossed, and went to the kitchen. In her absence, no one spoke. Yet a great chattering filled the house on Grizzly Street. It was as if twenty people had just entered the room.

Maha approached the front window. Outside, the sky was purpling. The Lord returned to the great room, with an even more profound air of disappointment about him. Several hundred people were gathered on the front lawn and on neighbouring property. A CBC broadcasting van was parked in among the crowd, its doors wide open. There were tents going up on the lawn, the street, and adjacent to the cemetery. A group of men and women with two long ladders was hanging a banner between trees. "No Blasphemy In Our Backyard" it read, bookended by a couple of unevenly painted yellow "Support Our Troops" ribbons.

"I should have mentioned," said the Lord. "I was followed."

FORTY-NINE

Kal and Alok sat on a park bench outside the Mineral Springs Hospital. The sun glinted off the decorative chrome band on the accordion. A small crowd of tourists and what the media were calling "pilgrims" took digital photographs from the other side of a police line erected by the Mounties.

Given the audience, Kal was too nervous to play the song he had memorized that morning, "In Every Neighbourhood in Paris."

"Did you know the Vatican has a squad?"

Alok fingered the IV hookup on the back of his wrist, and rolled the tower slightly with his shoe. "I'm not surprised, really."

"It's to investigate satanic crimes, mostly. But they're here."

"They think we're a satanic crime?"

"I guess."

It was probably the drugs, but it seemed to Kal that Alok's posture wasn't what it used to be. He was also sweaty and slightly grey coloured.

The last thing Alok needed was bad news, so Kal didn't tell him anything else about the Squadra Anti Sette that had arrived from Rome. He didn't tell Alok about their information meeting that morning with the Mounties, either. Footage from the night in the Eric Harvie Theatre had spread, by way of YouTube, all the way to a man called Abu Hafiza, whose online condemnation of Stanley had provoked some Hezb-e Islami Gulbuddin militants. Then there were the infrastructure concerns. Banff didn't have enough parking spots, hotel rooms, campsites, and helicopter landing pads for all the people who were arriving daily from around the world. A multi-faith coalition of fundamentalist Christians, Jews, Hindus, Sikhs, and Muslims, originally formed to battle same-sex marriage legislation in North America, had set up a twenty-four-hour vigil and prayer centre two houses away from the B & B on Grizzly Street.

"I was doing some reading yesterday afternoon," Alok said. "Confucius, when he summed up his wisdom, asked his disciples to look into their hearts and discover what caused them the most sincere pain."

Kal took a moment. The thought of losing Layla forever, to Elias Shymanski. The thought of Maha leaving Banff for Toronto and her fiancé. Loneliness and darkness and alcohol and hash and prostitutes, the very life he had been heading for.

"Then Confucius asked his disciples never to inflict *that pain* on others. We discussed it, last night, Stan and I. It's really good, isn't it?"

"Totally."

"A fellow's gotta wonder." Alok leaned back on the bench and looked up. "Maybe all the great ideas are already out there, always have been. The plight of humans is to ignore and forsake them, to bury them below the impulse to consume."

"Nah."

"It's psychotic, you know, this drive to expand and commodify. Capitalism, which has infected the human heart, Kal, is destroying us."

"Come on, buddy. Cheer up."

In the crowd beyond the police line, a woman bared her breasts. Alok waved to her. "Thank you so much!" The cameras turned toward her and she lifted a sign, promoting a website.

Kal reached down and produced a mournful minor-C on his accordion. "When do you get out of here?"

"Really soon. Tomorrow, I hope."

"We need you, Alok, real bad. Maha and Swooping Eagle are making up some rituals for The Stan. Every religion needs some, I guess. It's a competitive marketplace, Tanya says. People are done reading The Testament now, and you got to give them something more. Otherwise they head to the Internet or whatever, for the next big religion, or for pictures of singers not wearing any underpants. It's the next big step in the strategic plan."

"There's a strategic plan?"

"Tanya whipped it up."

"You're right, I gotta get out of here. You can't save the land from dying with a strategic plan."

"Amen."

Two men ducked under the yellow police line and sprinted toward Kal and Alok. Kal stood up, right away, to prevent them from touching or blowing up Alok. But three Mounties tackled them on the grass several paces away. There were flashes, from the cameras, and some of the tourists and pilgrims booed the police as they led the two men toward a squad car.

A fourth policeman asked Kal and Alok to go back inside the hospital, so Kal hugged Alok. "Let me know if you want me to sneak down here and spring your ass."

"That won't be necessary. I'll be out of here lickety-split."

A good part of the crowd followed Kal through the streets and avenues, as he made his way toward the house on Grizzly Street. They melded with the larger crowd and touched him, gave him letters for Stanley, pressed Safeway bags filled with gifts for Stanley into his hands, and kissed him, and cursed him. Most just asked questions as he hurried past without making eye contact, as the Mounties had suggested. *What miracles have you witnessed? What songs can you play? Will he give me powers? Is this the end of the world?*

FIFTY

The gorgeous young man with a fresh manicure and diamond earrings stared deeply into Tanya's pores. "It's absolutely disgusting," he said, in the pale-yellow light of an exhibition tent next to the house on Grizzly Street. "They wallow in their own crap, Tanya, and those pellets they eat are filled with PCBs and dioxin and – who knows? – any number of other concentrated cancers. You and I probably have tumours *right now* because of farmed salmon. It's a sign, you ask me. If you can't trust your food, you can't trust anything."

Tanya was preparing to make a formal statement to the media about The Stan, and she wanted to do it outdoors, with mountains in the background, to impress and attract the pantheists. But in natural light, without special *maquillage*, she would end up looking like a celebrity picked up on a drunk driving charge. Tanya enjoyed the young makeup artist she had hired, and this process. For too long, as a producer and executive, she'd been on the other side of the camera. It was hot outside, but there was an air conditioner in the tent. By next Friday, she would be sitting across from the great Morley Safer. She felt like an early investor in Google.

Until her idyll was interrupted by a voice. Kal's voice. Kal, in conversation with reporters.

Tanya jumped out of her chair and knocked the makeup artist into a steel support beam. Near the door of the tent, Tanya tripped over the portable air conditioner and fell on a sound mixer. She sprained her thumb and got a grass stain on the left knee of her white slacks. "Damn it!"

"Easy, girl," said the makeup artist.

There was Kal, with Maha, surrounded by television and print reporters.

"Oh, yeah, he can pretty much do anything he wants. He's super-awesome, and not only in making people float or whatever. First and foremost, he's about not inflicting the worst pain you can imagine on other people. And capitalism, of course, is psychotic. Anyway, Stan's got this vibe. You always want to be around him." Kal lifted his accordion while Tanya fought through the crowd. He played the introductory notes to "Strangers In The Night," and before he sang the opening line, he said, "Two weeks ago, I couldn't play any instruments at all. But now, dig it . . ."

Tanya did not want Stanley to be known strictly as a musical miracle-worker, and she did not want a former professional hockey player speaking for the organization, saying, "He's super-awesome" and "Capitalism, of course, is psychotic," on international television. So she burst through the final skein of media and reached for Kal. Off balance, Tanya missed his shoulder and connected with his left cheek and lip, neither of which had healed. Kal cried out in pain and drove himself backward, taking two female reporters and a cameraman down with him.

The accordion grunted.

Screams rang out. One of the reporters crushed in the melee was hurt. A small cut opened above her eye, and some of the blood smeared on her colleague's bare right arm. "Oh my God, oh my God," said the woman with blood on her arm. She sprinted toward the road, leaving her microphone behind. "AIDS test!"

Five cellphones came out like guns at the OK Corral. The various descriptions of the incident, for the emergency dispatchers, squeezed the goodwill out of Tanya's heart.

"There's been an aggravated assault on Grizzly Street."

"Massive head trauma."

"Bloodbath!"

"*Le trouble schizo-affectif.*"

"Attempted murder."

The reporters bumped into one another trying to get a statement from Tanya, Maha, or Kal himself. To simplify the message and direct the microphones and cameras toward herself, Tanya began to call out, "Accident. Accident. Ha ha! It was a funny accident."

It worked. She moved backwards, toward the tent next to the house on Grizzly Street, and the reporters followed her like hyenas stalking a wounded zebra. Tanya stopped walking and forced a smile. On the other side of the reporters, Kal was tending to the woman with the cut on her forehead.

The first question was simple. "Why did you attack Kal?"

"I didn't attack Kal." Tanya laughed. "I love Kal! I was trying to pull him in to kiss him on the cheek – he's so adorable – when I tripped on a shoe."

"That's a filthy lie," said one of the male reporters.

"Who said that? Who said that?"

"Why were you trying to kiss him?"

"Like I just said, he's adorable."

"So there *is* a sexual component to this cult?"

"This isn't a cult."

The sun went behind a cloud and Tanya saw her reflection in a camera lens. Her hair was tied back, and only one of her eyes had any mascara. Her foundation was uneven and she was not wearing lipstick. She desperately wanted to kick someone, or something, but if she did kick one of the reporters – preferably the man who had called her a filthy liar – she would need further reputation management. Tanya remembered her yoga. She found her centre and breathed and focused.

"I worked in the media my entire career, so I understand what you're doing here." Tanya smiled as warmly as she could manage. "But how can you all stand before us, this beautiful afternoon, in judgment? What we are doing here is trying to build a spiritual organization unlike any other, a group of like-minded Canadians committed to saving this country, and the larger world, from itself. We want individuals to come out from behind their television sets, to stop being customers and clients of a crooked government and an even more crooked corporate infrastructure, and begin a new and authentic life. With us. With Stanley Moss and The Stan."

"How much does it cost?"

"What?"

"How much does it cost to join?"

"Nothing. We're a collective."

"So you're Communists?"

"No."

"Socialists, then?"

"We're apolitical."

Several of the reporters laughed sarcastically. "An apolitical religious organization?"

"Do you hate Jesus?"

Tanya smiled, authentically this time. "Not at all."

"How do you feel about Jesus?"

"Me, personally? I think he's terrific."

"When will The Stan perform his next miracle?"

"Soon."

The reporters grumbled. A young man in the front raised his hand. "What do you think of the religious leaders gathered here to denounce you as minions of the Devil?"

Tanya could not tell the young man what she really thought of them. "Pity," she said, addressing the camera with a valiant attempt at genuine concern. "We feel pity."

FIFTY-ONE

Stanley could tell, by the background noise, that Frieda was in the garden. In the summer months, she pulled up new dandelions every morning with a long screwdriver. As neighbours passed in the alley, she would rise on her knees and say hello, talk about the weather, ask about children, offer to babysit. Stanley heard a bumblebee pass by his wife, and the wind.

"The new neighbours across the alley don't do a damn thing about their lawn," she said. "Dandelion seeds sail over with every gust."

"You could write a note, leave it in the mailbox."

"On Friday nights, the man of the house hosts backyard parties. Firepit and country music. You can hear him, when the windows are open, cussing away. I don't think he'd appreciate a note."

"Does he have a wife?"

"Yes, poor thing. And two girls."

Stanley savoured his wife's voice like chocolate. He couldn't remember any neighbours or the design of their garden, apart from the plum and apple trees blooming in the spring. All he really wanted to do was beg Frieda to come back to Banff, just for a few days. But if he launched into a new campaign, she would just hang up. Stanley imagined she was on the grass, lying on her back, a splash of morning sun on her face.

What Stanley did remember was watching his wife from the kitchen window, last summer and summers previous. He had often thought she looked like a sapper, digging for the long root of a dandelion as though removing the fuse from a landmine. She would lie on her side, with her thin elbow in the air. Always a sun hat, and either a pair of old shorts or blue jeans. Frieda had four stained T-shirts for summer gardening, each one a gift from a charity walk.

"Is it warm there?"

"Sure is," Frieda said. "And there?"

"It takes a little longer to heat up in the mornings. Is the ground dewy?"

She laughed. "Not too dewy, Stan, no."

When the others woke up, they were going on an excursion to a nearby lake. But he didn't want Frieda to think he was doing anything remarkable without her. Stanley wanted his wife to know what she already knew, that he needed her, just more so. "I'm just going to do some studying today."

"You could do that from home."

"I could."

Silence vibrated and crackled on the phone line.

"I've been watching old movies on DVD. Things you don't like. Musicals, mostly. Last night I rented *Footlight Parade*. You would've fallen asleep. Back when you slept."

"That's good."

"What's good?"

This was where the conversation would turn sour. Stanley would begin to feel guilty, and again he would explain why he felt compelled to stay in Banff. Frieda would say without saying that she was lonesome. That she felt abandoned and betrayed. And then it would become an ugly transition toward goodbye, again, until the following day's similarly grim conversation.

"How is Alok?"

"Still in the hospital."

"Send him my love. Or admiration. Something."

Stanley heard the engine of a car passing slowly through the back lane. He couldn't help himself. "I wish you were here."

"Television vans are parked outside the house. It's not neighbourly. I can't go to the store without cameras following me around. Twice now, I've seen myself on television, walking past the picture window. Which is filthy, by the way, and I'm not getting on a ladder. You know what? I've had to order groceries on the Internet. Charles sent me a link."

"All right, I'll get Tanya to call –"

"I'm moving to New York. I don't know for how long. There's a one-bedroom apartment I can sublet across the street from Charles's building."

"Frieda."

"I can't wait any more, Stanley."

There was a knock on his door. "Rise and shine," said Swooping Eagle. "We're off to see the wizard!"

Frieda cleared her throat. "I'll let you go."

"A few more minutes."

"I have a lunch date, and I have to pull up another fifteen dandelions before my shower, so –"

"A lunch date with who?"

"I love you," said Frieda, and there was a click, and a dial tone.

FIFTY-TWO

Maha told herself, again and again, not to despise Tanya. She tried to forbid thoughts like, *Go away, Tanya*, and *It makes me want to throw up when you flirt with the Lord, Tanya*, and *I hope a bear chews your stupid selfish face off, Tanya*.

With the other disciples, Maha stood on the shore of what was, according to a witch, the most haunted lake in North America. Swooping Eagle had driven them out in her minivan, both to escape the crowds in front of the house on Grizzly Street and to demonstrate some of the rituals of her own religion – in case The Stan was looking to borrow a thing or two.

The green water crackled with light. According to Swooping Eagle, and recent archaeological digs, the shores of this long and deep lake had been inhabited for ten thousand years before Europeans arrived to develop it into a resort village. A dam had submerged the village in 1941.

Swooping Eagle finished thanking the spirits for hosting them, and then she swept the large rock on which they stood with a magic broom. Maha glanced at Kal, who appeared to be on the verge of both laughing and crying. Swooping Eagle swept the rock and chanted quietly.

On a hill nearby, five sheep caused a mini-avalanche of dirt. Maha noticed a bear on the opposite bank of the lake, but she didn't want to break the spell of odd quiet that Swooping Eagle had created. Swooping Eagle took a white stone from her pocket, kissed it, and drew a circle on their ritual rock.

"Now," said the Wiccan, "what I've done here is I've cast a circle. As observers, this time, you'll stay outside it. This is a sacred space, a space between the worlds. It takes care of our energy while we are here."

"Oy." By the reddish half-moons under her eyes, it was clear Tanya hadn't slept much. The previous evening's television news, with the makeup horror, had apparently been hard on her sense of self. And unlike other spiritual devotees through the ages, around the world, Tanya did not seem eager to lose her sense of self. She pulled out her cellphone, for the third time in as many minutes, and checked it for missed calls.

Swooping Eagle cleared her throat loudly. "You mind turning that off, dear? If there's one thing the spirits don't like –"

"The spirits seem to be fine with your pink slacks, Swoopster. Just get on with it."

Up until now, the Lord had seemed preoccupied. He'd been watching and listening to Swooping Eagle, but Maha could tell his attention was focused elsewhere – on something down the beach, closer to the water. He tiptoed across the rock, careful not to step inside the circle, and whispered something in Tanya's ear.

Tanya sighed. "I'm really sorry I said that, Swoop," she said, in the monotone of a chastised eight-year-old. "It was mean."

Swooping Eagle bowed her head. "Tanya, since you're standing in the west, you'll be the western guard. Kal, stand a quarter-turn away from her. You're the southern guard. Maha, you're next, in the east. Stanley, I'd like you to stand in the north."

She placed a bowl of salt in front of Stanley, some incense before Maha, a lava rock at Kal's feet, and a cup of water at Tanya's. In the centre of the circle, Swooping Eagle laid down a white cloth and covered it with a number of items. "These are our working tools," she said, and gestured to a pentacle, a bell, a crystal, a wand, and a small black cauldron.

Then Swooping Eagle pulled her pink sweatpants off. After the pants came her sweater. Maha had trouble looking at Swooping Eagle in her bra and panties, and it was even more difficult when she removed those. Tanya slapped herself on the forehead.

"Can I say something?"

"Absolutely not," said the Lord.

In the centre of the circle, in front of her altar of cloth and working tools, the naked witch muttered and pointed and swung her arms about for some time. Then she faced north and bent over. Maha did not envy Kal's view from the south.

Some consecrations came next, and then Swooping Eagle called the mighty spirits to attend to the circle with their powers.

Swooping Eagle burned some incense, a scent that had always made Maha faint. The Wiccan thanked the goddess, other spirits, and her four quarters. She wiped the circle away, and they all sat down on the large rock to eat a carrot cake.

Swooping Eagle took a bottle of champagne and a carton of orange juice out of her bag, with five plastic cups. "We usually drink ceremonial wine, but considering the hour I thought we'd go for mimosas. I love mimosas. Don't you guys?"

"That was really quite terrific, Swoop." Tanya looked down at her hands. "But with all respect, could you put your clothes back on? Please?"

Maha wondered if life, a way of life, or even a religion, could be sacred without rituals.

Swooping Eagle, still naked, distributed the mimosas. She pulled out a knife to cut the cake. "That's just the way my coven does it. There's a thousand variations. We always have the circle, though, and the tools. We summon the –"

"It was very educational," said the Lord. "Thank you."

Kal drank his mimosa in one gulp and said, "Is there any more booze and juice?"

"I was lost before this," said Swooping Eagle. "Eating poorly, addicted to TV, married to an idiot. Wicca's given me a way of looking at the world without any malice or negativity or disharmony. The first year I . . ."

The Lord, who had been staring beyond the circle, started away. "Thanks again, Swooping Eagle. My friends. If you'll just excuse me." He climbed over the rocks toward the other side of the beach, removed his shirt, put it back on, and walked into the water.

FIFTY-THREE

Mary Schäffer and young Darlene stood on the beach with a number of other men and women. Most were aboriginal, but some were white, others Asian, still others of indeterminate origin. They had waited on the beach during Swooping Eagle's ritual. Patiently, Stanley thought. He had found it difficult to pay attention to the ritual as, from time to time, one of the beach people would take off into the air, float over the water, and drop into Lake Minnewanka without a splash. As Swooping Eagle had finished up, what seemed to be a sasquatch had stood on the lake's edge among the humans. Stunned by the Wiccan's dance of gratitude, Stanley had looked away, and when he'd turned his attention back to the beach the sasquatch was gone.

The beach people seemed to know when the ritual was over, as a number of them now eased into the water. Mary Schäffer waved at him to follow, so Stanley declined the offer of carrot cake and mimosas. Most everyone had gone in by the time he reached the shore.

"How cold is it?"

Mary Schäffer shook her head. "Don't be cute."

"It's a glacier-fed lake and I –"

"Listen, I don't like this any more than you do."

"Just a minute." Stanley removed his shirt.

"What are you *doing*?"

"You won't get wet," said Darlene. She stayed on the beach and motioned for Stanley to put his shirt back on. "Not really."

"Aren't you coming?"

Darlene shrugged. "Maybe later." She wore white linen pants and a smart tan jacket, with perfectly clean sneakers. "It's not my scene."

Mary Schäffer, in a pink dress, was the last to step into Lake Minnewanka. Stanley hesitated and Mary Schäffer sighed, yanked on his hand. "I don't know why everyone's so concerned about you. You obviously don't have a clue."

The water was not cold. It was as comfortable as the morning air in the valley, and though Stanley held his breath when he finally put his head under, it seemed unnecessary. As they walked along the gooey bottom, deeper into the green murk of the lake, the light becoming weaker, Mary Schäffer turned to him and said, "Go ahead, breathe."

It took a few attempts to gather the courage and then Stanley did breathe underwater. For the first time since Frieda had left Banff, Stanley laughed.

The floor dropped off suddenly and the expanse of the lake opened before them. Their hair and clothing fluttered. The sun rippled through the water just enough to reveal a series of ruins far below. Stanley assumed this was the Minnewanka Landing townsite, submerged by a dam in 1941. Yet by the time he'd called out to Mary Schäffer, to ask if this was indeed the case, light had returned. Stanley blocked his eyes from the suddenness of the change, from almost total darkness to brilliant daylight. Ten feet from the absolute bottom of the lake, as his eyes adjusted, Stanley saw it wasn't Lake Minnewanka any more. There was no sign of water. He was descending, slowly, into a town. A city.

They landed on greener-than-green grass, and Mary Schäffer pulled her hand away from Stanley's. There were trees, of both temperate and tropical origin. Buildings of ancient and modern styles lined a Main Street, where thousands of pedestrians passed in both directions. Some of them noticed Stanley and Mary Schäffer, and pointed. There were homes built on the edges of the lush valley. Stanley saw the sasquatch again, and another.

He closed his eyes, and when he opened them again, Mary Schäffer was standing beside him, fixing her hair. "What?"

"I don't believe this."

"You don't believe what?"

Stanley pivoted, gestured to the people and the infrastructure on the bottom of Lake Minnewanka. "This isn't happening. What did you do to me? Where's Darlene?"

"As usual, I don't know what you're talking about."

What Stanley really wanted was to share this moment with Frieda. Of everything that had happened to him since that morning in the backyard, this was most frightening.

Mary Schäffer seemed to anticipate Stanley's next series of questions and led him to what appeared to be the town's information centre across the street. "It's built according to the dimensions of King Solomon's Temple," said Mary Schäffer. "Half size, of course, and without any timber from the forests of Lebanon. I'm sure you've seen nothing like it."

They walked up the steps, past the pillars, and through the vestibule. There was one clerk, sitting at a stone desk in the central chamber. The walls of the large room were lined with cedar, with carved trees and angels in gold. Books were everywhere, though Stanley could not focus on their titles. "How can I help you?" said the clerk, a bearded man dressed in the leather garb of a nineteenth-century explorer.

"What is this place?"

The clerk laughed. "This is the library, information centre, and temple."

"No. I mean, what is this *everything*?"

"You didn't see the sign? You're in Svarga."

"Svarga?"

"Svarga. Welcome!"

Mary Schäffer and the clerk discussed between themselves something about a meeting, so Stanley wandered alone through the temple. He came to the end of the central chamber and started up a series of steps. The smaller room beyond, from what he could see, had cedar wainscotting and gold floors, with a great carved angel. He was drawn to this place, which felt lonesome and empty.

"Stop."

Mary Schäffer yanked Stanley by the collar and pulled him back into the central chamber. "That's the holy of holies, you moron. The dwelling place of God."

"There's a God?"

Mary Schäffer looked at the bearded clerk with a blank expression. It was clear no one was going to answer his question. So he asked another.

"Are you all dead?"

There didn't seem to be a yes-or-no answer to this one, but they almost spoke. The clerk grunted and rubbed at his grey-black hair as though a good response might be hidden under there.

"All right, how about this. Why did you bring me here?"

Mary Schäffer seemed pleased with this question, as did the clerk. "We're having a meeting, to discuss you in a more formal manner. You've been little more than petulant with me, in private."

"Ms. Schäffer, I haven't been petulant. But I don't think I'll have any illuminating answers for you. I'm just starting to get a handle on all this myself."

She turned to the clerk. "You see? Diabolical."

"So who are you people? Are you people?"

The bearded man smiled. "Of course, Mr. Moss. Everyone but the sasquatches. But you know what they say: sasquatches are people too."

Back out on Main Street, Stanley entered a procession. Thousands of people – dressed, like the clerk in Solomon's Temple, in period clothing – walked and floated in a direction that Stanley guessed to be north.

Though most of the people of Svarga were subtle about it, they seemed to regard him as a stranger and an alien. They allowed a pocket to form around him, as though he were contagious. Some whispered about him and stared openly. Others called out. He could not understand all of the languages, but he understood one man very clearly.

"Chop off his fecking head!"

Mary Schäffer said, "You have become something of a celebrity here. You're not one of us and you're not one of them, either." Mary Schäffer pointed straight up, to the murky, blue-green sky that was, in some sense, the undersurface of Lake Minnewanka. "When we planned this meeting, we weren't able to gauge the demand. At first we thought we'd hold it at the information centre, then public interest in you absolutely exploded. We've moved this meeting to the only room big enough."

Over the crowd, Stanley could now see a red gateway and wall, and beyond it a white-domed building. It took him some time to realize how and why he recognized this place. As they approached, the crowd paused to allow

Stanley and Mary Schäffer to pass under the sandstone arch.

They entered the gardens and pools of the Taj Mahal.

"Have you been?" said Mary Schäffer.

Stanley stopped, and covered his eyes with the palms of his hands. "I don't get this, and you're not telling me anything."

"Why should I tell you anything? You haven't told me anything."

He pulled his hands away. "I don't know anything."

"Poppycock. Poppycock. Poppycock." Mary Schäffer adjusted the white collar of her pink dress, and directed Stanley to the vegetation in each of the four corners. "These are the Gardens of Paradise. And up ahead, here in the central square, is the Celestial Pool of Abundance."

They reached the Celestial Pool of Abundance. There was a single lotus blossom floating on its surface.

"It represents the place where man met God."

Stanley did not know how to respond. Here he was, on the terrace of the Taj Mahal, with a Rocky Mountain explorer from Philadelphia who died in 1939. The crowd continued to leave space around him, even though they themselves were packed in tightly. Not far from the Celestial Pool of Abundance, Stanley spotted another sasquatch. "So I gather they're real, the sasquatches?"

"There are maybe five of them left up there. Down here, we have plenty. But most moved on, back when we were permitted to move on."

"Moved where?"

Mary Schäffer shook her head. "You are bloody infuriating."

They walked up the steps and entered the octagonal central chamber of the Taj Mahal. The translucent white

marble was decorated with Arabic inscriptions in black. A
giant brass lamp hung from the dome. As Stanley oriented
himself among the crowds, the symmetry of the chamber
made him dizzy.

Mary Schäffer directed Stanley to a chair in the centre of
the room, up on a riser. "Usually we'd have the cenotaphs
here, but we needed a stage."

"Right," said Stanley.

There was a long table to his right, where a man and two
women sat. The man and one of the women were aboriginals. The other woman, stunningly gorgeous, with a fierce
look of concentration, was Chinese. Mary Schäffer sat in the
remaining chair. In front of her, on the table, the nameplate
said "Mayor." She introduced Stanley to the three others.
Neither of the aboriginals seemed to speak English and they
weren't particularly friendly.

"Jin Ting Zhang," said the Chinese woman. "Or Clara,
whichever you prefer."

Stanley smiled. "Which do you prefer?"

"That's what I said."

"Yes, but I'm asking."

"Asking *what*, pray tell, Mr. Moss?"

"Which name you –"

"Stop talking to me. You're filled with drivel."

They waited several minutes for the central chamber of
the Taj Mahal to fill up. During this time, Jin Ting Zhang
spoke merrily to the aboriginal couple in what could have
been their language. Mary Schäffer signed some papers for
a man with stiff posture, dressed like photographs of
Benjamin Franklin.

Quiet settled over the full room. The only times Stanley
had seen this many people in one building were during

Edmonton Oilers playoff games. Mary Schäffer stood up. "We all know why we're here, so I won't waste any time with introductory speeches."

"Good!" said someone in the crowd.

"I'd like to formally present Stanley Moss. On your feet, Mr. Moss."

The crowd did not applaud. People below him, on all sides, simply stared in silence.

"We have invited Stanley Moss here to answer our questions. I informed Mr. Moss, some days ago, that he was creating an unprecedented spiritual interruption. On your behalf, I politely asked him to explain himself. He refused."

"Why?" said someone in the audience below. This inspired an outburst of more and louder "Why?"s, shouts of disapproval, threats, and insults.

Mary Schäffer stared at Stanley with a raised chin. Just below, on the floor of the Taj Mahal, Darlene appeared. "Speak up," she said, over the chaos. "Say something."

Stanley waved the crowd silent. "I sincerely apologize if I've offended you in some way with my *spiritual interruption*. But I assure you, this was not my choice. To be honest, I don't know why I have these powers or what they mean. I don't know what I am, or who you are, or if there's a God. Maybe you can help me. I have these followers. One had a heart attack and I'm quite worried about him."

"Liar!" said a man.

"Leave us alone!" said a woman.

"Chop that head off ASAP!"

The aboriginal man onstage with Stanley denounced him and spat on the table. Once he'd finished this loud and clearly angry speech, the crowd roared in approval.

"Let's put it to a vote," said Mary Schäffer. "How many

of you wish Mr. Stanley Moss to be banished from the Bow Valley?"

Nearly every arm in the Taj Mahal rose up. All but Darlene's.

"It's decided, then," said Mary Schäffer. "Take your people elsewhere, to Aspen, maybe, or Lake Tahoe, or Sharm El Sheikh."

That marked the end of the gathering. The citizens of Svarga shook one another's hands, slapped each other on the back, and started out of the Taj Mahal. Mary Schäffer and the other leaders joined their constituents. Stanley waited until nearly everyone was gone. The shifting of his feet echoed in the great marble tomb.

Darlene called out from below. "Are you all right?"

"I've had better mornings."

"Let's get you back to the surface."

Stanley hopped down from the stage and walked with Darlene to the entrance. He turned back, and the stage had already transformed back into the screened cenotaphs of Shah Jehan and his wife Arjuman Banu Begum.

FIFTY-FOUR

When the old man had been under the surface for a full minute, Kal got up from the mimosa-and-cake picnic and bounced across the rocks toward shore. He looked over the water, but couldn't see Stanley. There were no footsteps or clouds of disturbed sand.

"Is he there?" said Tanya, back at the rock.

"No."

Swimming was not Kal's chief talent but he had to try. He pulled off his shirt, shoes, and jeans and stepped into the clear green water. It was much colder than he had anticipated. But this was serious business, so Kal dove in and opened his eyes.

The water was not just cold. Kal's bones ached, and then he felt as if his skin were actually burning. Underwater, he found it nearly impossible to concentrate on his search for Stanley. Anyway, there was no sign of him. So Kal thrashed back to the rocky shore and, once he was fully out of the water, screamed involuntarily.

Kal hugged himself and tears filled his eyes. If there were anything left of Stanley that was normal and human, he would already be dead. The ripples of Kal's short swim lapped out into the lake and dissipated entirely.

A large white boat approached the shore and moored itself, several hundred yards out, to a buoy Kal had not noticed. Several people stood up, dressed in black. Scuba divers. He called out to the scuba divers on the boat and waved, hoping they might poke around under the surface for Stanley, but they did not hear him.

Kal called out, over and over, and jumped on the rocks. For a moment, he rested his voice and stared at the sun reflecting in crooked checkmarks on the surface of the lake. He had brought his hands to his mouth and was prepared to yell again when Stanley walked out of the water. There was hardly a ripple. Stanley was not there and then he was there, completely dry and smiling.

"What's going on?"

Kal looked down at himself in his wet, drooping underwear and rushed in to hug Stanley. It reminded Kal of a recurring dream through his teen years, of his father walking unexpectedly through the door in Thunder Bay. Running to his father, both angry and ecstatic. The desire to hide his father away from death.

"God damn it," he said, and slapped Stanley's back. "Don't do that to us."

FIFTY-FIVE

The Banff Community High School gymnasium and soccer field did not come cheap. Though Kal had given part of his loan to The Stan to cover the rental, Tanya never paid retail.

"This is a non-profit organization, Mr. Thiessen, a religion."

The school principal, a tall, sunburned man in his summer uniform of red vinyl short-shorts and a white tank top advertising Mexican beer, smiled sardonically. "Right."

"You disagree?"

Mr. Thiessen looked around the room. "I do."

"In what way?"

"It's all so transparent. The media circus you've created here. You're certainly not in this for the spiritual reward, Ms. Gervais."

"What is that supposed to mean, sir?"

They were standing in the centre of the gym, on top of a bear-head design. How inventive, thought Tanya. The Banff high school basketball team was called the Bears. She blamed this – the ugly banners on the wall, the motivational posters, and the anti-bullying propaganda in the hallway – on Mr. Thiessen.

"Nothing." Mr. Thiessen walked toward the doors. "Nothing at all."

"You're not a believer?" said Tanya, as she followed him.

"I've been a believer all my life, Ms. Gervais." He did not turn around as he spoke. He opened the door for her, however. "But I believe in an actual deity, a holy book, a tradition, a religion. Not a profitable hoax, if you'll pardon my frankness."

Tanya stopped. "I will pardon your frankness, sir, but not your arrogance. Not your chauvinism. Why are your miraculous prophet and rich religion more worthy of respect than my prophet and poor religion?"

"My prophet is the son of God."

Tanya knew, instinctively, that she should stop arguing with Mr. Thiessen. He would not be converted. And her goal at the Banff Community High School was not to discuss theological concerns. She was there to get a good price on an evening's rental of the field.

What would Stanley do? Tanya paused to wonder about this, and to her consternation she discovered that she did not know what Stanley would do. She made a note on the back of one of her Leap business cards: "Make guide for ethical living, and quick."

In the late 1980s, Tanya had worked as a production assistant for six months in Hollywood. She'd shared a tiny apartment in Studio City with two other women and briefly dated a young actor who was active in Scientology. The young actor was very secretive about his religion, but he did encourage Tanya to take a personality test. Usually when she took personality tests Tanya lied in order to make herself seem more attractive, powerful, and mysterious, but since she knew there would be no future with the young actor she answered honestly.

To her great surprise, the test showed she was unhappy. Deeply unhappy, out of balance, and divided from her fellow human beings. For three days these results echoed in her mind until Tanya nearly made an appointment at the nearest Church of Scientology for a detailed assessment.

Then, one night, just before sleep, the marketer in Tanya understood what was happening to her. She had been lured by fear: the great genius of missionary religion. Instead of signing up for an assessment, for improvement and reward, she broke up with the young actor, quit her job, moved to Toronto, and got seriously involved in cocaine for a year or two.

Stunned by this memory in the hallway of the Banff Community High School, she smiled. Then laughed. Tanya slapped Mr. Thiessen on the back. "Amazing," she said.

"What's amazing?"

She decided not to explain, and excused herself. Tanya rushed down Banff Avenue to the High Country Inn. That morning she had opened the Cascade Conference Room at the inn as a media centre, and had booked a Q & A.

When she arrived, thirty minutes early for the session, the room was already half full. Kal and Maha were distributing copies of The Testament, which Tanya now saw as an insufficient strategic expression of The Stan.

Tanya pulled Maha and Kal to the back of the room.

"What do you want?" she said.

Maha and Kal looked at one another, and then back at Tanya. Neither of them, apparently, understood the question. Tanya wanted to knock their heads together and ask again, but instead she reframed it.

"Search your hearts. If there was one thing you wanted for yourselves and the world, more than anything, what would it be?"

Kal brightened. "It used to be an NHL career. Then it was accordion powers. I have that now. I suppose, more than anything, I want the love of a good woman. And a better relationship with my daughter."

"Maha?"

"To serve the Lord to the utmost of my ability."

Maha and Kal were ripe to be plucked by a serious young actor who believed wholeheartedly in the rather expensive spiritual journey of Scientology. A religion for today had to be intensely personal. Stanley had to be a personal god, and the message had to be pliable enough to promise individual perfection.

"Maha, you're a princess." Tanya placed her palms on Maha's cheeks and kissed her on the mouth.

"Thanks," she said, "I guess."

"Now, get back to work."

At the appointed hour, Tanya stood behind the podium with her notes. "Many of you have been waiting to hear and see something substantial since the night at the Banff Centre. Well, I have *good* news."

FIFTY-SIX

Though she knew it was naughty, Maha stood outside the Lord's room in the house on Grizzly Street and listened to his conversation with Frieda. Maha knew they spoke on the phone every day, and that these calls were disappointing for the Lord. From the street came the usual chanting in a variety of languages. Maha leaned close to the keyhole. The Lord was attempting to convince Frieda that New York was ridiculously hot and humid at this time of year, to wait, to come back. To try, for a day or two. To *please*. . . . No, *please*. He tried to compromise with her, and to Maha it sounded as though his voice broke into weeping. But Frieda seemed to refuse, and the call ended without the Lord saying goodbye. Maha waited a few minutes and then knocked on his door.

"Yes?"

Maha opened it and stepped inside his bedroom. The Lord held the receiver aloft, as though he had forgotten it was in his hand. All at once he sat up straight and hung up the phone. Maha knew he had read her thoughts, and knew it would be redundant to apologize and articulate her sympathies. But she could not help herself. "That is the most difficult part of all this. Leaving what we've left behind."

"Yes," said the Lord, very gently.

"Not that my situation is anything like yours. I was happy to leave." Maha picked at her cuticles. "But I miss the city at sunset, the sound of French, my parents and my brother, the falafel place on Saint-Laurent . . ." All this, compared to the Lord's wife, seemed pathetic. So Maha nodded a couple of times and inspected the three pictures above the fireplace. "Have you been outside today?"

"I looked out."

"The crowds."

"Yes." The Lord smiled and gestured at the adjacent wicker chair. "You have come to discuss something. A problem?"

"Not a problem, exactly."

"Tanya."

"Yes. Tanya." Maha drew blood from the side of her index finger. There was a teapot on the table between them, and a couple of scones. A pile of religious books, from the Banff Public Library, lay on the floor in front of the Lord's feet. Maha took a scone and bit into it, feeling like a snitch or a betrayer. "No."

"No?"

Maha stood up and started for the door. "No. I won't say what I had planned to say. It is premature and . . . malicious. I'm sorry to bother you."

"You're not bothering me." The Lord laughed. "Never think that way. This isn't a corporation and I'm not a busy CEO. No matter what happens, we're still who we came here to be."

"Thank you."

On her way out of the room, Maha felt a sense of withdrawal she associated with smokers and drug addicts. Being in the same space as the Lord, alone with him, filled her with an uneasy pleasure. It was almost too much, and invariably it became queer if it lasted too long. But as soon as she was away from the Lord, Maha wanted to be near him again.

Maha put on a large pair of sunglasses. Still, outside the door, they recognized and swarmed her. There were growing vigils set up for the sick and desperate, and the men and women sitting on the Mexican blankets and in cheap plastic lawn furniture petitioned her for help. They held up photographs and shouted the names of children dying with horrible diseases. As usual, the demonstrators reminded Maha that she was bound for Hell. Thanks to Tanya's agreement with the major media outlets, Maha went unharassed by reporters. However, pilgrims and protesters followed her, and a number of photographers snapped pictures as she started down Grizzly Street.

There was an RCMP guard at the hospital stationed in front of Alok's door, at the request of The Stan's new lawyer, Tanya's friend from Calgary. Inside the room, Alok sat on the edge of his bed staring out at a woman picking up the feces of her Great Dane.

"Hey, good-looking."

Alok turned slowly. "Maha."

In truth, Alok was far from good-looking. There were dark bags under his eyes. He looked older, thinner, and bluer than the man she had met. Maha sat in the chair. "Are you feeling better?"

He smiled. "Absolutely."

"Can the Lord cure you? I mean, if you start to feel bad again?"

"He tried yesterday and the day before. It's upsetting to him, I can see that. But it's completely unnecessary, sweetheart. I'm feeling terrific. Really terrific."

Maha sat in the chair at the foot of Alok's bed. "Tanya is taking over."

"Taking over?"

"Yesterday she held a press conference and said The Stan is about perfecting the self. Making your dreams come true. Pushing through that barrier. You know late at night, on TV, those commercials about becoming energetic and sexy and rich?"

"If only you'll buy the book and tapes."

"That's what Tanya sounded like. The reporters seemed bored, actually. All they want is to see the Lord fly around and make birds talk."

Alok sat back and placed his hands together. There was a new peacefulness about him that Maha both admired and feared. "Having this distance from you all these past few days, I've realized something. I know *why* Stanley has been chosen – for his humility and his confusion. When we sit around and talk about the *purpose* of a religion, we're killing it. We've strip-mined God. Spiritual matters are so literal and functional today, and political, that they're abhorrent. There's no mystery left, Maha, and that's why we're here. To restore wonder and fear and confusion. To allow science to be science, history to be history, rituals to be rituals, myths to be myths. Religions aren't meant to answer the hard questions. Religion *is* the hard question. I'm so comforted by this."

A loud *whoosh* went through the room as a medical helicopter took off. A glass of water shook on the bedside table and Maha ducked, instinctively. But Alok didn't move. Maha didn't see how it could be comforting, what Alok had said.

"I don't think Tanya will agree with you."

Alok smiled. "It's moved beyond her now."

"When you get out of here, you can get rid of Tanya."

"I'm not getting out of here, Maha. You know it."

"Yes you are. Don't say that."

"We can't explain death away, like the great failed religions do. It's terrifying and dark. I can see it now, in my dreams, and it's wonderful. My death is perfect."

Maha looked out the window, not at the mountains or the Great Dane or the cars and trucks and pedestrians with cameras. She looked at nothing, and blew into her cold hands. "There isn't a Heaven or a Paradise. It's here. This is it. The genuine search for meaning –"

"You're talking about meaninglessness."

Alok's forehead was now covered in sweat, and his eyes had narrowed.

"The land isn't dying," he said, sleepily. "It's coming back to life."

"*You're* not dying." Maha slapped his leg, to wake him. "You'll get well again and we'll figure all this out."

"We won't figure it out, Maha. We can't. Isn't that beautiful?"

There was a layer of dust on the windowsill, illuminated by the sunlight. As Alok fell asleep, Maha addressed herself to the unknowable complexity of dust on the windowsill – the anonymous skin cells of sick people. And she didn't see what was so beautiful about it.

FIFTY-SEVEN

Overall, Stanley's time in Svarga reminded him of his visits to New York City. Nonchalant hairy people, architectural marvels, mad conversations. Only this particular trip lacked the merry debrief in his son's guest room with Frieda.

Stanley had now received separate, confused visits from Maha and Kal, both of whom had expressed misgivings about Tanya. Stanley didn't know exactly what Tanya was planning, but he was cautiously supportive of her marketing plan. A spiritual movement needed supporters. More important, and this was his job, a religion needed a comprehensive mythology and a promise; turning Canadians into sopranos wasn't enough.

None of the books he consulted adequately explained the in-between place he had just visited. Applying logic and reason to Svarga, figuring it out, made it seem dark and malicious. He stared at the off-white wall before him, a pen in hand, and waited.

The Stan had to be *new*, a reaction to the spiritual status quo. He would consult with Alok.

"What do you expect to accomplish?" Frieda had said, at least five times now, her voice smoked and dry on the digital line.

For most of the afternoon, various residents of Svarga had walked past his window – aboriginals, explorers, Chinese labourers, King Edward VIII. Stanley tried not to acknowledge them. The sky, and the house, grew dark. Thunder cracked and boomed through the valley. Stanley walked out of his bedroom as the rain began to fall and, through the picture window, watched the petitioners and pilgrims and protesters rush for cover. He took the opportunity to leave the house on Grizzly Street and take a stroll.

Stanley walked up past the Banff Centre and began climbing Tunnel Mountain in the rain. Halfway up, the storm grew nasty. The rain fell in heavy drops, from various directions, as the wind howled through the valley. Spruce bows lashed. Near the summit, a bolt of lightning flicked and the air smelled both wet and scorched. Typical of Alberta, the storm eased as quickly as it had come. By the time it had passed over Stanley, the town below was bathed again in mercifully warm sunlight. He sat on a flat rock on the small mountain overlooking town and watched the returning pedestrians.

One moment Stanley was looking down at Banff, alone on his rock, and the next Darlene was with him. She sat next to Stanley in a baby-blue dress and white hat. Her legs dangled without touching the ground.

"Did you make that storm, Mr. Moss?"

He laughed.

"So how does it feel to be the Lord?"

"I've completely forgotten aspects of my former life. Friends' names, my parents, the 1960s. But I feel healthy. Powerful. Clear. I feel ready to do something extraordinary. Help people. Make things better." Stanley took in the warm, wet air. "It's driving me a little bit crazy, I think. These people expect a lot from me, and I don't know how to *be* for them. A friend? A leader? A distant miracle-worker, speaking through codes and prophecies and metaphors and thunder?"

Darlene took her white hat off and spun it on her index finger.

"So you don't live down there, in Svarga?"

"Oh no," said Darlene.

"Where do you live?"

"Here and there."

Stanley removed his soaked sweater and wrung it out over the fine gravel in front of the rock. He looked at the girl, who had closed her eyes to face the sun. She appeared presidential. "It must be strange, being dead," he said.

Darlene smiled. "Strange is a good word for it."

"Do you know why I'm here, Darlene? What I'm here to do?"

She did not respond.

"Do you know?"

"I'm sure it isn't to float around and throw boulders, Mr. Moss."

"God damn it." Stanley looked up at the blue of the sky, source of inspiration for every prophet and poet in history. He saw only sky.

"Whoever did this to me, I'd like some hint." Stanley addressed the blue of the sky again. "Please. What do you want me to do? Hello? Where should I start? I'm ready! Hi!"

"Excellent strategy, Mr. Moss."

"I'm a florist. That must mean something, right? I think it's the central metaphor of our time, our destination."

"Flower arrangement?"

"Ecology. A new spiritual outlook, organized around ecology, could enshrine complexity, instead of simplicity. We could have rituals, even outdoor rituals, and offer religious experiences that are based in the present tense. Powerful, communal experiences instead of a strategy for easy personal and political wish-fulfillment. I don't know if anyone really *believes* any more – least of all the believers."

Stanley wondered if Darlene understood what he was saying, or cared. She just stared at him, and blinked.

"There's a contradiction," he said. "It's fine for me to think this up. But how do you create a religion that offers little of what people recognize as *religious*?"

Darlene put her hat back on and stood up from the rock. "Good luck."

"Where are you going?"

She shrugged and disappeared into some alders.

When he was a florist, Stanley had loved to be alone in his sales tents. Especially near the solstice, when dusk lasted for hours. He remembered watering the flowers, and the explosive scent at the end of a hot day. Young men and women in the strip mall parking lot, leaning against their cars and kissing. Skateboarding teenagers jumping curbs. Lost dogs. Professional drunks who installed themselves near the Safeway dumpsters after closing time to drink mickeys of vodka and eat expired bread.

Some nights, Frieda would surprise him as he locked up and they would take an overpriced glass of wine on the terrace of the Hotel Macdonald. They would talk, or not talk, and Stanley would sit there with his wife and marvel at his luck. Stanley knew, during those divine middle-class evenings of simple, undeclared beauty, that he and Frieda had discovered and unravelled a secret.

This, just this, Stanley thought, should be the promise of every religion.

FIFTY-EIGHT

The Cave and Basin hot spring, on the side of a giant mountain overlooking the town, was the birthplace of Banff. Kal had read some pamphlets, to impress Maha. The first documented European to discover the misty hot springs had said, "It's like some fantastic dream from a tale of the *Arabian Nights*." Kal repeated this line to himself, as he waded in the far less dreamy chlorinated pool the hot springs had become, waiting for Maha as she changed into her bathing suit. At first, he had installed himself in a particularly egg-smelling corner to watch Maha exit the change room in her white bikini. But the mist had enchanted him, just as it had enchanted that railway worker in the fall of 1883, so he turned around to watch it obscure the pale spruce trees lit by floodlights.

When a gust of wind blew off the steam and low cloud, a number of people who shared the pool seemed to recognize Kal from television and newspapers. He smiled at them and turned away, hoping they wouldn't wade over. So many of the pilgrims spoke poor English. For once he wanted to speak to Maha, privately and intimately, not to a bunch of Italians and South Koreans.

Tomorrow he would open for Stanley at the high school, with an accordion performance. The Stan lacked a proper hymn, so Kal thought he might put together a theme song. Sad, happy, romantic, like a sweet yet unplaceable smell you recognize from grade four. A light touch on his left shoulder interrupted the music in his head.

"What are you looking at?"

"The clouds."

Maha bobbed in the water as she looked around. Wet black hair clung to her ears and neck.

"Don't you think it's out of the *Arabian Nights*?"

"What?"

"The, uh, you know. The mist?"

"I've never read the *Arabian Nights*."

"You're Arab, though, originally?"

"My family descended from the Canaanites. Ethnically, I'm Lebanese."

Kal had meant to sound poetic. Now he was just uncomfortable. No matter what he did, Kal couldn't make his feelings seem natural and right in her presence. It wasn't even enough that he had spent $1,100 to remove his back, chest, and excessive crotch hair. It wasn't enough that he had done thirty-six push-ups and forty-four sit-ups in the change room.

In a desperate attempt to be alluring, Kal pretended he was too hot, hopped up on the edge of the pool, and straightened his posture to minimize any chub and maximize his pectoral muscles. He also flexed his biceps a bit, just enough so that he could still breathe and talk normally.

"What do you think about tomorrow?"

Maha raised her hands out of the water and performed a teeter-totter with them.

Kal had thoughts. Instead of revealing them he said, "You are so, so awesome."

For a long, long time Maha didn't respond. Then she took a breath and it seemed as though she was about to respond, negatively, but she didn't respond. Maha stayed quiet and moved the water around in front of her as though she were performing a slow, gentle breaststroke.

Kal wanted to tell Maha she was beyond pretty, in fact, she was the best hope for the future of the human race. The blood in her veins was sweeter than any music he could play.

But just as Kal started to tell her all of these things – the feeling of delicious loss she conjured up in him – Maha pushed herself off and swam toward the opposite side of the pool. Once she reached it, she climbed out. The mist had already enveloped her, so Kal barely saw Maha tiptoe along the platform and into the women's change room.

FIFTY-NINE

Tanya asked for the bill at Melissa's Restaurant, and smiled one last time. The producer from *60 Minutes* was a man called Francis – which Tanya had always taken to be a girl's name. He wore a vigorously chopped sandy beard and a pressed blue shirt. When he'd arrived at the restaurant for their pre-interview dinner, Francis had been wearing a sports jacket and a patterned grey tie. A plate of chicken cordon bleu, a bottle of Okanagan white wine, and two glasses of cognac later, Francis had removed his tie, his jacket, and his wedding ring.

"Can you answer me one final question?" he said, in a flinty New York accent. "Completely off the record?"

"Of course, Francis." She thought he was more of a Douglas. A Robert. His teeth and lips appeared glued by sugary cognac. "Anything."

"You're exactly like those pretty girls working for hard-core Republicans, aren't you? This is all a role. Right?" Francis leaned over the table and snarled merrily. "Not to diminish the power of what you've evoked here. It's a very resonant story about contemporary Americans' pathetic need for spiritual connection. But really," he whispered, "you're having us on, here, all us media dopes, aren't you?"

Tanya had been careful to sip her wine, and to pretend to fill her glass when she filled Francis's. In her experience, East Coast American media people were adventurous drunks whereas West Coasters drank fizzy water and held eye contact too long.

"If you don't believe what's happening here, Francis, why are you doing the story?"

His eyes, the foundation of his smile, opened and shut slowly. This routine, Tanya saw, often worked for Francis. Francis had partaken in a number of drunk, syrupy, sleepy, and utterly awkward affairs with colleagues and interview subjects. Such affairs weren't completely unknown to her. Francis lifted his hands from the table, as though Tanya had a gun on him. "I'll reserve judgment. I'll be a good journalist. But you really buy this thing?"

"I do. I've seen it and felt it."

"What does it mean to you?"

"Before this," said Tanya, her eyes fixed on him, "I was completely hollow. Completely."

"I'm sorry I missed that. Hollowness makes a person seem trustworthy to me." Francis took his last sip of cognac, the glass shivering slightly. An audible gulp. "Make sure you say it just like that to Safer tomorrow. Just like that."

Outside, on the corner of Lynx and Caribou, in an odd mist, Francis closed his eyes and moved in quite deftly, considering his condition, for a kiss. Tanya didn't open her mouth, and made it quick. The secret, in this situation, when the story had not yet appeared, was to be noncommittal.

"My room is massive," he said. "Jacuzzi. The mini-bar is stacked."

Tanya placed her hand on Francis's chest. "That is a lovely offer, thank you, but I have a lot of work to do before tomorrow night. I don't imagine I'll sleep."

"Another time? We leave Friday."

"Certainly."

Francis winked and, in one motion, turned and waved at the street. To hail a taxi that would not come. Tanya might have informed him that he would have to go back inside Melissa's and call a cab, or better yet walk to the Banff Springs Hotel, but she felt a certain amount of hostility toward Francis. So she left him and walked up Caribou to Grizzly Street, weaving through the tents on the front lawn and gravel driveway.

Swooping Eagle was in the great room, looking at the Calgary newspaper. She stood up to greet Tanya. "I'm so glad you're here."

The heat inside the house and the memory of Francis's kiss made Tanya feel slightly nauseous, and she burped a soup of cognac, fish, and stomach acid. "Why?"

"The mayor came, with some RCMP. They want you out of here."

Tanya didn't have to ask why. The street out front was nearly blocked. People were milling about, with liquor, in the cemetery. But Banff probably didn't have bylaws on the books to break crowds like these. She wondered about the persecution angle. "Did they give you a timeline?"

"The end of the week." Swooping Eagle rubbed her hands together. "Now, I don't want to be presumptuous, but I do have a few spells that might be relevant. That is, if Stanley doesn't want to . . ."

Tanya didn't pay attention. She was writing the morning's

press release in her head, and imagining the spin for *60 Minutes*. For the second time, they'd been evicted for their beliefs. Here in freedom-loving America.

On the way to her room, Tanya's desire for multi-platform communications strategizing faded. It might have been the wine, she thought, or something Francis had said. Maybe it was the reverberations of the word *hollow*. Either way, the gathering, the *60 Minutes* interview, the mayor, Swooping Eagle's tie-dye T-shirt with the elk on it, the prospect of finding new lodging, and press release complications all passed away. Tanya changed into her black teddy, splashed some cold water on her face, reapplied her eye makeup, and dabbed a subtle hint of perfume behind her left ear. Then she pranced down the hall to Stanley's suite.

She did not knock.

Inside, Tanya closed the door behind her and smiled. Stanley was on the bed, with a notepad and *The Book of Mormon*. He looked genuinely shocked to see her in a black teddy. This displeased Tanya; wasn't he supposed to read her mind and anticipate such things?

Stanley said nothing. The overwhelming biological and intellectual force that had led Tanya to his room had not abated, but she was more anxious than usual. "Mark Twain reviewed *The Book of Mormon* as a novel. Did you know that?"

"No."

"The angel Moroni. Do you think Joseph Smith and the boys knew the Greek root *moros*? Of all the names they could have chosen for their . . ."

"I know."

". . . angel."

"I know why you're here, Tanya."

Stanley said this resignedly. The timbre of his voice brought a new desire forth. Tanya now wanted to click her heels three times, close her eyes, clutch a terrier, and wake up in the Dominican Republic.

"And I'm afraid I can't do it."

She walked around the bed and sat next to him. "It's not like you'd be betraying Frieda. This is just a transaction, really, to make sure your seed – your holy seed – continues on." It actually caused Tanya physical pain to say the phrase *your holy seed.* "The son or daughter of a prophet or a God. Of a . . . very special, and attractive, man."

"I'm sorry, Tanya. I can't."

"How do you know? You haven't tried." Tanya leaned in to kiss him and stopped when she made eye contact. His lack of interest was an insult. She stood up off the bed. The muscles in her legs grew weak and a spike of heat passed through her. At the door, she turned. "You'd better be careful this whole thing doesn't go to your head. You're not going to find better, no matter who you are."

"Tanya –"

"This was a one-chance deal and you forfeit. You could have had it. All this." Tanya motioned to herself in the teddy and grasped the door handle. She sought the perfect goodbye phrase, something that would cut Stanley and leave him simmering in regret all night if not longer. All that came to mind, unfortunately, was, "You snooze, you lose."

In the room Tanya shared with Maha, a bottle of sparkling water sat like a consolation prize on her nightstand. Tanya's whole body felt as her legs had before, and the room went dark. In bed she considered removing the teddy, walking to Stanley's room, and asking him, one last

time, if he could deny himself these myriad pleasures. But
when Tanya opened her eyes again all was dark, and she
could hear Maha breathing in the bed across from her.

SIXTY

At the sound of glass breaking, Stanley gathered his most
prized belongings: two photos of Frieda and a painted rock
Charles had given him in kindergarten. If he lost these, he
would forget everything. Then Stanley moved through the
house to rouse the others, so quickly he hardly touched
the floor.

Swooping Eagle did not want to leave. There were too
many sacred objects in the house. Wasn't he God, or an
approximation? Surely he could stop a fire.

"I tried," he said, in the kitchen, as Swooping Eagle
pulled crystals from a cupboard. Creaks echoed from the
second floor and smoke swirled through the upper half of
the room. Swooping Eagle ignored his demands and continued to pack, so Stanley carried her out and met the others
on the front lawn.

Outside, the pilgrims and protesters dragged their tents
and displays away from the house. Maha consoled Swooping
Eagle. "Who would do this to me?" She turned to Stanley
and wiped the tears away with her blackened hands. "Why
am I being punished?"

The fire department arrived and attempted to save the house, but it was too late. The volunteers had blankets for everyone, and words of encouragement for Swooping Eagle. Protesters claimed they were reaping what they had sown, and a small fight broke out. Police officers rushed over to break it up. A neighbour came out with coffee cups on a tray, and crackers with sliced cheddar, for Swooping Eagle and her guests.

Stanley took this opportunity to sneak away. He slipped out of the yard, past several spooked pilgrims, and up the side of Tunnel Mountain.

He reached a spot above the Banff Centre, deserted and covered by trees. In the darkness, Stanley jumped up. The wind, atop and above Tunnel Mountain, was warmer than he had expected. Over the mountain and the golf course, into the deep valley and along the highway, he flew. The night was faintly lit by a crescent moon and the occasional flash of headlights.

It felt presumptuous and arrogant to fly horizontally, so Stanley moved through the July air with his feet down and his head up. There was a small body of water adjacent to the railroad tracks that he could not name, as he was familiar only with the highway view. From above, at night, this was a baffling and – Alok was right – haunted place.

Just outside the Banff Park gates, Stanley crossed the highway and entered Harvie Heights. He lowered himself to the ground in the sandbox of a children's playground, between the swing set and a blue slide. The hamlet on the side of a mountain between Banff and Canmore was perfectly silent and still at three in the morning. Now and then, a warm breeze shook the pine boughs. A bat, and another, fluttered overhead. Stanley couldn't help himself; as he always did with Frieda, in holiday destinations, he wondered about real estate prices.

, The log house was down the road from the playground and community centre. The truck was still warm, from its trip to Banff and back, and Stanley could hear muffled voices inside the house. Around back, there were two large shovels propped up against the garage.

Darlene leaned against the cedar fence that lined the large yard, wearing a baseball uniform. "What are you going to do?"

"Help me," he said.

In the vast backyard, where the property met the forest, Stanley began to dig. Darlene joined him. "What's your goal here?"

"Punishment, I guess." Stanley dug quickly, while Darlene was more deliberate and careful. Her pace seemed more reasonable, so he slowed down. "They have to know I'm serious. Someone might have been killed."

She sighed. "Eye for an eye?"

"Exactly."

"Very novel of you."

She had stopped shovelling and regarded him with a flat, even bored expression. Stanley dropped his shovel. "If you know what I'm supposed to be doing here, tell me. All right? These lunatics tried to kill my friends, and me. The world is full of these assholes, always has been, and since I'm . . ."

Darlene climbed out of the shallow hole, walked toward the house, and returned the shovel.

"Where are you going?"

"Mexico, maybe."

"Should I be Mr. Compassionate? Mr. Empathy? What's the point of empathizing with zealots?"

Darlene didn't answer. The yard was empty.

"Fuck!" Stanley said, into the air, and picked up his shovel again. He finished the hole and ran to the house. Without slowing down, he crashed through a large pane of sliding glass. The cowboys came running. One by one, Stanley yanked their arms out of their sockets and left them to howl and writhe on the floor.

Overbite stared up at the ceiling and said, even in his agony, "How long, O Lord, holy and true, dost thou not judge and avenge our blood on them that dwell on the earth?"

The woman was upstairs, sitting in her bed. She held up a cross and screamed. "Get back, Satan. Get back. For I am protected."

Stanley lifted the woman out of her bed and tossed her into the nearest wall, with just enough force to stun her. She moaned and cursed him. Then Stanley sent her floating downstairs with the others. He did not harm them further, and felt a bit nauseous over what he had already done. They continued to call out and castigate him, quoting from Revelation.

He tossed them outside and dropped them into the hole. Just fleetingly he thought, as they cursed and damned him, that they should not be allowed to speak. And in the next instant they were silent. They opened their mouths and no sounds came out.

"Well," said Stanley, "that's new."

SIXTY-ONE

Maha sat across from two police officers, a man and a woman. Both wore uniforms, which surprised her. On television, the interrogators always wore cheap suits. And offered their subjects something to drink.

They had been asking if anyone at the house had discussed insurance settlements recently, and Maha had been saying no. She was impressed by the number of ways they could ask the same question. They had already spoken to Kal and Tanya so it must have been at least their twentieth time.

"Someone is trying to kill us. Isn't it obvious?"

The policewoman tapped the table with her fingers. "Why would someone want to do that?"

"Because we frighten them. We have genuine faith. We have a leader. We –"

"Thanks," said the policeman, a tall man with perfectly clear skin and rosy cheeks. "You already told us all that, and so did your boyfriend."

"He's not my boyfriend."

The police officers looked at one another briefly, and smiled.

"Did you hear anything?" said the policewoman. "Breaking glass?"

"Something, but I couldn't tell if it was real or in my dream. Then the Lord came and whisked us out." Maha squeezed the plush white lamb she had rescued, her sleeping companion since the third grade. "There wasn't time to take much."

"And the Lord's name is Stanley Moss." The policeman wrote something in his notepad. "The other two didn't call him 'the Lord.' What is he the Lord of?"

"What do you think? The universe. All creation."

"Gosh, we're lucky to have him here in Banff. But why, do you think, would the Lord allow someone to burn his house down? The Lord is omniscient and omnipotent, isn't he?"

Maha looked down at her hands, which were still black. They hadn't given her time to wash them. All she could taste and smell were smoke and fire. "The Lord has a sort of amnesia. He doesn't remember Mohammed, for example. His powers are growing slowly."

"Our research suggests that the Lord is a retired florist from Edmonton."

"Oh, that's just his corporeal form."

The policeman looked up from his notepad. "His what?"

"*Corpo* and then *real*. Put them together and it's a new word."

The policewoman ignored this. "What has the Lord asked of you, Maha?"

"Nothing."

"Nothing, really?"

"Nothing."

The policewoman leaned over the table and spoke in a near-whisper. "You're a pretty girl. He never asks you to show him anything, or to touch him?"

Maha wanted them punished. "Never."

"You don't have an intimate relationship?"

"It's very intimate." Tears flooded into Maha's eyes. "I

grew up feeling him, but I thought he was someone else. Now I know him, personally. I live with him. My heart is his and I am here to serve him."

Maha felt as though she had been too honest, as though she had somehow betrayed the Lord by telling the police about him. But she pushed the feeling away. The Lord embodied honesty and his disciples ought to follow his example.

"What do your parents think of your new religion?"

"I don't know."

"You aren't speaking to them?"

"Not at the moment."

The policewoman made a note and shook her head. "Do you know where we can find the Lord, have a chat with him?"

"No."

"Where had you planned to meet?"

"We didn't. But the Lord knows our minds and he can find us anywhere."

The policeman looked up from the notepad. His partner nodded. "You sure are lucky, to be close to the Lord."

"I am blessed to have been called here." Something occurred to Maha. "If you want to speak to the Lord, just come to the gathering."

"That's at the high school." The policewoman turned to the policeman. "We heard about that from your pals. What do you think will happen?"

"I think we'll all be transformed. Alok says the Lord is here because the land is dying. Or coming back to life, one or the other. Alok says he's going to reinvent the atmosphere of sacredness in the world. Ritual and myth and intuition are lost to us, because we've literalized our religions."

"Who's Alok?"

Maha sighed. She did not want the police bothering Alok. "He's sort of our spiritual guide, but leave him alone. Some fundamentalists – not Muslim ones – kidnapped him and he had a heart attack. We're an oppressed people, you see? That's why I'm here, covered in smoke."

"Where is he?"

"I'm not telling."

The policeman laughed without looking up from the notepad. "Ten to one he's the big guy we're guarding at the hospital."

"Leave him alone. He's sick and doesn't need to be patronized."

"Is that what we're doing?" The policewoman sounded sympathetic but to Maha it was really the opposite of sympathetic. Maha was glad the Lord was not here to discover how she really felt about the policewoman. "We're patronizing you?"

"Yes."

"Would that be z or s in patronizing?"

"It depends," said Maha. "Do your sympathies lie with America or the United Kingdom?"

The policeman shrugged. "America."

"Then z."

"Thanks."

"I suspect," said the policewoman, "that you just patronized my partner."

"Can I leave now?"

The officers looked at one another, and seemed to come to a silent decision. Then the policewoman offered her hand to shake. "Would you do us the courtesy of phoning in and telling us when your Lord returns?"

"When he returns from the desert." The policeman slapped

his partner lightly on the shoulder with the back of his hand. "Get it? Jesus, in the desert, tempted by the Devil?"

The policewoman said, "Yes. We get it."

SIXTY-TWO

One afternoon, in her late twenties, Tanya Gervais was honest with her therapist. At the end of the session, he declared her a possible sex addict. She laughed at her therapist in his East Vancouver strip mall office and laughed for days afterward, recounting the story to her girlfriends. Alcoholics didn't play with their bottles, or withhold booze to cause frustration. If anything, she said, she was addicted to strategic frigidity.

In the hotel shower, a few hours after the fire, the diagnosis came back to her. It felt as though Tanya had succumbed to a cigarette after three weeks of clean air – here, in the room of Francis, the producer. Cigarettes were wrong, sure, but they were right for Tanya. All her old motivations returned in the shower, and she regretted her weak and maudlin response to the slab of concrete that had nearly crushed her. The true message of that rainy day was simpler than she had originally thought: be Tanya, only more so. Don't waste time or squander your gifts on increasing the net worth and global influence of a thirty-six-year-old. It was time to work, and work hard, for Tanya.

She dried herself and wiped the steam off her watch. It was 6:45 in the morning and she had slept for an hour. Tonight could prove to be the most important of her life, and it wouldn't do to be fatigued.

Francis lay sprawled on his bed, naked and snoring, the sheets wrapped around him like a python preparing to squeeze. Looking at him there and smelling the regurgitated alcohol vapour and cigarette smoke that filled the room, Tanya recognized another old feeling. Not shame, exactly, or self-loathing. But wonder. Wonder that she could have touched someone so beastly. Wonder that she could remain a heterosexual, all things considered.

Fortunately, *60 Minutes* had an American-network-sized travel budget. This was no guest room, it was a junior suite in the manor wing of the Banff Springs Hotel. Tanya found some covers and pillows in the closet, pulled out the sofa bed, closed the curtains in the main room, and flopped.

She imagined the multiple successes that awaited her later that day. For a birthday present during university, Tanya's mother had bought her a series of motivational cassette tapes that outlined tactics for personal mastery. This was one of them: *If you do not dream victory, it will not come.*

The phone rang just as Tanya punched through the membrane of sleep. In her confusion, she assumed it was Morley Safer. Who else could it be? She had to make a brilliant first impression, as the great man was surely the contact she needed to succeed in New York City. Morley Safer, a Canadian striver himself, would understand.

"Hello?"

There was a pause, and then a long inhalation. "Who is this?" said a woman with a Brooklyn accent.

"This is Tanya Gervais."

"Who are *you*, Tanya Gervais?"

Tanya was awake now, and she knew who was on the line. "That's not an easy question to answer."

"An interview subject, I suppose. Are you part of the religious cult, then?"

"It isn't a cult."

The woman sighed. "Where is he?"

"Sleeping, in the next room."

"We were supposed to be finished with this. He's had help."

"I'm sorry."

"Oh shut up." The click of a lighter and a deep inhale. Tanya imagined her sitting in the bright kitchen of an apartment in TriBeCa, cleverly purchased before the real estate boom. The woman exhaled with a faint whistle. "Do me a favour and tell me how it happened. Was he drunk?"

"Very drunk."

"Who initiated it?"

"He did."

"Explain."

"You know how it is." Tanya sat up in bed. "He took his tie off, started smiling a lot. With each drink he became more charming and handsome to himself and, in his fantasy, to me. He took off his wedding ring."

The woman moaned with either pain or humiliation, and most likely a mixture of both.

"He was very inelegant about that. I had already seen the ring."

The woman smoked. "So what's your excuse?"

"I have no excuse."

"You knew he was married. Does it give you pleasure to hurt people? I'm Francis's wife, so I know – that must have been the only real pleasure on offer."

Tanya thought about that.

"Aren't religious people supposed to be good? Isn't morality a part of religion any more, or is everyone an admitted hypocrite now? Will you see your shaman and find forgiveness?"

"Our house was burned down. I had nowhere else to stay."

"What does that mean?"

"I mean, Francis was kind enough to let me stay here."

"You didn't sleep with him?"

"He's in the other room. I'm on the sofa bed."

"Liar."

"I swear to you. I'm on the sofa bed."

Without telling a lie, Tanya convinced Francis's wife that they were not sleeping in the same bed. Francis's wife wanted to believe Tanya. So she did. They ended the call amicably, with Tanya promising to write a note to Francis about their oldest child's piano recital. The date had changed.

Tanya lay in bed again, harbouring no ill will toward Francis and his wife. If anything, Tanya was perfectly neutral on the subject of Francis's rampant infidelity. Would it have been better to tell Francis's wife the truth about the evening's sexual adventure, which was a few steps below mediocre? According to the sketchy precepts of The Stan, what was a woman to do in such a circumstance?

For a start, she could stay out of the hotel rooms of married men.

Tanya debated with herself so long that she forgot to visualize her coming victories. Sleep came midway between completely wrong and almost right.

SIXTY-THREE

Kal lurched from hotel to hotel, on and off Banff Avenue, looking for a sympathetic night-desk clerk. Between stops, mightily tired, he contended with disinterested drunks, starstruck pilgrims, and even a university professor from the Greater Boston area devoted to studying "popular delusions." The woman, who wore black-framed glasses that seemed upside down, insisted they get a coffee to discuss his role in the particular madness of this crowd. She left her business card in Kal's hand and, as he walked, it seemed to grow heavy, along with his sneakers and accordion and hair. He dropped it in a garbage can on the banks of the Bow.

It was cold and quiet in the town now. The sun had come up. Kal's breath was visible and his teeth chattered involuntarily. He could taste the smoke on his teeth. There were deer along the river, sleeping on a bed of high grasses. Kal was about to climb in and curl up among them when he passed one final hotel. A motel, actually, a couple of blocks away from the action.

Inside the cramped lobby, the desk clerk was asleep on his arms. Kal put his accordion on a plastic chair and stood in the quiet. It was warm, so Kal blew on his hands and held them over the electric heater on the floor. His shuffling footsteps woke the clerk, who called out, "Help you?"

Kal gave his hands one last rub and addressed the clerk. He had been rejected so many times, at full hotels and inns, he held exactly no hope. "I was just wondering if –"

"You're with Stan."

"I am. My name's –"

"Kal. I've seen you on the news." The clerk gestured at the small television unit behind the counter, which showed two blond teenagers climbing out of a limousine. It was a celebrity gossip show, the sort Kal used to watch in his Saskatoon apartment. "This is a great honour, Kal. I'm a believer myself."

"Well, that's terrific."

"Stick it to the man, I say. They've been trying to keep *the truth* from us for too long." The clerk, who wore enormous eyeglasses and a Calgary Flames hat, smiled and held the smile. His gums seemed an odd colour, in the fluorescent light. "Someone's got to stand up to them, the oil companies and the Chinese. Who do they think we are? Stupid peasants? Feeding us this shit?"

"Our house burned down tonight."

"Your house burned down or *they* burned it down?" He shook his head. "These mofos really don't know who they're up against, do they?"

"We need a place to stay and I was wondering if –"

"It'd be an honour." The clerk, a surprisingly short man, walked around the counter and hugged Kal. "You smell like a fire."

The contrast from cold to hot and dry, here in the tiny lobby, exhausted Kal even more. He didn't know if he could talk. "Four rooms, if you have them."

"I got one. But it's my biggest room, two queens and a cot. I usually reserve it for family and friends, so they don't have to stay with me. My sister and her kids are coming in from Winnipeg this afternoon but I'll put her up. It's a sacrifice, but hell." The clerk punched Kal in the shoulder. "I

have trouble with kids, to be honest. Those goddamn goldfish crackers, they get everywhere."

Kal moved the accordion and sat on the small plastic
chair.

"That's why Stanley's here, to wake us up. This is the revolution we've all been waiting for. Fuck 'em, right?"

"The goldfish crackers?"

"No, man. The military industrial complex."

Kal was really ready to catch some shut-eye. The clerk
could keep talking and wake up Kal later, after he was finished. Then, mercifully, the clerk went back behind the
desk and pulled the key from a wooden slot. "Is Stan
staying too?"

"We got split up after the fire. Everyone had to talk to the
cops. Do I have to sign anything?"

As they crossed the parking lot in the early-morning light,
the clerk asked about The Stan and adultery. Bad or good?
Kal found himself telling the clerk about how Maha had
rebuffed him in the hot springs. Love, Kal, explained, was
hazardous. The heart was a brittle thing, liable to turn hard
and bumpy like a mandarin orange in January.

He was startled out of his story by the sound of a door
closing. Somehow, Kal had taken all his clothes off save the
underwear, and he was in bed with his Roland FR-7 V.
The phone was next to the bed. Kal dialed 911 and asked
the operator to tell the police he was at – where was he? –
some motel. Room 201. There was a bed for Maha and she
didn't have to sleep with him or anything.

"You ever been in love?" Kal said, to the operator.

Someone else was in the room with him.

Kal covered the mouthpiece and Stanley spoke with a
serious voice. His voice was so serious it echoed and hurt

Kal's ears. He told the operator he had to go, and softly
hung up the phone.

SIXTY-FOUR

Stanley was hit with a feeling so wretched he fell out of the
sky north of Banff and landed in a thick cluster of Jack
pines. He extracted himself from the branches and brambles
and ran to the Mineral Springs Hospital, without bothering
to clean the debris from his suit jacket, slacks, and tie.

At the hospital, the security official at the information
desk lifted his hand. "No, no, no. No access until 8:00 a.m."

"I believe my friend may be in serious medical trouble,
and I can help him."

"You a doctor, then?"

There were a number of ways to handle this. Stanley could
sit in a waiting-room chair and watch the clock for two
hours. He could ignore the feeling that had struck him in the
air, that Alok was in trouble. That Alok needed him, desperately. Of course, the feeling had diminished. It was gone,
actually. Maybe this was nothing at all. Maybe Alok had suffered through a nightmare.

"What happened to your suit, sir?" The guard had an
accent. Newfoundland, maybe, or the hint of an upbringing in a rural corner of the United Kingdom. "You're
covered in stuff."

This poorly lit corner of the hospital, with the "Employees Only" door, was nearly deserted. He might have knocked the security guard out. Instead, he sought permission. Stanley concentrated on the guard's long face and moustache, eased his way through his skull, and lodged himself inside for a moment.

"Go right in, sir." The security guard stepped out from behind his oval desk and chuckled, tapped Stanley on the back, and asked him to keep good and quiet on the ward. "Good luck."

Stanley ran down the corridor, reading the handwritten name tags outside each room. It was a small hospital; Alok's room was the fourth on the right. Inside, there were two beds. An Asian gentleman snored in one of the beds, his wife in the chair beside. A book of crossword puzzles had fallen, haphazardly, to her sandalled feet. The second bed was made, the linens folded tightly around, and the curtains on the window were closed.

Outside the room, a porter mopped the floor.

"Alok Chandra?"

"My name's Steve."

"I'm looking for Alok Chandra. He was in this room. A big Indian man?"

The porter shrugged.

Stanley continued down the hall. What he realized, as his black shoes squeaked on the wet floor, was that he could not locate Alok in his mental map of the hospital. A thread had always tied him to Frieda and his friends but, suddenly, his communication with Alok had ended. Stanley hoped he had been discharged, that he had given in to some wild scheme and had driven or flown outside the contact area. Back to Toronto, perhaps, or Nepal.

It was a dim hope. Stanley checked every room and checked a few of them twice, in case Alok was in the washroom. He couldn't see or hear or feel Alok, and the blankness was confusing. Terrifying. Back in the hallway, he prepared to call out for his friend, in case he was missing something obvious. Stanley wanted to turn around and see the big goof, his arms out. *Stan! You're here!*

A man and a woman in white coats stepped through a set of folding doors and stopped. "What are you doing? You're not allowed in here," said the woman. "Who let you through?"

"I need to find Alok Chandra."

Stanley knew, from the instant he said the name and the way the woman's mouth twitched, that he would not find Alok. Her expression shifted from guarded to concerned. She stepped away and led Stanley into an empty room. As she did, the man said, "Aren't you Stanley Moss?"

The woman clicked her tongue in exasperation and closed the door. "I'm very sorry."

"Where is he?"

"Downstairs, I'm afraid. Your friend passed not long ago, a massive heart attack. The surgeon attempted a coronary artery bypass operation, but it was too late. Your friend was –"

"Where is he?"

"He went back to Calgary fifteen or twenty minutes ago."

"I mean Alok."

"Uh . . ." The woman opened the door and stepped back into the hallway. Her colleague was gone.

"I want to be with him."

"Mr. Moss, I understand what you're –"

"Take me to him!"

"I realize you're upset, but it's against hospital procedure. You're not a family member, I assume, and even if you were . . ."

The woman was pretty and stout, with curly black hair and big green eyes. She could not stop him, physically, if he wanted to go downstairs. His first instinct was to shove her aside, into the wall, like the crucifix-clutcher in the log cabin. His second instinct was to grieve for his first instinct, and for Alok. Stanley backed up against the wall.

"I'm sorry," the woman said, again. She checked her watch and swallowed loudly. "But you'll have to leave."

Stanley sneaked inside the woman just long enough. "Take me to him," he said.

The woman led Stanley through a door that required a card. They went down a set of stairs. After his cancer diagnosis, Stanley's last thought before sleep had often been of a morgue. This was where they would take him after he finally, mercifully, died on the palliative care ward of the Grey Nuns Hospital. A perfectly silent room, cold and concrete. Not haunted, like in the horror movies. What ghost would choose to linger here?

There were two bodies, on portable beds, covered in white sheets. "Leave me," said Stanley, and the woman did.

Of the two, it was abundantly clear which was Alok. Stanley lifted the sheet and touched his old friend's face. It was cool and sunken and waxy, and needed a shave. He remembered his grandparents' funerals, his parents', Kitty's, the simple bewilderment. Here but not here. My father but not my father. Alok but not Alok.

Stanley pulled the sheet back a little farther and revealed a giant stitch over Alok's chest. He looked around, to make sure he was alone, and placed his forehead on the stitch.

Stanley put all of his energy into making the heart come back to life. He listened and concentrated and spoke to the heart, coaxed the heart, and pleaded with it. Stanley cursed the heart, and Alok, and whatever god or force had done this to them.

After some time, ten minutes or an hour, Stanley sat in a metal chair in the corner. He did not wonder why, but Stanley did wonder how, for thousands of years, men and woman had created theologies of hope out of the emptiness and failure and deep, ancient, shattering silence that filled the room.

SIXTY-FIVE

The principal of the Banff Community High School, Mr. Thiessen, worked his way through the crowd, hopping up and down. Onstage, Tanya Gervais pretended not to see him. Mr. Thiessen was out of breath and purple-faced when he finally accosted her.

"Where's the security? Who's counting the people coming in?"

Tanya looked down at the gymnasium full of pilgrims and protesters. The gathering was not due to begin for another hour but the space was already filled beyond capacity. It felt like a sauna, only smellier and more humid. There were some sincere-looking old people, squeezed in near the stage, who had faraway looks on their faces. Another hour and they would surely faint. Or die.

"All right, Principal. Can we move the party outside?"

"We don't have a permit for that, Ms. Gervais."

"Come on, grow a pair. This is an historic night, with millions of dollars in free global advertising for Banff. You think the bureaucrats are going to object?"

He turned to the crowd and shook his head. "This is a disaster. You weren't honest with me."

"Sorry. I was thinking five hundred people, tops."

"There are five hundred people in the hallway, Ms. Gervais. And very few of them seem to speak English."

"Really?" Tanya smiled. She was, quite possibly, the greatest communicator in the country.

Mr. Thiessen looked down at his feet and bit his index finger. "All right," he said, weakly.

Tanya had heard him, but she wanted to hear it again. "Pardon?"

"You win, you win. Let's move it outside."

She clicked the microphone on and tapped it with a newly painted fingernail. "Good people, thank you so much for coming."

"Blasphemer!"

Others joined in, with dire predictions for the fate of Tanya's soul. They were quickly overwhelmed by pilgrims, who asked for Stanley.

Tanya waved her arms and spoke loudly and clearly, as if to a crowd of nine-year-olds. "Due to overwhelming interest and safety concerns, we're moving the event to the football field. Please make your way outside, in an orderly fashion.

Once the gymnasium is empty, we'll move the sound equipment and get started."

This news inspired a rumble of dissatisfaction. One of the banners strung up along the gym walls, with an A inserted between the S and T in STAN, fell to the floor. A scuffle started around it.

The project manager demanded more lucrative overtime rates. Tanya pulled a copy of the contract out of her purse, showed him the relevant subsection, and endured some cussing. As the gymnasium cleared out, and the labourers began to take the stage apart, Tanya walked through the storage room and out the emergency exit, avoiding the crowds. Outside the high school, she basked in the fresh air. She took off her shoes and enjoyed the cool of the grass on her bare feet.

According to her watch, Stanley was already two hours late. She flipped open her cellphone and called Kal, who was in one of the classrooms with Maha, working on his performance. "Any sign of him?"

"No," said Kal. "Is that bad?"

Tanya laughed. "We're moving it all outside. Are you ready?"

"I'll start quick and then move into a slow, European cabaret thing. Kind of big and showy."

"Just don't make it boring." Tanya looked up and east, at Tunnel Mountain. She would have bet the Gervais fortune that Stanley was up there, looking down on them. Feeling sorry for himself. "What's Maha doing?"

"Sitting. And, uh, staring."

"At what?"

"I don't know. The window and whatever's outside it. Trees, I guess."

"Is she all right?"

"She's sad about Alok."

"I have a job for her."

SIXTY-SIX

Stanley inspected a pale-yellow flower that grew on the mossy peak of Tunnel Mountain. The sun had set, but he was able to detect a wash of pink in the yellow of the drooping bloom. Thinking about the flower, the *why* of it, was deeply satisfying. The intricacies of the flower, from its tiniest cells to the clarity of its petals, mocked his ambitions. Its interactions with the soil of the mountain, with nearby shrubs and trees, with the rain and the snow and the bees that pollinated it in the heat of the afternoon, exploded with ungraspable meaning. It was the line of poetry that would never be written.

In Banff, below, a massive crowd had gathered at the high school football field. People in the audience had booed Kal's accordion performance, and now the great majority chanted Stanley's name. When he was in high school, this would have been his most potent fantasy. Now, in the absence of Frieda and Alok, it didn't matter how many gathered in Banff. Millions of needy swimsuit models could fill the Bow Valley and still he would be alone.

Once or twice, Stanley and Frieda had eaten dinner in front of singing competitions like *American Idol* on television. They were barrages of disappointment, as the attractive young singers bounced around in the latest fashions, massacring songs written and recorded by other people. As they watched, Stanley and Frieda commented on themselves watching. What it *meant* to share this experience with 35 million people. They made sport out of their moods and emotions: embarrassment, disappointment, anger, a rare hop of pleasure. It seemed a potent marker of North American culture, this television format. Unironic youth desperate to be famous, exalting the easy and grotesque songs of the late twentieth century as though they were hymns.

No doubt, these were the moods and emotions of God, if he allowed himself to feel: embarrassment, disappointment, anger, a rare hop of pleasure. Only God didn't have the luxury of feeling detached and superior, like viewers of reality television. He was implicated in every shot fired by every zealot. Every rape and holocaust and starving child was his.

Stanley was ready to accept the role of spiritual liaison and, in Alok's honour, return to human beings the possibility of transcendence. Moral action would be based on individual experience, self-awareness, and mythology in The Stan, not the literal interpretation of ancient books. He would do away with apocalyptic visions and teach his followers to engage with the earth and its mysteries, to seek meaning in the relationships among flowers and sex and death. Stanley didn't want to be a tyrant about it, but he would ask people whether or not *American Idol* allowed them to feel complete.

The roar of the crowd intensified. Nearby, an owl hooted. Maha appeared at the top of the trail, jogging. She stopped and lifted her hand when she saw him, bent over to catch her breath. Stanley pulled the flower from the soil, placed it in his lapel, and joined Maha. Together, they started down Tunnel Mountain.

Stanley knew she desperately wanted to ask a question. He also knew Maha didn't want to hear, or believe, the answer. A bat flew low overhead and gulped a mosquito. Stanley placed his hand on Maha's shoulder.

"Why didn't you save Alok?" she said.

"I tried, Maha. I'm sorry."

"What do you mean you tried? You're the Lord."

"No. I'm not the Lord."

"Don't say that."

"It's true and you know it's true."

"Please. Stop."

Halfway down, Stanley reached inside his suit jacket for Alok's note. According to the big man's will, written on Mineral Springs Hospital stationery, all of his material possessions went to The Stan. He wanted to be cremated and have the ashes scattered atop Tunnel Mountain. The manager of a funeral home in Canmore had been only too happy to offer inauthentic condolences in muted tones and provide a quote. What had Stanley wanted in an urn?

Stanley passed the note to Maha and she read it by moonlight.

"The crowd, down there, they don't deserve you. If Alok died for this, for them, well –"

"He didn't die for anything, Maha. He just died."

She shook her head in disagreement and put the note in her pocket. Even in a pair of poorly fitting jeans and an old sweatshirt, Maha was beautiful. "What are you going to do? Can you fix them?"

"I don't think it works that way. What I plan to do is explain what I've been thinking. If they don't go for it, I guess I'll go home."

"Do you think Frieda'll see you on TV?"

Stanley tried to imagine Frieda in front of their television, but he couldn't see it. In what part of the house did they keep the television? He couldn't see the television or the house. "She's probably watching a musical."

They reached the bottom of the mountain and walked through the neighbourhoods. The chanting became louder and louder.

"What are you going to tell them?"

"I'm going to tell them about the flower on the mountain."

Maha nodded and said, "Oh, good," but she wasn't thrilled with that answer.

Black smoke rose up from the environs of Banff Avenue. People screamed. It looked and sounded like a hockey riot. A block away from the high school, Stanley passed three youths in the midst of overturning a car.

This was Stanley's fault, so he did not punish the teenagers. Politely, he asked them to stop. They did, and followed him. Outside the fence, there was a scuffle. One of the combatants, a large and angry man who had removed his shirt, knocked out a protester with a single punch. The victim lay unconscious on the sidewalk, in the midst of a seizure, protected from further harm by friends while the assailant hurled biblical invective upon them.

The shirtless man recognized Stanley.

"He's here. Oh, he's here, he's here, great God almighty he's finally –!"

Stanley blinded him. The man screamed and fell to his knees.

Quickly, word spread that Stanley had arrived. The people conversed in whispers. Stanley hopped the chain-link fence and made his way along the outer wall of the high school until he reached the stage.

"Finally." Tanya's eyes were red and fierce. Her smile was monstrously artificial. The sound from the crowd was nearly deafening, and there were two camera operators behind her, so she had to speak directly into his ear. "Get your ass on that stage."

Stanley ignored her and took Maha's hand. "Are we ready?"

SIXTY-SEVEN

Maha could not go five seconds without coughing. It felt as though she had swallowed an ant colony of doubt, and its citizens were biting their way out of her.

The night had turned cold, and her sweatshirt reeked of stale beer. The jog up Tunnel Mountain had made her too hot, but now she shivered with chilly anxiety. A number of people in the audience, impatient and possibly crazy, had broken limbs and bloody faces. And the Lord was going to tell them about a flower?

Onstage, Kal sat slouched in a dark corner. The Lord embraced him, and whispered in his ear. Kal stood straight up and plugged his accordion back into the public address system. A hollow whine sounded as the Lord approached the microphone. The blue and green lights of cellular phones, held aloft to take photographs and short movies, made it difficult to see the audience.

A shot, and its echo. Maha had never heard a gunshot before, so she had no instinctual response. She didn't duck or cover her ears. There was a second bang, and a third. A series of screams rose up from the audience. The people in front of Maha, in the first rows, were pressed against the iron barricades in front of the little stage.

"Stop," said the Lord. "Stop moving. Please, relax."

The Lord dropped what appeared to be three bullets on the stage. He then raised his arms. Two men, one on the Lord's right and the other on the Lord's left, rose up out of the audience. They held guns. As he floated up, one of the men fired his gun into the air. The other dropped his weapon and merely flailed and screamed.

Maha wondered if the Lord would drop the men to their deaths, but they continued to rise up. The schoolyard went quiet again, and those in the front rows breathed normally, as everyone watched the two men rise up, and up, and up until they were two spots in the blackness – obscuring the stars, and then, with a final gunshot, disappearing.

Chanting began anew. The flashes from cameras and cellphones had a strobe effect. Maha was compelled to run up onstage and apologize to the Lord for the way she had been feeling on the walk down the mountain. Millions of people died every day, and it would have been indulgent and iniquitous to single out Alok. It *had* been a lesson.

From every direction, people clamoured and called out for miracles. They screamed for cancer, for global warming, for animal rights, for tougher drug laws, for weaker drug

laws, for revolution and partition, for lottery winnings, for
their dead loved ones, for the Prime Minister, for police bru-
tality, urban sprawl, poverty, abortion, Palestine, water
supplies, Sunnis, air pollution, Trisomy 18, sex tourism, the
end of the world.

Those who had come to denounce the Lord as the Devil
exploded in anger. They jumped up and down with their
signs, and Maha could see their spit silhouetted in the floodlights, along with the bugs. The Lord took several steps back
from the microphone and watched, in apparent fascination.

She climbed up onstage. "Do something."

The Lord turned to her and blinked. He nodded, cleared
his throat, and grasped the microphone. "I want you to
know that your religions, your prophets, will be welcome in
The Stan. So will your experiences and opinions. I'm not
here to tell you what to do, or give you a set of rules."

With the sound of his voice, the crowd quieted. "For most
of my life, I was a florist. I want you to calm yourselves and
think, for a moment, about a simple flower." The Lord pulled
the microphone off the stand and walked to the front of the
stage. "A simple flower that is inconceivably complex."

Maha walked back off the stage and down the small set
of stairs. There were shouts from the audience again, taunts
and demands.

"My daughter has leukemia!"

"Affordable housing!"

"Cure my acne!"

"Save us!"

The Lord said nothing for a while. The requests from the
audience became a general roar. Finally, he interrupted.
"Please, stop. I can't give you these things. God cannot give
you these things. That's not what He's here for, if He's here

at all. Now, please, consider a flower, the tiniest part of the tiniest flower in the most unnoticed corner of your garden."

He continued speaking, but the cries from the audience overwhelmed him. Next to Maha, the gentleman from *60 Minutes*, in jeans and a blazer, crossed his arms and smiled. Someone threw a cup of coffee and it splashed onstage before the Lord. Coffee splattered his grey slacks below the knees.

"They don't give a shit about flowers!" said Tanya, and the camera operators laughed.

Kal stood at the back of the stage. His accordion was still plugged into the public address system, though he hadn't played a note. Maha stood on the bottom step. "It's not working," she said. "Go tell him to do something."

"Like what?"

"He's the Lord."

Kal approached him and they spoke, near the microphone. The noise from the crowd became louder than ever, and a number of items landed on the stage. Coins, Slurpees, baseball caps, empty bottles. Amid the chaos, Kal started to play his accordion. It was a deep, slow, and simple waltz.

The Lord began to sway. A few notes into the song, the crowd fell eerily quiet. From where Maha stood on the first step, it was difficult to see. She assumed the Lord had quieted them, so he could explain more fully the nature of the religion. For a better view, she climbed up two more metal stairs. And at first, she didn't believe it. Everyone on the football field – the young, the old, the sick, the angry – had partnered up, and they were dancing a Viennese waltz, in absolute synchronicity.

Both camera operators climbed the stage scaffolding to get shots of the crowd from above. The waltz was soothing to Maha, after the deafening selfishness and malice of the crowd. The Lord turned to Kal and winked, and he transitioned from a waltz to a jolly, old-time jazz song. The people broke away from their partners and began to tap dance on the grass. Again, the Lord choreographed it so that each dancer was in time with the next. Children and the elderly tap danced with equal skill and enthusiasm, with beatific smiles on their faces. The ground shook. Again, Kal switched the tempo, slower this time, and the audience formed an enormous, moving pinwheel. The pinwheel transformed itself, like the beads in a kaleidoscope, into other complex, symmetrical patterns. All the while, the dancers smiled.

In time with the music, which Maha recognized from long-ago violin lessons as Bach's "Toccata and Fugue in D Minor," the dancers formed giant concentric circles in the middle of the field. The two outside lines moved one way, the next two lines moved the opposite way, and so on, like a spinning target. Then, gradually, the circle rose up from the centre, level by level. The four dancers in the middle floated at the top, while the outside lines remained on the grass. It was an enormous human wedding cake.

Finally, Kal began to play a triumphant song. It reminded Maha of a national anthem, but she couldn't place the nation. In groups of six, the dancers flew into the air, holding hands, spinning like fireworks. It sounded like the finale, and it was the finale. As the song eased toward its conclusion, the dancers eased down to the grass. And then, for a moment, silence. Kal wiped his hands on his jeans and the people looked at one another, and up at the Lord.

"You have to think of yourselves as part of something grand and holy. There is no man, or Lord, who can save you." Stanley pulled a flower from his lapel. "This is God." He pointed at Kal. "This is God." He pointed to

Tunnel Mountain and, presumably, the sky. "That is God."
And, finally, he pointed at the audience. "You are God. Take
one of these away, and there is no God. The pursuit of God
is God."

For a moment, it seemed the Lord had them. It seemed
they understood, or were at least willing to try. And then,
like an erupting volcano, it started again: requests,
demands, prayers, cries of desperation. The Lord turned off
the microphone and jumped off the stage, into the crowd.
He disappeared into the darkness.

SIXTY-EIGHT

The morning after the big dance number on the football
field, Tanya argued with a bearded man in a corner of the
Banff Springs Hotel parking lot. They interrupted each other.
She tried to finish a phrase beginning with, "Francis, I'm not
responsible for . . ." while Francis said, again and again, "But
you're the flack. How else are we supposed to . . ."

Several paces away, Kal and the gentleman from *60
Minutes* sipped coffee. They had already talked about the
weather, twice. To Kal's surprise, the gentleman from
60 Minutes – whose name was Mr. Safer – was a Canadian.

"The mountains used to be colder in August," said Mr.
Safer. "Didn't they?"

Kal shrugged. "I'm twenty-four."

"Not nostalgic for a better time yet?"

"Oh, sure," said Kal. "I was nine years old once, like everyone else."

Mr. Safer nodded and sipped his coffee.

The bearded man and Tanya approached. It didn't seem possible that they could have agreed, but something had been decided. "Let's go," said the bearded man.

In the grey SUV, similar to his ex-wife's, Kal sat next to Tanya in the back seat. "What's happening?"

"Stanley disappeared. I received his consent, set it all up, and now he's gone." Tanya punched the back of the seat in front of her. "I am going to sue his ass, and I mean it. What does he think this is?" She whispered in Kal's ear, so the two men up front wouldn't hear. "After last night, we have an opportunity to engage the world here. That's a market of 6 billion people. Do you understand how much *money* comes with this sort of attention? He's the number-one search term on Google."

"I never thought of it that way."

Tanya stopped whispering. "Jesus, Kal. Wake the hell up."

The accordion was on the floor at his feet. Kal was careful not to get the soles of his shoes anywhere near it. The longer it stayed clean, the better. Tanya's breath smelled of coffee and mint. He wished Tanya had sat up front, or walked.

Stanley had left a small urn containing Alok's ashes in the motel room, along with a note. The following morning, they were to scatter his ashes from the top of Tunnel Mountain. Maha was supposed to carry it, according to the note. Kal wished *she* were next to him in the SUV, instead of Tanya. But Maha was out looking for Stanley.

"I promised these guys an exclusive." Tanya resumed whispering. "Do you know what that means? The ramifications of it? Now that Stanley's pulling a diva routine on me, they have nothing."

"But last night –"

"Everyone got that footage. It's everywhere."

Kal understood, but when he searched his heart he discovered he didn't care. In fact, television interviews and money and markets and the sound of the word "exclusive" infuriated him. They were only a few blocks away from the burned house on Grizzly Street and Kal realized he didn't want money and Google – because Stanley wouldn't. Alok wouldn't.

"Let me out, please."

"What?" said Tanya.

Kal leaned forward and tapped the bearded man on the shoulder. "Stop the truck, please. I'm gonna help Maha look for Stanley."

"Imbeciles!" Tanya clutched his jacket. "If Stanley doesn't want to be found, he won't be found."

With a chuckle devoid of glee, the bearded man pulled over. Kal unfastened his seatbelt, removed Tanya's long white fingers from his jacket, picked up his accordion, and opened the door.

"This is so bush," said Tanya. "Are you choosing to be a loser?"

Kal slammed the door shut. The SUV idled for a moment. Inside, Tanya and the bearded man screamed at one another. Mr. Safer waved at Kal through the passenger window as the rear wheels spun gravel and they took off up the hill.

SIXTY-NINE

According to Islam, to incinerate a corpse is abhorrent. It is like laying a body out in the summertime to be devoured by crows and raccoons. Maha felt somewhat disgusted by the shiny pot of ashes in her hands. It was not a sacred privilege for her, as Stanley had assumed it would be.

In his absence, she had come to believe the awful words he had said. Stanley was *someone* but he was not the Lord. Maha still loved him, of course, and basked in his power like the heat of the sun, but if the Lord was not the Lord, who was he? What was his mission, and what was her role? She needed clarification.

For the last two nights, lying in a bed three feet from Kal's, she'd hardly slept. Stanley's disappearance, the void of comfort and meaning, was like hunger. In bed, the words came back: *The Lord is God, the one and only. Allah, the Eternal, the Absolute, the Self-Sufficient master. He begetteth not, nor is He begotten. And there is none like unto Him.*

Maha wanted to be alone on the hike up Tunnel Mountain, but Kal would not leave her side. Neither of them wanted Tanya to be there, but it was Alok's funeral, they couldn't command Tanya to smoke cigarettes and talk on her cellphone somewhere else. Kal rubbed Maha's back and said, again and again, "How you doing? Any better?"

"The same as five minutes ago."

"Cool," said Kal. "Cool."

The urn was a small aluminum jar with a lid that did not quite fit. There was a sticker on the side advertising the funeral home, and another sticker on the bottom of the jar identifying its origin in China.

It was somewhere between warm and chilly, this day in late August. A new contingent of the curious was beginning to arrive in Banff. There were fewer Canadians and more Europeans and Asians now, attracted by the dance number broadcast around the world. If Banff was at full capacity before, now it was ludicrous. The mayor had declared a state of emergency. There was a new noise about the town, a city noise: a constant rumble of vehicles and voices.

Maha had overheard a newspaper reporter ask one of the new arrivals, a pretty American woman, why she had come the morning after Stanley's speech.

"If this is the start of the next great religion, I want to be part of it," she had said. "You can be on *The Amazing Race*, but people forget you by the next season. Religions last a really long time."

A middle-aged couple descended and Kal stepped back so they could pass on the trail. The man wore a cowboy hat. He started to pass and then stopped. "You people are with The Stan."

"Yep," said Kal.

"We flew up from Portland to see him." The man smiled. His teeth were yellow and crooked, as were his wife's. They wore new hiking boots and jackets. It occurred to Maha that they would die soon. So would she and so would Kal. "When's his next big to-do?"

"You're wasting your time and money," Maha told them. "Stanley isn't coming back."

Tanya, in the middle of a phone conversation, jogged down to them. But she had gained too much speed, so she crashed into Kal. "Don't listen to her," said Tanya. "She's suffering from post-traumatic stress syndrome, like so many of your brave troops in Iraq. The truth is, Stanley will have another public address very soon."

"No, he won't," said Maha.

The man and woman continued to smile, though an aspect of discomfort had sneaked into their facial muscles. "Can we join you?" said the woman.

Maha displayed the urn. "Scattering ashes, sorta private."

"Next time!" said Tanya, with a fake laugh. "Keep watching for news. It's coming soon, bigger and better than last time."

The couple continued down the mountain, slowly, as the man suffered from a limp. Maha felt sorry for him and for his wife, sorry for infecting them with Tanya, who resumed her phone conversation.

"I really want a big animal to eat her," Maha said to Kal as they followed Tanya. "I wouldn't even turn away."

"Come on."

"All right, I'd turn away. But I wouldn't cry."

Kal shook his head.

"All right, I'd cry."

At the top of the mountain, they waited for Tanya to finish her phone call. She promised Stanley would be back in town in two days. Stan was seeking wisdom in the wilderness, like all the really top-shelf prophets.

Tanya folded her phone shut and dropped her red cigarette pack on a flat rock.

"Please pick that up," said Maha.

"The garbage?"

Maha wanted to shove Tanya off the edge. "Yes, the garbage."

"Go fuck yourself." Tanya pointed her phone at Maha like a gun. Then, slowly, she picked up the cigarette package and dropped it in her purse. "Satisfied? Everyone satisfied?"

Now that they were up there, it was obvious no one knew what to do. If Stanley was right and God was a *process*, then it did not matter what they said about Alok. As long as they said something. But Maha felt – no, she knew – that Stanley was wrong. It rested in her shoulders, this unhappy certainty, and pounded in the back of her head. She fiddled with the lid of the urn.

The wind blew their hair into their eyes. Tanya opened her cellphone, looked at the screen, and closed it again. She and Maha made quick eye contact with each other and then regarded their footwear and the riverbank below, where Stanley had jumped.

Kal stepped between the women. "Alok, uh, was a super guy. I just want to say I wish I knew him better, and I'll always remember him." He cleared his throat and nodded, and looked up. "I love you, pal, wherever you are!"

"I love you too." Maha wiped her eyes and fiddled with the urn some more.

Tanya slipped her cellphone into her pocket and clasped her hands, looked down. "Well, Alok, we went through a lot together, didn't we, old buddy? And –"

The urn popped open and Maha jostled it violently as she attempted to grasp the lid. Alok's ashes twisted out and into the air. Some drifted over the edge and into the valley. Other bits settled on the rock of Tunnel Mountain. The remainder, like a naughty ghost, blew into Tanya's face and hair.

SEVENTY

On his first visit to Svarga, Stanley had not noticed the diversity of architecture on the town's fringes. Mexican adobes, minimalist Japanese dwellings, sod houses, New York brownstones, twisting two-storey brick houses with bistros on the street level. He also had not noticed the sasquatches' dark eyes. Up close, there was a distinct sadness in them, and something like wisdom.

The sasquatches led Stanley down a long white stone road surrounded by plane trees. They came to a white château, with two turrets, built as a bridge across the river. Several men and women in matching uniforms tended its gardens.

"What is this place?" Stanley asked, breathing in the Svarga air hesitantly. He couldn't help wondering if it might revert to water.

The sasquatches did not answer. Standing between two of them, Stanley found they smelled like the hair of a seven-year-old boy with neglectful parents. At the entrance of the château, the sasquatches stopped and bowed, and a woman in a tattered man's business suit appeared in the murky sunshine of the inner castle.

"Welcome to Chenonceau," she said, with a strong French accent. "Have you been here before, or to the original in the Loire?"

"No."

"My name is Aurore." The woman in the suit offered her hand in such a way that Stanley did not know whether to shake it or kiss it. So he kissed it, and the woman laughed. "We are curious about you."

"Do the sasquatches talk?"

Aurore ignored his question and led Stanley deeper into the castle and up a set of stone stairs. "Underneath the castle, you may have noticed the River Cher."

"Yes." Stanley waited for a pertinent piece of information about the River Cher, but there was none.

"The gardens outside are reproductions of those enjoyed by Diane de Poitiers and Catherine de' Medici. Are they not beautiful?"

"I didn't get a good look at them, to be honest. The sasquatches –"

"After Versailles, this is certainly the most beautiful château in France."

Stanley decided it was futile to attempt anything like a conversation with Aurore. As she walked, her legs made a clicking sound. Walking behind her, Stanley could see through a hole in her neck.

On the second floor of the château, Aurore stood outside a darkened room. "When Catherine de' Medici died, she left Chenonceau to Louise de Lorraine, wife of Catherine's son Henry III. Of course, King Henry III was homosexual."

"Of course."

"But Louise de Lorraine was completely devoted to him. When Henry was assassinated in Saint-Cloud, she had this room designed as the site of her grieving, and a great darkness settled over Chenonceau." Aurore waved him inside with a curtsy. "Please."

"Thank you."

Mary Schäffer stood in a window. She was not wearing

her characteristic clothing. Instead, she wore a pair of baby-blue yoga pants and a white T-shirt. Mary Schäffer turned and smiled. "I've been waiting for you."

The ceiling of the room was black and decorated with silver tears and adorned crosses. In a corner of the room, a four-poster bed with blue sheets and a green tapestry.

"Queen Louise did nothing but pray after her husband died. She surrounded herself with woe."

Stanley admired the room, the window, the view of the gardens, and the river from the window. "I didn't leave the Bow Valley."

"No, you didn't. And you weren't kind to those lunatics I sent after you. By the way, it wasn't easy to return to them the power of speech. I had to erase their memories!"

"What did you ask them to do?"

"To capture and kill you, obviously. It would be much simpler and much more pleasant if you were dead, as you're attracting even more idiots to the valley. I trust you'll make another public appearance and send them away, this time without any of your magic tricks." Mary Schäffer rearranged a couple of the flowers in the bouquet before her. "Get things back to normal."

"What is normal?"

"You know what normal is."

"I don't."

"If you start a new religion, it will only make things worse. They aren't interested in an *actual religion*, you must know that. It's an insult, what you're doing."

"To whom?"

"Shut up, immediately. For you, that is an unanswerable question." Mary Schäffer did not make eye contact with Stanley. She continued to fuss with the bouquet.

Stanley waited for Mary Schäffer to answer his unanswerable question. Svarga made him feel dizzy and he wasn't sure how long he would last there. Time did not seem to be an issue for Mary Schäffer. So Stanley picked up the vase and tossed it out the window.

"Now then."

"You're a madman, Mr. Moss."

"If I stay here much longer, I will be."

Mary Schäffer swallowed and shook her head. It took some time for her to recover her smile. She turned to the door. "Aurore, would you please fetch us some tea? Nothing with caffeine?"

"*Oui, madame.*"

Mary Schäffer sat across from Stanley, at a wooden table. When Aurore was gone, Mary Schäffer pounded the table. "Some discretion, Mr. Moss, please. What do you think this is?"

"I don't know. That's why I'm asking you."

"It's very painful for us, Mr. Moss. Like you up there, we endeavour to forget painful realities we cannot change. We create diversions. Soccer matches, bullfights, Chinese operas. Once a year, Shakespeare comes and directs one of his plays using the original London cast. Unlike you up there, we don't have death as a balm. Things being as they are, we know we will be here in Svarga forever."

"Things being as they are?"

"God has abandoned us."

SEVENTY-ONE

Aurore brought the tea, rooibos with licorice, and pleasantries were exchanged. Mary Schäffer asked if Stanley enjoyed rooibos tea, as it was packed with antioxidants and other disease-fighting agents.

There wasn't space in Stanley for rooibos tea. He considered tossing the teapot, after the vase and bouquet, out the window. To squeeze this desire out of his mind, he considered the decommissioned fireplace with its two giant logs.

Mary Schäffer dismissed Aurore and poured the tea. There were also biscuits and dark chocolates in the shape of pyramids. "That's why we don't know who you are or what force created you. God has been gone for too long."

"Uh-huh."

"We hoped that by killing or expelling you we would gather some insight."

Stanley laughed. What else could he do? "So this is Hell."

"I resent that." Mary Schäffer gestured at Stanley's glass. "Drink, Mr. Moss."

"You first."

"We don't eat or drink. We're dead people!"

"Then why do you have rooibos tea, and biscuits, and tiny chocolates?"

"Why, for visitors. Like yourself."

"You get others?"

"Occasionally scuba divers will go too deep and pass through the membrane. We can't let them go back, of course, so we have to kill them. Drink up!"

Stanley sipped the tea. It struck him that Frieda would love it. "Is it Purgatory?"

"Now you're getting warmer. It's like a border town, between Canada and the United States. Or Kashmir. Yes, it's like Kashmir."

"And on the other side of the border?"

"There are theories." Mary Schäffer lifted a hand and touched her hair. "Do you know? Have you heard something?"

"No."

A sequence of loud noises floated through the window and Stanley looked out. A line of people and sasquatches wound its way through the gardens of Diane de Poitiers and Catherine de' Medici. At the front of the line, several men and women played drums and blew a variety of horns.

"What's this?"

"The parade of gloom. They've been doing it since God abandoned us. Ignore them."

"Why did God abandon you?"

"He abandoned *you*, *too*. What arrogance! If it weren't for you, up there, God would still be with us. Taking us over the border into Paradise." Mary Schäffer joined Stanley at the window. "I have half a mind to kill you myself, for your impertinence."

"Did you ever see God?"

"No, not me. They say God's assistant visited a few times after I arrived but I wasn't mayor then. There were a few closed-door meetings, a reception in Central Park. By the time I found my way out of the desert and understood Svarga, even God's assistant was gone."

"What did God look like? The white hair, the beard?"

Mary Schäffer laughed. "There's no point killing you. You're too young and naive to be anyone, or anything, of importance." She left the room and Stanley followed her. They walked along the corridor, down the stairs, and into a large room decorated with painted tapestries and an engraved oak door. "This is the guards' room," said Mary Schäffer. On the other side was the entrance to what looked like a chapel.

"The original is filled with depictions of the Virgin. When we built this Chenonceau, we substituted God for the Virgin."

Stanley did not understand what he was seeing. The paintings, the stained-glass windows, the marble statues all depicted a young girl. They weren't exact representations, as the clothes were all wrong, but the artists were clearly inspired by Darlene.

"Darlene?"

"What?"

Stanley laughed. "That's Darlene."

"What's Darlene, you silly man? Who is Darlene?"

"No one. Nothing. It must be the tea."

"It must be the tea!" Mary Schäffer pushed Stanley aside. "God has taken many forms, of course, but sometime in the 1500s God became a twelve-year-old girl."

"Why?"

"I won't talk to you any more if you don't stop asking inane questions."

"Sorry. I'll try to do better."

"Now, I suppose you came down to Svarga to see your friend."

"My friend?"

"Your friend. The portly one, with the brown skin. Alok."

"Alok's here?"

"Of course he's here! He's in the desert. That's why you came, isn't it?"

They stood in front of the chapel, and its depictions of God, for a long while. The sound of the parade, which had briefly faded, started up again. "You'll take me."

"On one condition."

"Anything."

Mary Schäffer led Stanley out of the château and on to the grounds. The parade of gloom, which had wound its way around the gardens and beyond, turned out and down the road lined with plane trees. "When you get back up there, you go out of the valley and leave us in peace. I can't ask you to commit suicide, which would be my preference, because I'm sure you lack the inner strength. But I've already expelled you and wasted no end of energy having you killed. Please, be a gentleman."

"And leave."

"Yes! Yes! Go back home."

They walked past the forecourt and the marques tower, beyond the gardens. Ahead of them, the parade musicians played an off-key version of "Louie, Louie." In the back, sasquatches clapped their hands and danced for God's return.

SEVENTY-TWO

The lush, continental climate of the Loire Valley gave way, in an instant, to a stiflingly hot desert. Stanley and Mary Schäffer passed from rivers and drooping trees into the sands of what appeared to be the Sahara. He looked back, and the Loire Valley had disappeared.

The Svarga sky looked how the sky *up there* ought to look in the middle of the Sahara, deep blue and streaked with mysterious white blotches. They walked for what seemed like several hours, in deep sand. To Stanley's delight, he grew neither tired nor sweaty. There were smooth hills and spines in every direction, extending in bleary mists. Over one last giant hill of sand, a slightly more forgiving landscape appeared, with short grasses and scorched, leafless acacia trees, their branches twisted like falcons' nests.

Ahead in the shimmering heat, another parade of gloom snaked its way around a small hill. Three goats with bells tied around their necks stood near the parade and ignored its singing, dancing, drumming, and horn blowing. It was easier to walk on this sand; Mary Schäffer adjusted her dress. Just beyond the hill, Stanley made out a few lopsided, windowless stone houses.

"This is as far as I go," said Mary Schäffer, as she walked back toward the hills of the Sahara. "This is a miserable place, with scorpions and rodents. Do you like horned vipers? I hope so."

Stanley was about to call out to Mary Schäffer, to thank her for bringing him to this place, when he heard a familiar voice behind him. A familiar yawn. Alok stood, stooped, in the entrance of the poorest-looking house. With a gush of relief, Stanley ran to his friend. They embraced. "I thought you were gone."

"I am gone." There was no wildness or joy in Alok's voice.

"I'm so sorry I wasn't there. If only I could have . . ."

Stanley wanted to continue but Alok had turned away. He wore a yellow muumuu, with reproductions of cave paintings. "Would you like to come inside?"

"I'd love to."

Alok allowed Stanley to enter the stone house first. It smelled of rotting meat and feces. To spare Alok's feelings, Stanley pretended he did not smell the smell. There was a stone bed and a mattress built with twigs. There was a broken chair and a giant wooden bowl and several blankets. In the middle of the house, a firepit.

The living arrangements were, in sum, horrifying. "Are you being punished?"

"You can't choose when, where, or to whom you're born. Near as I can tell, it's the same down here." Alok kicked at ashes in the firepit. "I've done everything to get rid of that smell."

"There's no water. Do you want or need some?"

Alok sighed. "I do *not* like being dead, Stanley."

"Surely, you can earn your way out with good works. You aren't stuck here forever."

"That's a nice thought, but there's no real logic to this. Near as I can tell."

Alok led Stanley out of the stone house, to the best place for sitting, in front of an acacia tree. The heat didn't seem to bother Alok, but there was an atmosphere of monotony in the windless air of the desert community. They sat, and Alok pulled out a small, rusted knife. He whittled a twig that had fallen nearby, and sighed.

"Did you hear?"

"Hear what?"

"No God."

Stanley nodded.

"People don't talk about it. But what a kick in the teeth. I mean, all the things I could have done differently. Sex, travel, hunting. A New Age store? How humiliating."

One of Alok's neighbours, a bald white man wearing Bermuda shorts and a floral-print shirt, stepped out of another stone house and stretched and waved. He walked over to a black goat and rubbed its head. "Some kind of weather!"

"Yeah, that's a good one, Irving." Alok tossed his whittled twig in the sand and addressed Stanley. "Same joke every day – if this *is* a day. I don't know."

They sat together, leaning against the tree, watching the goats. Stanley put his hand on Alok's shoulder and held it there. He wanted to say something, to make his friend feel better. But nothing seemed right. Alok sighed some more and time, or something like it, passed.

"How often does the parade of gloom come by?" Stanley hoped to instigate some liveliness in Alok. Perhaps there were benefits to joining.

"Time to time. They're assholes."

They sat for several more hours, until it began to seem pointless to Stanley, his being there. He watched Alok whittle, and nearly laughed out loud as he recalled his conversations with Darlene. "I know what I have to do."

"It really doesn't matter what you do," said Alok, without looking up from his gleaming twig. He wasn't whittling it for any purpose. Soon, it wouldn't be a twig any more. It would be scrapings on Alok's lap.

"Maybe I can come back."

"Don't. Don't come back here. It doesn't help."

Eventually, when it appeared Alok was asleep with his eyes open, Stanley kissed his friend on the cheek and stood up. Stanley waved to Irving, who responded with a hearty, "See you soon, Jake!" and returned to his stone house.

Several minutes, or hours, or days later, Stanley passed out of the desert and into the bottom of Lake Minnewanka. The sunken village appeared before Stanley, so he jumped and rose to the surface.

SEVENTY-THREE

How many times had Tanya Gervais said hello, in a chirpy voice, to Carol the executive assistant? How many times had Tanya asked about Carol's chubby daughter with the lisp? How many times had Tanya called Carol's chubby daughter with the lisp *a beautiful girl*?

Too many to count. Yet here she was, two weeks after Stanley's disappearance, begging.

"You know how he is, Tanya. If I put you through, and you make him angry, it's my ass."

"No, it isn't. I'll vouch for you. Darryl knows you and I are old friends."

"Old friends?"

"Please, Carol. Five minutes, what's it worth?"

Carol said nothing for a while. There were some clicking sounds. "Approximately seventeen dollars."

"Are you bribable, Carol?"

"Meaning?"

"I would like to help you and your beautiful daughter out. It isn't easy being a single mother, I know that. And Vancouver isn't getting any cheaper. How does a crisp one-hundred-dollar bill sound? You could buy Annie a new dress."

"Who's Annie?"

Tanya covered the receiver and said, "Fuckass," so loudly she worried the Banff Springs Hotel management would kindly ask her to vacate the premises. There had been enough money left over in the The Stan account to take over Francis's room. Francis, like a lot of the media based in New York, London, and Paris, had given up on Stanley returning. And so had Tanya. "Suzie. I meant Suzie."

"My daughter's name is Miriam."

"Of course it is, Carol. Of course it is."

The executive assistant took a deep breath. "Tanya, I told him this morning that you'd been calling. You know what he said?"

"No."

"Well, I'm not sure I can repeat it, in good conscience."

"I've had a change of heart. Tell Darryl this: I've got some great ideas about Leap's strategic vision, moving forward into the twenty-first century, and –"

"The vice-president position has been filled."

"What?"

"I'm sorry, Tanya."

The blood vacated her brain and landed in Neanderthal stress locations like the stomach and thighs. Tanya wasn't about to give up. "He can make up a new position. Vice-president of brand awareness. Vice-president of audience relations. Minister of propaganda."

Carol was clearly embarrassed for Tanya. She made a wet sound with her mouth, and delivered a pity-sigh over the digital phone line. "I'm sorry," she said again, and hung up.

To the ensuing dial tone, Tanya retorted, "I hope your fat fucking daughter gets diabetes."

And then Tanya went to the hotel gym. It had been several months and she was out of shape. She had to use five-pound barbells instead of ten-pounders for lunges, and she produced at least double her normal amount of lower-back sweat on the stationary bicycle. In the pool, treading water after a few laps, Tanya briefly considered going under and staying under. She wouldn't die, as the pool was full of potential rescuers. But her convalescence would be deliciously restful.

Tanya sat in the sauna with several other naked women, all of them talking about their children. Upstairs, after her shower, Tanya put on the white bathrobe provided by the preposterously expensive hotel and stared out her window at the river, the harsh mountains, the endless fields of pine and spruce trees. It all made her feel claustrophobic and nauseous. She missed the ocean.

The phone rang.

No one knew she was there, except for Francis the adulterer and Darryl Lantz. Francis the adulterer was on the airplane to New York, drunk most likely, so it had to be the thirty-six-year-old genius.

It was a voice she did not recognize, saying her name with a hint of an accent. He introduced himself so quickly Tanya did not catch his name. "I am in the lobby of your hotel, and I have a business proposition for you. May I come up, or should I meet you in the lounge?"

Tanya was still registering her disappointment at not hearing the voice of Darryl Lantz. It was dreamlike, her disappointment, a power outlet of wretchedness. She did not listen closely, but she agreed to everything. Yes, fifteen minutes. Yes, the lounge. Yes, see you soon.

All of her clothes had burned in the fire. To work out, she had worn a rented bikini and bare feet. Now Tanya put on her panties inside out and slipped into the outfit she had been wearing for two weeks straight – a black skirt, a tight-fitting red shirt with a stylized dragon on it, and a little blazer. She dried her hair and stared in the mirror, fascinated by the dark ovals under her eyes.

Tanya had never understood homelessness. In Vancouver, she had been surrounded by it. They slept in the alley behind her building and shopped in its dumpsters. They broke into her Hummer, twice, even though there was nothing to steal. She saw it and felt it now, how the reversal could come at you like a kung fu chop. How it could tear you out of yourself and leave a shell, an envelope of dry skin, behind.

In the elevator, a man in expensive eyeglasses looked variously at his Blackberry, his shoes, and her breasts. Her bra was so dirty it itched, so Tanya had decided to go without it.

"You like Banff?" said the man, whose suit and hair and skin were grey.

"Piss off."

The man did not look up from his Blackberry again.

There was a large window in the lounge. Something about the quality of light prompted in Tanya an instant thirst for a dry gin martini.

It was impossible to see anyone, as they were all backlit. One of the silhouettes stood up from a chair near the window and approached her. He was not a large man, though he had a confident gait. Tanya placed the accent when she saw his face, and remembered seeing him on the television news.

The man smiled without showing his teeth. He shook Tanya's hand and slipped her a card. "My name is Dr. Lam. I am a psychiatrist, palliative care specialist, and, from time to time, an entrepreneur."

SEVENTY-FOUR

Maha lay awake for hours every night, listening to Kal snore. It was a quiet and gentle snore, compared to her father's, but she knew it would increase in power and intensity with every grey hair that appeared on his head. In the long days after Stanley's disappearance, filled with miserable interviews and appearances in Banff, Maha grew suspicious that she had been part of a delusion. She watched Kal in the adjacent bed, his mouth open, his hands folded across his chest like the dead.

University professors met with her. Media outlets interviewed her. The president of the Muslim Canadian Congress took Maha out for southwestern cuisine and begged her to stop talking about her conversion to The Stan. It was insulting to her community and the religion of her blood. And though she did not admit it to him, Maha agreed. She stopped.

On the September day *60 Minutes* was to air its investigation of The Stan, Maha walked the Mount Rundle Trail alone, up to the point where climbers – equipped with ropes and helmets and Gore-Tex – played on the rocks. A thick band of cloud eased over the valley, darkening the day. It began to snow, and her feet were cold and soaking wet by the time she'd reached the motel parking lot. Where she decided to make a decision.

Option one: buy a bus ticket to Montreal. Option two: walk out of Banff to the Trans-Canada Highway, lift her thumb, acquire illegal narcotics, and live the life of a hobo, thereby insulting her community and the religion of her blood with even greater force. Option three: stay in Banff and wait for Stanley.

The third option could entail an unalterable rejection of Islam. The longer she stayed with Kal, in the motel room, as the snow fell around them, the more it seemed inevitable that they would move into the same bed. She knew how desperately Kal wanted to be with her, and his sincerity and devotion were endearing. He was handsome and kind, unlikely to turn on her. To enter into a romantic relationship with a white man who grew up Christian and dropped out of high school would not only further horrify her parents, it was also contrary to every one of Maha's girlhood dreams. Their children would be stuck between two ethnicities. They would live in squalor, possibly in rural Saskatchewan. Kal's snore would progress, along with the size of his waist. His grammar would not improve substantially, despite her ministration, and slowly he would begin to resent her. Upon her death the privation would be eternal. From the prairies to Hell.

Maha climbed the stairs and stood before the motel room door. Inside, television noises. The dull murmurings and chuckles of Kal and Swooping Eagle, over what sounded like an antidepressant advertisement. She put her hand on the door handle and, for what she knew would be the last time, attempted to engage in a conversation with Stanley. A request for guidance, an argument, a renunciation.

In response, more television noises. The wind, gusting through the courtyard parking lot. A diesel truck. Silence.

SEVENTY-FIVE

The real estate agent dismissed the country music ringtone blaring from his cellphone. He made it seem like a sacrifice, the sort of thing he did only for his most valued clients. "A Calgarian," said the agent, looking down at the number. "Dude can wait."

Dr. Lam smiled politely. "We really appreciate that. Thank you."

"Yes," said Tanya, with less enthusiasm. "Thanks."

The storefront was a few blocks off Banff Avenue, on Squirrel, but it was spacious and well priced. There were large street-front windows and new hardwood floors. The light fixtures were tasteful. Tanya walked through a swinging door in the back and discovered a small kitchen with a sink and a stove.

"It was a snowboard shop," said the agent. "Before that it was a café."

Dr. Lam discussed Internet hookups and phone lines with the agent while Tanya inspected the kitchen and opened a heavier door in the back. There was another street, Big Horn Street, and beyond that the railroad tracks and wilderness. She wondered if a bear had ever been hit by the train.

She heard Dr. Lam tell the agent to wait. Then they stood together in the small kitchen. "What do you think?"

"It's the best we've seen," said Tanya. Philosophically, she had always considered herself a businesswoman. An independent. But the reality of investing her own money and time and future in a business – a religion – suddenly frightened her. "But maybe something even better, and cheaper, will open up."

"This isn't about money, Tanya."

Though she disagreed wholeheartedly, Tanya nodded.

"So?" Dr. Lam turned on the water. The tap sputtered and water gushed forth. "Shall we?"

"I hate to give cash to that little weasel out there."

Dr. Lam smiled. He was a constant smiler. "Tanya. We're building a church of positive thinking here. Of graciousness and good humour."

"Oops. What I meant to say was: This is our first step in changing the world, and becoming ridiculously, fabulously wealthy."

Dr. Lam paused momentarily and frowned. From now on, Tanya decided, she would keep the brutal-realist thinking to herself. He pushed through the swinging door and Tanya followed.

The agent was on his cellphone now, looking out the window. "You have to seize this opportunity, Larry. *Seize it.*"

As a producer, Tanya had learned how to discern good acting from bad. This was bad acting. She would have bet the first two lease payments on the Squirrel Street store that Larry, if he existed, was not on the other line.

"Listen, Larry. Can I call you back? Excellent." The agent clamped the phone shut. "So?"

Dr. Lam glanced at Tanya and flipped the agent a thumbs-up.

On the way to Starbucks, where they would fill out the paperwork, Dr. Lam explained The Stan to the agent. The agent was confused. How could they run a religion without a leader?

"You can have a leader without a *leader*," said Dr. Lam. "How many movements thrive with a leader versus movements that have thrived in the very creative absence of a leader? It is preferable to have a pliable leader, a leader without any human weaknesses, so our teaching is pure. For that, we need the memory of a leader. All praise be to the greatness of Stanley Moss, but he has the ability to circumvent himself."

This seemed to be too much for the agent. He stopped asking about The Stan and talked instead about the idiots in Ottawa who put strict limits on condominium development in national parks.

At a table crowded with contracts, Dr. Lam wrote a

cheque for the first month and Tanya wrote one for the second month. Of course, the agent didn't have time for a celebratory coffee; he had another client waiting. The agent put on his sunglasses and, on the way out the door, advised them to "Stay out of trouble."

"Thanks for the meaningless cliché," said Tanya, in a chirpy voice.

It was happy hour at Starbucks. For the price of a tall, one could upgrade to a grande. So the café was full, and loud. Even with her large sunglasses on, a number of the customers recognized Tanya. Future paying clients of The Stan, she told herself, and the image of the smug, lying agent passed.

Dr. Lam, in what Tanya would soon see as a characteristic tone of voice, warned her against disdainfulness. "Sincerity is the beating heart of The Stan," he said.

They acquired coffees and pastry, and Tanya pulled out her checklist. The computer geek was already designing their website. Dr. Lam was working on the multiple-choice psychological profile that would welcome the unhappy and the curious to The Stan. Tanya was writing up a second draft of The Testament. That night, they would brainstorm and coin a series of new words, at once religious and scientific, to augment their recipes for maximum human performance. Each word would be a marriage of Hebrew, Latin, and computer programming.

All they had left now was the most difficult task: convincing Stanley Moss to co-operate.

Out the window, the snow was beginning to melt. Still, summer was over and autumn did not really exist at this elevation. Tanya sipped her medium-roast drip coffee, the cheapest item on the menu, a tax write-off under the "Entertainment" column. The coffee was bitter and comforting, too hot, a Vancouver sensation. Tanya looked at her watch and surveyed Starbucks, to see if anyone was watching her. The urge to check her nonexistent Blackberry warmed and quickened her further, and she discovered she both loved and despised the Joni Mitchell song playing in the café. Tanya was back in entertainment.

SEVENTY-SIX

The water at the surface of Lake Minnewanka seemed much colder than he remembered. Stanley had not expected to see snow on the ground. It hung wet and heavy in the valley and topped each peak. Branches of poplar and pine trees around the lake bowed to Stanley as he walked up the beach.

A man in a bright-yellow ski jacket stood nearby with his standard poodle. The dog hopped and growled, waiting for his master to throw the ball.

"Hello."

Stanley waved. There was no sign of Swooping Eagle or the end of summer. "Do you know the date?"

For some time, the man simply stared at Stanley. Then he reached blindly behind him until he found his station wagon, and supported himself on it. The poodle gamely attacked the ball, picking it up, tossing it on the rocks, and chasing it. "It's September. The twenty-first."

Stanley thought about that for a minute, marvelled at the weeks he had spent underwater. "You live in Banff?"

The man, somewhat recovered, nodded.

"Can I get a ride?"

"You're that guy, aren't you?"

Stanley nodded. "I am that guy."

Driving toward Banff on the Minnewanka Loop, the driver did not look away from the road. The dog, from its blanket on the back seat, licked Stanley's hand as though it were covered in beef.

As they crossed the highway, the man swallowed. "People're gonna go crazy, with you coming back like this."

It was an older car and it smelled strongly of dog. Stanley knew, from the interstices between the frightened man's words, that he was in some financial trouble. An investment had gone bad.

Knowing what he knew about Darlene, and the powers she had bestowed on him, Stanley closed his eyes and wished contentment and a measure of success upon the man, whose name was Marcel.

They entered Banff town limits and crossed the railroad tracks with a bump. Stanley pulled his hand away and the poodle, in the back, howled. "I'm sorry," said Marcel. "She never does that."

Stanley allowed the dog to lick his hand some more, and addressed himself to Kal, Maha, and Tanya. "Can you turn right?"

"I surely can."

Maha pulled a black suitcase along the sidewalk of Lynx Street, near the hospital. Anxious to speak to her, Stanley opened the door before Marcel could stop.

"Mister –!"

"Thanks, Marcel." The car halted and Stanley stepped out. "You're going to be all right, Marcel. Better than all right. Don't despair."

"Don't?" Marcel's mouth drooped.

"Don't."

Marcel smiled, feebly.

It was a cool day and they were far from the bustle of the shopping district. He closed Marcel's door, waved him away, and jogged to Maha. Stanley was thrilled to see her, and hugged her before she had a chance to adjust to his presence.

Maha wriggled out of the embrace and squinted at him. "Where did you go?"

"Lake Minnewanka." Stanley considered telling her about Svarga, and Alok. But she was already upset. Her eyes were dark and sore with fatigue, and her hair was pulled up in a wild bun.

"Why?" She teared up.

"It's difficult to explain."

"You gave up on us."

"No, Maha. Not on you."

"I looked all over. I tried to talk to you." Now she initiated a hug, and then pushed him away.

"You're leaving?" he said.

"There's no reason to stay, is there? To me, God's not a *process*. That's not why I'm here. I came here to do something pure and honourable for you. For God." Maha kicked her luggage. "A process? Do you know what it's like to be seventeen today?"

How had Darlene, when she was an active God, gone about making her children feel whole? Perhaps Stanley had just condemned Marcel to an uncritical and dangerous happiness that would lead him straight to a mental institution or jail.

There was a bench nearby, and Stanley led Maha to it. Two joggers passed, and lifted their athletic sunglasses to make sure they were seeing what they were seeing. Maha adjusted the lapel of Stanley's suit, which she had tousled.

"You're a Muslim again."

Maha nodded. "I always was."

There was no point warning Maha against any errors she might make. Stanley had enjoyed several conversations with God and he was no closer to understanding her plan. "I'm very sorry I disappointed you, Maha. That wasn't my intention. But of all of you, you're really the one I shouldn't worry about."

"It was my own fault, for thinking you were . . ."

"You're going back to Montreal."

"I guess so."

"Kal's pretty upset?"

Maha shrugged.

"You could stay a little longer and help me finish this."

"I don't know what *this* is any more, Stanley. They had to bring the army in, just after you left, because so many people were showing up with nowhere to stay. They all just wanted to . . . actually, I don't even know what they wanted. To dance, I guess, and fly around."

"They weren't listening, Maha. I tried to tell them, and show them, about The Stan. But there's still a great opportunity here, and I want you to help me."

Maha stood up. "My bus leaves in half an hour."

They hugged again. "You sure you won't stay?"

THE BOOK OF STANLEY

Maha pulled her suitcase down Lynx Street, turned a corner, and disappeared.

SEVENTY-SEVEN

A camera operator discovered Stanley Moss on the bench. Squawks erupted from the man's pockets. He was tall and hesitant, with a moustache and a cleft palate. "I got him, I got him," he whispered into his vest.

Another arrived, from the opposite direction.

The cameramen stepped in front of each other without taking their eyes from the viewfinders. Female reporters came running, their high heels click-clacking on the sidewalk, one from the north and one from the south. Stanley got up and started back to Banff Avenue. At least this way, they weren't bothering Maha.

Even in September, with neither warm air nor snowy ski hills, the crowds in central Banff were mad. Much of the media had given up on him, but many had stayed. Word moved quickly that Stanley Moss was back, and two more cameras appeared. Non-media approached: women running with babies, the elderly in motorized wheelchairs, sales professionals, hippies.

How did you learn to float?

Are you the messiah and, if so, which one?

Any chance you want to fight crime?

Is The Stan a religious system or a philosophy?
Bird flu: is it really coming?
So what's up with Jesus?
Are you an illusionist?
Is time travel possible?
Can I have three wishes?
Is there any way to stop Iran from developing nuclear weapons?
Are you happy?

The final question stopped him. Stanley thought immediately of his wife and, in that instant, he could not see her face, hear the timbre of her voice, or remember her name. Around him, the crowd seemed suddenly vicious. Stanley pushed his way out and commanded them to stop following. He walked down Bow Avenue, along the river. Many of the picnic tables were taken by young people, drinking beer and rye whisky, but one was empty. Stanley sat in a puddle of cola and watched and listened to the water passing. He tried to remember something – anything. Her name had two syllables. Her hair had been blond.

Once, long ago, he'd known where this water stopped flowing. He had even fished in the Bow as a child. His father had told him that the trout stocks had been accidentally dumped in the river on a hot day in 1925, when a truck broke down on its shore and the driver had to do something with the slowly dying fish fry.

Stanley approached the river and briefly lost himself in time. He was with his father, with his faceless, voiceless, nameless wife, in 1925. The truck was broken, the day was hot, and the fry were slowly dying.

Teenage cackles startled him out of his thoughts, and he walked around the corner to the motel. The door on the second floor was open. As he entered, Kal was sitting with his back to Stanley, playing his accordion and singing. "*I offered to convert, I offered to convert, I offered to convert to her religion.*"

"Kal."

The young man hopped off the bed and jogged across the room. "Finally," he said. When he reached Stan, he fell to his knees. "Make her come back."

Stanley couldn't hold it back. He smiled.

"Make her love me. No, don't *make* her. I don't know. Just do something."

"I'm sorry she left, Kal."

"How can you let her? And where have you been? When you're around, Maha's happy."

"What was that song?" Stanley extended a hand and helped the young man to his feet.

Kal pulled a can of ginger ale from the mini-fridge, opened it, and took a long swig. The way he stood, the abandon in the gesture, and his choice of poison proved that Stanley had not actually ruined Kal's life. "It's called 'She Rejected Me Because I'm White And Stupid.'"

"Play it for me."

"All right, but picture violins and one of those old-fashioned, ringing carnival sounds. The accordion is the big dog in this song, but there's an overall funhouse vibe."

Stanley listened intently, and imagined the funhouse vibe. It was a song of self-pity, with lyrics about the explosive beauty of Maha. The curtains were closed and the lights were dim, with an orange tint. His wife had always treasured moments like this, with a lick of genuine oddness about them, especially when they experienced them together during vacations. One morning in Santa Fe, for instance, they'd been sitting outdoors at a café when a small, one-legged dog, apparently unaccompanied by its owner, had wheeled by on a modified skateboard.

What was her name?

At the end of the song, Stanley applauded and whistled. "That was magnificent."

"Yeah, well, thanks for the musical ability."

"I am very proud of you, Kal."

"Really?" Kal sniffed and wiped his nose. "Did you know my dad died when I was small? My next song will be about him, I think. I never grieved right. Then there's songs about Layla, of course. And all the time I wasted on video games, and –"

There was a knock on the door. Kal wiped his eyes with the sleeves of his shirt and gulped back sobs. He slapped himself in the face and ran on the spot for a while.

"Am I good?"

His eyes were red and his cheeks were flushed. The tear-streaks were visible. "You're good," said Stanley.

"It'll be the motel manager. He's mad at you for not being a proper God and wants next week's rent."

Kal opened the door and Tanya was standing there, with new snow falling behind her. Dusk had arrived; she was lit by the old-fashioned yellow lantern on the landing. Tanya entered, and then, so did Dr. Lam.

It took only a moment to read their intentions, but Stanley was genuinely surprised to see the doctor. "What are you doing?"

"Mr. Moss, Stan, I'm here to help." Dr. Lam wore a leather jacket and tan pants. Heavy flakes of snow melted in his hair and on his shoulders. He stepped forward, shook Stanley's hand formally, and stepped back again. "A lot has happened since that first visit in my office. You're a home-town hero."

Kal returned to his seat on the bed. "You guys want ginger ale? Tap water?"

"It's a pleasure, Kal," said Dr. Lam. "I'm a real fan of your work."

"Sincerely? 'Cause I have a new song."

Tanya sat in the desk chair. "Super."

SEVENTY-EIGHT

Dr. Lam pretended to enjoy the French cabaret song with lunatic lyrics, and Tanya saw him for what he was – her saviour. Her true saviour. It never was Darryl Lantz, and Stanley Moss was an amateur. A typical Canadian, afraid to go big.

Not only was the doctor determined and savvy, he was also earnest and heartfelt about helping people. This combination of traits would free Tanya to sell her vision without compromising for the Aloks and Mahas of the world, who wanted to undo the Industrial Revolution and live in stupid bliss like a bunch of yaks.

She applauded when Kal finished his song. Dr. Lam said, "Bravo, my friend, bravo."

"Yeah, I'm putting together a whole album about my broken heart."

While Kal and Dr. Lam continued to exchange pleasantries about his accordion music, Tanya searched her bag for some eau de cologne. The room smelled of armpits, ginger ale, cheap shampoo, and disappointment. She looked up and discovered that Stanley was staring at her. Reading and judging her, with those tiny, dark eyes. That suit. *Get another suit, for Christ's sake.* She wanted to stop thinking thoughts that came naturally to her, so she smiled. "How *are* you, Stan, anyway? It's been ages."

"Get on with it."

"Right then." Tanya pulled out the legal documents and placed them in a pile on the table. "What do you know about Scientology?"

"Nothing," said Kal.

Stanley continued to stare. She experienced some discomfort in the area of her bladder, and wondered briefly if he'd hexed her with an infection. "How about Buddhism?"

"My ex-wife did yoga." Kal bit his bottom lip. "It started in India, right?"

Tanya decided to stop looking at Stanley altogether. Kal was there, as was the stained and worn-out carpet. "Unlike the three western religions, Scientology and Buddhism operate without a specific, named deity – per se. They have truth-tellers, of course, in L. Ron Hubbard and Buddha, and there's the vague higher power thing. But despite the golden rule, which appears in every religion with roots in the Axial Age, Christians, Muslims, and Jews would find little in common with Scientologists and Buddhists, as far as how their systems work."

"We already tried to start a religion," said Stanley. "It failed."

"How did it fail, exactly?"

"They wanted a spectacle. They wanted miraculous fa-vours. They weren't interested in a story, or a mythology, or a guide for ethical behaviour suited to the new century and its challenges."

Dr. Lam took notes as Stanley spoke. "Fascinating," he said.

"I know that hurt you, Stan. That's why you ran away." Tanya motioned to the papers on the table. "We're proposing to relieve you of that pain with a wholesale takeover of The Stan. All we need are signatures from you, authorizing it."

Again, he stared.

"We don't need your signatures, actually. Our legal advice suggests we can run with this, if we like. But we wanted to be fair and transparent with you."

Stanley shook his head. "Don't lie to me. It doesn't work."

"Heh heh." Dr. Lam rubbed Tanya's back. "She's been under a great deal of stress. It won't happen again."

Kal played a low note on his accordion.

The conversation had turned sour. Tanya had under-estimated Stanley's capacity for rage, his interest in her undoing. It was sad, really, the way he tried to blame her for his own mismanagement of The Stan. She had done everything within her power to mould the religion into a pliable and digestible commodity. Only that wasn't good enough for Stanley. He went off-message, out of hubris, like failed politicians and CEOs. Without market research, without reliable advice from an experienced marketing and publicity professional, no one could survive the critical rigors of the digital age. *Not even you*, Tanya thought.

Kal fumbled with the accordion on his lap, possibly preparing to sing another song. As much as Tanya wanted to speak, she saw that it merely frustrated Stanley. Like *she* was the only liar in the world. Her knight, her redeemer, destroyed the uncomfortable silence.

"In the United States, the most extreme warmongers are supported by evangelical Christians. In Europe, the secular state is under attack by fundamentalists. Then you have the Middle East, where a prerequisite for violence and destruction is what?" Dr. Lam waited a beat. "Faith. Yes, my friends, everywhere you look, goodness is under attack by the faithful. Now, how could this be?"

Kal looked up at the ceiling. "I don't know."

"Splendid." Dr. Lam winked at Kal. "Only the most cynical and manipulative among us know the answers to these questions. Unless, of course, you happen to be an award-winning psychiatrist, palliative care specialist, and author, with rigorously researched insights into these questions."

Dr. Lam sat next to Kal on the bed and faced Stanley. He spoke quietly. "Everything you have said is correct, Stan. As a species, we have progressed in certain ways and regressed in other ways. We have insulted our prophets and our gods, haven't we, by demanding personal and political favours from them? We begin with a political and social philosophy, one that empowers us and validates our way of life, and then we chauvinistically apply an old-time religion to that philosophy. We have collectively forgotten the true role of spirituality in our lives. It happened centuries ago, didn't it?"

An almost imperceptible nod from Stanley.

Tanya saw their books in the front window of every store in the developed world. Their infomercials on every television, every computer screen, every iPod. She saw her photo in *O, The Oprah Magazine*. There would be a long profile, written by an amateur sociologist, in *The New Yorker*. Eventually, the BBC would stop being so fucking snotty. Tanya would be the Saint Paul of The Stan. As soon as Stanley Moss stepped aside, she would make him into *Stanley Moss*.

She handed the legal papers to Dr. Lam and he pitched Stanley and Kal. What they needed was permission to use his name, his image, his history, and his likeness. Film rights, of course.

There was another long silence as Stanley flipped through the papers. He looked up at Kal and smiled. "What do you think of this?"

The motel room door swung open. Snow spun around Maha as she closed the door behind her. She stomped her feet on the mat, shook the white out of her hair, and went to Stanley. She took his hand. "Let's finish this."

"Good little helper," said Tanya.

Maha looked up and frowned at Tanya, as though the former VP of marketing and development were a rotting side of pork.

"What are you doing here?"

Tanya answered in the most polite tone she could manufacture. "We're here to save the land from dying, just as Alok wanted."

SEVENTY-NINE

In the snow, now twirling in a blizzard, Stanley walked past shops and restaurants through the dim lamplight. Servers and cooks sat at the otherwise empty tables, their feet up, sipping wine. All was silent but for the dull rumble of heaters and the distant engines of four-by-four trucks. The snow on the sidewalks was thick and wet, almost untrampled, as the uncommonly fierce storm had chased everyone off Banff Avenue.

Stanley turned up Caribou Street. The snow swirled around him in gusts. Darlene was waiting on a tombstone in the middle of the cemetery, wearing a dark-brown skirt and what appeared to be black ballet shoes. Her denim jacket was undone, over a cable-knit sweater. Her skin was so pale and she sat so still that Stanley thought she had become a doll. The snow did not seem to touch her.

Now that he knew Darlene, Stanley did not know how to address her. He averted his eyes, like a weak wolf addressing the alpha. "Your scarf is pretty."

Darlene tugged on it. The scarf was off-white, perhaps silk. "I was in Paris yesterday. Have you been there in October?"

"No."

"If you're on a budget, the hotels are much cheaper than in springtime."

"That's good to know."

Stanley could not see the town from the cemetery, or even a hint of its existence. There was only snow, the outline of trees, and God. "I was in Svarga, and Mary Schäffer told me –"

"I know."

"They have pictures of you. They say –"

"I know, I know."

"Well. You might have said something."

"What? What could I have said?"

"Whatever it is you say to people. *I am the Lord your God who took you out of Egypt, the house of bondage,* whatever."

"And then what? You tell two friends and they tell two friends and twenty years later someone writes a bestselling book and it's a load of clichés dressed up as prophecy." Darlene slid off the tombstone and adjusted her skirt. "I guess nothing takes twenty years any more."

"Why me? Could you tell me *that* at least?"

"Not in any satisfying way."

"Why have you hidden yourself?"

"Why didn't you save the land from dying? Why didn't you create a perfect new religion using the principles of ecology? Isn't that what you came here to do? Thousands upon thousands of people came when you called. You gathered them together and choreographed a dance number."

"I tried, you know I did, but they weren't listening. They didn't understand. They aren't willing to change, not for me, anyway."

Darlene played with her scarf. She had hidden herself for good reason. It was like raising a child to be a decent human being, a kind and honest man, only to have him move to New York City and become an asexual investment banker with no time for a proper dinner with his parents. Only for Darlene, or Yahweh, it was 6.5 billion times worse, 6.5 billion times over.

"Is there anything, in particular, you wanted me to do?"

She smiled up at the snow.

"I have a plan." Stanley sat next to Darlene on the flat rock, exhausted. "This isn't news to you, but I'm the wrong person for the job. I can't remember my wife's face.

I miss my life. I'm pleased that you gave me this opportunity but I –"

"Of course."

A long silence passed between them. Darlene sat up on the rock and waved her hand. In an instant, the snow stopped falling. The stars appeared in the sky and the glow of Banff reflected off the snowy boughs of the cemetery. Stanley wished he could have pleased Darlene. But if she couldn't prevent the land from dying, in all her thousands of years, surely Darlene could not have expected much from him – an old man, an agnostic florist, dying of lung cancer.

"I did and didn't." Darlene stood up off the rock, removed her scarf, and retied it. "I'm going to Israel."

Darlene did not offer encouragement. Stanley watched her walk to the gate of the cemetery, reinforced to keep the bears out, and then he followed her. He knew he would not see her again, that this was his last chance to seek wisdom. He wanted to know if he had permission to choose his successor. He wanted to know what would happen to him, and his wife, if he gave this up. Where would he end up?

A layer of snow covered the blackened husk of a house across the street. Darlene kicked some of it away, revealing ashes and shards. "You build it and you burn it down," she said.

Stanley decided not to seek wisdom. Instead, he apologized.

EIGHTY

Charles Allen Moss sat at the small table in the motel suite, drinking a glass of tap water. At first he seemed not to recognize his father. He looked up at Stanley with a mixture of confusion and resentment, and crossed his arms.

"What am I to do, bow or salute?"

It was inconceivable that Charles would fly across the continent, rent a car, and hunt his father down. But here he was, in charcoal suit pants and a white shirt. The tie, blue and yellow, was knotted yet loose. It hung below his unfastened top button. Stanley smiled. "My boy."

"At least he recognizes me."

"Get up."

Charles did as he was told, and Stanley hurried over to his son and hugged him. Mid-hug, he slapped Charles on the back of his head. To his own astonishment, Stanley began to cry.

"I'm sorry I didn't get in touch when you were sick. I was called away to a meeting in Washington and –"

"Shush. I'm just so glad you're here. Have you seen your mother? How is she?"

"Mortified." Charles wiggled out of the hug and unconsciously wiped the nonexistent creases out of his shirt.

"Did you bring a picture?"

"Of what?"

"Of your mom."

Charles touched his nose. "What the hell is going on here, Dad, really?"

His son looked old in this light, greyer and thinner on top. The skin around his neck had gone loose. Stanley was surprised that Charles hadn't sought treatments, for the hair and wrinkles. It wasn't pleasant to grow old in New York City in the twenty-first century.

Since Stanley could not answer his son's question, he didn't try. He went to the window and looked down at the massive crowd that had gathered in the snowy parking lot. A few people had spotted him on his way through town, and a few people had become a thousand.

"Mom wants to come live with me."

"I heard. Won't she cramp your style?"

Charles joined Stanley at the window and fumbled with the knot of his tie. "You know me, I barely have a style. *This* is my style. And besides, she wants to get her own place. What I don't want is you two separated unnecessarily, even if you are currently the most famous man in America." Charles finished his glass of water and winced. "God, what are you people putting in the pipes these days?"

"I'm almost finished."

"Finished what, Dad?"

"One of my colleagues and a former doctor have offered to buy my rights today."

"Rights to . . ."

"To me. My words, actions, name, likeness, story. They want to transform everything I did into myths and metaphors for better living. Halt the spiritual collapse of western culture."

"How much are they offering you?"

"Half a million dollars and a condominium in Puerto Vallarta."

Charles laughed. "You could get a hundred times that."

"I don't need the money. You don't need the money. I was going to give it to Maha and Kal. You've met them?"

"They were here when I arrived. I gave them two hundred dollars and sent them out to the French restaurant."

Stanley felt weak all of a sudden, and curiously enjoyed the sensation. The sight of his son. "I am so glad you came. Leaving work behind to see your dad."

Charles lifted a black item out of the front pocket of his slacks and displayed it. A personal communication device. "No one leaves work behind any more." Charles looked down at his little computer. "It's a phone, a web browser, an e-mail retriever. I can keep track of the markets. On particularly lonely nights, it sneaks into bed and fellates me."

"Where are you staying?"

"*We* are staying at the Fairmont. You can't share a room with a couple of kids any more."

Stanley adored this sensation, of his son taking care of him. "What's our room number?"

Charles pulled two keycards out of his pocket and gave one to Stanley. They agreed to meet at the hotel in the morning and hugged again. Charles opened the door, and the noisy crowd, alternating between chaos and organized chants, like British soccer fans, went silent.

"Who are you?" someone said.

"Nobody," said Charles.

There was an ovation. Stanley worried for his son's safety, so he sent him floating – screaming all the way – over the crowd. Watching through the window, Stanley dropped Charles on the bank of the river, not far from the bridge.

Stanley exited the motel through the fire door in the back and made his way through the dark alleys west of Banff Avenue to a beige condominium complex. Swooping Eagle welcomed him effusively into the refuge provided by her insurance company and boiled a pot of yerba maté, "the ancient drink of peace, health, and friendship." To Stanley, it tasted like hot water squeezed out of a whole wheat bun.

Stanley phoned Le Beaujolais and left a message for Maha and Kal. They were to avoid the motel and meet at Swooping Eagle's condominium.

While they waited for their friends, Swooping Eagle outlined her mission. "I've decided, since the fire, to get out of the historical bed-and-breakfast racket and start something new. I think you're here, *we're here*, as a last chance for the species. If we continue on our present track, we'll use up all our resources and poison the land and air completely. We'll be extinct in a few generations, Stanley. That isn't just intuition, either. It's science. Given that, how can I run a bed-and-breakfast?" She sipped her yerba maté. "You like this?"

"Not so much, Swooping Eagle. Sorry."

"Coffee? I have a bottle of Pineau des Charentes."

"I'm all right, really."

Swooping Eagle poured more tea into her cup. "We need to be transformed, not amused by historical anecdotes and the smell of lavender in our bleached pillows. I have a dream, an inspiration, to bring my philosophies to the people. To save them."

"How?"

"Maybe we could partner up, you and me, really focus. Failing that, I could use abstract landscape painting and interpretive dance."

"I have a better idea."

There was a knock on the door, and Maha and Kal entered. Kal's eyes looked even redder than before, and Stanley realized that Maha had said what she needed to say – that she did not love him.

"We've been talking, Stanley, and as much as we appreciate the gesture, Kal and I aren't interested in moving to Puerto Vallarta together. We want to stay here and help you, be your disciples."

"As friends," said Kal, "really terrific, awesome friends. Right, Maha?"

Maha sighed. "Please don't let Tanya and that doctor buy The Stan."

"Come with me." Stanley had planned to take them along the river, near the bridge, but he worried someone would spot them. So instead, they walked a few blocks west, past a number of old houses, and then through the thick snow into the trees. Stanley found a bare spot protected by pine boughs, and when they were gathered, he smiled. "Thank you."

"For what?" said Kal.

"For supporting me. For believing."

They could not read minds, but his friends seemed to understand. Maha placed her hands on his chest. "Don't leave."

Stanley asked them to form a circle, as they had on the banks of Lake Minnewanka. He stood in the south, Swooping Eagle in the north.

"No." Maha wiped her eyes with the sleeve of her fleece jacket. "Don't do this. You don't have to."

Stanley smiled. "Please don't worry. This is the way it must be. If you believe, Maha, you have to believe in it all."

The pale light of the moon half lit their faces. There were

crackles throughout the forest, as branches thawed. Without speaking, Stanley asked Swooping Eagle to concentrate. To distill her thoughts. Her vision. It took a long time, and from the corner of his eye Stanley could see Maha crying and Kal clutching his accordion nervously. He whispered, across the circle, to Maha. "What's happening?"

Several minutes later, with a scream, Swooping Eagle fell in the slush. She lay silent for some time, then sat up and wiped her nose, which had begun to bleed. "When I was a kid, at my uncle's farm, sometimes I'd grab the electric fence. That was worse. Or, I guess, better."

"How do you feel?"

"I'm tingling. It's like I just sobered up, all of a sudden."

"Were you drinking?" said Kal.

"Not at all."

Swooping Eagle was sober and Stanley was tired. When he blinked, his eyes wanted to stay closed. "Try something."

"Like what?"

Kal closed his accordion. "What's going on here?"

Swooping Eagle took a few steps back and stretched her arms out, as though she wanted to make sure she wouldn't hit anyone. Slowly she began to shine, brighter and brighter, a Vitruvian Woman, until Kal and Maha covered their eyes. Stanley asked her to say something.

"It's *The Muppet Show*," she said, in a voice that rumbled so deeply a couple of car alarms went off on nearby streets, "with our very special guest star, Carol Burnett."

Stanley applauded. "Very prophetic."

The light faded and, a minute later, went out like an extinguished candle. An afterglow remained around her. "I'll have to think of some more profound things to say."

"There's climate change," said Maha.

"Bad viruses," said Kal. "It was on TV."

"You'll know exactly what to say and do, when the time comes." Stanley took her hand in both of his and tried with all his strength to accept his words as the truth. "God chose me so I could choose you."

They walked back to the condominium complex together and, while they did, Swooping Eagle and Maha and Kal organized a meeting for the following day. A luncheon in the condominium, tabouli salad and cucumber sandwiches. No one wanted to acknowledge the fact that Stanley was leaving. They stood in another circle, in front of Swooping Eagle's building, looking down at the melting snow and up at the stars.

"Sure turned into a nice night," said Kal.

Stanley couldn't bear to talk about the weather so he hugged Swooping Eagle. "Don't do anything until you're ready. Make sure you know exactly what The Stan should be. Don't make the mistakes I made."

Swooping Eagle kissed him on the cheek. "I appreciate your trust in me, and I will not squander it. I'll bring it all together, Stanley, all the gods and communities. Your ideas about the earth and ecological mythology, moral action –"

"Maybe keep your clothes on, though. I'm not sure the world is quite ready for that."

"Note taken."

Stanley, Maha, and Kal walked slowly through the dark alleys. It was suddenly too cold for Stanley, without a winter jacket. *Frieda* came to him like a gust of wind and he laughed, clapped his hands. How could he have forgotten? Undone by the nervous silence, Kal scouted ahead, to see if the crowds were still in front of the motel. While he did, Maha wiped the tears from her eyes and hugged Stanley. "I'm so angry with you, for doing that."

"You have to help."

"I don't know."

"Promise me."

Maha's tears wet Stanley's neck. She rolled a melting snowball around with the toe of her boot. "What happens to you now?"

"I go home to Frieda."

Kal returned, sliding around as he ran. "There's only a couple of them, sitting with some candles and singing songs. I'll protect you, Maha."

Instead of hugging Stanley, Kal insisted on playing a goodbye song. It was an instrumental, blending classical, tango, and continental melancholy. He shook Stanley's hand.

For the first time in months, a firm handshake actually hurt. Stanley watched them round the corner. He waved, but they didn't turn around.

It remained a clear night, crisp and quiet. He walked across the bridge and down Spray Avenue, leading to the Banff Springs Hotel. A fog rose up off the flats near the river. As a child, on camping trips with Kitty and his parents, he had wanted so badly to stay in this stone castle. Entering the imposing lobby, with its high rock ceilings and opulent chandeliers, Stanley realized he had never actually been inside the hotel. The uniformed concierge bowed faintly. There was no awe in his eyes. He said hello, just hello. He desired nothing from Stanley as he directed him toward the elevators.

The room on the second floor was decorated with luxurious furniture. Charles, looking tired and dishevelled, was at his computer. He spoke into his small, black device. "I want us out of oil for the time being."

The greenhouse-style windows in the living room offered a view of the Bow Valley, faintly green in the moonlight. Stanley braced himself on the windows and looked out, noticing the sound and rhythm of his breaths, until Charles was off the phone.

"Your grandfather, my dad, never could have imagined a hotel room like this."

Charles joined Stanley at the window. "Are you finished what you had to do here?"

"Yes."

"How are you sleeping these days?"

"Really well."

EIGHTY-ONE

William and Rosa.

Stanley recalled them during breakfast, as he dipped his final morsel of fried potato into salsa. He was on the verge of saying, aloud, that the Banff Springs Hotel was too sophisticated for mere ketchup, when they reinstated themselves. William grew up near Grande Prairie, the fourth son of a farmer, and Rosa was originally from Ottawa. A clerk's daughter whose mother died of tuberculosis. William and Rosa met at a community picnic shortly after they finished school and entered into a long, cautious courtship. William became a carpenter and Rosa a French tutor for the rich children of Garneau.

His sister, Kitty, whose hair was somewhere in-between blond and red. Pigtails. The three houses where they grew up, two on the north side of the river and one on the south. Skeleton Lake every weekend all summer, the gravel roads and bright-yellow canola fields and grasshoppers. The smell of the trees in the rain along the lake, walking with Kitty in their rubber boots and slickers. Birch woodsmoke rising out of the cabin. The funeral of his second sister at a funeral home in downtown Edmonton, next to the Masonic Hall. William and Rosa hiding their grief like an ugly secret.

A server came around to pick up Stanley's dirty plate. Charles had finished eating long ago. He stared at his father. On their way out of the hotel, they passed a grand bouquet of flowers in the entrance hall. Stanley smelled them and, in a shock of delight that was almost painful, remembered each of their names. Stanley went through them, one by one, for Charles. Chinese aster, globe thistle, zinnia and gladiolus, scabious and hypericum, red hot poker, cockscomb, achillea, love-lies-bleeding.

The rental car, a silver Mercedes sedan, was parked far from the hotel. It wasn't a particularly long and difficult walk but Stanley's lungs were aflame. He was dizzy. He leaned on the hood of a minivan and waited for his breath to come back.

Charles was patient with him. "Should we stop at the hospital, on the way out?"

"Absolutely not."

Stanley sat back in the heated leather passenger seat. They crossed the bridge and he regarded the Chalet Du

Bois longingly. He closed his eyes and treasured his regrets, as Charles took another phone call from New York.

He remembered his affair with the customer, whose name was Heather. She was a divorced schoolteacher, ten years younger than him and of more generous proportions than Frieda. It went on for a long time, piteously long, and he endured a swampful of her tears and Frieda's tears because he had been too cowardly to end it sooner.

Once, when Charles was a baby, crying inconsolably of an afternoon, Stanley had screamed at him. Screamed at the baby, as loud as he could. "Leave us alone!"

Not long before his father died, Stanley had wished his father would die.

There was more.

Charles, his mother's son, chose the long mountain route of Highway 93 through Lake Louise and up the Icefields Parkway. "They say it'll melt completely in my lifetime," he said, as they passed the retreating glacier. "The rivers of the mid-continental plains will dry up. Alberta and Montana will be deserts. I'm investing accordingly."

"I'm so lucky I don't have grandchildren."

"Ouch, Dad."

"It's not too late."

"What will they drink, these grandchildren of yours, when the water is gone? What'll they eat?"

Stanley couldn't tell if his son was being facetious. Ten years ago, the boy would have called this sort of talk left-wing nonsense. "Maybe the land won't die. I've made certain arrangements."

Charles laughed.

They stopped for gas and snacks in Jasper. The snow had not reached the valley and the sun was out. Most leaves had fallen from the trees but a few crisp, deep-red flakes of foliage held on.

Stanley purchased a bottle of water, an act that would never feel natural, and leaned against an aspen tree along the railroad tracks. His mother's father, a Ukrainian, had been interned here during the First World War. With his countrymen and other unwanted immigrants, he'd built Jasper as a slave. As they prepared to leave Jasper, Stanley related this story to Charles.

"Not that I'm keeping track, Dad, but I think you told me that every time we came out here. I've heard it somewhere between thirty and forty times."

"You won't forget, will you?"

There were mountain goats on the highway, so they had to wait for several minutes while a woman got out of her station wagon up ahead and shooed them away. With each kilometre, Stanley grew more exhausted, more nauseous. His lung capacity continued to shrink, so that by the time they passed out of the national park and into the smelly suburbia of Hinton, Stanley was sure he would soon stop breathing.

He closed his eyes. Charles made a few more phone calls. The pull of Stanley's dream, an incomprehensible thing about flowers and floating and Frieda and New York, was unpleasant. But Stanley preferred the promise of sleep to nausea and panic, so he lowered his leather chair and lay on his side.

Moments later, it seemed, Charles was whispering and squeezing his arm. "We're home."

Stanley sat up. They were parked in front of the house, in front of the two Douglas fir trees. In his fatigue and confusion, Stanley felt, for a moment, like an eight-year-old boy, returning home from a weekend trip to Skeleton Lake.

The front lawn had been ravaged by dandelions, and no one had shovelled and bagged the cones. It was dark now. His house keys had been lost in the fire so Stanley followed the steps: take the key from under the deck. With it, open the garage.

Charles went into the garage and found the spare in the red toolbox, under the old ratchet set. The brown and white vinyl siding was dirty. Tomorrow, Stanley would take the high-pressure hose and wash summer's grit from the house.

Inside, his own smell, their smell, nearly knocked Stanley down. How exotic and familiar it was, all at once. Stanley closed the door behind him quietly, carefully, as Charles took his suitcase downstairs to the spare room. The act of closing the door like this reminded him, cruelly, of late nights during his affair with Heather, the retired schoolteacher. Sneaking into the house and hoping, shamefully, that Frieda was asleep.

The kitchen shone by the light of the lantern in the lane. Frieda had acquired a new stainless-steel coffee maker, and she had left a box of Raisin Bran on the counter. During her pregnancy, his wife had enjoyed a late-night snack of cereal, a habit that never left her. Stanley stood in the kitchen long enough to smile at the box of Raisin Bran, to raise it and admire it like a talisman.

Then, a scream. A war cry. He backed into the stove and instinctively lowered himself to the floor. The light clicked on, disoriented him. "Frieda?"

She stood before him in her blue flannel nightgown, holding what appeared to be a paring knife.

"What are you going to do with that? I thought I told you: a *big* knife."

Frieda looked down at her weapon. "It's all I had upstairs. I cut up an orange a couple of nights ago, before bed, and forgot to bring it down."

"Can you help me up?"

She put the knife on the counter, crossed her arms, and then helped him up. "God," she said, as she yanked, "where did all that strength go?"

"It went."

Frieda hesitated, so Stanley pulled her in for a hug. They stayed like that, hugging in the kitchen. Stanley explored her lower back, the way he liked. They kissed and she gently pushed him away so she could look him in the eye, her hands grasping his arms. "Where have you been?"

EIGHTY-TWO

They took their morning coffee in the backyard. Frieda read aloud from the newspaper, about superbugs, casualties in Afghanistan, gang murders, the health benefits of consuming wild blueberries on a daily basis.

Frieda had purchased a radio for the kitchen, and it sat near the open window so they could listen to classical music and the hourly news on the deck. It was on a quiet setting so Charles, who worked on his laptop in the dining room, would not be disturbed by what he called "inane Canadian boosterism." Crows and magpies hopped about in the yard, edging closer to a few dropped cherry tomatoes. Shortly, after they ate a couple of the muffins that were baking in the oven, Frieda and perhaps Stanley would pull up the dead sunflowers and fold them into clear plastic bags, rake the leaves and fir cones, and wrap burlap around the lavender so it might survive the winter. They would go out for dinner with Charles. Malaysian, most likely – his childhood favourite. He had never been a hamburgers-and-roller-coasters sort of boy. More like Assam Ayam and Verdi. And as much as he would enjoy it, Charles couldn't stay much longer.

A voice echoed through the neighbourhood. "Susan, line three. Susan, line three."

Stanley interrupted Frieda's reading. "Did they hire someone new at the Ford dealership?"

"Susan."

It was not a warm morning but it was pleasant enough to be on the deck. The sky was white with cloud. Stanley understood that he had been in this moment, this exact moment, thousands of times. The smells of decomposition, oil refineries, raspberry bran muffins.

With his wife, he did not feel obliged to speak. Stanley thought, perhaps, if it began to rain and they could not work in the garden they could go to the Bonnie Doon pool or the Kinsmen Centre. Frieda could do laps and Stanley could sit in the hot tub and admire her form. Look up at the clock and watch the second hand's *click click click*.

The timer on the oven beeped. Stanley wanted to get up and pull the muffins out, remove them from the pan, and put them in the basket. He wanted to pull the butter and margarine out of the fridge – butter for him and margarine for his wife – and bring it all outside. He wanted to glance at the digital clock on the stove, even though he knew the time, and he wanted to look at the thermometer and top up their coffees. He wanted to wash his hands and dry his hands, look at himself briefly in the mirror on his way outside and think, *Yes, I am* that *man.*

Of course, he could not fetch the muffins. It would take too long. His breath would fail him and he would become woozy and lower himself to the kitchen floor. The muffins would tip, or the coffee would spill, or the butter would smear on the white linoleum. He would be too bashful at first to call for help and he would sit there until Frieda came in to check on him.

"Should we go to Emergency today, just to see?" Frieda had finished reading. Her coffee mug was empty and she was on her way to the back door. "No big deal. Just . . ."

"We'd sit in the waiting room for hours, and for what?"

Frieda nodded and went inside.

In the distance, the sound of a leaf-blower. The neighbour kid who had adjusted the muffler on his Honda Civic opened the garage door and revved his engine. The bass on his stereo thumped so deeply Stanley could feel it in his stomach. Under the newspaper on the patio table, a novel set in Colombia. Had Frieda and the members of her book club grown tired of India?

She came back outside without the muffins or the butter and margarine or the coffee. Frieda leaned back against the door and squinted. The sun was bright, even through the cloud. "I've been wondering about something. Is this a choice you made?"

"I don't know what you mean."

"Stan, I think you do."

"It's a choice I made."

She went back inside.

A white helicopter passed overhead. Stanley could not imagine how there could be traffic at this hour, mid-morning, and he stopped himself. He realized: *I am thinking about a helicopter.*

The muffins were in the dark-brown basket, lined with wax paper. The coffee was in its new black-and-steel warmer. Butter and margarine. The smell of butter and margarine. Frieda arranged everything on the table and shooed a bug away.

"Is there anything else you want? Water?"

"No, this looks great."

"Stan, just tell me if there's something. I'm up anyway."

"There's nothing. This is already too much. Is Charles joining us?"

"I don't want to disturb him."

"Charlie!" Stanley called out again, "Charles," and paused to catch his breath. The talking had exhausted and delighted him, the fullness and emptiness at once, the ordinary ritual. His chest burned. He reached across the patio table and touched his wife's hand, and smiled. Over the loudspeaker, the secretary announced another phone call for Susan, this time on line two.

ACKNOWLEDGEMENTS

I want to thank Jennifer Lambert, my editor, for her brilliance and for her respect.

Thank you to Ellen Seligman, Ashley Dunn, Terri Nimmo, and my other friends at McClelland & Stewart in Toronto for their continued, superlative support. I want to thank my friend Shawn Ohler in Edmonton, for his fine eye and endless energy. Again, I want to thank my mentors, coaches, and colleagues at the *Edmonton Journal* for allowing me the time, when I needed it, to nurture this second career.

A number of friends, across Canada and in France, have generously offered advice and editorial support in reading early drafts of *The Book of Stanley*, including a lot of Albertans whose names I wish I could provide here. Thanks to all of you.

Thank you to Anne McDermid and to Martha Magor, for all the wisdom and cheerleading.

The Canada Council and the Alberta Foundation for the Arts provided much-needed funds some years ago, when I started working on a novel about Stanley Moss. Thank you for that, and long live public arts funding in Canada. The country would be unimaginable without it.

Thank you doesn't seem sufficient for Gina and Avia, and the rest of my little family. But thank you, with love.